Irish author **Abby Green** [...] career in film and TV—wh[...] of a lot of standing in the [...] trailers—to pursue her love of romance. After she'd bombarded Mills & Boon with manuscripts they kindly accepted one, and an author was born. She lives in Dublin, Ireland, and loves any excuse for distraction. Visit abby-green.com or email abbygreenauthor@gmail.com.

USA TODAY bestselling, RITA®-nominated and critically acclaimed author **Caitlin Crews** has written more than one hundred books and counting. She has a Master's and a PhD in English Literature, thinks everyone should read more category romance, and is always available to discuss her beloved alpha heroes. Just ask! She lives in the Pacific Northwest with her comic book artist husband, she is always planning her next trip, and she will never, ever, read all the books in her 'to-be-read' pile. Thank goodness.

RINGS THAT BIND

ABBY GREEN

CAITLIN CREWS

MILLS & BOON

First published in Great Britain 2025
by Mills & Boon, an imprint of HarperCollins*Publishers* Ltd,
1 London Bridge Street, London, SE1 9GF

www.harpercollins.co.uk

HarperCollins*Publishers*, Macken House, 39/40 Mayor Street Upper,
Dublin 1, D01 C9W8, Ireland

Rings That Bind © 2025 Harlequin Enterprises ULC

On His Bride's Terms © 2025 Abby Green

Carrying a Sicilian Secret © 2025 Caitlin Crews

ISBN: 978-0-263-34450-9

02/25

This book contains FSC™ certified paper
and other controlled sources to ensure responsible forest management.

For more information visit www.harpercollins.co.uk/green.

Printed and Bound in the UK using 100% Renewable Electricity
at CPI Group (UK) Ltd, Croydon, CR0 4YY

ON HIS BRIDE'S TERMS

ABBY GREEN

MILLS & BOON

PROLOGUE

SHE WASN'T THE most striking woman in the room, but that was largely because she was dressed with understated elegance and not to draw attention, unlike most of the women here. But, nevertheless, there was something very compelling about her. He saw how she drew second glances. Third.

She was undoubtedly a beauty, but Primo Holt had to concede he *was* judging her from a distance. He'd never met Faye MacKenzie, or seen her up close, in spite of the fact that their worlds intersected on a regular basis.

But very soon they would interact on a much more personal level because he had every intention of asking her to marry him.

He'd known he would have to marry sooner or later—as the scion of one of North America's most notable families, it was a duty he couldn't escape—but he'd managed to put it off for a long time. However, lately he'd had to acknowledge that sooner or later was now.

Not marrying was generating headlines and speculation about his personal life that he did not need. It was detracting from the business. And once his personal life began to affect the bottom line, it was time to face reality.

Faye MacKenzie was the perfect candidate, whittled down from a list carefully curated by his closest advisors. She came from an impeccable family line, dating back into

American history almost as far as Primo's. People said his kin had come in on the *Mayflower*. He knew that was just a myth, but they weren't far off the mark.

Her Scottish/English ancestry was evident not only in her name but also her colouring. Pale skin—a rarity in these circles of golden skin that spoke of regular holidays in various exotic climes. Black hair, flowing in silken waves over her bare shoulders. She wore a classic strapless black dress, moulding to her slim curves with a deceptive simplicity that could only have come from one of the world's top designers. Discreet jewellery, but impressive nonetheless and no doubt from the family vault.

She was a divorcée, but Primo didn't care about that. She'd married young and divorced young. No children. Apart from that there was no hint of impropriety. She was thirty, to his thirty-five. She was experienced. Mature. Also, appealingly, she was independent. She had a job. She was a highly respected private art broker. She had a degree in art history and a Master's specialising in art business.

He had no time for taking on a wife who would be intimidated by him, or unused to his world. He needed to hit the ground running with this marriage—and, crucially, he knew just how to appeal to Faye MacKenzie to entice her to agree.

CHAPTER ONE

'HOW IS YOUR dear father? It's been a while since we've seen him, and one hears things…'

Faye MacKenzie forced a bright smile in the face of this man and his cronies who had surrounded her before she could escape. She knew well that the solicitous question and their veneer of concern was just that—a very thin veneer—and that underneath it was a desire for any kind of hint that all was not well, and that her father was on the way out—of life and off the board of MacKenzie Enterprises, upon which he'd sat since his own father had died some forty years before.

'Gentlemen, I will pass on your regards. My father is just fine—never better, in fact. And as for what you've heard… You'll have to forgive my ignorance, because I am not privy to such things. And now, if you'll excuse me, there's someone I need to catch before they leave.'

Faye slipped through a gap in the circle of vultures around her and her smile faded, to be replaced by pursed lips and a set jaw. She snagged a full glass of champagne from a passing waiter's tray and ducked behind an exuberant plant on the edge of the ballroom, so she could take a break and absorb the fact that all was *not* well, and coming to this function in the centre of Manhattan this evening had proved her and her father's suspicions right. People were talking.

She took a gulp of sparkling wine, hoping it might soothe

her frayed nerves. A breeze skated over her skin and she looked behind her to see open doors leading out onto a terrace. Air... Air would be good.

She went outside and stood at the wall and tipped her head back for a moment, closing her eyes. The sounds behind her from the packed ballroom—people chatting, laughing, gossiping against the backdrop of classical music—fell away, to be replaced with the sounds of the city far below. A siren, a car horn.

Whenever she was home now, and not travelling for work, she spent most of her time with her father in their upstate family home in Westchester, so she usually enjoyed coming into the city as a diversion. But this evening the sounds of the city weren't soothing. They were jarring. Because she knew she would have to go home and confirm her father's worst fears.

She dropped her head back again, opened her eyes and looked out over the view of Manhattan's glittering skyline unseeingly. Frustration mixed with anxiety churned in her gut again. Why had he been so foolish as to—?

'Not enjoying the party? I can't say I blame you.'

Faye went very still. A bizarre thought struck her—the fact that she knew exactly who had just spoken, even though she'd never met him face to face, close up. She'd seen him across the room earlier—it would have been hard to miss him, head and shoulders above everyone else, making her pulse trip with dismaying ease. Dismaying because it was such a cliché to be affected by one of the richest and most gorgeous men in the world as easily as if she was an innocent debutante.

She was no innocent debutante.

She took a breath and turned to the man who was standing beside her, looking at her. She had to tip her head back because he was well over a foot taller than her. And she wasn't that small. He was far taller and broader up close, and it made her skin feel hot. He was solid. All muscle and bone.

He held out a hand. 'Primo Holt. I don't believe we've actually ever met?'

Faye might have laughed out loud. Anyone who didn't know who this man was most likely didn't have a pulse. But shock kept her from breaking into laughter. She almost wanted to look around them, to see if there was a camera crew capturing her reaction for some kind of a prank show. She might inhabit the same world as Primo Holt, but she was a lot further down the food chain.

She put out her own hand, but just before they made physical contact she had a strange sense that her life was going to be changed for ever the moment they touched. She didn't have time to pooh-pooh the audacious thought before he was clasping her hand in his, and a powerful surge of electricity ignited her blood and made her skin prickle into goosebumps.

Faye couldn't help the intake of shocked breath. She saw how his eyes widened a little, as if he too had felt it. They were beautiful eyes. Blue. Piercing and direct. They stood out against the tan of his skin and the stunning architecture of his face. Thick dark golden hair swept back from a broad brow. He really was ridiculously gorgeous—as if the gods had decided to bestow upon this man even more than his birthright of incredible wealth and fortune.

And yet any sense of *beauty* was diluted by a hard jaw and the sheer power field around him that was almost tangible. He was ridiculously masculine, in a world where most men were soft from privilege.

She struggled to make her brain function and somehow managed to say, 'I'm Faye MacKenzie.'

His hand squeezed hers minutely before letting her go. 'Yes, I know who you are.'

Faye instinctively brought her hand back into her chest, almost cradling it, as if to keep the sense of his hand holding hers for as long as possible. Dimly she wondered what on earth was wrong with her. She was behaving like a starstruck groupie.

She blinked and dropped her hand to her side. He was still there, but she felt marginally more in control of her reaction.

'How can I help you?'

He frowned a little and his mouth tipped up, which only brought Faye's attention there. Her belly did a swooping somersault. Mother. Of. God. The man's mouth was pure sin. Sculpted and full and firm. And he was laughing at her. Teeth straight and white. He was quite literally an angel in human form. But he wasn't a benign angel... She sensed that he could very much cause havoc.

Faye dragged her gaze back up. She bristled at the way he was affecting her so easily, making her take leave of her sanity and senses, and she seized it—anything to feel less unmoored by this man's presence.

'Is that amusing?'

His mouth straightened, but there was still a glint in his eye. 'No, not at all, but actually there is something you can help me with.'

'I find that a little unbelievable.'

Primo leaned against the wall beside Faye, supremely nonchalant. To be under this man's laser-like gaze was beyond disconcerting. She felt very conscious of the fact that she wasn't half as glittering as other women at the party. She wished she'd put on more make-up.

'And why would that be?' he asked. 'Aren't you one of the world's foremost art experts?'

Her insides jolted. He knew what she did? She couldn't help a small frisson of pleasure from the compliment. 'I wouldn't know about that, but it is my sphere of interest, yes.'

'I've looked you up. You have an impressive list of satisfied clients and have brokered some of the biggest deals in the last decade.'

Now Faye felt embarrassed, and she ducked her head slightly. 'It's something I'm passionate about, which makes it easy to do it for a living.'

'Passion certainly makes things more interesting, no?'

Faye looked at him. Was he...flirting with her? The expression on his face was inscrutable, but there was a twinkle in his eyes. An incendiary image of her and this man with naked limbs entwined flashed into her head before she could stop it. It left her even more disconcerted and breathless. Men didn't have this kind of viscerally physical effect on her.

Clearly oblivious to her wayward imagination, Primo glanced behind them at the party and then back to her. 'What would you say if I asked if you'd like to come for a drink with me?'

Faye's heart thumped and she felt momentarily dizzy. Was Primo Holt, one of the world's most eligible bachelors, really asking her out for a drink?

'Not here,' he added. 'Somewhere close. I'd like to get your professional opinion on something.'

The dizziness subsided. It wasn't a date. It was work-related. It wasn't his fault that his every utterance sounded like something far more decadent and illicit. But a small rogue part of her pointed out that if it was entirely professional he'd have asked if she would meet him at his office, or during work hours. Not late at night. For a drink.

But maybe this was how he conducted business. How would she know? The man was famously discreet in his business and personal life. He'd never been linked with a woman long enough to cause speculation to mount, and the women he did get pictured with all seemed to be as discreet as him.

He was looking at her, waiting for an answer. Even though he'd said he wanted to discuss something, a giddy excitement gripped her. It scared her. Faye got asked out on dates. She even went on some. She even spent the night in some men's beds. But rarely—and not for a long while.

'You want to go for a drink to discuss something?' It was as if she had to have it confirmed.

He nodded. 'That is unless you need to stay at the party. We could arrange another time?'

Faye couldn't see over Primo's shoulder, but she didn't need to to know what was behind him. More vultures circling to ask her about her father. And there was something else. An urge to seize this moment. Because she was intrigued and more than a little intoxicated by his interest. Even if it did turn out to be purely professional.

She racked her brains for when she might have heard anyone in the art world discuss working with him, but drew a blank. If Primo Holt wanted to work with her then it would be a massive feather in her cap. His family had an extensive private art collection that not many had ever seen. If she could persuade him to open it up, loan some works to galleries, it would be a massive coup.

So when she said, 'No, I'm happy to leave now,' she told herself that it was purely out of curiosity and for the potential professional connection. Not because he was the most beautiful man she'd ever seen up close.

Primo was already taking a phone out of his pocket saying, 'Good, I'll instruct my driver to be ready. Meet you in the lobby in ten minutes? I just have to say goodbye to the host.'

Of course he did. Because he was Primo Holt and he was automatically a guest of honour. Unlike Faye, who the host would know of, but wouldn't care less about if she ducked out early. With Primo Holt.

She must have nodded her assent, or said something, because she watched him walk back towards the party with a long-legged stride. Back broad. Classic tuxedo moulding to his body like a second skin. Long legs. Narrow waist.

She saw how the crowd parted to admit him, and then closed behind him again like a sea of adoring acolytes. She could see people looking at her, whispering, and suddenly she wanted to escape.

She made her way to the cloakroom and got the jacket that matched her dress—loose cape-style, with sleeves—and slipped it on. When she got to the lobby she didn't have time to worry if Primo Holt might have changed his mind or come to his senses, because he was already waiting for her, wearing a long overcoat. He was intimidatingly suave.

He saw her and watched her walk towards him. Faye prayed she wouldn't fall flat on her face and somehow managed not to. Primo put out a hand for her to precede him and she went out and down the steps, to be guided into the back of a sleek SUV with tinted windows.

It was early spring, and the air still had a nip, but she knew that wasn't why her skin prickled. It was the man sliding into the back alongside her now, issuing instructions to the driver, who nodded, and then they were moving out smoothly into the night-time Manhattan traffic.

Faye was still too stunned to say anything, not really believing she was in the back of Primo Holt's car being driven across town.

'There's a private club where we can have a drink without being bothered, is that okay?'

Faye turned to look at the man who seemed so huge on the other side of the car. His scent was crisp and unmistakably masculine. She nodded. 'That sounds fine.'

Before long they were pulling to a stop outside a discreet building. She found that she liked the fact that he hadn't tried to make superficial conversation to fill the time en route. She rarely met people who could sit in silence with such ease.

The driver opened her door and she got out. Once again Primo put out a hand to let her precede him to a doorway under an awning that opened as if by magic as she approached. She heard Primo address the suited man in the doorway in fluent French.

Then he said, 'Marcel, I'd like you to meet Faye MacKenzie. I think we'll just be having drinks—unless you're hungry?'

Faye shook her head. The thought of trying to eat in this man's company made her stomach flip-flop. 'No, just drinks is fine.'

Their coats were taken. Faye guessed this was a private members' club and maybe a guesthouse. It was sumptuously decorated with soft carpets, muted colours, hand-painted wallpaper, and luxurious drapes that were pulled back at the entrance to the bar. It had dimly lit booths and tables, around which sat at least a couple of A-listers whom Faye recognised.

They were directed to a booth near the far end of the bar, tucked away but with a view of the room. Faye sat down and Primo slid in from the other side.

Low music accompanied the murmur of chatter and laughter. It was decadent and ultra luxe. Discreet glamour. No wonder Primo Holt's personal life was a well-kept mystery if this is where he conducted his liaisons.

Faye's face grew warm under the soft lights. Who said this was a liaison? And since when was she so hungry for male attention? She'd been burned a long time ago with her first—and only—marriage, and she'd carved out a life for herself in which her independence was the most prized thing.

She hadn't felt the need to follow a man in such a long time that it was only now she was realising she hadn't even hesitated to acquiesce to his invitation. As if her brain had decamped and allowed her body to dictate her actions. She could tell herself it was purely professional curiosity, but she knew that wasn't true.

A waiter approached the table. Primo looked at Faye. 'What would you like?'

She said, 'A classic gin martini—and some water, please.'

She hadn't drunk much at all this evening, but this situation was too surreal. She felt she needed the alcohol, but at the same time wanted to maintain a clear head.

He ordered a whisky.

When the waiter left Faye forced herself to look at Primo Holt, even if it did feel like looking directly into sunlight. Her mind blanked and that was unnerving, because it wasn't as if she wasn't used to talking to VIPs.

As if hearing her thoughts he said, 'I read about the deal you just negotiated for a Picasso for a client rumoured to be part of the British Royal Family.'

Faye couldn't help but feel a little glow of pride. It *had* been a monumental deal. She inclined her head and said, 'I can confirm it was a Picasso, but as for who my client was... I couldn't possibly comment.'

'Someone who knows how to be discreet? I like that.'

Faye felt more than a frisson this time. She had a sense that he wasn't just talking about professional discretion. Right now, Primo Holt was managing to eclipse even royalty.

His hand went to his bow-tie and he made a small face as he said, 'Do you mind? These infernal things always make me feel like I'm being strangled.'

Faye shook her head and watched wordlessly as long fingers undid his tie and he opened a top button, revealing the strong, bronzed column of his throat. It jogged her memory. Hadn't his mother been a Brazilian supermodel?

He lifted his glass and said, 'Cheers.'

Faye looked around. Her drink was on the table on an embossed coaster. She hadn't even noticed the waiter's return. Too busy ogling Primo Holt.

She lifted her glass and let it touch his. She echoed his *cheers*, then took a sip, relishing the slight burn of the alcohol. It gave her the courage to say, 'I'm surprised you didn't have a date with you.'

He put his own glass down and shook his head. 'I was there alone. I'm not seeing anyone at the moment. Are you?'

The bluntness of his question took her by surprise. But she found she liked it. She shook her head. 'No, I'm not with anyone right now.'

Hadn't been for ages. But he didn't need to know that. She struggled to remember the last time he'd been linked with someone. He always seemed to choose women who were intimidatingly beautiful and accomplished. Something Faye had obviously absorbed subliminally over the years.

'It's strange that we've never met face to face before,' he noted. 'When we've been present at many of the same events over the years.'

Faye bit back a wry smile. 'That might be the case, but I don't think we're quite on the same…level.'

'Your family name is about as old as mine.'

Faye shrugged. 'Nevertheless, MacKenzie Enterprises is a minnow compared to Holt Industries.'

'Smaller, maybe, but no less successful in its own right. How is your father, by the way? I've always had a lot of respect for him. He's straight-talking.'

Faye pushed aside her niggling anxieties. 'He's fine. Slower now, but no less able.'

Her father had been involved in a car accident some years

previously and had damaged his legs, so he was now confined to a wheelchair, or walking frame.

'It's just you and him?'

Faye nodded, wondering where this was going. 'Yes. I'm an only child, and my mother passed away when I was still a teenager.'

'I'm sorry...you were young to lose her.'

Faye shrugged minutely. 'My father and I had each other.'

'He never remarried?'

Faye shook her head. 'No, he adored her. They were an urban legend...a love-match.'

'You were lucky to have that. My parents were most definitely not a love-match, and my father has never been the paternal type.'

'They divorced, didn't they?'

Primo nodded. 'When I was much younger. Our mother walked out the door one day and never came back. I've only seen her sporadically since then.'

Faye sucked in a breath at the easy way he'd revealed an undoubtedly traumatic incident in his life. 'That's tough.'

Primo seemed unconcerned. 'It was a long time ago. I don't like to dwell on the past. It holds us back.'

Faye took the hint.

Move on.

Emboldened by this frank exchange, she said, 'I read that you have full control of your family business now.'

'My father never really did care about the legacy. He just did his job and retired as soon as he could.' Primo's mouth twisted a little. 'No problem with succession in our family.'

Faye frowned. 'Don't you have a brother?' She vaguely recalled something about him walking away from the family business some years ago.

'Yes, Quintano. But he's never been interested in the family business—and he became even less so when he found out our father wasn't his father.'

Faye had heard about this, but had never been sure how true it was. 'He doesn't live here, does he?'

'No, he lives in Brazil with his wife and his son. And they had twin girls a few months ago.'

Faye felt a familiar clutch of pain down low in her abdomen. A mixture of emotion and the memory of the pain she'd suffered. 'Do you see them much?'

A shadow crossed Primo's face. The first time this evening she'd seen it.

He lifted his glass and said, 'No.' He took a sip of his drink.

Faye felt a little light-headed. They were discussing subjects that seemed awfully personal for a first conversation between relative strangers.

Afraid that she was getting lost in a little fantasy that this was a date, she said, 'It's very nice that you asked me here for a drink…but you mentioned needing my opinion on something?'

To her surprise, Primo suddenly looked a little abashed—if such a man could look abashed.

He said, 'I have to admit that while I *would* be interested in your professional opinion, it's not the primary reason I asked you here, which is for something along more personal lines.'

There was no mistaking the gleam of interest in his eyes now. There was a slow thump of Faye's heart. 'Oh?' She couldn't help asking. 'I'm a little curious…why me?'

Why not one of the vastly younger and more beautiful women who had been at that function, simpering and pouting and looking for their next rich and powerful boyfriend?

Primo looked at her. 'You're a very beautiful woman.'

Faye didn't like how those words made her insides fizz

and jump like a young girl's. She was too old for these games, and her impression of Primo so far was that he wasn't a game-player.

Her gaze narrowed. 'Thank you for the compliment, but we both know you could be sitting here with someone far more wide-eyed than me.'

Primo felt a surge of adrenalin go through him. *This* was why he wanted to marry Faye MacKenzie—precisely because she wasn't some wide-eyed ingenue. And she was extraordinarily beautiful. Far more than he'd given her credit for. No wonder she'd been drawing looks at the party.

Her eyes were huge, and the most unusual shade of hazel, turning from gold to brown to green within a second. Finely drawn dark brows. Exquisite bone structure. But it was her mouth that had captivated Primo the minute he'd seen her up close. It was full. Lush. At odds with such a refined face. Hinting at a level of sensuality that was backed up by a refreshing earthiness he didn't usually encounter in women from this milieu.

He shook his head slowly and said, 'On the contrary, I knew I wanted to ask you for a drink before I introduced myself.'

He saw how she tensed slightly, drew back. 'What does that mean?'

'It means that I already knew I wanted to talk to you. To meet you.'

Primo knew instinctively that the only way to play it with this woman was to put his cards on the table. She wouldn't appreciate games.

'It's quite simple. I would like you to consider marrying me.'

Those stunning eyes widened and Primo noticed how long her lashes were. She was shocked. Colour left her cheeks.

She said a little faintly, 'Did I just hear you say…?' She trailed off.

'That I would like you to consider a marriage proposal? Yes, you did.'

She was visibly tense now. Primo had to curb a strange urge to touch her, as if to comfort her in some way. Reassure her.

She shook her head slowly, as if trying to clear it of something, and then she said, 'That's the most preposterous thing I've ever heard. We don't even know each other.'

'Hence the reason why I wanted to meet you. To ascertain what I already suspected: that you and I have the potential to make a great match.'

The fact that his blood was humming with electricity and awareness only added to the sense of rightness. He wanted her. As he hadn't wanted a woman in a long time. The soft golden lights turned her dark hair and pale skin lustrous. From a distance earlier, the elegantly simple dress had only hinted at the body underneath, but up close she was all woman, with tantalising curves.

But as he watched her he could see the shock fade and her jaw tighten. She said, 'Thank you for the drink, Mr Holt, but if you've had your fun, I'm going to leave now.'

She turned away and started to move out of the booth. It took a second for Primo to realise she was really leaving. He was so unused to anyone walking away from him.

Something unfamiliar made his gut lurch. Was it…panic?

He cursed himself. He had misread this situation badly. He was usually a lot more suave than this.

Before he knew what he was doing, he'd put his hand on her arm and was saying, 'Stop, please… I'm not making fun of you. This isn't a joke.'

CHAPTER TWO

THE FOLLOWING DAY, Faye paced up and down in the reception room at the family home. She hadn't slept a wink. Her head was full of questions and revelations and sheer... shock. Still.

Primo Holt had asked her for a drink under false pretences.

Her anger and humiliation still burned bright.

He wanted to marry her.

Faye stopped pacing as she recalled how he'd tried to persuade her to stay at the bar, but she'd insisted on leaving.

He'd said to her before she'd left, 'I may have made an error in being so upfront, but after meeting you I thought you'd appreciate this approach more.'

More than what? Faye had asked herself as she'd made her way back to the family home in Westchester. He'd insisted on his driver taking her. In the end she'd accepted that offer, feeling that after inviting her out to have a joke at her expense it was the least he could do.

But it had been no joke.

He'd been deadly serious, because he'd had an agenda all along, while she'd been staring lustfully at his mouth. The memory made her burn. And she hadn't even known the full extent of his agenda until this morning, when he'd arrived at the house to have a meeting with her father.

A *prearranged* meeting.

The sense of exposure made her insides curdle. She'd believed that Primo Holt had fancied her, and that that was why he'd asked her for a drink. It had been a total charade. He'd just wanted to see her up close before going into a meeting with her father, and she knew exactly what that would be about. Because, as those men last night had alluded to, her father was in a weak position and Primo Holt was making his real intentions very clear.

To take over MacKenzie Enterprises.

Faye cursed herself. *How* could she have been so blind? So naive? God knew, she more than most women knew what this world was like and how everyone in it was a commodity. She'd learned that lesson after her first marriage, because as soon as she'd become a worthless commodity her husband had cut her loose. Less than a year into their marriage.

She veered away from that particular memory, focusing her ire on Primo Holt again. She'd been distracted by a hard body and a pretty—*no*—a spectacular face. Proving that in spite of everything she really was as weak and susceptible as any blushing debutante.

At least he didn't woo you, pointed out a little voice.

Faye shuddered delicately. There was that, at least. He hadn't drawn out the charade. That would have been worse. At least she'd only been under the illusion that he fancied her for about an hour, and not for weeks. She would have exposed herself even more.

Because the truth was that she'd found him far too exciting and thrilling, and if he'd tried to do something like kiss her— Her face burned at the knowledge that she would have let him.

He'd awoken a dormant fire inside her. A fire she'd buried ever since she'd been so badly burned by her marriage.

A fire that she wasn't entirely sure she'd ever felt before. Not even with her husband.

There was a light knock on the door and Faye tensed. 'Come in.'

Mary, their housekeeper, appeared in the doorway. 'Mr Holt has finished his meeting with your father. He'd like to see you before he leaves.'

I bet he would.

Faye felt like petulantly refusing to see him, but she knew she couldn't. This was so much bigger now than their mortifying non-date last night.

'Of course. Please show him in.'

Mary stood back, and Faye could see the way the older woman's eyes widened as she admitted the tall, powerful form of Primo Holt. He was wearing a steel-grey three-piece suit. Hair brushed back from his forehead. He looked as if he'd stepped out of a photoshoot for male models—except he was no male model. He was too big…too imposing. She realised then that in spite of his veneer of civility there was something wild about him. Untamed. It excited her.

He walked in and Faye crossed her arms over her chest. When she'd found out that he was due to visit her father that day she'd dressed carefully in tailored trousers and a silk shirt, buttoned up. Hair pulled back into a bun. The thought of giving him any kind of impression that she fancied him made her cringe.

That sense of exposure made her say now, 'Why the great charade last night? Why didn't you tell me you already had a meeting planned with my father?'

He shook his head. 'It wasn't a charade. I did want to meet you face to face.'

She arched a brow. 'And what? Do a bit of tyre-kicking before you pursued your real agenda? Which I presume is to take advantage of my father's current situation?' Before he could answer, she said, 'You're no better than those other vultures who were there last night, feigning concern for his welfare. You're more devious.'

He winced. 'I guess I deserved that.' His expression cleared. 'I meant what I said, though. I respect your father and I respect the business your family have built up. The truth is that, yes, I had a plan to meet with your father, but it just so happens that I'm also in need of a wife. I hadn't specifically planned on meeting you before talking with your father, but when I found out you'd been invited to that party last night it was too good an opportunity to pass up.'

This only made Faye's sense of humiliation more intense—especially when she remembered her reaction to him. 'And what, pray tell, were you going to do if you decided after meeting me that I was not someone you cared to propose to?'

He made a minute movement with one broad shoulder. 'I would have still spoken to your father, but I would have been pursuing a wife elsewhere.'

Faye smiled tightly. 'How convenient for you that you deemed me suitable after...what...?' She lifted her wrist and pretended to look at a watch, then looked back to him. 'About an hour? How could you have been so sure you want me as a wife?'

A muscle in his jaw ticked. Faye didn't care.

And then, before he could speak, something struck her and she felt slightly nauseous. 'You had me investigated, didn't you?'

She turned away and started to pace, her mind spinning with recrimination. *Of course! How could I be so stupid?*

She turned to face Primo again, folding her arms across her chest again. 'No one in our world acts spontaneously. Tell me, where was I on the list?'

That muscle ticked again, but he had the grace not to

feign ignorance. 'You were top. Because of your association with your father.'

'Lucky me,' Faye said caustically. 'And lucky you to have had such a quick search. Pity, though, that it's come to nothing.'

'I wouldn't be so quick to reject a perfectly good offer.'

Faye's jaw dropped. When she could manage it, she said, 'You are unbelievably arrogant.'

'Yes,' he agreed easily, 'I am arrogant. But I think you'll find it's born out of knowing I work hard. I'm very good at what I do and it's not out of a sense of entitlement.'

His easy acceptance of what she'd just accused him of took the wind out of her sails a little. She couldn't imagine many people accusing Primo Holt of arrogance. And getting away with it.

She hated to admit it, but he intrigued her—and he was right. He'd always had a reputation for working as hard as his employees, not expecting them to do anything he wouldn't, and as Holt Industries encompassed everything from real estate to media corporations, that was some feat.

'So, you're hoping for some kind of value package deal? Is that it? Bag a wife and take over MacKenzie Enterprises at the same time?'

He put his hands in his pockets, and that made Faye want to look down. But she resisted the urge. He rocked back on his heels. Supremely at ease, in spite of the crackling undercurrents. Maybe she was the only one who could feel them?

'You have to admit that it would be a convenient solution all round,' he said.

Faye scoffed. 'Convenient for you, you mean.'

Primo suddenly looked serious. 'Do you realise how weakened your father is right now? The board could force him out within weeks if he continues as he is. He should never have taken the advice to sell off so many shares.'

Faye felt sick again. Primo spoke the stark truth. She'd said as much to her father herself. He'd given in to the lure of handing over a little more control, and at the urging of a bad advisor he'd let go of more than he'd intended.

Faye couldn't help sounding a little bitter. 'I suppose you'd like us to believe you have only our best interests at heart?'

'I won't lie and tell you that, no. Right now, you and your father have no personal relevance for me. But I do have the company's best interests at heart because it's a good business opportunity.'

You have no personal relevance for me.

Those words struck at Faye in a place they shouldn't be striking. This man was a stranger.

'Am I to read between the lines and surmise that if we were married we *would* have more "personal relevance"? Which would then translate into a sense of responsibility to our family legacy?'

Primo's eyes flashed. A ghost of a smile made one corner of his mouth quirk. 'That would be one way of looking at it, yes.'

Faye's eyes went wide. He was making those vultures from last night look like bunny rabbits. 'I don't think I've ever met someone so cynical and arrogant and downright—'

Primo held up a hand. 'Please, save your breath. I know exactly what I am.'

Faye closed her mouth. She'd always considered herself a pretty level person, but this man managed to get her worked up in a way that no one else ever had. He made her feel defensive, exposed, and full of hot, volatile things.

Fighting to regain some semblance of control in the face of Primo Holt's nonchalance, Faye asked, 'Why do you think it's such a good business opportunity?'

He answered without missing a beat. 'You're a legacy

brand that's been a cornerstone of supplying and managing the construction industry since the eighteen-hundreds. That's the kind of name and reputation money can't buy. By letting me take majority control, your father can be assured of its survival for another couple of generations, hopefully. And, yes, it will add to the Holt Industries portfolio. Anyone else will likely not have the same respect for your father or the name.'

He went on.

'I won't lie. We would restructure—we'd have to. The reason your father came so close to handing over his majority share was because you're haemorrhaging liquidity. This way your father would get to see out the business he's cultivated his whole life and can ensure it lasts on into the future.'

'Positively altruistic,' Faye commented dryly.

Primo shook his head. 'Not at all. I fully expect it to become a thriving profitable company again, but if it doesn't I will carve it up and parcel it off without hesitation.' He smiled, and it was a shark's smile. 'However, I have every confidence it won't come to that. Your father's company has just diversified too much. It needs to focus on what it was always known for before, as an iron and steel foundry.'

Once again a little jolt of recognition went through Faye. That was what she'd been saying to her father for years. But he'd always tell her that she couldn't possibly understand the intricacies of a billion-dollar business. He'd never resented her for being an only child and a girl, and not being interested in taking her place on the board, but she knew he'd been disappointed the business would essentially die out with him.

But maybe now...it wouldn't.

As if hearing her thoughts, Primo added, 'Your father isn't going to live for ever, Faye. By doing this deal with me, he'll protect the MacKenzie name and reputation after he's gone.'

Faye's insides twisted. She knew her father *was* getting old. And tired. His weariness was what had led to his making a bad decision to trust someone else's advice.

But this was only part of the reason Primo Holt was here.

'And that, I presume, is contingent on our marriage?'

'I'm not saying the marriage is a prerequisite for the business deal...but, as I've pointed out, it would ensure a certain level of loyalty and security and commitment to a long-term investment that can't be bought or negotiated.'

Faye pretended to sniff the air. 'Maybe I'm going a little crazy, but I could swear there's a smell of...of *blackmail* in the air, with base notes of cynicism.'

Primo let out a bark of laughter. 'Hardly! I'd call it... an incentive.'

He looked at her, eyes twinkling. She was amusing him.

He said, 'I don't know how you can be born into our world and not be cynical. At least then one isn't at the mercy of delusion and disappointment. I wouldn't be offering to marry you if I didn't feel like we'd make a good couple, Faye. Two of America's foremost families forming a union, both personally and professionally, would be considered quite a sweet incentive by most.'

Sweet. A little shiver went through Faye. Nothing about this man said *sweet*. He conjured up words like *hard... ruthless*. Not *sweet*.

She looked at him, more curious than she'd like to admit considering the subject of this conversation. 'And what do *you* get out of the marriage?'

'Reputational stability. I'm thirty-five. My single status has been having an adverse effect on some of my deals lately. I'm not considered trustworthy. It's old-fashioned,

and a bit archaic, but it's there. And I want to marry someone who is my equal, not some debutante.'

Faye wasn't sure if she should feel flattered or not. But
she had to admit that she liked it that he wasn't one of those
men who seemed to think it would make him look more
virile to marry a woman a decade younger.

'Why haven't you married before now?'

He answered without hesitation. 'It's not an institution
I have any interest in. I have no delusions about love, or
romance. I saw only toxicity in my parents' marriage, and
I've never had any desire to risk repeating that. However,
I have always known that one day I would have to marry,
and the longer I remain single, the more speculation about
my personal life is eclipsing the business—and that's not
acceptable.'

He continued.

'As much as I see it as a necessary evil, I do think that
with the right kind of wife one's standing, socially and professionally, can be enhanced, and that's what I'd be hoping for.'

Wow, that's cold.

Faye hadn't expected such a brutally clinical answer, but
at least he wasn't pretending that it would be anything but
a marriage of convenience.

She said, 'As I'm sure your team informed you when
collating their dossier on my suitability, I *was* married and
I am now divorced. I don't particularly want to repeat the
experience.'

'It wasn't good?'

No. She'd believed herself in love with her husband, and
he with her, but she'd been wrong. Getting divorced within
a year of her wedding day had been humiliating and hurtful.

Faye lifted her chin. 'Not particularly, no. Hence my lack
of desire to jump into another marriage.'

'This would be different.'

'How?'

'As you said, you're no wide-eyed ingenue. Neither am I. We'd be going into this with the understanding that it is an agreement made between two adults who can see the benefits of such a union. No emotional artifice.'

Faye felt a little breathless all of a sudden. No, there was no emotional artifice, and he wasn't wide-eyed. He was worldly-wise and experienced.

Once again she had a disconcerting flash of his head coming closer to hers...how he might take her face in his hands, angling it up towards him so he could kiss her so deeply that—

'You must be fielding curiosity about your personal life too,' he noted.

Faye smiled thinly. 'At the age of thirty, I think most people consider me irrelevant.'

Primo's gaze dropped over her body and then moved back up again, so thoroughly and slowly that it was bordering on insolent. When his eyes met hers again he said, very clearly, 'You are most definitely not irrelevant.'

Faye hated how that affected her. Because she had no doubt that he turned this easy charm on everyone, bending them to his will.

Deep down, she had been feeling an increasing sense of becoming invisible. Of resigning herself to the fact that she might be alone for the rest of her life. Too independent for some men, too intelligent for others. Too burned by her marriage to let anyone get too close. Too afraid of exposing herself like that again in a world where love-matches didn't really exist.

She'd somehow forgotten that when she'd met her husband, and had thought that maybe she'd buck the trend, like her parents had, and would have a real marriage.

But it had become clear pretty quickly—at the first bump in the road—that their marriage hadn't been founded on much at all. A lesson Faye hadn't forgotten and wouldn't ever forget.

So in some ways, much as it galled her to admit it, what Primo was proposing wasn't altogether unappealing. Faye knew her father worried about her. He was an old conservative romantic, and she knew that he would be happier if she were married. She would do anything to make her father happy. But this...?

Then she thought of something Primo hadn't mentioned and her insides twisted. She knew how to put him off the idea of marrying her.

'What about children? I presume they're a part of your long-term plan? You have responsibilities to your own family legacy.'

'Of course—and, yes, that's also part of why I'm inclined to consider marriage at this point. I know I have a duty to create a lasting legacy in the form of a family.'

Faye couldn't help but feel a little sad when she heard the way he laid that out, as if it were just something on a checklist. It was the way most of their peers in their milieu behaved towards having children—it was a strategic thing to secure bloodlines and fortunes. Not—heaven forbid—because they might actually want to invest in the notion of creating a family out of love.

But that was how she'd always envisaged having a family. Not because it was strategic, but because she wanted to recreate the love and security her parents had given to her.

Faye wanted to feel relief that she was about to end this... whatever this was with Primo Holt...before it had even started, but what she did feel was a little more conflicted.

She said, 'Well, I'm not in the market for having children. Under no circumstances. I won't provide you with heirs, so ultimately this marriage would have no long-term benefit for you or your family name. It'll have to be a business deal without the marital benefits, I'm afraid.'

Primo looked at Faye for a long moment. She epitomised sleek elegance, with her hair pulled back. She wore a silk shirt. Tailored trousers nipped in at her waist that drew the eye to her long legs.

The fire he'd sensed last night under the surface of that elegance was on full display now. He imagined the pulse throbbing at sensitive points of her body and his own body responded. He had to grit his jaw and call on every ounce of control he possessed not to embarrass himself.

He'd been curious to see if she'd have the same effect on him today, and if anything it was stronger. And what was disconcerting was the realisation that they'd orbited each other for years—all their lives—and this chemistry had been lying in wait until they'd come close enough to touch.

He focused on what she'd just said. She didn't want children. That didn't cause him a huge amount of concern at this point. They barely knew each other, after all. Surely after time spent together they would discuss the matter again and she might feel differently.

Primo's philosophy on having a family was basically: do no harm. The bar of parenting he'd experienced had been so low as to be practically non-existent. His mother's abandonment of her two sons hadn't been preceded by much care and attention, and yet Primo could remember having to pull his brother Quin away from where he'd been clinging on to their mother's legs as she'd tried to leave. Primo always carried that memory with him, as a reminder never to let his emotions get in the way of reality.

And their father might as well have abandoned them for all the care and attention *he'd* given them.

So, as far as Primo was concerned, if he did have a family, he would do his utmost to treat his children with respect and give them a sense of inclusion that he'd never experienced. As for anything more than that? That was in the realm of fiction and fantasies.

'Children...family...that's not something we have to discuss now. I realise that this is a lot to absorb.'

Faye was still tense. 'I don't think you're listening to me.'

Oh, Primo was listening. But she was telling him one thing with her mouth and another thing entirely with her eyes and the flush in her cheeks. While the electricity between them was strong enough to light up an entire state. He had an urge to close the distance between them and slide his hand around to the back of her neck, cover her mouth. He wanted to taste her. He imagined she was spicy and tart and sweet all at once. She would surprise him. He was sure of it. And he was still sure, in spite of her protestations, that she was the right choice for him.

She wasn't remotely intimidated by him. Anticipation burned low in his gut. He had to have her.

He said, 'I've told you that I think a union between us would be advantageous to any deal with your father, but if you don't want to marry me it won't affect that. I don't play games.'

She inclined her head slightly. 'I appreciate that. Even if you have admitted that a marriage *would* make the deal more binding.'

'All I ask is that you at least give this proposal some thought.'

He could almost see the inner struggle on her face behind those gold and green eyes. Mesmerising.

'Fine,' she eventually said, tight-lipped. 'I'll think about it. But I wouldn't hold your breath.'

Primo looked at her and said. 'I wouldn't dream of it. I think you'd enjoy watching my demise from lack of oxygen.'

To his surprise, Faye let out a helpless burst of laughter before quickly covering her mouth and sobering.

She wanted him.

He knew it.

He took a step backwards, even though everything in him resisted moving away from her, and said, 'Regardless of what you decide, Faye, you can't deny that there is something between us.'

Before she could respond to that, either to agree or deny, Primo turned and walked out of the room.

It was only when he was in his car on the way back into town that he was able to reflect and realise that for the first time in a long time—if ever—he couldn't foretell what would happen.

Oh, he knew her father would agree to the deal—he'd be a fool not to. But as for Faye? Primo genuinely had no clue. She could go either way.

There was a tingling tightness in his gut…a sense of something shimmering just out of reach. It was so unusual and so rare that at first he didn't even know what it was. But then it struck him… What he was experiencing was as banal and common as a cold. It was excitement.

He let out a bark of surprised laughter at the notion, causing his driver to send him a concerned glance in the rearview mirror.

CHAPTER THREE

FAYE HAD JUST returned to her Manhattan apartment from
visiting her father, after a trip to Los Angeles to secure a
piece of sculpture for a client at an auction. It had been a
week since she'd seen Primo Holt. But he'd started texting
her twenty-four hours after they'd spoken.

Messages like:

Have you had a time to think about it yet?

She'd replied:

How did you get my number?

Your assistant was very helpful when I told him I needed
to get some urgent assistance with an art purchase.

That's underhand.

I would have said enterprising. Well? Have you thought
about it?

A decision like this requires more than twenty-four hours.

Twenty-four hours later, Primo had sent:

How about now?

I'm in LA. You just woke me up.

There's a great breakfast spot on Sunset. Angie's. Tell them I sent you.

Thanks for the rec but I know it already.

You're welcome. Think about my proposal on the flight home.

I'll be sleeping.

Pity.

That provocative flirty response had sent flutters through Faye's body. No, not flutters. Something distinctly stronger and earthier. Something that scared her with its intensity. And it annoyed her because she had no doubt that he was just playing with her.

It had been a long time since anyone had been so direct. *Since someone had wanted her.* Even if it was for a marriage of convenience. But those last words he'd issued to her face had revolved in her head like a mantra all week.

'You can't deny that there is something between us.'

Disturbing. Intoxicating. Unbelievable.

Faye hated to admit it, but she'd spent much of her time when not working looking the man up online. There were scant details of his mother and father's divorce. Acrimonious. How his father had married again, numerous times. How his brother had refused his inheritance and become a self-made billionaire with his tech business and was now based in São Paulo. How Primo had taken the reins of the family business and within just a few years had tripled its fortunes and importance. Thousands of employees globally.

The man seemed to be indefatigable. In one twenty-four-hour period a journalist had accompanied him as he'd done a deal over breakfast in London, another in New York that afternoon, and by the same evening had been hosting a charity ball in Miami.

Faye could remember seeing him at that event, because it had taken place during a famous art fair held annually in the city. She remembered him wearing a white tuxedo jacket and looking vital and gorgeous. Not as if he'd just traversed the globe.

As for his private life—it was locked up tight. There were only a few photographs of him online with beautiful women. Each one more accomplished and impressive than the last. A human rights lawyer. A famous model turned philanthropist. An interior decorator. A fashion designer.

There were no salacious kiss-and-tells. No tabloid rumours. Only endless speculation as to when he was going to settle down and with whom.

And he wants you.

As his wife. Not a lover. It was probably second nature to a man like him to make a woman feel desired. He could have seduced her that first night and she probably would have succumbed, much to her shame.

Faye walked over to the window in her living room and took in the view of Central Park in the distance. She worried her lower lip—a bad habit.

While she'd been in Los Angeles her father had agreed to the deal with Primo. Her father looked years younger already...as if a huge weight had been lifted off his shoulders. Faye's conscience pricked. She hadn't truly noticed how much of a burden the business had become.

She'd had lunch with her father after that conversation with Primo, and she'd told him about the proposal.

He'd responded, 'You don't even know the man.'

Faye had explained about Primo taking her for a drink.

Her father had frowned, 'Is he using marriage as a bargaining chip?'

'Not exactly,' Faye had had to admit. 'He would still do the deal with you, to take over majority control of MacKenzie Enterprises, but…as he pointed out…a marriage would ensure his *personal* investment as well as the business deal.'

Her father has asked, 'What do you think of him?'

Faye had avoided answering that directly by asking, '*Would* it be beneficial to you? If we married?'

Her father had shifted a little uncomfortably and hadn't been able to meet her eye. Faye's insides had sunk. Primo himself had confirmed it already. Of course it would be beneficial.

Eventually her father had sighed and looked at her. 'It *would* give us an added level of protection. He'd naturally be more invested in protecting his wife and father-in-law.'

Her father had reached for her hand with his and Faye had noticed how fragile he felt.

He'd said, 'I do worry about you, my dear. What are we going to do about you?'

'Daddy, you don't need to worry about me, I'm perfectly fine as I am.'

'Aren't you lonely, though? I was so lonely after your mother died… I know what it is to be alone.'

His words echoed in her now, with a kind of hollow truth. In spite of her hectic work schedule she *was* lonely. More than she'd like to admit. And one of the most exciting men she'd met was expressing an interest in her.

No, she corrected herself. He was expressing an interest

in acquiring a convenient wife along with his new business venture.

At that moment her phone pinged with a message and she looked at it.

I want to marry you, Faye, so you're going to have to come up with something more compelling than a lack of desire to have children. Primo.

Faye put her hand to her mouth and let out a little helpless sound somewhere between laughter and a sob. It was as if he was inside her head, hearing her innermost thoughts.

It wasn't just that she wouldn't agree to have children. *She couldn't have children.* It was the reason why her first marriage had broken down. She'd got pregnant in textbook style, practically on their wedding night, but very early into the pregnancy she'd started bleeding and had been in intense pain. She'd been rushed to hospital for emergency surgery, where she'd had a miscarriage. There had been complications, and a few days later she'd had to have a partial hysterectomy. Her womb had been removed.

It had been utterly devastating and her relationship with her husband hadn't been strong enough to survive.

Faye had vowed never to put herself through that pain again—the pain of finding out so cruelly just how naive she'd been in believing that her husband loved her enough to want her just for herself. All she'd been to him was a trophy wife to stand by his side and a vessel to bear his heirs.

So why on earth would she agree to dive headlong into a marriage with someone who wanted her for the same thing? The only difference this time was that she was under no illusions that Primo Holt loved her. And she certainly didn't love him. She barely knew him.

He was bold, uncompromising. Faye should hate it that

he was being so pushy. Demanding. But it wasn't hate she felt. It was something a lot more complicated. And, perhaps even more disturbingly, she felt a sense of curiosity.

In spite of every misgiving, Faye was filled with a sudden desire to consider taking something for herself. Reclaiming a part of her womanhood and reputation that had been decimated with the divorce. She could still remember the looks and whispers as people had wondered what on earth was wrong with her that she hadn't been able to hang on to her husband for even a year.

It had been so cruel. She'd felt like a failure as a woman because she'd failed to bring a pregnancy to term and would never bear a child.

The truth of her medical condition had never been made public, thankfully. Not even her father knew the full extent of her operation. It had been too raw and painful to share.

And so Faye had just held her head high and weathered the scrutiny and gossip until the next inevitable scandal had come along and she'd become yesterday's news.

But even today, after she'd healed so much from that early raw pain, there was an air of failure that seemed to cling to her in public. And pity. Maybe a marriage with Primo Holt would give her a chance to redeem herself. Not that she'd ever really needed that validation, but a small part of her still felt that pitying scrutiny whenever she stepped into a public space. Alone. And it did get to her, deep inside, down to the part of the wound that had never been allowed to fully heal.

Not only that, it would secure the business deal with her father and the family business. Protect them on another level. As Primo had said himself, he'd be *more personally invested*.

A sense of illicit excitement gripped her as she entertained the notion of actually acquiescing to Primo's proposal. But the excitement dissolved a little when she thought of how she couldn't possibly offer him what he would ultimately need to secure his position—the next generation.

But maybe she could ensure that that would never be an issue. If he was willing to agree to *her* terms for a marriage.

Before she lost her nerve, Faye typed back a response to his last text:

I'm willing to discuss things further.

A text came back almost immediately.

Good, my assistant will be in touch to arrange a meeting.

Two weeks later, Manhattan

It was her wedding day. Faye's head was still spinning at the speed with which things had moved since she'd sent that text to Primo.

The speed of light.

The speed of Primo.

She was in the luxuriously spacious en suite bathroom of the penthouse suite in one of Manhattan's oldest and most iconic hotels.

Primo had booked her and her father in, insisting that they stay there rather than travel in and out of the city. A thoughtful gesture. They could have used Faye's Manhattan apartment, but this was far more convenient and comfortable.

On this same floor there was a function room where guests were already mingling. It was a small crowd. Intimate. Her father, some of their closest friends and their legal team. On Primo's side he had no family, just his legal team as witnesses.

Faye looked at her reflection in the mirror, feeling as if she was looking at someone else. She was wearing cream high-waisted tailored trousers, wide legged, teamed with a midriff-skimming long-sleeved sheer top overlaid with lace and intricate beading. Her hair was pulled back into a low chignon, and she wore classic pearls and the engagement ring Primo had surprised her with a couple of days after she'd agreed to marry him. A square yellow diamond with smaller triangular white diamonds on each side in a gold setting. It was an antique, from his family vault, and yet it felt surprisingly modern and very elegant. It also fitted snugly, without needing alteration. Something that had unsettled Faye a little—especially as she didn't consider herself to be remotely superstitious.

Just the previous day she had signed the final legal papers—a marriage agreement setting out the parameters of this union. She'd met with Primo in his offices over a week ago and laid out her terms for a marriage, all of which he'd agreed to—which had taken her by surprise.

Because there, in black and white, she'd made it clear that she would only agree to a marriage if they could review the situation in six months' time and decide at that point whether to carry on or divorce.

It gave Faye a get-out clause, and she was sure that Primo would want to get out by then too. Because she'd also made it clear that under no circumstances would she consider having children, so at least she could feel that she hadn't deceived him.

But you didn't tell him the full truth, pointed out a little voice.

No, she hadn't divulged the full extent of her infertility.

She had no intention of baring her innermost pain to someone who she hardly knew. After all, she wasn't planning on this being a long-term union. If Primo was so determined to marry her then this was how she was doing it. On *her* terms.

Six months of a marriage between the two families would solidify the business deal between her father and Primo, and give them added protection and security for the future. She'd ensured that there was a clause in the marriage agreement that, in the event of a divorce, it wouldn't have any detrimental effect on the business deal. And, as little as she knew Primo, he didn't strike her as a vindictive man.

Faye knew what she was doing was ruthless on some level, but it was no more ruthless than Primo expecting that he could secure himself a convenient wife on the back of a deal. And he'd made it very clear that this marriage had nothing to do with emotions, so there was no danger of *hurting* him. If anything, divorcing in six months would be an annoyance, but she was sure he could go to number two on his list of potential wives and secure another bride.

And in the meantime you'll be married to a man you want for the next six months.

Faye flushed at that incendiary thought.

Her mind slipped back to Primo's offices a week ago. He'd looked at her from across his desk, leaning back in his chair, supremely relaxed. Fingers steepled before him. She'd noticed how masculine his hands were. Short, blunt nails. She'd imagined they'd be slightly calloused. Not soft. Hard. Like the rest of him.

'So you're saying that you don't want to cohabit and that you'll only agree to us appearing together in public at pre-agreed events?'

She'd nodded, a quiver in her belly, knowing that she must be pushing him to the edges of his patience with her list of requirements for their marriage agreement.

She'd said, 'I've been independent for a long time and I won't give that up. I've also got a busy work schedule, so I simply won't be available for every public outing. I might not even be in the same country. But I'm sure if an event is important enough, and organised far enough in advance, we can ensure you get what you need out of the arrangement.'

His eyes had flashed at that, sending more than a quiver through Faye.

He'd commented dryly, 'What I'm getting, by the sounds of it, is a part-time wife.'

He'd stood up then, and walked over to one of his floor-to-ceiling windows. His loose-limbed grace had caught Faye's eye more than the commanding views of lower Manhattan. The way his shirt pulled across his broad back and shoulders, hinting at the muscles underneath, the narrow waist and the firm buttocks—

He'd turned around to face her and Faye's face had flamed guiltily.

He'd said, 'If we don't live together, and only meet intermittently, then how do you suppose we'll consummate our marriage? Or will you do me the honour of cohabiting with me on our wedding night? I have every intention of this marriage being a real one, Faye. I don't sleep around and I'm not unfaithful. And I like sex.'

'I like sex.'

At that blunt pronouncement, Faye hadn't been able to stop a slew of images of their limbs entwined from spooling out in her head.

But he'd made it sound so…functional. Like something they'd do that was part of the agreement, to tick a box. He hadn't alluded to what he'd said before, about there being *something* between them. Did he know she wanted him and so he didn't feel the need to feign his own desire any more? She'd felt vulnerable. Exposed.

'No one needs to know the intimate details of where we're living. We both have busy lives.'

Primo had stalked back towards his desk and Faye had felt herself tensing against the way her skin prickled with anticipation. He'd perched on the edge of the desk, one strong thigh in Faye's peripheral vision. It had taken all of her strength and control to keep her gaze up. He'd been striking a dominant pose and yet she hadn't felt intimidated. She'd felt very keenly that he was curious about her reactions to him.

'That's not really answering my question.'

Faye's throat had suddenly been dry as sandpaper. 'I'm not saying we can't…consummate the marriage…'

After all, whispered a little voice, *isn't this what you want too? Something out of this arrangement for you?*

But the thought of surrendering to him on a more intimate level had been terrifying. Because without even touching her he'd made her feel things she'd never felt before—a kind of wild yearning. An awareness of herself that no other man had ever made her feel. A sense of not being fully in control. When he seemed to be scarily in control.

She'd forced her brain to work. 'I'm open to discussing making plans, but if you want to get married on the date you've specified, I'm afraid I'm already booked on a flight to Venice that evening. I have clients lined up to meet during Carnival.'

Primo had narrowed his gaze on her before saying dryly, 'Discussing making plans to consummate our marriage? How romantic.'

The disdain in his voice when he'd said that had made Faye stand up. She'd shot back, 'We both know this isn't about romance, but if you're going to mock me then perhaps you need to look for another convenient bride.'

Primo had stood up too and regarded her. 'Forgive me. I don't mean to mock. You know where I stand on the fantasy of romance in marriage. But I would like this marriage to function, and for it to function we need to be aligned in public and in private. If you don't think that is possible then maybe this is not a good idea.'

She'd overreacted. And Faye had felt even more exposed. Primo had agreed to all of her terms, and it obviously made sense for their marriage to appear as real as possible.

Aware of the stakes if she pulled out at that point, she'd taken a breath and said, 'I do think it's possible. I want this marriage to work too.'

For six months at the most.

There was a knock on the door at that moment, jolting Faye out of her memories of last week. She said absently, 'Come in.'

It was her father, stooped and walking unsteadily with two sticks. Even so, he looked dapper in his steel-grey three-piece suit. He was determined to walk her down the aisle. Her father knew well that this was no love-match, but she could see that he hoped it might become something enduring. She hadn't told him of her terms. Her conscience pricked, but she told herself that the long-term benefits of having been married to Primo Holt even for a brief period would be worth it.

Her father looked at her with suspiciously shiny eyes. 'You remind me so much of your mother...you look beautiful.'

Now Faye's eyes stung. 'No one was as beautiful as Mother.'

Her father said a little gruffly, 'They're ready for us.'

Faye sucked in a breath and gathered up her matching cropped jacket and the posy of flowers—yellow and cream, matching her outfit and the engagement ring. She hadn't even thought to organise flowers. Primo had done it.

She went to her father and forced a smile, slipping an arm through one of his. 'Let's go, then, shall we?'

* * *

Primo didn't like how on edge he felt. Almost...nervous. Which was ridiculous. He couldn't ever remember feeling nervous in his life. But right now he was definitely not feeling his usual level of confidence.

Arrogance.

Faye had accused him of being arrogant. As he'd told her, he'd be the first to admit to it. But he wasn't so arrogant that it made him blind to things. He certainly wasn't blind to the fact that Faye MacKenzie was an enigma.

He knew she was marrying him for her own ends—to shore up the business deal with her father and to bolster her own reputation after a failed early marriage and years of being something of a social outlier. In spite of professing not to care what people thought, she was human, and no one was immune to the lingering toxicity of an old scandal.

But apart from that...? He knew she wasn't mercenary. She had a family fortune of her own to inherit. Not to mention a very lucrative and successful career as one of the world's most respected art brokers.

So, was she marrying him because she was also getting something more personal out of it? He wasn't so sure after she'd informed him that they'd have to *make plans* to consummate their marriage.

Usually women were only too happy to bare all with him as soon as possible—physically and emotionally. But not this woman. She looked at him with those gold and green eyes warily.

He knew there was heat between them. The moment they were in the same room he felt it like a live current. Maybe he should have kissed her that day when she'd come to his office, looking so prim in a trouser suit. Accusing him of mocking her. He'd wanted to kiss her. To muss up her hair. Undo the buttons of her blouse. Mess with that pristine elegant surface and demonstrate the physical benefits of a marriage that had nothing to do with *romance*.

The prospect of that made his blood hum with anticipation.

But at that moment a hush went over the group of people in the function room. The back of Primo's neck prickled as the celebrant came and stood before him and gave a cue to the string quartet, who started playing music.

For a moment Primo felt an almost superstitious reluctance to turn around to see his bride. But then, telling himself he was being ridiculous, because this really was just a slightly more personal and intimate form of a business deal, he turned around and was instantly awe-struck.

Faye was stunning.

Primo barely noticed her father, or how slowly she walked with him to keep pace. He drank her in. She was elegant and cool and sexy all at once in a wide-legged trouser suit. Hair pulled back. Make-up discreet. He saw the flash of her yellow diamond engagement ring and felt a surge of possessiveness to think of one of his ancestor's rings on *her* hand, marking her as his. It was a deeply primal and uncool sentiment to feel, but he couldn't help it. Primo had never felt possessive of a woman in his life; when those games started he would be gone.

She wore a top under her jacket that at first sight looked transparent, sending his pulse into overdrive, but then he realised it was sheer, not transparent, and overlaid with beaded lace. Edgy. Sophisticated. He hadn't known what she would wear, and from what he'd seen of her so far she clearly favoured a modern kind of elegance.

She reached him. Her scent was subtle and made him want to lean closer. Roses and musk...and something much more sharp cutting through those classic notes.

She looked at him with those wide hazel eyes. They

glowed green today, enhanced by her subtle make-up. Long lashes. Mouth slick with a colour that looked like wine.

Primo suddenly had an image of taking a glass of wine and tipping it over her bare skin before licking it—

'Take care of her. She's precious to me.'

Primo's wayward imaginings dissolved under the unmistakably steely tone of Faye's father as he handed his daughter to her fiancé. He forced himself to meet the man's eyes and said with full sincerity, 'I intend to take very good care of her.' His gaze went to Faye's. 'If she allows me.'

Faye made a slightly strangled-sounding noise as her father put her hand into Primo's. He curled his fingers around it securely, not even sure at this late moment that she wouldn't try to walk away. The fact that he still wasn't sure of her after she'd laid down a slew of ultimatums before agreeing to this marriage told him all he needed to know about how exciting it would be to marry her.

As for those ultimatums—no cohabiting and only going to prearranged social events. They didn't perturb him. It wasn't as if he was suddenly ready to cohabit either, but it would be more practical, long-term. In six months she'd have grown comfortable in his world—he was sure of it.

What if she wants out? asked a little voice.

He dismissed it immediately. She wouldn't want out. He could only enhance her social standing and add to her business contacts. Her father would be reaping the benefits of not having to worry about the family business.

Primo slid her a glance now, as the celebrant welcomed them. Faye was presenting him with her very perfect side profile, not a hair out of place. Once again, her remoteness made his fingers itch to undo her—literally. Because he could see the pulse under her skin. Fast. He imagined it as hot as his.

Turning this marriage from part-time into full-time, and

revealing the woman under the sky-high walls she hid behind, was a challenge that fizzed in his veins. And her insistence about not having a family? He wasn't too bothered
about that... Let him persuade her first that they could be
good together, and then they could move on to the next
phase: to build an enduring marriage with a legacy that
would last for generations.

Primo faced forward, Faye's hand in his, and vowed that
this marriage would be as successful as every other venture he'd ever invested in. Failure wasn't an option. Not
for Primo Holt.

CHAPTER FOUR

Venice Carnival, two days later

FAYE HATED THAT she felt so conspicuously alone. Especially as she was now a married woman and the reason she was alone was her insistence on coming here for work.

She could be on her honeymoon; even arranged marriages indulged in arranged honeymoons. But she'd insisted on sticking to her work schedule, and now she felt a bit like a child who had overplayed her hand.

The simple gold wedding band that Primo had slipped onto her finger only two days ago was heavy. She resisted the urge to look at it and see how it nestled against the engagement ring. Markers of his possession of her. When he hadn't yet possessed her at all. Not like that.

She felt a little breathless. They'd only shared a kiss. But that kiss would be burned onto her memory for ever. The civil wedding ceremony had passed in a blur of vows and promises that she'd been too conscious of Primo to focus on. Standing beside her. So tall and broad.

If she hadn't had to walk down that aisle at a snail's pace to meet Primo she might have stumbled at her first view of him waiting for her. He'd been dressed in a light grey three-piece suit, with a slightly darker silk tie and a white shirt. He'd had a small sprig of flowers in his lapel matching her posy. A touch that had made Faye feel inordinately emotional and somehow guilty. She'd put no thought into the wedding plans, leaving it all up to Primo's team.

But apart from all of that he'd been almost too beautiful to look at directly. Not beautiful. Gorgeous. And sexy. Filling out his suit in a way that drew the eye to his powerful physique. Hard jaw. Firm mouth.

And then that mouth had been coming towards hers before she'd been able to prepare herself, and the kiss that she'd thought about from the moment she'd met him had been every bit as terrifyingly exposing as she'd feared it would be.

Faye had been on dates in the decade since her divorce. She'd even taken some lovers. But not one had ever ignited such a burning inferno inside her. Not even her husband had done that, she'd realised in that moment. It was as if there'd been a spark deep within her, just waiting for Primo to ignite it fully.

When Primo had pulled back, it had taken an age for her to open her own eyes. She'd realised he was practically supporting her as her legs had turned to jelly. Mortifyingly, before she'd been able to gather her wits, he'd leant close again and said, for her ears only, 'See? I told you there was something between us. I look forward to getting to know you better...*wife*.'

Those words had made her insides swoop and dive like a besotted teenager's. She'd pulled back, terrified he'd see just how much his kiss had impacted her. How much the knowledge that he *did* want her impacted her.

But he'd simply smirked, as if he could hear her every thought, and taken her hand, tucking it under his arm, making sure she was all but welded to his side as he'd strolled back down the makeshift aisle and the quartet had played a sunny, joyful tune.

A short time later they'd sat together for lunch. Primo

had taken a sip of wine and said, 'You're still insisting on going to Venice this evening?'

Faye had only had to think of that kiss and the way he'd smirked at her to nod her head fervently and say, 'Absolutely. I can't let my clients down.'

'Shame. Maybe I could come with you? I'm due to take a short break, actually. I could play house husband while you work?'

Faye had immediately been rewarded with an image of a naked Primo lounging amongst rumpled sheets in the midst of the fading grandeur of a palazzo, awaiting her return like some louche playboy, there for her pleasure...

Faye shook her head to dislodge the memory.

At that moment a waiter in an all-black silk Pierrot suit with a mask covering his face passed by with a tray, and she swiped a glass of sparkling wine before her imagination went any more rampant. She took a big sip.

She was here at the Carnival to meet with some clients and visit art galleries. She'd just negotiated a couple of deals totalling in the millions, and she should be savouring her success, but it felt hollow. Because for the first time she was noticing that she had no one to share it with.

Damn Primo Holt for awakening a weakness inside her. *And more. Desire.*

It just went to show that she didn't have to scratch far beneath the surface to unearth vulnerabilities she hadn't felt in a long time. So much for her prized independence!

She took in her surroundings, forcing her mind away from thinking of *him*. The masked ball was taking place in a centuries-old palazzo, right on the Grand Canal. Candles and soft lighting turned everything golden. The costumes people wore were as elaborate as the palazzo, with its wall murals, frescoed ceilings and Murano glass chandeliers. Some men were in simple classic tuxedoes and some in

capes and silk shirts, like heroes from a romantic histori-
cal novel, all wearing masks.

The women's dresses ranged from modern evening
gowns to costumes that would have made Marie Antoi-
nette look shy and retiring, complete with wigs and stunning decorative masks with feathers and jewels.

Soft music came from a masked string quartet.

There wasn't a jarring note of modernity anywhere. Faye
could easily imagine that she'd been transported back in
time by a couple of hundred years.

She rolled her eyes at herself, glad of the scarlet lace
mask that covered half her face. It matched her dress, and
the lace choker around her throat. Her hair was piled high
into a chignon—she'd aimed for artfully rough and messy,
because she'd had to do it herself. The dress was strapless.
Lace over silk. The bodice was fitted over her chest and
to her waist and then fell in voluminous folds to the floor.
It wasn't as eye-catching as some of the costumes, but she
didn't mind that. She'd never particularly liked to draw attention.

But you like the attention Primo gives you.

Faye's insides clenched. Perhaps she'd been too hasty, insisting on coming to Venice. Because right now she could
be consummating her marriage, and not feeling this awful
sense of regret and hollowness spreading throughout her—

'Waiting for someone?'

Faye's racing mind stopped dead. The little hairs rose up
all over her exposed skin. *His voice.* No. It couldn't be. Was
she so desperate that she was imagining him?

The back of her neck tingled. She turned around and
came face to chest with a tall, broad man dressed all in
black, with a cape tied at his throat and thrown carelessly
over one shoulder. She looked up. His face was half covered with a hawk-like mask, revealing a firm jaw and that

mouth. That mouth she could probably pick out of a line-up even though they'd only kissed once.

For an incredible moment Faye could almost imagine that a couple of hundred years *had* melted away and they'd slipped back in time. He looked like a buccaneer. A marauding pirate. She felt breathless. Her heart was pounding. Her insides were melting, turning hot and languorous.

Somehow she managed to say, 'No, I'm not waiting for anyone.'

He cocked his head to one side. 'Shame. You look a little lonely.'

Faye felt her faculties return and lied through her teeth. 'Not lonely at all.'

'A woman as beautiful as you shouldn't be here alone.'

Faye almost rolled her eyes. 'Have you said that to many women this evening?'

He shook his head. 'No, just you. But perhaps I have it wrong, maybe you're avoiding someone.'

Faye smiled sweetly. 'Wrong on both counts. I'm here for work, actually, at the invitation of a kind client.'

'Who has left you here alone? Very remiss of her.'

'Him, actually.'

His eyes flashed behind his mask. The black made them look very blue, and his skin look even darker. 'This...client... Was he trying to foster a more personal relationship?'

'That's really none of your business.'

'Isn't it?' was the swift response.

After all, even though they hadn't acknowledged each other's identity, this *was* her husband. For the first time Faye felt a thrill go through her at the thought that this was *her man*. And he had come all the way here for her. And he might be jealous.

Or maybe he hadn't and wasn't. She felt exposed...a far too common sensation around this man...

'Tell me,' she asked, 'are you here for business too?'

He shook his head. 'Would you believe that up until this morning I had no plans to come here. I can't explain it, but I felt a calling…maybe it was because I saw you in a dream and I wanted to see if you could be real.'

Faye hated how those words affected her. Because he'd said them blithely, with no care, and because it highlighted the part of her that reacted to words like that. Wanting the sentiment to be real.

'I am real, and I'm pretty certain I didn't appear in your dreams.'

He looked at her. 'I wouldn't be so sure about that.'

A moment tautened between them, alive with electricity. A waiter came by and the man in black—Faye refused to acknowledge who he really was just yet, like a coward—took a drink and deftly swapped her half-finished one for a fresh glass.

Then he said, 'Join me on the balcony? It's a little stuffy in here.'

Faye nodded and let him take her gloved hand, leading her through the crowd to open French doors leading to a balcony. Another couple were at the other end, heads close together.

She still couldn't quite believe that he was here. That she'd been lamenting acting too hastily only a moment before he'd appeared.

They stood together and for a moment nothing was said. They took in the iconic and impressive view of the Grand Canal and the palazzos on the other side, lights shining from windows, each one a portal into another life, or lives, being played out as they had been here for hundreds of years.

'The history of this place has always humbled me.'

Faye looked at the man in surprise, and then almost felt

irritation. *Would he stop reading her mind?* She shook her head at her own ridiculousness.

He obviously saw her reaction and said, 'What? Did I say something wrong?'

'No.' She couldn't help smiling a little. 'I was just thinking the same thing.'

He was looking down at her. She couldn't read his expression. She was glad of their masks, creating this barrier between them. Then he reached out and touched her mouth with a finger, but it was so fleeting that she wasn't sure if she imagined it, even though her lip tingled.

He said, 'Look, let's stop this—

Before he could emit another word Faye blurted out, 'Can we not? Please?'

She knew he was about to dismantle this shimmering delicate facade of anonymity and she wasn't ready. She felt a little foolish, but she really, really wanted to preserve this moment, and she didn't want to analyse why it was so important to her. Something about not being ready to face the reality of why they'd married. For a business deal. She wanted him to want *her*, uniquely, and felt somehow protected behind the flimsy lace mask. As if it disguised the truth of their situation and how badly she wanted him.

'Can we leave?' she asked, before she lost her nerve. Before reality could return.

For a moment he said nothing, and Faye was afraid he'd make some flippant remark, but suddenly the air was infused with a sense of urgency. He just nodded, took her hand again and led her back into the room, dispensing with their glasses en route to the entrance. From there he led her down to the ground level, where a water taxi was waiting.

Faye hadn't even noticed that she'd left her cape behind until Primo was undoing the silk tie on his and taking it off and putting it around her bare shoulders. It still held the warmth of his body, imprinting onto her skin, making it rise up into goosebumps.

'Thank you.'

She glanced at him through the gauzy lace of her mask. His mouth looked firm.

'You're welcome.'

He sat beside her and put an arm across the back of the seat. Faye knew she should ask where they were going, but she was too afraid of shattering this illusion that they were strangers taking a moment out of time. When the reality was anything but that.

For a second, it struck Faye that perhaps this man she'd left the party with *was* in fact a stranger, and that she'd projected her desire for her husband onto him, willing him to be Primo. But when she sneaked a glance at him again, she could see the distinctive jaw under the mask. Hard and stern.

As if sensing her looking at him, he turned. The hawkish mask should have made him look scary against the backdrop of a moonlit Venice but she felt only excitement. His eyes were very blue. It was Primo. *Her husband.*

The boat's engine had stopped now, and they were being steered into a landing pier that was attached to a soaring four-storey palazzo.

'What is this place?' Faye asked, in spite of her wanting to maintain the charade of anonymity.

The fact that it was obviously one of Venice's older palazzos was obvious. It was one she'd noticed on her trips up and down the canal. She knew who owned most of them, but not this one. Which usually meant very old money.

Primo replied, 'I own the top-floor apartment. The rest of the palazzo is owned by the Monegazio family.'

Faye's sucked in breath of shock that was disguised by the fact that Primo was getting out of the boat. He extended a hand to her and she took it, holding her dress up with the other hand as she stepped onto concrete.

The Monegazio family were one of Venice's oldest and most venerated. They had a private art collection that was the stuff of legend. It had never been seen in public. And apparently her husband owned their top-floor apartment.

Primo bade *ciao* and *grazie* to the boat taxi driver and led her to huge ornate doors that opened as if by magic as they approached. An elegant older man was on the other side, dressed in black trousers and a long-sleeved black jumper.

Faye heard him address the man as Matteo, and they exchanged a few words in Italian. Cleary he was some kind of concierge. The man dipped his head towards Faye in greeting, and then disappeared through an open door off the main entrance hall. Presumably his apartment.

Primo led her deeper into the palazzo. Faye got a tantalising glimpse of vast canvases on the walls as they walked over faded ornate rugs. There was a big table with a massive vase of fresh flowers.

She suddenly realised they were standing at modern gleaming metal doors. Primo pressed a button. Faye let out a surprised huff of laughter. 'An elevator? Isn't that a little sacrilegious in a place like this?'

'This was part of what they needed my money for. The oldest member of the family, the matriarch, is confined to a wheelchair now, so the palazzo had to be made accessible. They're asset-rich and cash-poor.'

The elevator doors opened, revealing a very standard and modern interior. It was jarring after her feeling that they'd been transported back in time. The elevator ascended and the doors opened again into a large marble-floored entrance hall. There was a circular table there, upon which sat a piece of modern sculpture. Faye recognised the artist instantly, and would have stopped to inspect it more closely, but Primo was ahead of her, striding into a living area and turning on low lights.

She followed, and her jaw dropped. It was a vast open space with windows out to the canal on either side, as this palazzo was not adjoining any others. One side of the room was a sumptuous living space, and subtle dividers at the other end demarked a dining area with a big, generous table. Oriental rugs overlaid a traditional terrazzo floor. Everything was cream and gold and very, very, luxurious.

She looked up; the ceiling was ablaze with ornate frescoes. Cherubs and angels and clouds and skies. It should have looked ridiculous. It didn't.

'It's…' Faye struggled to find words to describe the beauty around her. She couldn't.

'It's a little more…ornate than I would normally go for, but it suits the surroundings.'

Faye nodded. 'It would have been criminal to turn this into a minimalist space.'

'Drink?'

Faye realised that Primo had moved over to a drinks cabinet. She felt unsteady, as if they were on a ship. And, considering the water all around them, it wasn't a totally ridiculous notion.

She relished the thought of some fortification. 'Sure.'

He looked at her. 'A gin martini?'

He remembered her drink of choice. She felt a little jolt in her belly but shook her head. 'Too strong. A glass of prosecco would be fine, if you have it.'

He inclined his head and was soon approaching her with a flute of golden sparkling wine and holding a glass of what looked like whisky for himself.

He held out his glass. *'Saluti.'*

Faye clinked her glass against his and echoed his toast. She took a sip. The effervescent wine bubbled down her throat. Perfectly chilled and fragrant. Like the excitement mixed with trepidation fizzing in her veins. She'd never felt like this before sleeping with other men. Not because she was so confident, but because none of them had ever affected her on such a deep, visceral level.

He lifted a hand and gestured towards his face. 'If you don't mind?'

Faye's heart thumped. It would be ridiculous to ask him to keep it on.

She shook her head. 'Not at all.'

But as he unmasked himself she moved away a little, and looked at the canvases on the walls. They were all impressive, all originals, and did not follow any discernible pattern.

Faye stood before one. 'You have a Renoir.'

Primo came and stood beside her. 'As you can see, my collection is somewhat...eclectic,' he said, and his tone was self-deprecating. 'I can't claim to have any great knowledge. I tend to choose something if I like it, rather than because it's of strategic importance or because it fits into a narrative.'

Faye continued around the walls, taking in a snowy Dutch landscape. 'Truly, that's the best way to buy art—not because you *should* or because something is in fashion.'

'Is that how you buy art?'

Faye looked at him. He was watching her, his face no longer hidden, a shoulder leaning against the wall. For a second she couldn't breathe. He looked so beautiful.

How could this man really want her?

She was nothing that special.

She struggled to remember what he'd just asked her. Art. How did she buy art.

She shook her head. 'Actually, apart from curating my own family's collection, I don't collect a lot of art. I'm too conscious of what my clients are looking for. I have bought pieces along the way, but invariably I end up selling them on.'

Primo took her glass out of her hand and put it down, then said, 'Give me your hands.'

Faye did so, bemused. Primo tugged off the gloves that matched the dress. Silly to feel so exposed when it was only her hands. Primo put the gloves aside and then took the hand upon which her engagement and wedding ring sat and lifted it.

He arched a brow. 'You're a married woman?'

Faye scowled at him and he let her hand go, putting his hands up. 'You're the one still hiding behind a mask.'

Reluctant to let go of the last shred of illusion, but knowing it was silly to keep it up, she turned around and presented Primo with her back. For a long moment Primo did nothing, and Faye almost turned around again, but then she felt his hands at the back of her head, undoing the mask. It fell into her hand.

She would have turned around then, but Primo's fingers were in her hair and he was pulling out the pins holding up her chignon. Strands of hair started to fall down around her shoulders. When all the pins were out, he speared her hair with his fingers and massaged her scalp.

Faye had not expected that. She closed her eyes at the delicious sensations of Primo's big hands on her head. She felt like purring. She forced her eyes open and turned, dislodging his hands.

His eyes were a very bright blue. He said, 'You're still wearing your cape.'

Faye lifted her chin in a silent gesture for him to undo it. He did, his fingers making light work of the tie. She shivered lightly as it fell to the floor, baring her shoulders and the top of her chest.

He put out a hand and Faye looked at it for a moment before putting her hand in his. His fingers closed around hers and he led her from the living area, down a corridor to another doorway.

His bedroom.

It was a feast for the senses. Parquet flooring. A Murano glass chandelier. Hand-painted wallpaper in the Chinoiserie style. Gold trim. French doors leading directly out to a balcony overlooking the Grand Canal. A vast bed with a Rococo-style headboard trimmed with gold. Pristine white linen.

Faye couldn't take her eyes off the bed, but then Primo said, 'Okay?'

He was giving her permission to say no. Something about that consideration, especially now that they were married, made a piece of Faye's defences crumble.

She nodded. She couldn't *not*. She wanted him.

But just when she thought he'd waste no time in getting her on her back, he said, 'Look up.'

She did, a little bemused, and gasped out loud. The ceiling was an explosion of colour and clouds and cherubs, much like the ceiling in the main room, but there was a subtle difference to this one. She recognised the artist and couldn't quite believe it.

'Tiepolo?' she asked, naming a famous Venetian painter known for his Rococo style. There'd been rumours that he'd worked on palazzos for private families, but she'd never seen the evidence.

'Yes.'

'This ceiling must be priceless,' she breathed.

'It is. I own this entire apartment, but I don't own this ceiling,' Primo revealed.

'Art like this belongs to the world, not to one person.'

'Indeed.'

Eventually Faye took her gaze down from the ceiling to look at Primo. The air seemed to quiver between them.

He reached out a hand and pushed a lock of hair over one shoulder. 'Do you know how exquisite you are?'

Faye ducked her head, but he tipped up her chin with a finger. She said, 'You don't need to say things...like that. I'm not here to be wooed. We're married. This is an arrangement.'

Primo's eyes flashed with something, but Faye couldn't decipher the emotion. He said, 'We wouldn't have to be married for me to have wanted you out of all the women at that party.'

Faye gulped. 'But I'm nothing—'

Primo put a finger to her mouth, stopping her words. And then, before she could take another breath, his finger was replaced with his mouth and she was pulled tight into his body, his hands around her waist.

After a long, drugging moment he pulled back. Faye struggled to open her eyes...focus. Primo's eyes were so hot she felt seared.

He said, 'Don't ever suggest you're nothing again.'

Faye swallowed. She could taste him. 'I...okay.'

This was a wholly new sensation for her. Not just because she hadn't had sex in a while, but also, she realised now, because she instinctively chose men she felt in control around. With this man, she was not in control. But she trusted him. And that was almost scarier to acknowledge, when she'd spent the last decade keeping herself very protected.

He took his hands down and without taking his gaze from hers started to undress. Slowly, methodically, taking every piece of his clothing off until he was naked.

Faye's blood was sizzling and it hurt to keep her gaze up.

He said, 'You can look. I won't break.'

There was a thread of amusement in his voice. It emboldened Faye to drop her gaze down and...

Oh. My. God. The man was hewn out of living, breathing rock.

Broad shoulders and chest. A smattering of hair. Muscles that could have been carved and shaded by an artist. Golden skin. Slim hips. The darker hair at his groin where his body was hard. Thick and long.

Faye's eyes widened. He was magnificent. Every inch of him virile and unashamedly masculine.

'I'm feeling a little underdressed here,' he said, reminding her that she was still in her own costume, which suddenly felt restrictive. She reached for the zip at the side of the dress, under her arm, and started to tug it down. But it got stuck.

Primo stepped forward. 'Let me.'

Faye lifted her arm and Primo tugged at the zip until it gave way under his fingers. Of course it did. She couldn't imagine this man touching anything—even an inanimate object—and it not giving way to his touch.

The dress loosened around her chest, but to her surprise Primo held her arm up and pressed his mouth against the underside of her arm. A shudder of pure desire went through Faye. It felt like a shockingly intimate act.

He let her arm go. Primo stood in front of her again and slowly peeled the dress from her chest and then down and then with a tug over her hips it was falling to the floor.

Now she stood before him in nothing but a matching underwear set—strapless bra—and her shoes. She kicked them off, which lowered her a few inches, making her feel tiny next to Primo's formidable height and bulk. But she didn't feel nervous or intimidated.

He was looking at her, that bright gaze lingering on her

breasts, spilling out of the flimsy bra cups, moving down to her belly and hips and thighs.

'You are beautiful.'

Faye wanted to say the same thing to him, but felt shy.

Thankfully Primo took her by the hand again and led her to the bed. He sat down and pulled her between his legs.

'Turn around,' he ordered gruffly.

She did, and felt him undo her bra, letting it fall to the floor. Then he tugged her panties over her hips and down. She stepped out of them. Now she was fully naked.

He gently urged her to turn around again, and when she did his mouth was at the same level as her breasts. He cupped one fleshy weight and leaned forward, placing his hot mouth around one straining peak. Faye's head fell back and her hands speared his hair in a bid to hold on to something.

She was lost in a vortex of sucking, drugging heat, with a wire of tension linking directly from her nipple to between her legs. She didn't even realise her legs had given way until she was in his lap with his arms around her. Her pulse was thundering.

He stood up, taking her with him, and laid her on the bed. He went to retrieve something from a drawer, muttering something about not being able to last, and when Faye realised it was protection she said, 'It's okay...'

He looked at her with the foil packet unopened in his hand.

She said, 'I won't get pregnant. It's okay.' She deliberately didn't elaborate, and knew he most likely assumed she meant she was taking the contraceptive pill.

He put down the protection and came over to the bed, 'I'm clean. I get tested, and it's been a while since I had a lover.'

'Me too,' said Faye, feeling shy again.

He came over her on both arms, muscles bunching under his gleaming skin. Faye couldn't quite believe that Primo Holt was looking at her with such...naked hunger.

He kissed her again, an arm going under her back, arching her up to him so that her breasts were pressed against his chest, the hair there a delicious abrasion against her sensitised skin.

She moved restlessly under him, growing bolder, a hand seeking and finding his erection, wrapping around him, and glorying in the sheer evidence of his arousal. *For her.* It was the biggest aphrodisiac in the world.

And then he took his hand from him, saying again, 'I won't last. I need to be inside you.'

Faye needed no encouragement. She spread her legs around him and he guided himself to the centre of her body. Their skin was slick. Faye was panting. Primo teased her for a moment, dragging the head of his erection along her folds. She lifted her hips, causing him to impale her a little. Her eyes nearly rolled to the back of her head.

He let out a huff of laughter and said something like, 'I knew we'd be good together.' But she couldn't be sure. She was half crazed.

'Please...'

'Open your eyes. I want you to be sure you know who you're making love to. Not some random stranger from a masked ball.'

She looked at him. 'Of course I knew it was you...'

Even as you tried to pretend it wasn't, reminded a little voice.

Faye put her hands on Primo's arms. 'Please, Primo...'

It was as if saying his name broke some last shred of his control and he was sinking into her, stretching her so wide that she gasped.

He stopped. 'Am I hurting you?'

She shook her head, unable to speak. She squeezed his arms, urging him on, and he sank deeper. Faye could feel her body accept him and mould around his length, taking him in all the way until she didn't know where he ended and she began.

She'd never known making love could be so…intense. And Primo had barely even moved. And then he did, pulling back out and then moving in again. Slow, methodical movements, making the tension wind tighter and tighter.

His movements got faster, and Faye's entire body was as taut as a bow. He put a hand under her bottom and squeezed the firm flesh, then brought his hand around to where their bodies met. With one flick of his finger, a storm broke inside Faye's body and she was sent flying so high she wasn't sure if she'd ever return to the woman she'd been.

Primo's movements were more frenzied, wild, and with a guttural cry he stilled inside her, his body jerking as he too was split apart by pleasure.

CHAPTER FIVE

WHEN PRIMO WOKE, he kept his eyes shut and savoured the feelings in his body. He couldn't remember the last time he'd felt so heavy. Replete. Images and sensations came back to him. Soft lips…sweet mouth. Firm breasts with spiky nipples…rolling them in his mouth and sucking… making her moan. Silky, heavy hair trailing through his fingers…wrapping that hair around his palm as he drove into the tightest, silkiest embrace…his body responding instantly, hardening…

Primo wanted her again. *Now.*

He squinted in the soft dawn light coming in through the curtains and put out a hand…but met nothing. His eyes opened fully and he came up on one arm. The bed was empty, but still faintly warm. She wasn't long gone.

He sank back. He didn't have to investigate further to know that she was already gone. His instinct had been right. Together, they'd been explosive. More than he'd even antici-pated. He'd never felt such chemistry with a woman before.

His gamble to come to Venice to seduce her had paid off.

He hadn't felt resentful or irritated that his new wife wouldn't give him a wedding night. He appreciated that they hardly knew each other. And that this marriage was founded on the back of a business deal.

He'd known she was skittish around him. Clearly her first marriage had burned her. She'd said it hadn't been good.

The lingering satisfaction in Primo's body made his mouth curve up in a smile. Maybe now that she'd seen how good they were together she would relax a little more into her role as his wife.

Primo sprang from the bed and walked naked over to the French doors, pulling them open. He stepped out onto the balcony and looked down to see a water taxi moving away from the landing pier, a distinctive head of black hair, tumbled over shoulders, and the scarlet flash of a dress. The taxi sped away, taking his wife to her next destination.

Primo's smile got wider.

He had no doubt that she was going to lead him a merry dance, but if last night was anything to go by he would enjoy every second of being married to Faye MacKenzie. And sooner or later, she would give up on those *terms*.

At that moment there was a sound of collective giggling, and Primo looked away from the taxi to see another taxi near the palazzo, full of tourists who were all looking up at him and pointing. He put his hands modestly over his groin area and, still grinning, bowed and went back inside.

Faye willed the boat taxi to go faster, so people wouldn't be able to look inside and see her sitting there still dressed in her costume, hair undone, make-up melted off in the heat of passion.

She groaned silently when she recalled the previous night. Not even the fresh air of the spring morning could dilute *those* memories.

She was doing the walk of shame—albeit in a boat in one of the most beautiful cities in the world. That didn't make it any less mortifying.

She'd never experienced sex like that. So…urgent. Raw. Powerful. After that first time, she was pretty sure she'd fallen into a deep sleep. And then at some point she'd woken in the night, to find Primo wrapped around her body. She'd tried to move, but his embrace had tightened, and then she'd felt his body, hardening against hers.

Within seconds they'd been entwined again, and this time it had been even more urgent. Mind-blowing. She'd never had a lover like him. He'd opened her eyes to a depth of sensuality inside her that she'd never known existed.

Her cheeks were still burning at the thought of how he'd react to find her gone. But she'd had to leave. The thought of sitting with him and doing something as banal as sharing breakfast had seemed—ridiculously—like an intimacy too far after what they'd shared.

And it wasn't as if she wasn't going to see him again. They were married! They were due to attend an annual charity gala ball in Manhattan later that week. A social staple. A chance, as Primo had put it, to introduce themselves to society as a married couple.

But right now Faye had no idea how she'd ever look him in the face again. She'd been so...wanton. Lustful. He'd turned her into some hungry, base creature. And yet as the sight of her hotel came into view, and the taxi started slowing down, she couldn't help a tiny secret smile forming on her mouth. Because he'd unlocked something inside her and she couldn't in all conscience be sorry. Her whole body was still tingling in the aftermath.

She was about as far removed from her usual pristinely put-together self as she could be, but the sense of languorous satisfaction in her blood drowned out any need to be concerned about it.

The boat landed at the pier. A hotel attendant stepped forward to help her out of the taxi. As she walked into the foyer she passed a couple whose eyes widened when they saw her. Faye swallowed back an urge to giggle. She felt like explaining to them that she wasn't coming back from an illicit night of debauchery with a total stranger—that she had, in fact, just spent the night with her husband...

But that thought sobered her.

As she ascended to her room in the elevator she had to remind herself that Primo following her to Venice and seeking her out merely demonstrated his determination to get this marriage started. It hadn't been a romantic gesture. It had been entirely practical. And she hadn't even hesitated to acquiesce, too blinded by his spontaneity and sheer charisma.

She couldn't afford to forget the terms she'd laid out for this marriage and the knowledge that it was short-term only. Because she was realising after last night that this man could destroy her in ways she'd never been destroyed before. There was too much at stake—her precious independence and her bone-deep need to protect herself from being hurt all over again.

The Griff Benefit, Manhattan

The annual benefit ball to raise funds for cancer research was one of New York's biggest social events. It was held in one of Manhattan's most iconic hotels. Invitations were sent out by a board made up of New York's oldest names, and receiving an invitation—or not—could make or break someone's reputation.

Faye stood on the stairs that led down to the ballroom where a crowd of beautiful people thronged. Gold-edged mirrors around the ballroom reflected the glittering scene a thousand times over.

She wished she could say otherwise, but she spotted Primo immediately. Hard not to when he towered above most people around him. The lights glinted off his thick head of hair, highlighting the blonder strands.

As if sensing her, he lifted his head and his eyes zeroed

in on her immediately. Faye felt it like a jolt of electricity straight into her blood. It was the first time she'd seen him since Venice. Admittedly it was only a few days, but it was as if she'd left his bed only that morning, the sensations were so immediate...and the memories.

He came straight to her, walking up the stairs. He was dressed in a black tuxedo and he looked gorgeous. She sensed everyone in the vicinity hush, all eyes on them. Primo had wanted them to arrive together, but Faye had been caught up at an art auction and, because she'd had to go to her apartment to change, wouldn't have made it to meet him in time. So they'd come separately.

When he reached her she couldn't look away. Those blue eyes held her captive. He reached for her, putting an arm around her waist and pulling her into him. She found herself cleaving to him before she could resist the pull.

Then he tipped up her chin and pressed a lingering kiss to her mouth. Faye was already dissolving and melting, in spite of every pep talk she'd given herself not to allow him to have such an effect on her again. Evidently she'd been wasting her time.

He pulled back. 'Good evening, *wife.*'

Faye made a face and tried not to be so aware of how her breasts were crushed against his chest. 'I have a name.'

He smiled. 'Smile...everyone is watching us.'

Faye smiled dutifully.

He pulled back a little further and his gaze swept down over her body. 'You look...stunning, *Faye.*'

A glow of pleasure lit her up before she could stop it. But she had chosen her dress carefully. And it did please her that he'd noticed. She was used to sticking to classic shapes and colours, nothing too eye-catching, but this dress had called to the little girl inside her when she'd seen it in a window of a shop near the auction house.

Dark pink, strapless but for one garlanded strap over one shoulder. It had a ruched bodice and then fell in soft silken folds to the floor. It was whimsical. She didn't want to say *romantic*, but the word whispered in her head. She'd matched it with a pearl necklace and earrings that had belonged to her mother, and her hair was twisted back into a low bun.

'Thank you,' she responded, too shy to tell Primo how gorgeous he looked. Surely he had to know?

'You didn't stay for breakfast in Venice.'

Faye's face grew hot as she remembered her fear of him waking and finding her trying to contort herself back into the dress. Flitting from his magnificent apartment as if she'd done something wrong.

'I had a meeting to get to. And a flight back to New York.'

'I felt like a cheap one-night stand.'

Faye scoffed. 'You're telling me that you routinely encourage your lovers to hang out the morning after?'

He lifted his hand, where his wedding ring gleamed. 'I'm a married man now.'

Faye couldn't help a pulse of pleasure at this sign that he was taken. By her. He'd also neatly deflected her question.

Primo tucked her hand into his arm and said, 'Let's go meet the jackals, shall we?'

Faye couldn't help her surprised huff of laughter as Primo led her down the stairs and into the crowd. It was only afterwards that she castigated herself. No doubt he'd done that on purpose, to ensure she looked suitably delighted to be on his arm. *The new Mrs Holt.*

After cocktails and canapés there was a lavish banquet, finished off by an auction. It included everything and anything, from the ownership of an unknown English football team to a vintage Aston Martin, last seen on screen in a world-famous spy movie.

As the auction was drawing to a raucous close Primo stood up, following others who were also starting to move to the dance floor. Faye looked up at him and felt dizzy, even though she was sitting down. He held out his hand in silent invitation.

Damn the man.

She put her hand in his. 'I'd love to.'

In the next room a band were playing smooth tunes, and Primo pulled her into his arms. He looked down at her. 'I believe this is officially our first dance.'

'And what better arena for it to play out? In front of the very people you want to impress with your newfound settled status.'

Primo made a *tsk*ing sound. 'I want more out of this marriage than just to convince people I'm settling down.'

Faye's conscience pricked. She avoided Primo's eye, helped by the fact that he'd spun her away from him with a little flourish and then pulled her back into his arms.

She was suddenly breathless. She could feel the way his body was responding to hers. He held her close. No escape. He was looking at her as if she was the only woman in the room. It was heady. Intoxicating.

Then he asked, 'Why *did* you leave the other morning? And don't fob me off with your itinerary.'

Faye couldn't hide. To avoid admitting how intense it had been, she said, 'Because I'm used to my own space.'

Primo frowned. 'You've been married. I can't imagine you crept out of your first husband's bed.'

Faye had a flashback to waking up in bed alone after she'd had the operation after her miscarriage. Her husband hadn't shared breakfast with her ever again. Or her bed. Their moments of marital bliss had been laughably brief.

She forced a smile, but it was brittle. 'It was so long ago I hardly care to remember.'

'And it's none of my business,' Primo conceded, surprising Faye. Then he said, 'What matters is the present moment, and the fact that *we* are married now.'

Faye felt absurdly grateful for how easily Primo was willing to let that go. And for the maturity he'd exhibited. 'Thank you.'

He swung her around to avoid colliding with another couple, and that only pressed Faye closer to his body, making her aware of the whipcord strength of every hard muscle. If she closed her eyes for a second she was transported back to Venice, and how it had felt when his body had joined hers for the first time.

Suddenly she was filled with desire—a desire to escape the hundreds of eyes watching their every move and the whispers.

Primo stopped moving and looked down at her. 'Had enough?'

This time Faye was grateful for the uncanny way he seemed to be able to read her mind.

She nodded. 'Yes.'

Primo took her hand and led her off the dance floor. They made their way to the foyer, where Faye collected her coat—a light three-quarter-length jacket matching the dress.

She was surprised that it was so late. Usually she found these events beyond tedious. But Primo hadn't been a clingy date, nor had he expected her to cling to him. He'd been happy to conduct his own conversations. A man who was confident in himself... A rarity in her experience.

As they waited for Primo's car to be brought round, Faye wondered if she should hail a cab. But Primo said, 'My driver is at your disposal, but I would like it if you accompanied me to my apartment. I seem to recall that you don't have any early engagements.'

Faye might have asked how he knew that, but at Primo's request her assistant and his now worked together to synchronise their social and work engagements. The fact that he now knew her schedule as intimately as she did was still a bit disconcerting, but then she realised that it worked both ways and smiled.

'I seem to recall that you have an early pick-up for a flight to London?'

He inclined his head. 'Indeed, but if you keep me up all night I can sleep on the plane.'

She shrugged minutely, belying the heat in her body at the excitement that gripped her at the thought of keeping him up all night. 'Why not?'

At that moment, as if on cue, Primo's driver appeared in front of them, jumping out to open the car's rear door. Faye got in, and Primo went around to the other side.

The journey to Primo's apartment didn't take long, and Faye had to concede that in practical terms it would probably make sense for her to move into Primo's apartment... but that wasn't a step she was ready to dive into.

Getting involved in the intimacy of day-to-day living would remind her far too painfully of her first marriage, and the way her husband had shut her out once she could no longer deliver the required heir.

The thought of something similar happening with Primo made her feel a little winded for a moment—and *that* was what kept her cautious. He'd already impacted on her in ways she didn't want to investigate.

The car was pulling to a smooth stop now, outside a tall building bordering the park. When Faye got out Primo was there to greet her, holding out a hand. As she took it, flashes of light alerted them to the paparazzi who must have followed.

Primo cursed softly under his breath, and when they were inside he said, 'I'm sorry about that. I had no idea we were being followed.'

Faye shrugged a little. 'It's just as well I agreed to come with you—otherwise there'd be a story on *Page Six* tomorrow, speculating as to why we're not living together.'

They were in a private elevator now. Primo leaned back against the wall. 'That's not why I asked you to come back with me. I want to make love to you. I haven't stopped thinking about you since Venice.'

Faye's heart sped up. She hadn't stopped thinking about it either, but the elevator doors opened at that moment so she didn't have to speak.

Primo led her into a circular entrance hall. Marble floor, walls painted a light soft grey with blue tones.

'Let me take your jacket.'

Faye let it slip from her shoulders. Primo took it and put it in a small cloakroom. He led her through one doorway into a large reception room. It was bright and airy, with sumptuous couches, coffee tables. Understated tones of blue and grey. Classic. Elegant.

Then she spotted something on one wall and gasped, walking over to stand before the massive canvas. Primo came and stood beside her, and handed her a glass of sparkling wine.

She said, 'It's a Monet. I didn't know you had one in your private collection. It's one of his Haystacks paintings.'

'You mean I could have lured you here before now with that?' Primo joked.

Faye tore her gaze from the luminously beautiful painting. 'He's one of my favourite artists.'

Primo looked at the painting. 'Mine too—although I'd say for far less knowledgeable reasons than you.'

Faye shook her head. 'It's nothing to do with knowledge. It's how it makes you feel.'

She felt her skin prickle and turned her head to find Primo watching her.

'Do you want to know how you make me feel?' he asked.

Faye's hand clutched the glass. 'Do I?'

Primo's gaze turned dark and explicit. 'Hungry.'

She was ravenous. She wanted his hands on her.

'I'm hungry too,' she admitted, although it felt as if saying that was chipping away at the walls inside her.

He smiled. 'That wasn't so hard, now, was it?'

Faye didn't have time to scowl, or react, or tell Primo that actually she'd changed her mind. Because the glass of wine was taken out of her hand and she was in his arms and he was kissing her. She felt a sigh of relief mixed with pure base pleasure move through her in a shudder of longing.

He pulled back and she felt herself become weightless as Primo lifted her into his arms so that he could carry her through the apartment. Faye caught glimpses of an outdoor terrace. A gleaming kitchen. A dining room. And then they were in a corridor and Primo had kicked open a door that led into a huge bedroom with possibly the biggest bed she'd ever seen in her life.

She had an impression of dark muted colours in a simply decorated space.

He put her down and she slipped off her shoes. Hunger propelled her to start pushing Primo's jacket off his wide shoulders until he shucked it off and it fell to the ground. Then she was undoing his bow-tie and the buttons on his shirt.

He was slipping the garlanded strap of the dress down her

shoulder and bending to press kisses against her skin. Faye gave up trying to take his shirt off and let him take over.

He found the zip at the back of the dress and pulled it down. He pulled the tie out of her hair so that it fell down around her shoulders and back. Then he straightened up and looked at her.

'Undress me.'

Faye needed no encouragement. She pushed aside his shirt and marvelled at the expanse of his muscular chest. She'd wondered in the last few days if maybe she'd imagined his beauty. But no. He was even more beautiful.

She pushed the shirt down over his shoulders and arms, coming close again. But Primo didn't touch her. He let her take her time, her gaze roving over his form. Hands splaying across his chest. Fingers trapping a blunt nipple.

She heard his indrawn breath and looked up, and she couldn't help smiling as she leant forward and flicked her tongue over the nub of flesh. Primo hissed. A sensitive spot. Faye made a mental note. She had a sense in that moment that a hundred years wouldn't be long enough to learn all of this man's sensitive spots, and she felt the most acute and peculiar pang of loss.

Faye pushed the notion aside, telling herself she was drunk on Primo—he was addling her brain. She put her hands to his belt and trousers, undoing them with an efficiency born of growing desperation. And then she was pushing trousers and underwear down over his hips. They fell to the floor and Primo stepped aside gracefully.

Her dress was loose around her chest, and she tugged it down until it too fell to the floor. She wasn't wearing a bra. Now all she wore was her underwear. Primo cupped her breasts in his hands and Faye shivered delicately. He rubbed her nipples with his thumbs and she had to bite her lip to stop moaning or begging.

'What do you want, Faye?'

She moved closer, dislodging his hands, pressing her body against his, moving against him, relishing the feel of his hard body against the softness of her belly and between her legs, where she ached.

'Touch me, Primo.'

He put his hands on her waist and together they tumbled onto the bed in a tangle of limbs, hard against soft. He moulded every curve with his hands, kissed, licked and sucked every erogenous point until she was incoherent with need.

And then he pushed her legs apart and hooked them over his shoulders. He put his mouth on her and Faye could no more keep it together than stop breathing. She cried out as wave after wave tore through her body, and then Primo entered her still clasping body with one smooth, devastating thrust and Faye was torn apart all over again.

When Faye woke, she was the one alone in the bed. She couldn't move for long moments, her limbs heavy with a kind of satisfaction she'd never experienced before.

Before Primo.

Once again, the intensity of the physicality between them stunned her. She'd heard about sex like this, but had always believed it to be a kind of myth. People boasting.

He was obviously an experienced lover, and not remotely shy—she blushed when she thought of how he stood before her unashamedly naked—so was it uniquely him? Did all his lovers feel the same as Faye?

That thought sent a tendril of something dark through her. Jealousy. She denied it. Jealousy had no place here. In six months she would be walking away, and she would have no hold over Primo. Their time was finite. A means to an end. And if she felt bad about it then she must reassure herself that she was no less ruthless than him for marrying her solely because he'd deemed her suitable. And because he was acquiring their family business.

To that end, her father was a transformed man. He was actually getting to enjoy a retirement of sorts, now that the burden of heavy decision-making had been lifted from his shoulders.

And the burden of worrying about you, whispered a voice.

Faye groaned a little and rolled over. She buried her face in Primo's exquisite bedlinen. All four hundred million thread count, or whatever it was.

When she could move, she sat up and pulled back the covers. She had no idea when they'd finally fallen asleep. And now he was on a plane somewhere over the Atlantic.

Faye got up and washed herself in the luxurious en suite bathroom and found a robe, pulling it on and belting it.

Back in the bedroom, she studiously ignored the fact that Primo had obviously picked up the detritus of her clothes and underwear and draped them over a chair. She was tempted to look in Primo's drawers for something to wear but hesitated, feeling it was too intimate.

After a night spent in your husband's bed? mocked a voice.

She ignored it.

She pulled the curtains back, finding French doors that led out to a terrace. She went outside in bare feet. The morning was bright and the air fresh. The streets were a long way below. From here Faye could look across Central Park. Her apartment was somewhere on the other side of the park, a block further back from this spectacular view. She'd bought her own place with her own hard-earned money and she was inordinately proud of that fact.

She went back into the bedroom and decided to explore

beyond it. She heard a sound coming from the main part of the apartment and went still. Had Primo not left?

The thought that he hadn't left because he wanted to spend more time with her was sending flutters into her belly... But when she got to the doorway leading into the kitchen there was an older woman there, dressed in dark trousers and shirt, her hair in a sleek, elegant grey-haired bob.

She turned to Faye, who immediately felt naked even though she wore the robe. 'Good morning, Mrs Holt. I'm Marjorie. Mr Holt's housekeeper and general domestic dogsbody.'

Faye couldn't help but respond to the woman's warm, easy manner and outstretched hand. 'Please, call me Faye... I'm still getting used to being Mrs Holt.'

To put it mildly.

The woman smiled at her. 'You must be hungry...please come with me.'

She led Faye through to an adjoining informal dining room, where a veritable feast had been laid out. Fresh fruit, granola, yoghurt, pastries, coffee, tea... And the daily news-papers.

'I can do you a cooked breakfast, if you'd like?'

Faye shook her head. She wasn't used to being waited on like this, and rarely had time for breakfast. 'Oh, no, that won't be necessary—but thank you.'

'Mr Holt has organised some clothes for you—he said you're still not fully moved in.'

Faye smiled weakly and looked at the designer bags by the door. 'Thank you.'

Marjorie left her to eat in peace, and Faye eyed the bags suspiciously while she had some fruit and granola and yo-ghurt. She forced herself to have coffee before looking. The man had left at the crack of dawn—not that Faye had woken out of her pleasure-induced coma. How on earth had he organised this?

Eventually curiosity overcame her. She got up and investigated, pulling out trousers, tops, underwear, flat shoes, heeled shoes, toiletries. There was also a choice of leisure wear, and even jeans. They were simple, elegant clothes—the kind she would have chosen herself.

Faye's mobile phone pinged from somewhere nearby and she found it in her evening bag, which had been left on a table in the hall. Her face flamed. She couldn't even remember discarding that when they'd arrived here. Too drunk on Primo. Too desperate.

There was a text from Primo—presumably from somewhere over the Atlantic.

Good morning, I hope you slept well. I arranged some clothes for you. I have to go to Paris from London for a cocktail function on Friday evening. It's not on the list of events for us to attend together but...they have art in Paris. P (Your husband)

Faye couldn't stop a silly smile spreading across her face. But as soon as she was aware of it she rearranged her features. Her initial reaction was, *No way!* They hadn't discussed it, she had prior engagements, and she couldn't just drop everything and be expected to fly across to Europe again so soon.

And yet with the lingering after-effects of Primo's very particular brand of expert lovemaking still humming in her blood, all she could see in her mind's eye was a rose-tinted view of Paris as the sun set over the Seine.

She knew that she could rearrange her schedule quite easily—the beauty of working for oneself. And he was right. They did have art in Paris. And she had clients.

She knew deep down that she'd made her decision instantly, and that it had not much at all to do with making arrangements to see clients and a lot more to do with a man who was fast becoming something of a distracting obsession.

She sent back a quick text.

Thanks for the clothes, that was thoughtful. I will see if I can rearrange some work engagements. F (Your wife)

Before she could delete the cutesy copycat *your wife*, she sent the text and threw the phone down.

Her insides were somersaulting like a teenager's. Ugh. This had so not been the plan when she'd signed up to this marriage.

CHAPTER SIX

Paris

'IS THERE A better time to be in Paris than in the spring?' The woman beside Primo at the cocktail party gave a slightly annoying laugh. 'I know it's such a cliché, but isn't Paris just so beautiful?'

Primo wasn't and hadn't ever been unaware of Paris's beauty, but to his shame he'd always taken it for granted. Today, for the first time ever, he'd had a little time after a lunch meeting and had taken a walk back to the hotel along the Seine. And he had noticed the trees in blossom, the people strolling along with dogs or just eating lunch.

He'd noticed lovers too, locked in passionate embraces. And that had made him think of Faye. And how, since the other night in Manhattan, he hadn't been able to get *their* passionate embraces out of his head.

In bed, she was everything that he'd thought she would be and more. Under that serene and elegant surface was an earthy, sensual woman whose appetites matched his. It was a little unexpected to find that he was married to the best lover he'd ever had. The most he'd hoped for was that they'd be compatible. What they actually were was combustible.

It would fade, Primo had told himself that afternoon, as he'd sat down for a few minutes and ordered an espresso from a riverside café. As if the coffee might help to burn away some of the anticipation he felt because he knew that Faye was coming to Paris to meet him.

Strange that it had felt like such a victory when she'd texted earlier.

I've managed to rearrange some of my meetings. I'll see you at the event. F

He'd been in an early meeting in London and he'd felt like a teenager whose crush had just agreed to go out with him.

Ridiculous.

He only realised he was scowling now when the *'Isn't Paris just so beautiful?'* woman beside him looked a little alarmed.

He rearranged his facial expression and said, 'You are right. It is absolutely the most beautiful city in the spring-time. Now, if you'll excuse me, please?'

He'd turned to walk away, and was just thinking to him-self *Where the hell is she?* when the little hairs went up on the back of his neck.

He looked up the stairs that led down into the room where the party was being held. Faye was standing at the top in a flowing black knee-length cocktail dress. Sleeveless. So far so classic. But it had a deep vee that cut between her breasts, and when she moved the dress shone and sparkled from the intricately beaded lace overlay.

She wore vertiginous high heels, and Primo couldn't take his eyes off her as she came down the stairs, her legs long and shapely. Deep within him he felt a very primal beat saying, *Mine, mine, mine.*

He walked to the bottom of the stairs to meet her. Stand-ing on the bottom step, she was at a slightly higher level than him, and Primo gave in to temptation and kissed her.

He felt her quickly indrawn breath and then, within a beat, her mouth had softened under his. If not for the crowded room behind him, he would have been hauling her closer and indulging in seeing how easy it would be to slide a hand under one side of her dress to cup a breast.

He drew back reluctantly. She blinked at him. Her hair was pulled back, sleek. In a low ponytail. She wore minimal jewellery, but he could see the engagement and wedding rings in his peripheral vision, and he was filled with such a strong sense of satisfaction that it was a little disconcerting.

He said, 'Thank you for coming. You look stunning.'

She suddenly looked a little shy, with an expression he hadn't noticed before because usually she was so confident. It made him think of how she could often appear a little shy before they started making love, but then she'd be all heat and fire and—

'Thank you. You look…lovely too.'

Primo felt a burgeoning sense of something very light and expansive filling his chest. He tucked Faye's arm into his and led her into the room. 'So, can I take it that you decided to join me because you missed me?'

'Not quite,' was her dry response.

Primo let her go to take two glasses of sparkling wine from a waiter and handed her one. *'Santé.'*

She arched a brow. 'You speak French?'

'Mais, bien sûr. I also speak Spanish, Italian, German and passable Mandarin.'

Faye looked a little smug. 'Me too. I also speak Arabic and passable Farsi. I did a few months' study of Persian Art in Iran a few years ago.'

Primo bowed his head. 'I defer to your superior linguistic abilities. So, tell me, what on earth else could have tempted you to come to Paris if it wasn't your insanely handsome and virile husband?'

Faye's face went pink. Primo realised he enjoyed getting under her skin by teasing her.

'I've arranged to visit the newly reopened Conti Art Gallery.'

'That's Modern Art, right?'

Faye nodded. 'Very good.'

'When are you going?'

'Tomorrow—early, before they open. A client has done me a favour in organising a private tour.'

'I'll come with you.'

Faye looked a little surprised. 'Are you interested in Modern Art?'

'Not especially, but I'm sure you can make it interesting.'

Faye cocked her head to one side. 'Do you know how much I charge for a personal appointment?'

Primo smiled. He really enjoyed this woman and her determination to cling on to her independence. She surprised him—and it had been a long time since he'd been surprised. He had no doubt that once she'd made her point about retaining her independence inevitably their lives would dovetail more. But for now he was enjoying the novelty.

He said, 'I'm sure I can make it up to you in kind.'

She went a little pink again. She opened her mouth, but before she could say something that he already knew would be tart they were interrupted by the host of the party.

'Primo, this must be your beautiful new bride! Please introduce us.'

Primo bit back a smile at Faye's thwarted expression and took her hand in his as he faced their host.

Faye didn't like how nice it felt to have Primo touch her back or take her hand. It was as if when they were in close proximity he couldn't *not* touch her, and she had to admit she felt the same. But she'd never have the nerve to claim him physically the way he did her.

It brought back painful memories of her first marriage. She was naturally a tactile person and, believing that she and her husband were both on the same page emotionally, she'd felt comfortable enough to touch him in public. Just little gestures…a hand on his back or, when sitting down, on his thigh…

But invariably he would tense and move away a little, and say to her, *sotto voce*, 'Not here, Faye.'

She'd learnt to curb her natural impulses, and since then no lover had enticed her to experiment again. But Primo did. And yet the thought of reaching for his hand and having him turn to look at her as if she was doing something wrong kept her impulse in check.

Dusk was falling over Paris, and outside the Eiffel Tower was twinkling in the distance. Faye was coming back from the bathroom and saw Primo was deep in conversation with a man. For a moment she was arrested by his sheer good looks and formidable build. He was dressed in a dark blue suit and a light blue shirt, open at the neck. Impossibly suave.

She hadn't really been breathing properly since she'd arrived and caught his eye, and he'd come to the stairs to meet her. She saw the open French doors and diverted to an outdoor terrace, relishing the thought of a moment to get some air and try and sort through all the tangled things Primo made her feel.

Chief of which was the ever-present humming desire.

She came within ten feet of the guy and it was as if an electrical switch had been turned on.

She was tingling all over at the thought of what the night would hold. Her assistant had told her that Primo had a suite booked here, at the hotel where the party was taking place, so she'd booked a room too.

She knew Primo would expect her to share with him, but there was a part of her that still resisted giving herself over completely to this arrangement.

Because you know it won't last.

She reassured herself that it wasn't as if Primo had been under any illusions that she'd married him with unabated enthusiasm. They both knew it was an ancillary deal alongside a much bigger one.

And he knew that she might decide to leave after six months. There was no guarantee she would stay. And if she kept her boundaries during that time then he couldn't say she'd deceived him.

Simple. And yet...not.

It felt as if every time she was with him he had a stronger pull on her.

She shouldn't have come to Paris. They had a function to attend together in Boston at the end of the following week. That would have been time enough for them to meet again. But Faye had given in to an impulse too strong to ignore...

'Here you are.'

A shiver of longing went down Faye's spine and directly into her gut at the sound of Primo's voice. She closed her eyes for a second, and then opened them as he came to stand beside her, facing her, one elbow resting on the wall of the terrace. Like this, his mouth was on the same level as hers, and all Faye would have to do would be to lean forward and—

He reached out and touched her jaw with a finger. 'You look very stern.'

Faye relaxed her facial expression, felt her skin tingle where Primo had touched her. 'I was admiring the view.'

Liar.

She found herself divulging, 'I spent a summer here as an au pair, between school and college.'

Primo looked at her. 'That's impressive. Why weren't you swanning around the Mediterranean on a yacht, presumably like the rest of your peers? You could have had an easier summer.'

Faye shrugged again. She felt pricklingly self-conscious under Primo's blue gaze. 'I was never into that kind of vacuous social life. And I didn't mind working.'

'Your independence means a lot to you,' he observed.

'I was an only child. I think I learnt from a young age to be comfortable on my own.'

Until she'd lost herself in her first marriage, believing herself to be in love.

Primo looked at her. 'You're not on your own now. I'm here.'

Faye's heart thumped unsteadily at the gleam in his eyes. 'I guess so.'

He arched a brow and moved closer, until there was no space between their bodies. 'Do you doubt it? Should I show you how real I am?'

In her head Faye said, *Please*... But all she could manage was a kind of pleading sound. No words.

Primo stood up straight and cupped her jaw and face with both hands. Something inside Faye melted. Relaxed. She spent so much time in her head that she was fast becoming addicted to the way Primo could silence everything with his touch.

His mouth covered hers, stealing her breath, and she was lost. The party just feet away was forgotten. The kiss started out chaste enough—as if Primo had intended it to be just a perfunctory thing—but neither broke contact, and then it became something far more incendiary and explicit.

His hands had moved down to her waist and he was pulling her closer, so she could feel the evidence of his arousal through their clothes. Faye moved her hips enticingly.

Primo pulled back and said in a rough voice, 'Witch.'

He lifted a hand and cupped her jaw again. Faye wanted to lean into his hand and purr like a cat.

'I think I've had enough of this party. You?' he asked.
Faye nodded.

Primo took her hand and led her back into the thronged room. They went to the host and said goodbye.

Outside the party, Primo still had Faye's hand in his. He lifted it and pressed a kiss to it, causing Faye to suck in a sharp breath. His easy tactility and affection were fast becoming addictive.

'Fancy a nightcap in my room? I presume you've booked your own room in the hotel?'

Faye nodded, almost feeling guilty now. But Primo said nothing. He just led them to an elevator.

It ascended to the very top level of the hotel. Naturally he had a penthouse suite that appeared to Faye to run across the entirety of the top floor, with views even more impressive than those a few floors below.

'What would you like?' Primo asked.

Faye looked across the room. He'd taken off his jacket, and his back and shoulders looked very broad.

Faye took off her shoes and sank down into a plush chair. 'A small white wine, please.'

Primo poured the drinks and came back over. He handed Faye hers and sat down at right angles to her chair. Faye tucked her legs under her. Primo's gaze dropped to her chest, and Faye looked down and realised the dress was gaping open slightly over one breast. Her skin prickled with awareness. She could have pulled it back over, to cover herself, but she left it.

Primo looked back up at her face. The air between them

sizzled, but she tried to feign nonchalance. 'You don't have an apartment in Paris?'

Primo shook his head. 'My father does, but I don't use it. We had a lot more properties, but I sold most of them off...just keeping a few strategic ones.'

'My apartment in Manhattan is the only property I own. We had more, but Father sold them off after Mother died. He didn't see the point in travelling much after she was gone.'

'He really loved her?'

Faye nodded, feeling a little emotional. She took a sip of wine to disguise it.

Primo was shaking his head. 'I can't imagine what it must be like to have two parents who aren't permanently at each other's throats. My parents' marriage was one of two states: either ice-cold, with tension thick enough to cut with a knife, or dramatic histrionics. The morning our mother left,' Primo went on, 'Quin was clinging to her, crying and begging her not to go. But I was numb. I had to peel him off her. To this day I can't stand dramatics.'

Feeling a little less exposed after hearing this, Faye said, 'That's a form of self-protection. Your brother acted out his anguish, but you pushed yours down.'

Primo arched a brow. 'Was psychology part of your art degree?'

But his words held no edge or defensiveness. Faye wondered what it would take to really ruffle the surface of this very self-contained man.

At that moment his gaze dropped again to her chest. His jaw tightened.

Feeling emboldened, Faye asked, 'Is something bothering you?'

His gaze came back up. His eyes were glittering. 'You know exactly what you're doing.'

She didn't, actually, but it felt heady to finally see some

evidence that she *could* ruffle Primo's feathers—even a little bit. She looked down and could see the curve of her breast. She pulled her dress apart a little bit more, exposing herself, and then very deliberately tipped her glass of wine so that the cold liquid fell on her breast, running in a rivulet around and over her nipple.

'Oops.'

'Faye…'

She looked up. Primo's face was stark. He'd put his drink down and his hands were on the arms of the chair, knuckles white.

'Come here,' he ordered softly.

Faye felt like saying, *You come here*, because she wasn't sure her legs would work when she stood up. But she found herself untucking her legs and obeying his order, until she was standing in front of him, her glass in her hand.

'Give me your glass.'

She handed it over and he put it on a side table. Then he looked at her and leaned forward, putting his hands on her waist and drawing her to him, so that she had to put her knees on the chair either side of his thighs.

Her hands went to his chest and she could feel the strong thud of his heart. Faye's own heart was palpitating.

Primo reached up and slid his hands under the wide straps of the dress. 'May I?' he said.

She was sitting on the man's lap, legs spread wide. She nodded, and bit her lip as he pushed the material down her arms, making the dress fall to her waist, exposing her bare breasts.

Faye lifted her arms from the straps.

Primo lifted the wine glass from the table and held it to Faye's hot skin, making her nipples pebble into tight buds of need. Then he slowly and deliberately poured more wine, first over one breast and then the other, before putting the glass back down. Then he cupped her breasts in his hands and proceeded to very thoroughly lick them clean of all traces of wine, lingering on her nipples, sucking and tugging on the sensitised flesh, until Faye was unconsciously moving her hips against him to assuage the ache.

As if reading her mind, Primo kept his mouth on her as one hand delved under the skirt of her dress and found her lace underwear, pushing it aside so that he could explore her flesh, finding where she was hot and moist, delving deep inside with first one and then two fingers.

Faye was feverish now as, with his tongue and mouth and wicked fingers, he brought her to a shuddering orgasm. She looked down at him, stunned, as her body shuddered with voluptuous aftershocks. But she was still hungry. And she could feel every muscle in his body was taut.

She lifted herself up and stood on shaky legs. She pulled her underwear off completely and then positioned herself over Primo again. She undid his shirt and pushed it open, spreading her hands and fingers across his chest. And then she reached down and undid his belt buckle and button.

He said with half a smile in his voice, 'We could go somewhere more comfortable...'

Faye shook her head. 'No, here. Now...'

While she was undoing him, finding his length and putting her hand around him, he was reaching for her hair and unpinning it so that it fell around her shoulders.

She came up on her knees, either side of his thighs, and he put his hands on her buttocks, squeezing the flesh as she slowly and carefully moved down onto his hard length.

They both sucked in a breath as her body took him in and sensitised muscles moulded around his flesh. For a moment Faye didn't move, too full of something that felt almost... emotional as she looked into his eyes.

And then, terrified of what that meant, she started to

move, up and down, making Primo's jaw clench. Their skin grew slick with perspiration and his hands squeezed harder, urging her on, allowing her to move but then holding her still so that he could surge up and into her. And all she could do was cling to his shoulders and bite back a low moan of pleasure.

This orgasm came less quickly than the last one, but it was no less devastating—like a massive body of water that kept surging and surging until it broke against her, her body clamping down on Primo's until he too found release, holding her still as he thrust up, touching her so deeply that she couldn't breathe for a long moment, and then fell, limp against him, her face buried in his neck.

Faye wasn't sure how or when they were able to move, but somehow, at some point, Primo was lifting her to his chest and walking them through the suite into a bedroom.

He put her down on the end of the bed and said, 'Wait there.'

Faye didn't have the strength to tell him she wasn't even sure if she could speak, never mind move. She was vaguely aware of her deshabille. Dress bunched up to her waist. Underwear gone. Breasts completely exposed. Hair down. Make-up…? Smeared into oblivion. But somehow she couldn't care less. She'd never felt so relaxed with a lover. When she was with Primo like this, boundaries dissolved and melted into nothing.

He came back and she realised he'd taken off his rumpled clothes. He pulled her up and led her into the bathroom, which was already steaming up from the shower. He pulled her dress down and then brought her into the shower, where he proceeded to wash her with thorough efficiency.

Even though she could barely move, she could already feel the flickers of a resurgence of desire as his hands moved over her backside and around to the front, dipping down briefly to that tender spot between her legs.

Sleepily she protested, 'I can wash myself...'

'Done.'

He turned the water off and wrapped her in a big soft towel. He'd pulled her hair up, twisting it into a knot to keep it dry. He let it down now. He briskly dried himself and then led her into the bedroom, to the bed.

Faye crawled into it and landed on her back. Primo lay beside her. She turned her head to look at him and saw he was watching her. She opened her mouth to say something... But she was asleep before she could articulate anything, her last image of Primo's bright blue eyes on her.

When Faye woke she felt so utterly heavy and at peace that she relished the feeling for a few moments—before snippets of the previous night came back to her. She was in Paris. As if to remind her of that, the very distinctive sound of a French police siren came faintly from the street far down below.

She opened her eyes. The bed beside her was rumpled, but empty. She breathed out. There were no sounds coming from the bathroom. Faye sat up and realised she was still in the towel from taking that shower. After the most torrid and urgent sex she could remember having.

She groaned. She was pretty sure Primo wasn't used to waking up with lovers still wearing a towel and with their hair all over the place.

She went into the bathroom and pulled on a voluminous robe. She found copious lavish beauty products. And a new toothbrush still in its packaging. Faye freshened up and pulled her hair back, and steeled herself to see Primo.

On bare feet—because of course she had nothing of her own with her in his suite—she padded through the generous rooms until she came to the main reception room. The French doors were open onto the terrace and curtains moved softly in the spring breeze. Faye heard deep voices and then a man appeared in a hotel uniform.

He bowed towards her. 'Good morning, Mrs Holt. Breakfast is served on the terrace.'

Faye mumbled something in return and went out to find Primo sitting at a laid table, dressed and shaved and not looking as if he'd unravelled her completely last night. She felt exposed.

He looked at her, an expression of something close to amusement on his face which didn't help her mood.

'Good morning. Don't worry—it's still early. You won't have missed your appointment.'

The appointment!

She'd forgotten. Not like her at all. The man was scrambling her brain. She felt on edge and prickly.

She sat down on the opposite side of the table. Coffee. She needed coffee.

As if reading her mind—because why not? He could read her body better than she could—Primo picked up the pot.

'Coffee?'

Faye held out her cup. She knew she was being ridiculous, but this was exactly why she'd pushed so hard to have boundaries between her and Primo—to avoid this kind of cosy domestic scene. For her it brought back too many painful memories of breakfasting on her own once her previous husband had decided she was no longer a viable wife.

'Thank you,' she said, as graciously as she could, and took a sip of the strong hot drink.

'Not a morning person?'

She looked at him and felt her irritation sapping away. She *was* being ridiculous. 'I guess I'm just used to my own space.'

'You don't like to hang out with lovers the morning after?'

Faye shuddered lightly. 'Not generally, no.' She looked at him over the rim of her cup. 'You?'

His mouth firmed a little. 'I've tended to avoid it, as it can signify a desire for an intimacy that I'm not interested in.'

He looked at her again.

'But this is different...we're married.' Primo gestured to the table full of fruit and tempting pastries. 'Look at us, having our first breakfast together. Cute.'

There was only the slightest hint of mockery in Primo's voice.

Faye desisted from making a face, or saying, *Don't get used to it.* But she wanted to turn the spotlight on him and asked, as she picked up a *pain au chocolat*, 'Based on what you told me about your thoughts on marriage and romance, I'm assuming you've never been in love?'

Primo took a sip of his own coffee. He shook his head. 'No. I don't believe in it. I think people form attachments... have things in common. They like to call it love as a justification for staying together, for choosing one person.'

He looked at her.

'*You* have been in love.'

CHAPTER SEVEN

FAYE FELT PANICKY. How did he know? What had she told him about her husband?

'I never told you that.'

'No,' he agreed. 'But your first marriage wounded you more than just on the surface. You were hurt.'

Faye avoided his eyes and picked at the pastry. Eventually she admitted, 'I thought I was in love with him, but I was just naive.'

'You were young, and you had a good example from your parents. Why wouldn't you have hoped for a successful relationship built on more than just strategy after seeing that?'

Faye looked at him. Sometimes she felt a lot older than her years, having gone through a marriage and a divorce and the trauma of becoming infertile. But here with Primo and his non-judgemental acceptance she felt lighter. Somehow...younger again. As if there were still possibilities.

She shook her head at the fanciful notion. Good sex. That was all it was. Addling her brain.

'Maybe,' she conceded, and put some of the pastry in her mouth in case she asked any more leading questions.

It didn't surprise her that he hadn't been in love, but she didn't like to admit that she felt a sense of relief. It disturbed her—the thought of someone being able to crack this man's generally serene exterior.

They managed to eat and finish their coffee companionably enough, but then Faye realised something. 'My clothes are all in my room, on another floor.'

Primo said, 'I've arranged for the butler to gain access to your room and bring over some things so you can dress.'

Once again he was demonstrating an easy and generous courtesy. It made something swoop dangerously inside her. Chipping away at her defences. Faye felt churlish for insisting on maintaining her own space, but after last night, and how easily he could make her lose herself, it was more important than ever.

She stood up. 'Thank you for doing that.'

'They're in the guest room.'

'I'll go back to my room before we head out, if that's okay? Meet you in the lobby in about twenty minutes?'

'Sounds good.'

Primo waited for Faye in the lobby. For the first time in a long time he was taking his foot off the unrelenting accelerator.

You mean the first time ever, prompted a little voice.

And it had happened without him really making a conscious decision. A little unsettling to realise now, even if Primo knew that everything was in good hands.

He'd handed over the responsibility for ensuring the smooth transition of absorbing MacKenzie Enterprises into Holt Industries. He knew Faye's father would be watching everything carefully, and he did trust his man. But still, for someone who had taken up his role as heir to his father and devoted his every waking moment to it for the better part of the last two decades, it was only now he was appreciating the extent to which he'd abdicated his responsibilities. For a woman. When no woman before had inspired any desire to spend more time with her than necessary.

This is different. You're married. You have to spend time together.

Primo shook his head at himself. He was being ridiculous. This *was* totally different. He was married to Faye. He had to get to know her. Surely this was to be expected of a marriage? A shifting of priorities into the more personal sphere?

He slipped sunglasses over his eyes. He couldn't deny that he was finding the chase aspect of their relationship... entertaining. And he really didn't think she was doing it for the thrill. His instinct all along about her had been that she didn't play games. But that unsettling realisation that he'd been acting without thinking lingered, making him feel a sense of exposure.

Asking her to come to Paris... Deviating from the schedule... *Enjoying her company* in a way that he hadn't expected.

She might turn to fire in his arms at night, but she was keeping him at arm's length by day—exactly as she'd laid out in their agreement. He told himself that that was what he wanted too. It wasn't as if he hoped for a more emotionally intimate relationship. But *some* emotional intimacy was unavoidable and necessary in order to cultivate a long-term union.

Clearly, she didn't fully trust him, and for them to have a successful marriage that would have to change. So he was just doing what he could to foster that trust.

Ultimately, what remained most important to Primo was protecting his family legacy and name. Consolidating the success and wealth he'd already achieved. Faye was just the next step in that process—taking him and Holt Industries to the next level.

At that moment, the tiny hairs went up on the back of his neck and he turned to see Faye walking towards him as if conjured out of his thoughts. She was dressed casually, in loose trousers and a short-sleeved fitted jumper that drew the eye to her small waist and perfectly shaped breasts. Flat shoes. Perfect for the Paris streets. Hair loose around her shoulders. A crossbody bag with an iconic designer logo on the clasp.

She oozed class and elegance. But after getting to know her—as much as she would allow—he knew of the passion beneath the surface. And the spikiness that he suspected she hid from most people.

He liked it. Like the way her nipples felt against his tongue. Sharp...

She stopped before him. 'What are you smiling at?'

He took her elbow to guide her out of the hotel. 'Nothing...nothing at all.'

He was doing the right thing—investing time in his wife. After all, now she was as much a part of the future of Holt Industries as he was, and any sense of exposure he'd been feeling dissolved as they walked into the early-morning beauty of Paris.

When the six months was up she would have forgotten all about reviewing their marriage. She would trust him enough to jettison those *terms* and they would be a solid, successful unit.

They'd finished their tour with the gallery director and Faye was lingering in front of a painting that had transfixed her. People were trickling in now—the first visitors of the day.

'You like that painting,' Primo commented from beside her.

Faye tore her gaze away from the swirling abstract in vivid reds and pinks. 'Lara Lopez. She's a Portuguese artist. Up and coming. She's becoming a name, and some clients have started collecting her work.'

Primo looked at the description plate. 'It's called *Life*, and donated by the artist.'

'It's a big coup to have your work displayed among some of the century's greatest modern artists.'

Faye felt a little exposed at the way something about the painting called to her so viscerally.

Primo said, 'That doesn't explain why you like it so much.'

Now Faye felt really exposed. 'I'm not sure...maybe the colours.'

'I think it's because it's like you.'

Faye looked at Primo sharply. 'What does that mean?'

'On the surface you're all cool and refined, but under the surface you burn—and you have a passion for life that I think you are afraid to show people.'

Faye's mouth dropped open, but she quickly shut it again and said, a little testily, 'Did *you* do a degree in psychology?'

Primo smiled easily. 'Nope, completely self-taught.'

Faye made a sound like *harrumph*. The truth was that Primo's assessment was scarily accurate. There *was* something about the painting that called to her because she felt its passion. Its hunger for life. All the things she was afraid of since failing at her first marriage and then becoming infertile.

She moved away and looked at her watch.

'Somewhere else to be?' he asked.

She glanced at Primo. He was too distracting. Dressed in casual trousers and a dark navy polo shirt that seemed to make his eyes pop even more. She'd been ultra-aware of him as the director had led them around the museum on a whistlestop tour.

She felt a little churlishly like asking, *Don't you?* Because he seemed all too happy to wander around and take in the sights. It unnerved her, because she hadn't factored in spending time with him like this.

Even so, she felt almost guilty when she said, 'I'm actually going to Dublin for the night. There's a dinner in

Dublin Castle to celebrate some of Ireland's biggest living artists as part of their annual culture week.'

Primo frowned. 'That wasn't in the diary.'

'No, because I thought I couldn't go. But since I'm in Paris, and it's less than a couple of hours' flight, I told them I could make it after all.'

His gaze narrowed on her for a moment, and then he said, 'That sounds like an interesting evening.'

Faye almost had the urge to say something crazy like, *Do you want to come?*

But he was looking at his watch and saying, 'I should get back to the hotel. I have one more meeting before I head back to New York. I have meetings there tomorrow.'

'Of course. I need to get back and pack too.'

She was glad she hadn't blurted out the invitation. That would really have been muddying the waters.

Primo said, 'I'm glad you came to Paris... You know, Faye, I'd like to get to know you better. I think we can really enjoy ourselves in this marriage if you give it a chance.'

Faye felt all at once gently chastened, guilty, and something far less identifiable. 'I... Okay.'

'You can smile too, if you want. Your face won't crack, I swear.'

It suddenly struck her to wonder when she'd started to hold herself so rigidly. After her divorce?

She forced herself to take a breath and smiled.

Primo shook his head. 'One day, Faye MacKenzie, you'll smile for real.'

Dublin

'One day...you'll smile for real.'

The words were still reverberating in Faye's head later that evening as she was guided to her dinner seat in Dublin

Castle's magnificent and historic St Patrick's Hall. There had been a drinks reception in the Portrait Gallery before the gala dinner, and Faye had met with some of Ireland's biggest artists.

Usually an event like this would consume all her energy, as she would be thinking of people she could link the artists up with—galleries or clients—but this evening she was distracted.

Why did Primo care if she smiled for real? Why couldn't he just accept the status quo, with them appearing together when necessary and spending the night together when it was convenient?

Although, that didn't quite capture the heat and intensity of their chemistry. It wasn't so much *spending the night together* as mutually combusting and passing out in a pleasure-induced coma.

Faye looked around her now and a sense of isolation struck her. Like at the Venice Carnival Ball, it seemed that everyone was paired off and chatting animatedly.

She was wearing a green silk evening gown, cut on the bias and low on the chest, with small capped sleeves. Flowing and romantic. She'd spotted it in a boutique window before leaving Paris and now, as she sat here, she realised she'd bought it because she'd imagined Primo seeing her in it and wanting her.

Now she felt silly. It was too whimsical and exposing— physically and emotionally.

Damn Primo Holt for making her behave like a teenager with a crush. And for making her more aware of her isolation and also of how tightly wound she was. She took a deep breath in a bid to force herself to relax. She took another sip of her sparkling wine that she'd carried into the dining room with her—and then promptly nearly spat it out again when she saw the object of her fevered thoughts being directed to the table where she sat and the empty chair beside her.

She couldn't quite believe it, but the somersaulting sensation in her belly told her he was real. And his scent. Crisp and spicy and earthy.

He was wearing a classic black tuxedo and smiling benignly at her, 'Hi.'

Then he looked down at her dress and back up. There was very explicit heat in his eyes.

'You look...amazing.'

Her wish was fulfilled. As if a fairy godmother had heard her thoughts.

There were a million and one reasons why Faye should be prickling at the sight of Primo so improbably here, in Dublin. But the last few moments of self-recrimination had dissolved, replaced by instant pure desire, and Faye was revelling in the very obvious desire in his gaze. Exactly as she'd fantasised.

The truth was she was happy to see him, and she was too surprised to fight it.

'Do you get a kick out of surprising people?' she asked.

Primo took a sip of the wine a waiter had just poured for him. 'Can't say that anyone has ever inspired me to want to surprise them before...it's uniquely you.'

She shook her head. 'How did you even—?'

'Once the organisers knew that I was your husband they were aghast that I hadn't been included in the invitation, and were only too happy to accommodate me at short notice.'

'What about your meetings in New York?'

'Moved them. Quite easy to do when you're the owner and CEO of the company.'

Everyone else around them faded away. Faye felt something inside her weaken. Maybe it would be okay to indulge in this...this crazy honeymoon period, or whatever it was, between them. She felt something bubbling up inside her—a lightness she couldn't repress. And then a smile broke across her face at the fact that Primo had come all the way to Dublin to surprise her.

Primo drew back, as if shocked, and put a hand to his chest. 'Could that really be a smile?'

Faye made a face then, and picked up a small bread roll as if to throw it at him. But her smile didn't fade.

After the lavish dinner, Faye and Primo walked the short distance from Dublin Castle back to her hotel on the banks of the River Liffey. He held her hand and she shamelessly luxuriated in the tactility that she was beginning to trust more and more.

She pushed away the voices warning her to be careful.

Dublin was a young, vibrant city, and people spilled out of bars and cafés enjoying the unseasonably warm spring weather.

A few people stopped and did a double-take at seeing Primo in his tuxedo, and Faye couldn't blame them. He'd opened his bow-tie and the top button of his shirt, and he looked as if he might have stepped off the cover of a book, with his dark golden hair and near-perfect features.

They passed a buzzing gay bar and Faye heard one man say to another sorrowfully, 'All the gorgeous ones are straight.'

She couldn't hold back a small laugh.

Primo said, 'Careful, if the wind changes you might stay like that.'

Still smiling, Faye said, 'My wee Scottish granny used to say that. Except she was a long way from her actual Scottish roots.'

'Do you ever go back there?'

She shook her head. 'No, we really have no links to the

place any more—apart from family stories and some very distant relatives. Although I did manage to do a semester at Edinburgh University, which I adored.'

They were at the hotel now, and Primo picked up the key. One key.

Faye looked at him and he said, 'I upgraded you—*us*—to the penthouse suite.'

She guessed Mark, her assistant, must have told Primo where she was staying. She had half a mind to resist Primo's all too magnetic pull, but that would have taken a strength she couldn't currently muster.

'Okay.'

They took the elevator to the top floor, its doors opening into a corridor with a room at the end. The suite was spacious, and decorated with lots of wood and elegant soft furnishings. A balcony ran along the outside of the living space, overlooking the river.

Faye heard the sound of a cork popping and watched Primo pour two glasses of champagne, bringing one to her where she stood on the balcony.

'Thank you,' she murmured, still a little overwhelmed that he was here. She said, 'You didn't have to come all the way here. We'll both be back in Manhattan next week. We have that function in Boston.'

Primo rested on an elbow beside her and looked at her. 'You don't get it, do you? I want you, Faye... I haven't wanted anyone like this in a long time. I find you exciting—and that doesn't happen very often for me either. The fact that we're married... I'd still want you even if we weren't.'

'You're saying this could have been just an affair?' Faye said, almost hopefully.

Primo shook his head. 'I'm glad it's not. I think marrying you is one of the smartest things I've done in a long time.'

Faye desperately tried to resist the spell he was weaving around her, making her think all sorts of things. She gestured at the invisible electricity between them. 'But *this* won't last...it never does.'

He didn't disagree with her. 'And then we'll still have enough to make a very successful marriage.'

'You don't like to fail, do you?' Faye observed.

He smiled, and it was a shark's smile. 'Not an option.'

She shivered slightly. She wondered what it must be like to be on the other side of this man's charm and interest. If you crossed him...

Like you, you mean? When you have every intention of walking away after six months? Not revealing the truth of your infertility?

Faye desperately reassured herself that she'd made it very clear what her terms were and couldn't be accused of deception.

To stop thinking about that, she leaned forward and kissed him, pressing her mouth to his, revelling in the firmness of his lips. For a moment he let her kiss him, and then he reached for her with his free arm and pulled her into him, taking control of the kiss and showing her that any sense of control she might have had was just an illusion.

The wine glasses were put down and that electricity crackled in the air around them as they blindly made their way to the bedroom, shedding and divesting themselves of clothes as they went.

Faye vaguely wondered if it had been less than twenty-four hours since she'd slept with him. It felt like years ago. She was desperate, hungry, reaching for Primo as soon as he was naked, putting her hand around him and hearing his sharp intake of breath.

She was naked too, and Primo cupped her breasts, feeding her tingling flesh into his mouth, making her moan softly with need. She took her hand off him and moved under him, spreading her legs around him, and Primo needed no further enticement to join their bodies in one deep thrust.

Faye's head was thrown back as pleasure climbed inexorably through her body, tightening every nerve-ending until she was held on the brink of shimmering ecstasy. But Primo wouldn't release her.

She looked at him, and his eyes were on her. She had nowhere to hide. Bared utterly. And yet she couldn't look away.

'Please... Primo...'

His face was flushed, a lock of hair falling onto his forehead. He was in her, and around her, and they were one in a way that she knew terrified her. But she couldn't unpack that now. When he reached down between their bodies, touched her where they were joined, he finally released her from the exquisite tension and they both fell over the edge and into pleasure so intense it almost hurt.

When Faye woke she was alone in the bed, like the previous morning in Paris, her body heavy with a bone-deep sense of satisfaction and her mind full of snapshots of the previous night. It had been as raw and elemental as the first few times and it didn't look to be waning any time soon.

He'd followed her to Dublin.

The lightness she'd felt on seeing him yesterday evening lingered. It was an unusual sensation for Faye, who'd got used to barricading herself behind protective walls since her first marriage.

She rolled over and buried her head in the pillow, letting out a groan of embarrassment but also feeling a fizzing kind of joy.

A tap on her bare shoulder made her go very still. She dug her face out of the pillow and squinted at Primo, standing by the bed in a robe, holding a coffee cup. She was very dishevelled and naked. She pulled up the sheet, feeling shy, which was ridiculous.

'Morning,' Primo said cheerfully, putting the cup down near the bed. 'Coffee. I seem to recall it having a positive effect.'

Faye might have scowled at him, but her face didn't seem able to arrange itself into that expression. She leaned over and picked up the cup, taking a sip. The coffee had an almost instantaneous effect, waking her out of the dreamy state she'd been in. *Good.*

She put the cup back down and looked at Primo. 'Don't you have meetings in New York?'

'I pushed them again. I'm extending our trip—if you can rearrange your schedule. We'll be back in America in time for the Boston event.'

Her mouth dropped open in shock at this pronouncement. When she'd recovered, she asked, 'And in the meantime we'll be…?'

Primo sat down on the edge of the bed and placed his hands either side of her. 'Enjoying a honeymoon—which I believe is a normal event for most newly married couples.'

Faye gulped. 'I thought we weren't most married couples, though.'

The sizzle in the air between them made a lie of Faye's words. Primo confirmed it when he said, 'On the contrary, I think we're proving to be no different to most newly-weds, and if anything it would serve us well to indulge this…phase.'

'Phase…?'

Primo very deliberately pulled the sheet down, exposing Faye's chest. His hungry gaze moved from her mouth to her breasts and back up. Instantly she was wide awake and burning inside.

He bent forward and pressed his mouth to the upper slope of one breast. Faye sank back against the pillows. Maybe Primo was right. Maybe if they did indulge in this…phase, it would burn out quickly and some kind of sanity might return. And then she could remember what this was supposed to be about. A means to an end.

Six months of marriage to ensure her family's legacy would be protected and secured for the long term.

Six months to indulge in this man, who was slowly but surely rewiring her brain to demand a level of pleasure that was truly unprecedented.

She reached for his robe and pushed it off his shoulders. Primo pulled back and shrugged it off, and then he was naked, his skin gleaming with dark golden perfection.

He whipped away the sheet completely, but before he touched her again he said, 'So, do you think you can rearrange your schedule?'

Faye had never been more exposed than she was right now, practically panting in her desperation for Primo. Her brain was too feverish to try and figure out why this might not be a good idea so she gave in, and a little more of those defensive walls crumbled in the face of Primo's bold charisma.

She said, 'I'm sure it won't be a problem.'

And then let herself be persuaded that indulging in a honeymoon was merely the most effective way to burn themselves free of this inconvenient chemistry as soon as possible.

Eight hours later

Faye's heart was pumping and her limbs were shaking. She fought to get her breath back and she couldn't stop smiling.

Breathless, sweaty, when she could speak again, she said, 'That was...amazing.'

Primo grinned, and there was a smugness to his expression that didn't even bother her.

'I aim to please.'

Between Faye's legs, the powerful and majestic horse shifted. She leant forward and patted her neck. Her horse was a little smaller than Primo's stallion, but no less impressive.

She looked around her, getting her breath back. They'd just galloped along the shore of an empty beach in the westernmost region of Ireland. Not another soul shared the space with them. The sky, in typical Irish fashion, had gone from blue to grey, sunshine to showers within minutes. And back again.

Primo had surprised her—after they'd started their day again—by taking her to a small private airfield just outside Dublin, where a plane had been waiting to fly them to Galway.

Then a chauffeur-driven car had taken them along the most unbelievably scenic coastal route to a small, fully staffed private castle, overlooking one of the most beautiful beaches Faye had ever seen. Windswept, with a wild sea foaming at the shore.

Primo was a superb horseman, sitting in the saddle with an easy grace. And for a tall man, that was saying something. It was also the first time Faye had seen him in jeans, and if she'd thought him sexy before, now he exuded something far more dangerous.

The horses started to walk back down the beach—clearly this was a regular run for them. When they'd arrived, the housekeeper had shown them around and fed them a delicious late lunch, and then they'd been shown to the stables and the horses, where a groom had kitted them out with boots, jackets and hats.

Faye looked out to the sea now and shook her head. 'I think I've dreamt of a place like this but never thought it could exist.' She looked at Primo who was watching her. 'How did you even know I could ride a horse?'

And then she thought of something, and for a moment she felt the tiniest prick of pain. A pain she really shouldn't be feeling.

Primo had opened his mouth, but Faye put up a hand, forcing a smile. 'No, you don't have to tell me. Presumably whoever did their research into my background saw that I had competed in cross-country horse trials.'

Primo had the grace to look a little shamefaced.

Faye told herself this was a good thing. It would be very easy to be totally swept away by this impromptu trip to one of the most beautiful places she'd ever seen. And she hated it that it felt a little tainted now. The bubble of joy burst.

She wasn't a fool. She knew Primo was investing his time and energy in her so he could turn her into an amenable bride.

She was more glad than ever that she'd laid out her terms from the start. If he hadn't insisted on marrying her, this really might just have been an affair, and that was how she needed to view it from now on.

Before he might read anything into her response, she gave the horse a gentle kick with her heels and said, 'Race you back to the castle.'

Primo sat in his saddle for a moment, watching the sheer beauty in motion that was Faye on a horse. She and the horse moved as one. Her hair streamed out from under her hat. Her face just now had been beaming with happiness, pink with exertion. Eyes shining. And it had caused an ache to form in Primo's chest so acute that he'd almost put a hand to it.

She'd literally taken his breath away.

He realised that Faye was infinitely more beautiful than he'd given her credit for.

He'd never experienced anything like this before, because he'd never have indulged a lover in case she got the wrong idea. And also, he had to concede, because no lover had ever inspired him to want to do something so fanciful.

To book an Irish castle for a night.

To ride horses on an empty sea-swept beach.

To eat oysters by a blazing fire.

But, as he'd told her, he intended for them to have a honeymoon—and wasn't this the kind of thing honeymooners did? After all, he had decided in Paris that forging as strong a bond as possible between them would be a good investment in this marriage. Hence his decision to follow her to Dublin and surprise her.

But at that moment a series of images from the previous night appeared in his head in Technicolor X-rated detail. As much as he'd like to think he was in control of his actions, he had a niggling sense that any sense of control was an illusion. That in fact he was being driven by far more base impulses.

Nonsense. Of course he was in control.

So why did it bother you so much to see that beaming joy disappear from her face when she'd realised how you knew about her prowess with horses?

Primo could have told her a white lie—that he'd had no idea. But he didn't lie. He had known from the file he'd had prepared on her.

He felt defensive now. Why should that be a problem? It wasn't as if either of them was under any illusions as to why they'd got married.

The point was how they'd forge a successful relationship from this point onwards.

Primo nudged his horse into a canter and swiftly caught up with Faye. He caught her horse's reins, bringing both animals to a halt.

She looked at him, eyes wide. 'What are you doing?'

He leaned forward and took her chin in his hand and kissed her hard. She tasted of sea salt, and he could feel the texture of sand on her face. His kiss gentled, and she resisted for a moment before softening. Something inside him exulted, but he fought temptation and pulled back.

'There was nothing in any file about *this* between us, Faye. This chemistry is what will take our marriage to another level.'

She looked at him, and her eyes were very green and gold, reflecting the landscape. He couldn't read her and it irritated him. Usually he found women easy to read.

But then she smiled and pulled back. 'If this is your attempt to try and beat me, it's pretty pathetic.'

She nudged her horse and cantered away from Primo towards the castle.

He shook his head at himself. There was nothing to be concerned about. He was letting the Irish mist rolling down off the hills get to him. He went after Faye, and she beat him back to the stable-yard by a nose.

CHAPTER EIGHT

THE RIDE BACK to the castle had helped elevate Faye's mood again. She really had no right to feel hurt by Primo. He'd never lied to her. And he was right. This chemistry between them was unprecedented, and she had every intention of making the most of it while it lasted.

In the stables, they handed back their hats to the groom and said goodbye to the horses, who were getting hosed down before being fed. Faye felt very dishevelled and wind-swept, but also happy. She hadn't indulged in horse riding for so long, and it had used to be one of her favourite activities. It made her think of how linear her life had become.

She came out of the stables and Primo was waiting for her, dressed in the same kind of waxy jacket she was wearing—loaned to them by the castle's housekeeper. In his snug worn jeans and boots, hair messy, he suddenly looked a lot younger. And sexier than she'd ever seen him.

Primo was looking at her as if he'd never seen her before, and it sent an electric jolt all the way through her body. He walked over to her and cupped her jaw, eyes roving over her face.

He said, 'Do you have any idea how beautiful you are?'

Faye might have laughed if Primo hadn't looked so serious. Her hair was a wild tangle, any make-up she'd had on had been sand and wind-blasted off her face, and she was pretty sure she'd just stepped in horse manure.

But he'd never looked more gorgeous to her too. The beauty of the landscape, the earthiness of the smell of the horses and salty tang of the wild sea...all seemed to combine to create a mutual urgency.

Primo took her hand and led her through the back door of the castle to the boot room, where they slipped off their boots. Then, without stopping, he took her hand again and led her up through the house, straight to their bedroom.

At this point Faye couldn't care less that they'd been given only one bedroom. She hardly noticed the gleaming dark wooden floors, overlaid with rugs. The heavy drapes. The blazing fire behind a guard. The huge, imposing four-poster bed. The portraits of strangers on the wall. The gold claw-footed bath by the window.

All she had eyes for was Primo, and all she could think about was how badly she needed to be naked with him. But instead of ripping off her clothes, he stepped up to her and cupped her jaw and her face. Then he kissed her, long and slow and deep, until her legs nearly gave way.

Only then did he start to pull off her jacket, as she did his. Hands tugged and pulled at shirts. Snaps on jeans. Underwear.

It was raining outside now, lashing against the window from an ever-darkening sky, but they were oblivious.

Primo lay down on the bed and pulled Faye over him so she was straddling his thighs. He cupped her breasts and she moved up so he could put his mouth on them. Her back arched and Primo moulded her body, waist and hips. He dipped a hand between her legs and felt how ready she was, and he positioned her over him, holding himself in his hand as she lowered herself onto him with slow, torturous care until he was fully sheathed in her.

They both stayed very still for a moment. Breathing in the sensation.

Faye couldn't look away from Primo's eyes, even though she wanted to. Because even here, in this fevered moment, she knew she should protect herself but it was impossible. He demanded her full attention and she had to give it.

Slowly, she started to move up and down, building the pleasure for as long as she could stand it. Until their skin was slick and their breathing was laboured.

Primo let out a guttural sound, and then, 'Faye, I can't… you're killing me.'

He put his hands on her hips and held her still, while he took over dictating their pace. Faye gave up any illusion that she'd had control at all and handed herself over to the primal rhythm that took over their bodies, bringing them to a soaring climax that had Primo sitting up and clasping Faye close, their bodies shuddering in unison as pleasure ripped through them and broke them apart.

Faye had a vague sensation of Primo collapsing back onto the bed, taking her with him, and she couldn't fight the urge to sink down into endless ebbing waves of pleasure.

When Faye woke it was dusk outside. Low lights were burning. The bedroom was empty, the fire low in the grate. She noticed a robe on the bed, and once again Primo's consideration made her chest feel a little tight. Her first husband had never thought of such small but important details. She'd put it down to the fact that they'd been much younger, but she knew in her heart of hearts that if her husband had been a good, kind person it would have been evident even then.

She pulled on the robe and went over to where the bathtub sat in front of the window, showcasing a magnificent view of the beach and the sea beyond. It was full of steaming water. Was that what had woken her up?

Faye pulled her hair up, slipped off the robe and stepped

into the bath, groaning softly as she sank down into the hot water and it instantly soothed tender muscles.

There was a range of luxury toiletries, and then she noticed a glass of chilled sparkling wine. This decadence truly was next level. She never indulged herself like this.

She picked up the glass and took a sip, relishing the bubbles slipping down her throat. She washed herself and sank back, glorying in the moment, still a little unbelieving that Primo had arranged all this so they could have... a *honeymoon*.

It wasn't supposed to be like this. She was meant to be getting on with her life and her work, and they were meant to be meeting up only at prearranged public events. But now...

Faye found that she couldn't quite find the thread of thought she should be worried about and sank deeper into the bath.

After a few minutes she realised that she was hungry, so she got out and dried herself. She pulled on the most casual clothes she had with her—a soft, loose pair of trousers and a shirt. She wasn't exactly prepared for this extended trip.

Leaving her hair up, Faye made her way down through the castle—thankfully it was on the modest side—to the kitchen and dining room area. She stopped in the doorway and her heart turned over before she could stop it.

Primo was dressed in low-slung jeans and a T-shirt, stirring something on the stove. There was an open bottle of wine and two glasses on the table. He looked outrageously sexy against the domestic backdrop, and Faye felt a little more of those precious defences crumbling into dust. At this rate she'd have nothing left to cling on to.

And then Primo turned around and she noticed the tea towel flung over his shoulder. Mentally, she sent up a plea to whatever gods were torturing her with this man.

Give me a break!

She came into the kitchen feeling shy. 'Hi.'

He said, 'I can't claim to have done anything but put this over the heat and stir it. That's about the extent of my domestic capabilities, I'm afraid.'

Faye's nose twitched. It smelled divine. She came closer. 'What is it?'

'Apparently it's Irish beef and Guinness stew. The house-keeper left it for us.'

Because they'd been too rampant to stop and discuss dinner with her earlier.

Faye busied herself finding bowls and plates. She poured the wine into glasses. The kitchen was large and pleasantly rustic, but with modern touches.

Primo dished the stew into the bowls. 'You're happy to eat here?'

'Of course,' Faye said. 'There's no point causing a mess in another room.'

They sat down and Faye ate some of the stew, closing her eyes in appreciation of the tender meat and delicious flavours. 'This is amazing.'

Primo made a similar sound. Then he observed, 'You're pretty unspoiled for the heiress to one of America's largest fortunes.'

Faye took a sip of wine. She felt deliciously relaxed. 'I could say the same of you. Why aren't you a playboy brat?'

Primo shrugged minutely as he broke a piece of bread off a loaf and dunked it into the stew. 'Like you, that lifestyle never really interested me. And I was aware of people gossiping about my father at an early age. If I went into work with him I used to see how he wasn't really respected, and that made an impression. I felt ashamed. I knew I didn't want that. From a young age I knew I wanted to restore respect in our family name.'

'That's a pretty profound revelation to have. And your brother wasn't interested at all?'

Primo shook his head. 'Quin was the nerd—always had his head buried in his computer, coding or gaming.'

'You were pretty good on that horse today,' she said. 'Where did you learn to ride?'

'Actually...' he said slowly, as if it was just occurring to him. 'My mother taught me. She was a brilliant horse-woman. Her family bred racehorses in Brazil.'

'Were you close before she left?'

Primo shook his head. 'She was generally too busy fighting with my father. But I'd forgotten about her taking me horse riding. Quin would have been too small.'

'Do you see her now?'

'Not much—sometimes at social events. I've forgotten what number husband she's on.'

Faye absorbed that. 'I was pretty lucky with my parents, but I always wished I had siblings. I was lonely.'

'What about friends?'

Faye shrugged. 'Sure, I had my friends. But when I wasn't at school the house always felt very empty, and I could tell my parents were sad.'

'They couldn't have more children?'

Faye's insides clenched. How had she let them get onto this topic? She shook her head. 'No. My mother had complications after my birth and couldn't...' She trailed off, because it was too painful to articulate the fact that Faye appeared to have inherited her mother's gynaecological issues.

'I'm sorry.'

Faye avoided Primo's eyes, because she could hear the genuine compassion in his voice. She busied herself clearing their plates, and quickly changed the subject in case his questions became even more personal.

'So, are you going to tell me where our next stop is on this magical mystery honeymoon tour?'

Primo sat back and watched Faye taking the plates over to the sink. He was well aware that she was deflecting talking any further on this topic of conversation, but even though he wanted to ask her if her family history had anything to do with why she was so adamant not to have a family, he decided not to.

A few things were striking him.

Such as how unlike any other woman he'd ever known she was.

She really was incredibly unspoiled. He couldn't think of anyone else who would be happy to sit at a well-loved kitchen table without a silver service and eat a humble, albeit delicious stew.

She was loading the dishwasher now. He didn't even know where his dishwasher was, and he felt a dart of shame.

She was barefoot. But not even the loose casual clothes could hide her beauty. Hair up, tendrils falling down. Face clear and fresh. It reminded him of how she'd looked on the horse...so happy.

He could get used to making this woman happy.

The thought appeared unbidden in his mind. He told himself it was an entirely legitimate thought to have about one's wife. But on a deeper level Primo knew that it wasn't necessarily just about making her happy for the sake of the relationship. It had something to do with making *him* happy too.

Happy. Since when had he needed to be happy?

He wasn't averse to the idea, obviously, but it wasn't something he'd ever given much thought to. And he realised now that perhaps there was something a bit sad about never acknowledging the need for happiness...

Faye was looking at him and waving a hand. 'Hi, where did you go?'

Primo shook his head. He was losing it. And it was all this woman's fault.

He stood up and topped up the wine glasses before giving one to Faye and taking the other for himself. Then he took her free hand and led her out of the kitchen, back through the castle to the bedroom.

She said, 'You haven't answered my question...where are we going from here?'

Primo brought them into the bedroom and closed the door. He put their glasses of wine down and stripped until he was naked. He directed an expressive look at Faye, and she slipped out of her clothes too.

A flush was rising over her skin and her nipples pebbled. Primo looked his fill, as she did him, and as the hunger clawed and bit at his gut, demanding to be slaked, he felt a frisson of unease. Shouldn't the edge have been taken off by now? But it was as if the more he had of her, the more he needed.

He struggled to control himself. His body was betraying him spectacularly. He dragged his gaze up and all he could see was gold and green, mirroring back the hunger he felt.

'You asked me where we're going from here?' he said.

'I did?'

He nodded.

Faye said, a little breathlessly, 'I'm not sure I care all that much any more.'

'That's good,' he said, and he moved forward and caught Faye's hips, pulling her towards him.

The moment her softer body touched his, he felt the beast roar within him.

Just before he kissed her, and threw them both back into the inferno, he said, 'That's good, because there's nowhere else I want to be other than right here, right now.'

* * *

'I have to go to London to take a meeting,' Primo said.

Faye tried to hide her disappointment. They were having breakfast in the formal dining room of the Irish castle the following morning. It was making Faye nostalgic for their cosy, informal dinner in the kitchen the previous evening.

And what had happened afterwards.

She fought down the inevitable reaction of heat rising in her body.

Every time they made love it seemed to eclipse the previous time and she couldn't figure it out. Surely it was meant to go the other way? That was how it had always happened for her before. Even with her first husband she couldn't remember it being like this... So intense. So urgent. Maybe it was no harm that this spontaneous honeymoon was coming to an end.

He said, 'You could come with me, and we could go back to New York together from there.'

She needed to get her wits back.

Faye shook her head. 'No, it's okay. I think I'll go back to Dublin for the day and check out some galleries—they have some really interesting artists showing at the moment.'

'London has galleries too,' Primo pointed out.

'I like to know what's going on outside of the big art hubs.'

'That's why you're so good at what you do.'

A burst of warm pleasure filled Faye's belly. She smiled. 'I try my best.'

'I can drop you off in Dublin and go on to London.'

Faye felt a spurt of regret already, but she said, 'That would be great, thank you.'

When she was getting off the private plane a couple of hours later, she was surprised by a burst of emotion.

Primo was standing with her, waiting for the door to be opened, and she turned to him and said, 'Thank you for that…the castle…the horses…' She was about to say, *It was magical*, but she amended it. 'I really enjoyed it.'

The door was being opened now, and he took her chin between his thumb and forefinger. He tipped her face up towards him. 'I enjoyed it too. I'm sorry we're cutting it short.'

He kissed her then, and Faye felt an urge to change her mind about staying in Dublin. But she resisted the pull. *His* pull. He was scrambling her brain. She needed to reassess what was happening here—because all she could see was Primo.

He pulled back. 'See you in Boston.'

She opened her eyes. 'See you in Boston.'

But a few hours later Primo was already texting her.

Faye was in a city centre art gallery, trying to get her mind back into work mode, when her phone vibrated.

She took it out of her bag.

Hi.

Faye rolled her eyes, but even as she did so her heart was beating fast.

Aren't you in a meeting?

Yes, but I'm bored. We should have stayed at the castle. It was fun.

Faye blushed. Yes, it had been fun.

She realised she was smiling. Because she was having

fun now, texting Primo. And she couldn't seem to care that it shouldn't be *fun*.

He texted again.

What are you looking at right now?

Faye took a picture of the painting in front of her and sent it.

A couple of seconds later:

Is that upside down or meant to be like that?

Faye let out a burst of spontaneous laughter and then quickly covered it with a cough when a couple of other people in the quiet gallery looked at her.

There was another message.

I have to go to a stuffy dinner tonight. I wish you were here. You'd make it so much more interesting.

Faye's heart thumped hard. She sent back:

We can't always get what we want.

Pity!

Faye cursed him, but smiled.

Then she put her phone away, so she wouldn't see any more cutesy texts from Primo.

She left the gallery and walked down the street, and tried to push out of her mind what he'd said.

We should have stayed at the castle.

She passed a boutique and glanced at it, then stopped

as something caught her eye. In the window was a dress. It was short and made out of sequins of different colours, giving it an iridescent quality—golds and silvers and rust colours. Exactly the kind of thing she would normally never go for. Too flashy. Too exposing.

Normally.

Following an urge too strong to ignore, Faye went into the boutique and came out twenty minutes later with a bag and a half-baked audacious idea in her head.

London

Primo was sitting at a dinner table in one of London's most famous restaurants. The sounds of the people around him chatting and laughing were muted, soaked up by the luxurious soft furnishings and thick carpet. The decor was dark and mostly leather. The atmosphere was hushed, discreet and very, very exclusive. He'd spotted one ex-American President on the way to his table—who, upon seeing Primo, had made a point of greeting him.

Primo never took things like this for granted. He'd worked to build respect for Holt Industries again after his father's lacklustre attention, and he had no intention of squandering it.

What if Faye wants to divorce you in six months? whispered a little voice.

The notion gave Primo an unpleasant jolt. As if his footing wasn't quite steady, even though he was sitting down. Not possible, he quickly reassured himself.

A kaleidoscope of images from the last few days came into his head. Faye was happy with him. Why on earth would she want to divorce?

His phone vibrated in his pocket and he took it out and looked at it.

How's your dinner going?

Primo smiled.

As boring as I predicted.

You don't look that bored.

Everything inside Primo went very still. Slowly, he looked up from his phone. He surveyed the tables nearby. Mostly men in suits. Like at his table.

His phone pinged again. He looked down.

You're getting colder.

No, he was getting hotter at the very thought that she might be here. Proof, if he even needed it, that this marriage was turning out to be more viable than he could have hoped for.

Primo turned his head the other way, to where there was a bar area. His gaze fell on a woman sitting alone. For a second he didn't recognise her—and then his heart stopped dead. Arrested by the sight of her.

She was sitting on a high stool, dressed in something that appeared to be poured onto her body like a glittering sheath of shimmering colours. Two straps. Low-cut. Long legs, crossed, drawing the eye to her thighs, sleek and toned. Hair down and wavy. She was looking at him, and as he caught her eye she smiled and lifted the delicate flute in her hand in a salute.

Primo's blood thrummed with adrenalin and shock and surprise and sheer...joy to see her.

And in that same moment, as if scenting competition,

Primo sensed lots of other males' gazes going to Faye. Alone at the bar. Looking like a vision. For the first time in his life, Primo felt a surge of something very primal. Possessiveness. A need to stake his claim.

He put down his napkin and cut through the conversation of the other men, saying, 'If you'll excuse me, please? There's something I have to attend to.'

He stood up without waiting for anyone to acknowledge what he'd said and strode straight over to Faye. He caught her scent. Flowery and musky and *her*.

She looked at him, a glimmer of mischief in her eyes. 'Hello, do I know you?'

Primo put his hands on the arms of her chair, caging her in. 'Oh, I think you know me very well. Intimately, in fact.'

Faye put her head on one side. 'Come to think of it, you do look a little familiar... Isn't it... Holden...something?'

Primo grinned. He realised he was having fun. A concept that he'd never really entertained before, much like whether or not he was *happy*.

He sent an explicit look to her hand. 'A married woman? In a bar alone? Dressed to tempt the devil?'

Faye opened her eyes wide. 'Are you the devil?'

'I wouldn't have thought so,' Primo responded. 'But right now I'm full of very sinful thoughts and desires.'

'Would you like a drink?'

'I'd love one. Whisky.'

Faye put out a hand. 'Please...join me.'

Primo let go of her stool and sat in the one beside her. He watched her order a drink from the barman and his hands itched to reach out and touch her, claim her. But he was also enjoying this little game.

The barman put his drink down. Primo lifted his glass.

Faye brought hers to his and clinked it gently. 'What are we drinking to?'

'You tell me—you're the one who enticed me over here.'

'Spontaneous encounters.'

He clinked her glass. 'Spontaneous encounters.'

They sipped their drinks.

Faye sent a glance towards the table where he'd been having dinner. 'Won't they be annoyed you've just walked away?'

Primo shook his head. 'I don't want to sound arrogant, but they need me more than I need them.'

Faye glanced quickly over again and back. 'They do look a little disappointed.'

Primo beckoned to the barman and asked, 'Can you send over a bottle of dessert wine—the 2009 Chateau d'Yquem—to my dinner companions, please.'

Faye made a low whistling noise. 'Are you sure they're worth it?'

'It'll ease the pain of my absence—as will the fact that dinner was on me,' Primo said dryly, and raised a glass towards the table as the wine was delivered by a waiter. He looked at Faye. 'So, are you here on business?'

'Mainly pleasure for this particular trip.'

Primo let his gaze drop over her body. The dress dipped low between her breasts and he wanted to pull the sparkly material to one side so he could taste her. His body throbbed. He shifted in his seat.

'And you?' she asked.

Primo looked at her. 'Business, ostensibly, but I'm fast being tempted to turn it into something more pleasurable.'

At that, Faye drained her glass of wine and stood up from the seat, bringing her body momentarily between Primo's thighs. His erection twitched. And then it did more than twitch when she put a hand on his thigh and he felt her squeeze it.

'I'm afraid I'm a married woman, so I'll have to go before you tempt me to do something I might regret.'

Primo drained his drink and caught her hand as she was leaving. She looked at him, a picture of innocence and wicked siren all in one.

He said, 'Let me tempt you. I promise it'll be worth it.'

She pretended to consider, and then she said, 'If you promise that no one will ever know.'

Primo made a cross shape on his chest. 'I promise.'

Faye tugged him with her, out of the bar, and Primo followed, leaving in his wake an aborted business dinner and not one ounce of regret.

When Faye woke in the morning she was face-down in the bed, her head turned to one side. She cracked open an eye and saw the bed was empty. The previous evening came back in a rush of images and sensations. Sitting in the bar waiting for Primo to notice her. The strength of the jolt of electricity when he had. And the adrenalin when he'd just walked away from his dinner for her.

She hadn't been sure what to expect. It was one thing, him surprising her, but she hadn't known how he'd take her interrupting his work life.

But he hadn't hesitated.

They'd left the restaurant, which was attached to one of London's most exclusive hotels, and when they'd walked into the lobby Primo had said, 'Please tell me you have a room here, or I'll have to book one right now.'

The hunger in his voice and on his face had almost brought her to her knees there and then. She'd silently pulled a room key out of her bag, and he'd taken her hand and led her straight over to the elevator.

In the elevator, he'd asked roughly, 'What floor.'

'The top,' Faye had answered, breathless. Apparently they weren't playing any more.

As the lift had ascended Primo had pressed the stop button and said, 'This is taking too long.'

It had been exactly the same thing she'd been thinking.

In the next second they'd been pressed together, mouths fused, kissing desperately. Primo's hands had moulded her body to his, finding the slit in the dress, exploring beneath to find the place between her legs where she was embarrassingly ready. She'd gasped into his mouth as he'd stroked his fingers into her, tilting her hips towards him.

She'd climaxed around his fingers, unable to stop herself. She would have drawn back, mortified, but Primo hadn't let her. He'd taken her hand and put it on him.

'Feel what you do to me,' he'd said. He'd rested his forehead against hers. 'You have a hold over me, Faye...like nothing I've ever known before.'

And you over me, she would have said, if she'd been able to speak.

She'd felt a moment of tenderness for him. He'd sounded almost bewildered for a moment. As if he genuinely didn't understand what was going on.

'Do you mind that I came?' she'd asked, before realising the double meaning and burying her face into his shoulder with fresh embarrassment.

He'd chuckled softly and tipped her chin up, not letting her hide. 'No,' he'd responded. 'I absolutely don't mind. I wonder if I'm dreaming you up.'

Faye had leant forward and nipped at his lower lip. She'd squeezed his firm flesh. 'I'm real. Make love to me, Primo.'

The air had been so white-hot around them, Faye had wondered how their clothes hadn't melted off.

Primo had said, 'Not here.'

He'd pressed the button again, and somehow they'd managed to get to her suite without scandalising the respectable residents of the hotel. And then it had become a heat haze of desperation, and sinking into flesh, and wrapping her legs around Primo's hips and begging, pleading for release, over and over again, until the dawn had streaked across the sky...

And now...

Faye lifted her head and squinted, and let out a little yelp. It was almost lunchtime. Then she noticed the note on stiff white hotel paper on the pillow.

She picked it up and turned onto her back to read it.

See you in Boston. P (Your husband)

It took Faye a second to realise she had a soppy smile on her face. And, as much as she tried, she couldn't seem to rearrange her facial muscles.

The notion that Primo had permanently altered something in her very cells was a little disconcerting.

CHAPTER NINE

WHILE FAYE WAS waking up, Primo was already high above the Atlantic Ocean—he had a meeting in Manhattan that evening, and Faye had arranged to meet a client in London before she left. He was still marvelling at the previous evening. It was the hottest thing any woman had ever done to him. Surprising him like that. In that dress. The image of her sitting on that high stool would be burned onto his brain for ever.

He felt a burst of pure satisfaction that went deeper than the lingering sensual pleasure—because he had chosen his wife well. He foresaw a long and happy union, in which inevitably this intensity of desire would wane—it had to—but would be replaced with something far more manageable. Not this...fevered need to have her, driving him—and *her*—to bouts of spontaneity that he was enjoying—there was no denying it—but which ultimately weren't sustainable.

Being distracted away from his business dinner meeting the previous evening had been an anomaly. It unsettled him a little now to acknowledge how easy it had been to walk away. And how unlike him. It was the kind of behaviour his father would have exhibited. Getting distracted by a beautiful woman.

But Faye was his wife. Not just a lover. Perhaps even she would have to concede that all the signs pointed to a sustainable union. But something niggled. Even though he knew every inch of her intimately, and knew how to push her over the edge with just a flick of his finger, she was keeping something in reserve.

After all, she was still maintaining her independence in the relationship. There was no talk of moving in together yet, and while Primo appreciated that on one level—because of course he didn't intend for this to be an emotional union—spending time with Faye had made him rethink the need for such boundaries. It wouldn't be a hardship to live with her. The thought of having her in his bed every night was…ridiculously seductive.

To his surprise, for the first time in his life he was actually envisaging having a family with someone. Not just as a duty to create the next generation of Holts, but really creating a family, even though he wasn't sure what that looked like. But Faye did. She'd grown up with loving parents. She would be a good mother—he knew that instinctively.

She was inspiring Primo to think that maybe—just maybe—there was a chance that their marriage would prove to be fulfilling in ways that he hadn't fully appreciated.

Boston, a few days later

Is it too much to hope we can arrive at events together one day soon?

Faye didn't answer Primo's text and shut down her phone. She sighed as the taxi crawled forward in the bumper-to-bumper traffic near the venue in Boston. She wasn't surprised that Primo had been irritated when she'd said she'd make her own way to this function, but her meeting *had* genuinely run over.

She shook her head again to try and dislodge the woolly

feeling. She'd felt an ominous prickling pain at the back of her throat all day today, and she'd been sniffling. She really hoped she wasn't coming down with a cold. She had a massive job the following week in Manhattan—helping a corporate client take delivery of their new art collection, curated by her—and she'd promised to be on hand to help them get it hung properly.

Her limbs felt a little achy. She told herself it was just the effects of the jetlag after her return from Europe.

That magical coastal castle in the West of Ireland felt like a long time ago. She wondered if she'd imagined it?

She hadn't seen Primo since London. She would have, if they'd lived together. The thought that they could have been sharing a bed for the last few days sent simultaneous thrills and trepidation through Faye.

Living together was just a step too far into making this whole arrangement more permanent.

You are married to the man—can't get more permanent than that, pointed out a voice.

Faye scowled at herself.

If anything, the more she got to know Primo, and the more she hungered for him, the more imperative it was to maintain these boundaries she'd put in place. Boundaries she'd never known would become so important.

Because she hadn't expected to want him.

To like him so much.

'We're here.'

'Thank you,' Faye said, jolted out of her spiralling thoughts.

She saw the flow of the immaculately clothed crowd going into one of Boston's oldest buildings for the charity benefit and curbed the urge to tell the driver to keep going.

Just then, her head started to pound. But she couldn't

leave. Primo was waiting for her, and every cell in her body was urging her up and out of the car, to go and be with him.

She cursed her weak body, but congratulated herself that he might have got to her physically, but she was still intact emotionally. He might have chipped away at those walls a little bit, but they were still strong enough to withstand all his considerable charm and powers of persuasion.

As she approached the main hall where the event was taking place, she spotted Primo immediately. Clad in a white tuxedo. Hair swept back from his forehead.

Her insides turned to jelly. And suddenly her confidence that she had somehow remained emotionally untouched by this man drained away, to be replaced with something far less certain. She knew him now in ways she never would have imagined she would. And he was so much more than she had thought a man like him could be.

He had got to her.

Faye clutched her evening bag. Maybe if she turned back now the taxi would still be there. She could jump in and—

But at that moment Primo turned to look at her. As if he'd known she was there all along. And she was caught. He was coming for her, the crowd parting to let him through like a sea.

And then he was in front of her and she couldn't breathe. *She'd missed him.*

'Hi…'

'Hi.' He looked stern, as if he was about to say something else, but then his expression relaxed. 'I was wondering where you were.'

'Stuck in traffic.'

He took her hand and Faye instinctively wanted to burrow closer. He brought out something very feminine in her that she'd repressed for a long time. A need to feel looked after. Safe. She instantly felt more at ease with her hand in his. And it should annoy her, but it didn't.

'Come on,' he said, tugging her into the room thronged with the beautiful and the famous and the rich. 'I'm having an argument with the governor about the merits of funding art programmes and he needs to hear from a passionate expert, not an idiot like me.'

Faye shoved down all the niggles, psychological and actual—the prickling at the back of her throat, her increasingly fuzzy head and the way she felt hot and cold at the same time—and let Primo lead her into the fray.

'Why insist on separate rooms when we know we'll end up in bed together?' Primo was asking Faye in the back of the car as they left the event a few hours later.

For the first time since Faye had met Primo she could actually say that making love to him wasn't foremost in her mind. But the car was pulling to a halt outside the hotel now and Primo had somehow magically appeared at her door in what seemed like a nanosecond to help her out.

She stumbled a little.

'Are you okay?' His hand tightened on her elbow.

'I'm fine. Just tired, I think…maybe coming down with something.'

They were in the elevator now and Primo looked at her. 'You look flushed.'

He put a hand to her forehead and Faye wanted to swat it away, but it felt like too much of an effort.

'I think I might have caught something. I'm sure it'll be gone in the morning.'

When they got to their rooms, and Faye stopped outside her door, Primo asked, 'Are you sure you're okay?'

Faye nodded, but winced slightly. It was starting to hurt when she moved her head. 'I'm just tired.'

'I'm coming in with you.'

Faye protested. 'Primo, I'm not sure I'm really feeling—'

'Not for that.'

He took the key out of her hand and swiped it, opening her door. Inside, he turned on some lights and then went to the connecting door that linked their rooms. He opened the lock on Faye's side and looked at her.

'I'm going to open the door on my side too. Let me know if you need anything, okay?'

He handed back her room key. Faye took it and watched him walk out again. A minute later he was unlocking the door on his side, so all Faye would have to do was open her door.

He called through the doors. 'Night, Faye.'

'Night, Primo.'

Somehow Faye managed to undress and wash herself, even though it felt like a monumental task. She fell into bed, hoping that by morning she'd be feeling better.

But she wasn't.

She was worse.

Much worse.

She woke to a persistent banging noise, and when she tried to speak nothing came out. Her throat was agony, as if filled with hot needles.

She managed to get up and go in the direction of the banging and pulled the door open. She was looking at a broad, bare chest that was vaguely familiar. Primo.

He put a hand on her forehead. 'Faye...you're burning up.'

Faye wanted to say, *Give it a rest, Primo, you're not that amazing.* But she felt herself become weightless, and then she was being deposited on a bed.

She realised that it wasn't her bed, and struggled to sit up, croaking out, 'Primo, I told you—'

'Yes, a doctor, please, ASAP.'

Faye sank back down. Oh. He wasn't trying to make love to her. He was calling a doctor. For some reason Faye found that momentarily hilarious—until she laughed and it hurt her ribs.

Everything seemed to happen in a bit of a blur after that. A doctor came—a nice lady, who poked and prodded Faye and looked at her throat. Faye's head was clearing marginally, and she heard the doctor say, 'It looks like you've picked up this virulent strain of flu going around.'

Primo's voice came. 'I'll take her home. I can take better care of her there.'

Home. The word floated around Faye's head but she couldn't pin it down. It felt comforting, and also slightly scary.

She was given some medication, and water to drink, and that helped to cushion the various symptoms.

At some point—she wasn't sure how—she found she was dressed and on a plane with Primo, shivering.

And then they were in a car, and there was a blast of cool air before she felt weightless again and realised Primo was carrying her.

She lifted her head. 'Hey, I can walk.'

'You're going straight to bed.'

Faye frowned. 'You have a one-track mind, mister. I told you I don't want...'

But the words disappeared out of her mouth and her head and Faye fell into a fractured sleep, punctuated by moments when someone held her up and made her swallow tablets and drink water. Other moments when she would feel boiling hot and cold all at the same time.

There were voices...but the main one she listened out for and found absurdly comforting was the deep one. It was never far away.

At some point Faye woke up. Suddenly her mind was relatively clear and she wasn't drenched in sweat. But she was weak.

She came up on one elbow.

'You're awake.'

A large shape detached itself from a chair in a room that Faye dimly recognised. Primo. He was wearing a shirt and jeans. Bare feet. Hair mussed. Stubble on his jaw.

'Where am I?'

He sat on the bed. 'My apartment. Manhattan.'

She struggled to focus. 'But we were in Boston.'

'Two days ago. We came back here. You have the flu pretty bad.'

'I need to go to the bathroom.'

Primo stood up and pulled back the covers.

Faye realised she was in a set of her own sleep clothes, shorts and a matching button-down top. She sat up and swung her legs over the side of the bed.

Primo put out a hand, but Faye said, 'It's fine. I'm sure I can—' But when she tried to stand, she promptly collapsed again.

Primo put his arm around her and supported her on cotton wool legs into the bathroom. Faye held on to the sink. She felt weak and shaky. She caught a glimpse of herself in the mirror. Pale, but with two bright red spots in her cheeks. Hair long and lank. She groaned inwardly. If this wasn't one way to potentially end this marriage, she didn't know what was.

Primo was hovering.

Faye said, 'I think I'll be okay.'

Primo backed away reluctantly. 'I'll be right outside the door.'

Faye managed to go to the toilet without incident, and washed her face and brushed her teeth. Those small activities were enough to make her feel as if she'd run a marathon.

Primo knocked. 'I'm coming in.'

Faye didn't have the energy to tell him not to, and it was a relief when he scooped her up and took her back to the freshly made bed. Daylight was streaming into the room now, and the French doors to the terrace outside were open, curtains fluttering a little in the breeze.

The housekeeper was just leaving with the bundled-up sheets and Primo said, 'Maybe we'll try some chicken soup?'

'Very well, Mr Holt. I'll be right back.'

A name popped into Faye's head. 'Marjorie.'

Primo was pulling clean sheets up over her waist. 'That's right. She's my housekeeper here. You've met her before.'

The woman came back with a tray that Primo took from her, saying, 'Thanks.'

Faye's voice still felt scratchy and a little sore. 'I've been really out of it…'

'You were. At one point I almost took you to the ER, but you told me not to.'

'I did?' Faye had no recollection.

'Here, try some of this.'

Primo was bringing a spoon to her mouth and Faye obediently opened up. The warm, tasty soup was the most delicious thing she'd ever tasted.

'Well, you haven't eaten in days.'

She hadn't realised she'd spoken out loud. Suspiciously, she asked, 'Was I saying things?'

Primo brought another spoonful to her mouth and she dutifully drank it down.

He said, 'There was a lot of muttering about fences and walls. And bricks crumbling.'

Faye cringed when she realised the significance of her ramblings. Primo knocking down her precious defences.

She asked, 'What day is it?'

'Tuesday.'

Faye calculated. The Boston event had been on a Friday. She'd lost a whole weekend. And then she realised something else and sat up straight.

'I'm meant to be curating the hanging of new art in the Goldman Law Practice downtown.'

Primo put a hand on her shoulder, pushing her back against the pillow gently. 'Your assistant has let them know you're unwell and they've put the installation on hold until you're better. All your other appointments are being rescheduled.'

She realised something else as Primo fed her another spoonful of soup. After she'd swallowed, she said, 'You've been taking care of me... What about your work?'

'It's fine. I rescheduled some meetings...worked from home.'

The enormity of how ill she'd been hit her—and the way Primo had taken care of her. 'I'm sorry. I had no idea I was coming down with something so bad. I shouldn't have gone to Boston.'

He looked at her. 'How on earth could you have known?'

'I'm feeling better now. I can go back to my own apartment today.'

Primo emitted a sound of exasperation. 'You aren't strong enough yet. You need at least another day...maybe two days...to rest and recuperate.'

'But I—'

Primo put down the tray and stood up, hands on his hips, 'Faye, dammit. I'm your husband. I'm supposed to take care of you. We made vows, remember? In sickness and in health?'

Faye's insides quivered. She'd never seen Primo like this. 'Yes, I know, but...it's not as if we were saying them...' She trailed off.

'For real?' he finished. 'They were real enough to me.'

That landed like a soft blow to her gut. 'But this is just a...a marriage of convenience...a business arrangement.'

Primo sat back down. A muscle was pulsing in his jaw. 'Is it, Faye? Really? When we can't keep our hands off each other?' He waved a hand. 'Current circumstances notwithstanding.'

'That's just chemistry.'

He looked at her for a long moment, as if he was going to say something, but then he took the tray back onto his lap and filled another spoon with soup. As he brought it to her mouth he said, 'It's non-negotiable, Faye. You're here under my care until you're strong enough to leave, so get used to it.'

Faye, unused to being spoken to like a recalcitrant child, obediently opened her mouth and let Primo feed her. Something had just shifted between them and she wasn't sure what it was. But by the time she'd finished the soup she was exhausted again, and only too happy to escape Primo's stern mood by slipping back into sleep.

Two days later, as Faye was recovering, she was also realising the true severity of her condition. She'd fallen in love with Primo. And how could she not have? It was as if the man had been specifically put on this Earth to get under every single one of Faye's walls until she was left utterly defenceless. No wonder she'd been raving about that in her delirium. She could only hope Primo had no idea what she'd been on about.

Her assistant had just left Primo's apartment, after going through Faye's rescheduled appointments and meetings, and he'd also brought over what had appeared to be half of Faye's possessions, which were now being installed in Primo's guest room. Faye had agreed that it would be practical to have some things here, because Primo wasn't letting her go anywhere until he was satisfied she was completely fine.

She was feeling inordinately vulnerable after this revelation on top of all the signs of Primo exerting his very skilful brand of taking over her life as well as her heart.

When he appeared in the informal living area where she'd had her meeting with her assistant, dressed in those jeans that should come with a health warning and a shirt, Faye—whose reviving libido only made her feel even more exposed—said waspishly, 'I'm not sure you didn't make me ill on purpose to engineer this campaign to all but move me into your apartment.'

Primo folded his arms. He looked far too smug for his own good. He said, 'I'll be the first to admit that I'm pretty much capable of anything, but I haven't quite perfected my skills in sorcery.'

Faye scowled at him, hoping that he wouldn't see the truth of her emotions. How had she let this happen?

As if to help her, a kaleidoscope of images raced through her mind—from that first meeting with Primo, to Venice, then Paris, Dublin, the castle in the West of Ireland, London… It was like a string of jewels laid out, twinkling at her and mocking her for believing she could remain immune to this man's undeniable charm.

Then he said, 'I have something for you—a little get-well gift.'

Faye sat up. She wished she was wearing something other than yoga pants and sweatshirt. But it was an improvement on nightclothes.

Primo bent down and retrieved something from behind a sofa. It was a square-shaped item, wrapped in brown paper, measuring about one foot square.

He handed it to her and she held it. Not too heavy. She started to undo the paper, pulling it open, and realised it was a small canvas that looked familiar. Striking deep red and pink tones. She held it up and away from her face—and then noticed the signature on the bottom.

'Lara Lopez...' Faye gasped when she realised what it was. A miniature of the original much larger painting she'd admired so much in Paris. *'Life.'* She looked at Primo. 'How...?'

'I got in touch with her to see if she'd sell the one in Paris, but she has an agreement with the gallery so she can't. But she told me she had this, which was the genesis of the bigger painting. Her trial run...'

Faye was struck dumb. Beyond moved that he'd not only remembered her loving that painting but that he'd gone to the trouble of trying to track it down. This one was smaller, yes, but it was perfect.

Faye looked at Primo again. 'I can't believe you did this...it's very special. Thank you.'

For a second she was terrified she might cry, when she'd thought she'd cried her last tears over her first husband and the devastation that she'd never give birth to her own children.

Primo took the painting from her and put it on the mantelpiece. 'You can decide where you want it. We can get it framed.'

Faye stood up, her limbs still feeling slightly wobbly. 'I love it. I'm glad the other one stays in the gallery, though, because people should get to see it. This is...perfect. Thank you, Primo. You didn't have to get me anything, but I do love it.'

He glanced at his watch. 'I have a meeting in the office. Do you mind if I leave the apartment for a couple of hours?'

Suddenly overwhelmed by everything—her revelation and this gesture—Faye said hurriedly, 'No, not at all. You really don't have to babysit me.'

Primo was about to leave when he turned back. 'You'll still be here when I get back?'

Faye tried to think of some pithy remark but in the end she just nodded. 'Yes, I'll be here.'

Primo walked out and Faye sank back onto the couch and gazed at the painting. There, laid bare, was every pulsing, beating bit of emotion she felt for Primo. But Faye knew that, as much as he would prefer her to be absorbed into his world, like an amenable wife, he wouldn't thank her for falling in love with him.

Primo came back to his apartment that evening and all was quiet. Marjorie would be gone for the day. For a second he imagined that Faye might be gone too, even though she'd said she wouldn't.

The surge of conflicting emotions that thought brought up propelled him into the main living area. Empty. As was the kitchen. He checked her bedroom. The bed hadn't been slept in all day. A good sign. But where was she?

Eventually he thought to check the media room and found her on the couch, asleep under a large shawl. Hair flowing around her head. Feet bare. One arm above her head. She was wearing the least enticing outfit imaginable, and yet Primo's blood leapt.

She stirred, as if sensing him, and opened her eyes. She looked deliciously drowsy and flushed. For a second, he saw a slow smile start to lift that tempting mouth—before her brain obviously kicked into gear and her eyes widened and she scrambled to sit up. Back behind those walls.

He put out a hand. 'Sorry I didn't mean to wake you.'

She pushed hair out of her face. 'What time is it?'

'After eight. I got held up.'

She sent him a look. 'Because you've been playing nurse-maid to me, no doubt.'

'I brought home some takeout.'

At that moment Faye's belly rumbled. Her appetite was obviously back with a vengeance. She blushed. Primo marvelled that she could still blush so easily.

'That sounds nice,' she said. 'What is it?'

He held out a hand and helped her up from the couch. He said, 'Thai. Is that okay?'

'I love Thai.'

They went into the kitchen and Faye sat on a stool on the other side of the counter to Primo, where he busied himself putting containers into the microwave to heat them up.

Faye said, 'I wonder who's in the Irish castle now? Are they having Irish stew too? Did they go on the beach with the horses?'

Primo ladled some rice and sauce into a bowl and handed it to Faye with cutlery. 'You really loved that place, didn't you?' he observed.

Faye nodded. 'Maybe my ancestry is Irish, not Scottish,' she joked. And then, 'I never go horse riding any more...it reminded me how much I loved it.'

'Nothing stopping you from taking it up again.'

Faye sighed. 'I guess not... But it's just easy to forget to carve out time for those things, you know? And then, before you know it, years have gone by...'

'Are you always so chipper after a bout of sickness?'

Faye sent Primo a sheepish look. 'Sorry. I guess I haven't had so much time off in a long time. I like to keep busy.'

Primo could empathise with that. Since marrying Faye, though, he'd taken more time off than he'd ever done before. He'd also—as he'd found out today—taken his eye off the ball to some extent. Deals had been languishing, waiting for his signature or decision.

His chief legal advisor had said, before leaving Primo's office, 'Maybe it's time to start delegating? After all, you're a married man now. Presumably you'll be starting a family…'

Primo had realised that he'd arrogantly assumed that even while investing some time in his new wife he wouldn't be letting anything slide, but he'd had to acknowledge that hadn't been realistic. Faye was a priority now—in a way he hadn't fully envisaged when he'd decided to marry her.

These last few days, while she'd been ill, he'd felt helpless. For a man who was rarely helpless, it had been an unwelcome and humbling experience. He'd had to watch as the virus worked its way through her system, not being able to negotiate with anyone for a speedier exit. And the relief he felt now, to see her return to health, was also humbling.

He liked having her here. And not just because she was his wife and he felt she *should* be here. There was an added dimension to coming home and knowing she would be around that he hadn't really anticipated, and it transcended even the notion of being able to sleep with her every night. Although that obviously appealed too.

He told himself this wasn't about emotions—it was purely practical.

Maybe now that she'd seen how they could be together even when it wasn't all about urgency and chemistry she would reconsider some things. Notably her reluctance to have a family. But Primo knew he would have to tread carefully. He'd gained some ground, and he had no intention of squandering it, but he also had every intention of getting her to agree to consider taking this marriage to the next level.

A far more permanent and enduring one.

CHAPTER TEN

'SÃO PAULO?' REPEATED FAYE, like a parrot.

She'd woken up that morning feeling almost fully normal again for the first time in days. But she still felt that lingering sense of frustration she'd felt last night, when after dinner she'd tried to subtly let Primo know that she was feeling a *lot* better, in almost every regard, especially where her desire was concerned.

Only to have him put his hands on her arms and move her away from him, saying, 'You still look a little tired.'

She'd lain in bed stewing with a mix of anger and fear that, after seeing her at her worst, he didn't fancy her any more.

Now they were having breakfast.

'Yes, São Paulo,' he said. 'My brother has extended an invitation for us to visit.'

Faye went still and looked at Primo. He was avoiding her eye. 'Oh, that's good...isn't it?'

Primo was brusque. 'I haven't seen him in a long time, or met his wife, so I guess it's a good thing.'

He was nervous. Faye could feel it. Her heart went out to him.

'It'd be nice to meet them,' she said.

He looked at her then. 'It would be good for your recuperation...some sun and relaxation.'

'I had the flu—not TB,' Faye pointed out.

Primo regarded her. 'It was a severe enough bout that you're not arguing with me about work.'

For once, that hadn't been uppermost in Faye's mind. She scowled at Primo, but he just smiled, and in that moment it was more important than anything to Faye that she'd distracted him from his trepidation about seeing his brother.

She was in so much trouble.

They left New York as dawn rose the following morning. Faye had dressed in soft jeans and a short-sleeved cashmere top. Primo was on the other side of the plane, engrossed in paperwork and on the phone to someone called John.

Faye was enjoying being able to watch him. To see how his lips pursed and the way he ran his hand through his hair, mussing it up. He was wearing a shirt and dark trousers. Every inch a successful titan of business. The fact that she knew the man underneath gave her a serious thrill.

Which fizzled a little when she thought of how caring for her through her illness had killed his desire for her. She made a quick calculation and felt a burst of despair. They'd only been married for just over a month and she'd already fallen for him so hard that it made whatever she'd felt for her first husband look like a teenage crush. And the demise of that relationship had all but dictated her entire last decade.

Primo made her want things she hadn't admitted to herself that she wanted in so long. Safety. Security. Companionship. A lover. *A family.*

No. She blocked that thought out immediately. That way lay only certain pain, and she would never expose herself to that again.

She would never know the pain of Primo looking at her as if she was an empty useless vessel, because he would never know the full extent of her painful history.

There was a minimum of five months left before Faye

could take advantage of the six-month get-out clause and obtain a divorce and move on. But, she reasoned, if her bout of sickness *had* given Primo the ick where the physical part of the marriage was concerned, then at least if Faye re-established their boundaries, and didn't agree to any more little impromptu trips like this, they could get back to the business of a convenient marriage.

An hour later Faye couldn't sleep, in spite of the comfortable bed where she'd retreated to stop herself ogling Primo while he worked. Her mind was going a hundred miles to a minute, mainly castigating herself for falling in love with Primo. For allowing him to open up deeply buried desires and dreams.

She heard a noise and came up on one elbow to see the object of her thoughts in the doorway.

'Hey...' Her voice still felt a little scratchy.

'Hey.'

Faye was still in her clothes, but Primo was looking at her as if he'd never seen her before. His gaze seemed navy in the low lights of the bedroom, and she could see how it dropped over her body, lingering on her breasts, belly, thighs. She could feel it like a physical touch.

'Why are you looking at me like that?'

Because he didn't want her any more. Right?

Then he asked, 'Can I join you?'

Very belatedly, Faye realised that he must be tired— they'd both been up early. She went to scramble off the bed. 'Of course. Sorry. You take the bed. I can go back out—'

'Where are you going?'

She was sitting on the side of the bed now, looking at him. 'To give you some space?'

He shook his head and started to undo his shirt. Faye's eyes helplessly tracked his fingers as his chest was revealed.

Did he think she was going to just stay here and lie next to him?

She stood up—but that only brought her to within an inch of his body.

He put his hands on her arms. 'Where are you going?' he asked again.

There was a gleam in his eye that she couldn't quite fully trust. But she heard herself blurting out, 'You don't want me any more.'

Primo's eyes widened incredulously. 'Why on earth would you think that?'

She avoided his eyes. 'I was sick…it wasn't a pretty sight.'

He caught her chin, made her look at him. 'Do you have any idea how hard it was not to touch you? Would you want me less if *I* was sick?'

Joy and relief bubbled up inside her, making her a little giddy. 'Well, I guess it would depend… I mean, if you had those nasty little—'

He cut off her words with his mouth, but she could feel his smile and her insides somersaulted and swooped. All the lectures she'd given herself about redrawing boundaries faded into the background when faced with the fact that Primo still wanted her.

Things escalated quickly. His shirt was off. He'd pulled her top up and she'd lifted her arms to help him remove it. Jeans and trousers were undone and kicked off.

They tumbled onto the bed and Primo drew back for a moment and looked at her, clad in the lace and satin of her underwear.

She said, 'I've never done it on a plane before.'

Primo arched a brow.

Suddenly Faye felt blindingly jealous. 'You have.'

Primo palmed a breast, pulling down the lace cup to expose the plump flesh, teasing a nipple between two fingers. Faye's back arched as she tried to hang on to her indignation.

Primo said, 'I admit it's not my first time, no. But if it's any consolation, I can't even remember the woman. And, as this is your first time, I'll be very, very gentle.'

Faye forgave him as he lowered his mouth to hers and drugged her with a very explicit kiss, hands moving over her body, removing the scraps of underwear.

They came together in a deliciously slow, sensual dance, as gentle as Primo had promised. Until, of course, neither one of them wanted *gentle* any more, and the pace of their movements and the glide of their bodies became more urgent and desperate.

She wrapped her arms around his neck, heels digging into his buttocks as he thrust in and out, taking them higher and higher, until the climax broke over them simultaneously, both too desperate for this pinnacle to eke it out.

Primo buried his head in her shoulder, breathing fast. 'I'm sorry…wanted to make it last…'

Faye felt a surge of tenderness and smiled dreamily. 'It was perfect. Amazing.'

Primo lifted his head and looked at her. 'What do you do to me, woman? I don't know who I am when I'm with you…'

Faye's gaze moved around his face, as if she wanted to imprint every feature on her mind for ever. She landed on his mouth and traced the shape with her finger. 'I know the feeling.'

They fell asleep, Faye tucked into Primo's body, his arms tight around her, as they chased the sun across the sky.

São Paulo

Late that afternoon they were in a car and waiting for the gates to Primo's brother's home to open. It was at that precise moment that Faye recalled Primo mentioning that they had a little boy and baby twin girls, about eight months old.

What had she been thinking?

She'd instinctively avoided being around babies and small children ever since her miscarriage and operation. But it was too late now. The gates were opening and they were driving between two verdant walls of lush foliage.

They emerged into a huge open space in front of a modern two-storey house. Lots of windows. Faye could see a green lawn, strewn with kids' toys. Her insides twisted.

Waiting for them was a tall man who Faye recognised instantly as Primo's brother, but his colouring was lighter, and he was infinitely more casual in low-slung board shorts and a T-shirt. A pretty woman with long reddish-blonde wavy hair stood beside him. Average height. Wearing short cut-off jeans and a pretty loose summer top. She looked nice.

The car came to a stop and a small blond-haired boy appeared and opened Faye's door. She didn't have time to react. He was holding out his hand.

'Hi, I'm Sol. Are you my Aunt Faye?'

Faye was instantly won over. She shook his hand. 'Yes, I believe I am. Nice to meet you, Sol.'

The woman appeared behind Sol and grabbed him. 'I'm so sorry. We told him to wait and not overwhelm you.'

Faye got out and the woman stuck out a hand. 'I'm Sadie. It's so nice to meet you.'

'You too.' Faye smiled, feeling shy.

Then she looked to see Primo approaching his brother. Both similar heights and builds. They were wary, but then Quin moved and pulled his brother into an embrace. Faye could see that Primo was taken by surprise, but he hugged his brother back.

Quin came and said hi to Faye. She noticed he had brown eyes.

He tucked his wife under his arm and she wrapped an arm around his waist.

'You guys must be hungry,' she said. 'Let's eat and then we can show you around.'

Faye sat back and observed the brothers and Sadie throughout most of the delicious early evening dinner, served in a vast open plan kitchen/dining space.

Before they'd landed in São Paulo, Primo had told her a little about Quin and his wife. That they'd been estranged for a few years but had now reunited. In that time, Quin had had sole care for his son, Primo had told Faye.

'I'm still not sure exactly why they had to split up, but they're back together now.'

To Faye's eye now, it didn't look as if anything could part Sadie and Quin again. They touched constantly and shared little looks in a way of communicating that could only come from a very intimate union. She hated herself for feeling a twinge of envy.

They had appeared with two sleepy dark-haired babies just before dinner was served. Stella and Luna—twin girls. Faye had felt the habitual pain on seeing them, but pushed it down deep. And then they'd gone to put them to bed with the help of a woman called Madalena, their nanny, who seemed to be almost a member of the family, as close as a grandparent.

'I can stay up for dinner with guests because I'm five now,' Sol had declared once Quin and Sadie had returned. They'd brought a baby monitor with them, presumably to keep an ear out for the babies.

Faye had smiled at the precocious young boy. 'You're very grown up indeed.'

Sol piped up now. 'Hey, do you like football, Uncle Primo? It's my favourite.'

Primo smiled. 'It's been a long time since I played, but maybe you can show me?'

'Cool! Tomorrow?'

'Of course—if your parents don't mind.'

Faye couldn't help noticing that Primo was a little stiff in his exchanges with Sol. Obviously he hadn't had much to do with children. She could see him being a good father, though. He was kind, and compassionate, and she felt that, if given the chance, he would want to do things differently from his own father.

She felt a pang of pain—because he wouldn't ever have that chance with her.

To distract herself, she got up to help Sadie clear up, pooh-poohing the woman's protests. She said to her in the kitchen, 'You have a beautiful home and family.'

Sadie looked a little dreamy, and then said, 'Thank you. I don't take it for granted for one second.'

After Sol had gone to bed, Quin said, 'I'll show you to the guest house. It's nice and private.'

He led them down through the garden, automatic lights coming on to guide their way. They walked through a small copse of trees to find a smaller version of the big house, and a pool nearby.

Quin gestured to it. 'Feel free to make yourselves at home. There's a pool hut with swimsuits and towels—whatever you need.'

He showed them into the guest house. Another open-plan, gorgeously decorated space. Understated luxury. A fully stocked kitchen.

'Thank you so much,' said Faye. 'This is truly lovely.'

'Like I said, make yourselves at home. I'm really glad you're here.'

He left them, and Faye noticed that all their stuff had already been unpacked and put away.

Primo was looking a little stunned.

Faye went up to him. 'Are you okay?'

He nodded. 'It's just a lot...to take in. He's younger than me, but I feel like he's older.'

'I guess having children will do that to you,' Faye joked.

Primo looked at her and pulled her close, she went willingly.

He said, 'Thank you for coming with me.'

'You'd have been fine on your own.'

'I think it helps to have people around to defuse the tension between me and Quin.'

Faye shook her head. 'I don't think he bears any grudges. And Sadie seems nice. Normal.'

'She's good for him.' Primo looked at the bed then, and said with faux innocence, 'I don't know about you, but I'm exhausted.'

Faye moved closer, pressing against Primo. 'Me too.' She reached up and pressed a kiss to his jaw. 'Absolutely wrecked.'

He started taking off her clothes, and Faye savoured every single moment leading up to them both being naked.

They made love in their own private tropical forest house, but afterwards, even as her body hummed with a sense of deep satisfaction, Faye couldn't escape the uneasy sensation that this was where things would come to a head.

There were so many raw emotions flying around, and she wasn't sure if she'd be able to escape unscathed. It was getting harder and harder to try and hide the depth of her feelings around Primo.

The following day, Primo surveyed the domestic scene before him on the lawn. His nephew, Sol, was shadowing his two crawling twin sisters like a mother hen. Gently manoeuvring them in a safer direction if he thought they were getting too close to danger. Sadie was talking to Faye, and both women were watching the little tableau.

Faye was relaxed here in this domestic situation. Not fazed. Not bored. Not sending him pointed looks as if to say, *When are we leaving?* He'd noticed that she did seem a little reluctant to get too close to the children, but he put it down to lack of experience, like him. Sol and the babies alternately fascinated and terrified him.

Absurdly, emotion rose. Emotion that he hadn't felt in years. In for ever. Not since he was a small boy, when he'd pushed it down deep, because he couldn't be the one to lose it over their mother leaving. Quin had done that for both of them. Primo had had to be strong.

'I'm sure this is nothing like you're used to,' said Quin.

His brother's dry tone cut into Primo's reflections. He shook his head, didn't dare look at his brother just yet, in case he saw something Primo wasn't quite ready to reveal. But things were sinking into place inside him, whispering of yearnings that he'd only recently allowed himself to think of. A life with Faye—a *whole* life.

Maybe this was why he'd gravitated towards seeing his brother. Because he'd needed to see this, feel it first-hand. Feel a desire for *this*. Something he and Quin had never really experienced and yet here he was—in this idyll of…a family. *Love*. For the first time he was seeing it up close, and he had to admit that for some…it could exist.

Primo said, 'Family is important, isn't it?'

Then he clarified, 'I mean, *this*.' He gestured to the scene before them where Sadie had now put the twins in a double buggy in a shaded area and was kicking a ball with Sol. 'Not what our father drummed into us.'

He looked at Quin, who was watching him carefully.

Quin said, 'It's everything. The only thing that matters.'

Primo blurted out, 'I'm sorry.'

Quin frowned. 'For what?'

'For not checking that you were okay after…everything.'

'After discovering our father wasn't *my* father?'

Primo nodded. 'And earlier…when we were younger. I should have taken more care over you. You're my baby brother.'

Quin smiled and shook his head. 'I was just thankful that I wasn't *you*. You took the pressure off me to be something I had no desire to be.'

Primo glanced at his nephew and his sister-in-law and said, 'Still, I'm sorry that we didn't have more of this… More time to be brothers without cares.'

'There's still time.'

Primo looked at Quin and felt the emotion rise again, swelling his chest. 'Thank you,' he said, his voice slightly rough.

'Hey, Uncle Primo! Come and play with us!'

Primo welcomed the distraction and went to join Sadie and his nephew.

The baby—one of the babies—was crying. Faye looked around helplessly, but everyone had disappeared. Quin had gone inside. Primo and Sadie and Sol were hunting for the ball that Primo had kicked into the copse of trees. And one of the babies was now wailing pitifully.

Faye got up and went over and peeked under the muslin net. A pair of dark eyes looked up at her. Beautiful eyes. Ringed with long lashes. A rosebud mouth. She'd stopped crying momentarily, but now her little face scrunched up again and the mouth opened.

Faye whispered, 'Oh, no, please don't. You'll wake your sister and I don't know what to do.'

But now she was wailing again and so, acting on an instinct too strong to ignore, Faye reached in and carefully extracted the baby. She was heavier than she'd expected, and she looked at Faye for a moment with tear-laden lashes before reaching out her pudgy arms.

Faye put her over her shoulder and awkwardly patted her back. She seemed to like that. She stopped crying. Faye walked up and down, jiggling her a little on her shoulder.

'You're a natural.'

Faye turned around to see Sadie. She was vaguely aware that Primo and Sol were playing football again. 'Oh, no, I'm not. Really, I'm not. I've hardly ever held a baby.'

Faye felt sure Sadie would rush to take her baby back, but the woman seemed utterly unconcerned.

She checked on the other twin and chuckled. 'Stella is the lazy one—she'll sleep through a tornado. Luna wants to know what's going on. She obviously wanted to meet you.'

Faye smiled, but it felt shaky. Holding this warm, trusting baby was bittersweet. Her head was nestled into Faye's neck. She could feel her breath against her skin.

Sadie asked, 'Are you and Primo…? Do you plan on having a family?' And then she put a hand over her face and said. 'Please—forgive me. You don't have to answer that. It's such an intrusive question and you're only just married.'

But Faye shook her head. With this baby in her arms, and Sadie's easy manner, she heard herself admitting, 'I've told Primo that I won't have children…but it's not that I won't… I *can't*.'

Sadie's hand went to her mouth. Her eyes filled with compassion. 'Oh, Faye, I'm so sorry. I had no idea…'

Much to Faye's horror, she could feel her eyes prickling. As if sensing Faye's unravelling, Sadie reached for the baby and deftly re-installed the now sleeping infant back into the pram.

She discreetly led Faye away from the garden. 'Are you okay?'

Faye nodded. 'I'm so sorry… It's just…'

It all tumbled out—how their marriage was really only a marriage of convenience, but that Primo did want a family at some point, and Faye had no intention of telling him that could never happen so she was going to leave when the six months was up.

'I'm so sorry, Faye… You're in love with him, aren't you?'

Faye nodded. 'Pathetic, isn't it?'

'Not really,' Sadie commiserated. 'I suffer from the same affliction.'

'But Quin adores you.'

Sadie made a face. 'It wasn't straightforward for us… But that story would require at least a bottle of wine.'

'Mama! Luna is awake again.'

They heard the sound of Luna crying and Sadie rolled her eyes. 'I'm sorry, it's actually time for a feed—that's why she's restless.'

'Go,' said Faye, pushing her emotions down. 'I'm sorry you had to hear all that.'

Sadie squeezed her hand. 'We're sisters now, no matter what happens. Okay?'

Faye nodded, feeling absurdly emotional again.

When she felt she was composed enough, she moved back around to the patio—and stopped dead in her tracks. Primo was holding one of the twins in his arms and Quin was showing him how to feed her with a bottle.

There was an awestruck look on Primo's face that Faye had never seen before. And never would see again. Because now she knew that she couldn't continue this charade. Coming here had broken something inside her, and she hadn't even thought she'd had anything left to break.

Faye felt a spreading sense of hollow loneliness.

Damn Primo Holt.

She wished in that moment that she'd never laid eyes on him.

CHAPTER ELEVEN

PRIMO WAS AFRAID to breathe.

Quin chuckled. 'They're quite sturdy you know.'

His little niece was staring up at him with huge dark eyes, as if he held all the knowledge in the world, as she greedily drank down the milk.

'Then you have to pat her on the back, Uncle Primo, but she might get sick on you.'

Primo tore his eyes away from the baby to look at Sol, who seemed like an old pro at this baby-feeding lark. Then something caught his peripheral vision, and he saw Faye walking quickly down the lawn towards the guest house.

She seemed in a hurry, and Primo would have called out, but he didn't want to upset the baby.

After he'd been schooled in the art of winding the baby, and she'd let out an impressive belch, Quin took her back and said, 'Well done, brother, your first feed. You can thank me for the practice when your firstborn comes along.'

Primo felt something uneasy settle in his gut.

He stood up. 'I'm going to check on Faye.'

'Come in for dinner around six? We'll have a barbecue this evening.'

Primo nodded and left Quin holding one daughter and Sadie with the other baby. He thought he noticed that Sadie looked at him slightly strangely, but told himself he was being paranoid.

Maybe now was the time to have that conversation with Faye. Surely by now she would have to admit that what they had was good. And that it could endure.

But when he walked into the guest house the first thing he saw was Faye packing her bag. She seemed agitated.

'Hey, what's going on? Did something happen? Your father...?'

She went still. And then she stood up straight and faced him. She was pale. Her eyes looked huge.

She shook her head. 'No, it's not my father...or anything like that. It's me. I have to go. I'm going to request a divorce, Primo. I'm sorry, but I can't wait for the six months.'

Primo was looking at her as if she was losing her mind. She was. She was in full panic mode. She needed to get away from here and from Primo *now*. This place was the manifestation of the dream she'd always had of what family life could be, but it was also—cruelly—her worst nightmare. Because she could never have this. And she certainly couldn't give it to Primo.

She took a breath in and forced herself to try and calm down. He deserved to know everything.

She said, 'I saw you with the baby just now...'

Primo was shaking his head as if trying to understand. 'A second ago you said you had to leave. You said you want a *divorce*.'

Faye nodded. 'I did.'

'What's going on? What on earth has seeing me with the baby got to do with anything?'

Faye was wringing her hands in front of her. 'That's just it. It has everything to do with everything. With us. I saw how you looked at her, Primo. How you've started to heal the rift with your brother. And that's amazing. But I can

see what you're thinking. That maybe you want this too...
what he has. A *real* life. Family.'

The word *love* was on her tongue, but she bit it back. He
might want more, but she was sure that love wasn't part of it.

He looked at her. 'Yes...maybe. And I have been wanting to talk to you. Can't you see that what we have between
us is so much stronger than we expected it would be? It's
made me think that perhaps...perhaps it could be possible
to do things differently. I'd never thought about children
before as anything but a means to an end...extending the
family legacy and name,' he went on. 'But creating a family
with you, Faye... You've inspired me to want something I
never thought I wanted before. Never thought I could have.'

Emotion rose, burning inside Faye. She did her best to
stop it from spilling over. 'That's just it, you see. I can't
give you that.'

Primo shook his head again. 'What is so awful about the
prospect of having a family with me, Faye?'

'You're not listening to me. I said, I *can't* give you that.
Literally, *cannot*.'

He made a snorting noise. 'You mean won't. What is it?
Are you using this as a bargaining chip to get something
even more?'

Faye was horrified. Never would she have thought he'd
go there. 'No! How could you think that?'

But you have deceived him.

'Primo, please listen to me. There's something I haven't
told you. I haven't been entirely...transparent.'

He opened his mouth, but she put up a hand to stop him.
He closed his mouth. She lowered her hand.

'When I was with my first husband, I got pregnant
straight away. A textbook conception.' Faye tried to keep
the bitterness out of her voice. 'But within a few weeks I
was bleeding. A miscarriage. It got complicated. I was taken

into hospital. They cleared the miscarriage, but they told me I needed an operation or I might die.'

She forced herself to look at Primo.

'I had to have a partial hysterectomy.'

Primo was looking at her blankly.

Faye forced herself to spell it out. 'They took my uterus, Primo. I have no uterus. I cannot bear children.'

After a long moment he asked, 'Why didn't you tell me this?'

Faye sank down on the end of the bed. 'Because I've never told anyone, really. Not even my father knows. I hardly knew you. I didn't think it was any of your business.' A little defensively, she said, 'And I told you right from the start that I wouldn't have children. So you *knew.*'

Primo was shaking his head. 'No, you don't get to pin this on me, Faye. You said *wouldn't.* There's a big difference between that and *couldn't.* And do you know what that difference is? The belief that there's a possibility that you'd change your mind.'

'I didn't think it would ever be an issue. I had no idea that our marriage would become something neither of us expected. I'm sorry, Primo. I should have told you the truth from the start.'

Even amidst the tension between them right now, Faye felt as if something heavy was lifting from her shoulders. The weight of her painful secret.

Primo looked at her, eyes widening. He snapped his fingers. '*That's* why you insisted on the six-month get-out clause. You never had any intention of this lasting longer than six months, did you?'

She couldn't lie. 'No.'

Primo's jaw was tight. 'I told you at the very beginning that I didn't play games, but this has all just been one long game to you, haven't they? All you were interested in were the short-term benefits, and yet you ensured you'd reap the long-term benefits for your father and your family business.'

Faye stood up again. 'Don't pretend you started out with any better intentions than I did. You got your business deal and your convenient wife as a bonus. Why would I have shared my most private pain with someone who had picked me out of a file of potential wives?'

'Because you knew very well that I always had the long term in my sights. And because as soon as we met it was clear that the spark between us was anything but *convenient*.'

'We could have just had an affair. Maybe that's all it should have been.'

'That horse has bolted, Faye. I don't usually let people get the better of me, but you blinded me.'

'I wasn't trying to blind you,' Faye said miserably.

I was too busy being blinded by you and falling in love.

'So what was your plan? Wait out the six months then take your leave, as per the get-out clause? No harm, no foul?'

Faye nodded. 'I didn't think it would be an issue. I believed we'd be living very separate lives, and that when it came to it you wouldn't want to stay married anyway. But then…it became something else.'

Everything.

'You didn't know that the best sex of your life would happen within a marriage of convenience?' Primo laughed harshly, 'Well, go figure…me neither.'

Faye winced. 'You'll find another wife and—'

He cut her off. 'That's what you thought? That I'd just weather the fallout of a failed marriage and get on with choosing wife number two?'

She winced. 'I'm sorry, Primo… It all happened so fast and I was sure it wouldn't last…'

Primo closed the distance between them so quickly that Faye couldn't speak. He took her arms in his hands.

'What wouldn't last, Faye? *This?*'

His mouth crashed down on hers, and even amidst the tension and the anger and the recriminations Faye melted into Primo, every cell singing to be close to him, to have him touch her.

He pulled back, eyes blazing. 'Does that feel like it's going anywhere?'

No. It felt stronger than ever. Like a live force.

She pulled free of Primo and put some distance between them. 'I never meant for this to happen,' she said. As if they could have controlled it!

'It happened,' Primo said flatly.

Faye lifted her gaze and forced herself to meet Primo's blistering blue one. Not hot anymore. Cold.

'I'm truly sorry, Primo, for not telling you the truth. It's a painful secret I've kept from almost everyone for ten years. It's part of the reason I haven't been in any relationships beyond the very superficial. After my husband rejected me, I didn't believe I'd be enough on my own for anyone. Maybe I didn't tell you because I didn't want you to be in a position where you felt you had to stay with me out of some sense of loyalty.'

She continued painfully.

'But it doesn't change the fact that I cannot give you a family, Primo, and there's not enough to sustain us without that family. It's better that I leave now. We'll get a quiet divorce and you can get on with choosing a more suitable wife. I don't think your reputation will be too damaged—men seem to have more leeway in that regard than women.'

Primo was reeling with everything he'd just learned. With how badly Faye had deceived him. It threw up stark questions. Like what would he have done if she had told him this from the start? Would he still have married her? If he'd had to sit down and seriously consider if he wanted a family would he have been happy to settle for an affair? And where would they be now if he'd done that?

He had a feeling they might still be exactly in this very place, and it was disconcerting. But all he could see when he looked at her was the face of treachery. Here in this place where a dream he'd never admitted to having, had just crystallised...only to be smashed to bits in the same instant.

He couldn't look at her, because looking at her was creating too much cognitive dissonance in his head.

He turned away from her.

'I'll go, Primo.'

He also couldn't *not* look at her.

He turned around again. 'It's that simple? You just walk out of here and what...? Get on with your life?'

She bit her lip. She looked pale, eyes huge, but he couldn't let that affect him.

She said, 'Whatever you think about me, you deserve to get on with your life and have everything you want. A family.'

But that dream was now tarnished. That angered him almost more than anything else. The fact that she'd been the one to inspire that dream only to destroy it.

And he had a suspicion that she wasn't experiencing the same inner implosion as him. Because suddenly Primo was having all the feelings, after a lifetime of pushing them down and believing himself immune. There was anger, rage, loss, joy, hope and awe. And they were all coalescing into a swirling black mass inside him.

But all he could think of right now was the day his mother had left, when Quin had been crying and begging and pleading and Primo had been so icy-cold. Numb. Pulling Quin back. Vowing never to be someone who would humiliate himself like that.

And there was another emotion swirling in the mix that Primo wasn't ready yet to name.

He couldn't.

It was unbelievable. Impossible.

And if he uttered it everything he knew, every tenet he'd built his life upon, would dissolve and he would be left behind. This woman would walk out through the door anyway, just as his mother had done, and Primo would be undone. And this time he wouldn't be able to stay numb. So he wouldn't utter it.

He moved back. Away from Faye. Shut himself off from that swirling mass inside him. He thought of how she'd taken up a place in his life that he'd never expected—to the point that he'd taken his eye off the ball. He'd never been so lax when it came to the business, and he felt a shiver down his spine.

Had he turned into his father after all?

The whole point of marrying her had been to enhance his life and work, not eclipse it. Maybe she was right. She'd deceived him, and now she was giving him a chance to reclaim his sanity, to remember what was important to him.

Except he wasn't sure what that was any more.

He felt the terrifying urge to go on his knees before her and beg her not to go. Ice entered his veins. A self-protective force he hadn't had to use in a long time.

He said, 'You're right. We're done.'

And then he turned and walked out through the door. He was still intact. Still himself. He hadn't dissolved into the mass of seething emotions in his gut.

CHAPTER TWELVE

Manhattan, a week later

FAYE WASN'T SURE what day it was. Time had become something elastic…hard to fathom. When she'd emerged from that little house in the forest with her bag, Sadie had been waiting for her. Primo and Quin and the children had gone to some other place. Because they were family and they belonged together.

She was the outlier. Not welcome.

Somehow, Faye had kept it together.

Sadie had taken her to the airport and put her on a plane. She'd hugged her and said, 'I really hope this isn't it, Faye.'

But it was. Faye had always known, from the moment that the spark between her and Primo had got stronger, that she was playing with fire by not telling him the full truth of her past.

If only the marriage had been one of two moving parts, orbiting around each other but never really meeting…

'Faye…?'

She looked up and saw Mark, her assistant, looking a little worried. 'Um…someone is here to see you.'

In her little office? Hardly anyone came here. She always went out to meet people. It was a perfectly serviceable office, but it wasn't all that interesting or sexy. It was in a building full of offices on the upper east side. Her window overlooked a tiny corner of Central Park that could just be spotted between two blocks.

'Who is it?'

She tried to make her sluggish brain work. Was there something she'd missed in her diary?

'It's Primo...your husband.'

For a second Faye's hearing and senses went. She felt as if she was under water, with everything muffled and sounding distorted. Mark was frowning, coming towards her. She waved her hands, sucked in breath. Came up for air.

She could do this. He was probably just here to discuss the divorce... But surely he could have done that through his lawyers?

'It's okay,' she said. 'Send him in.'

Because, pathetically, even when she knew he must despise her, Faye wanted to just look at him. Breathe the same air.

Mark went out and a few seconds later Primo appeared, sucking all the air and light out of the room. Faye would have stood up, but her legs felt like jelly.

He was holding something wrapped in brown paper and he put it down against a wall. He was dressed in a three-piece suit. He looked... She frowned. He looked tired. A little of his golden aura slightly dimmed. She blinked. No, he was still gorgeous. She was imagining things.

She forced her legs to work and stood up. 'Primo.'

He didn't come any closer. 'Faye. You look...'

She didn't want to know that she looked tired too. She felt tired, in a bone-deep existential way that she'd never experienced before. And yet, in spite of her heartbreak, she also felt a measure of peace, after finally unburdening herself. Not that Primo would thank her for that.

'Are you here to talk about the divorce?' she asked.

'No.'

She looked at him.

'But I am here to talk.' He started to pace. 'You see, the thing is, Faye, you shocked me in São Paulo… I had no idea what you'd been through.' He stopped and looked at her. 'That was horrific. I can't imagine what it must be like, at the very start of your young life, to be told that something as fundamental and basic as having a child is to be taken away from you.'

Faye sat down again, her legs giving way. 'It was…one of the worst days of my life.'

Primo paced again. 'And then, instead of supporting you, your husband turned his back.'

'Yes.'

He stopped. Looked at her. 'He made no attempt to understand it? To make you feel better?'

Faye stood up again. She couldn't wilt like this. She came around her desk but stayed close to it.

'No. Look, Primo, are you here to remind me of what happened as some kind of punishment? Because if you are, it's working…and, believe me, it's not as if these memories are ever that far from my mind.'

He looked at her, and his face was stark with something she couldn't interpret. It made her broken in pieces heart pulsate a little.

'No, I'm no…, I'm sorry… I just had to try and piece together what happened…'

She had to know. She could already feel the treacherous sprouting of hope. 'Why are you here?'

He looked at her, his eyes very blue. 'Because I'm not prepared to give up so easily. You thought that I'd fall at that hurdle? Just because your first husband did?'

Faye looked at Primo and remembered those moments when he'd joked about winning, not quitting.

'This isn't a game, Primo. You don't have to try and beat

him. If it's any consolation, he really didn't turn out to be all that great. I believe he's on wife number three, and he's locked in bitter custody battles to see his children from the first two marriages.'

Primo waved a hand. 'I'm not trying to beat him—he's a fool. I'm just saying that having children can happen in so many ways.'

Faye's insides clenched painfully. This man had made her want to dream of that again, of the possibilities. Even if she would never actually give birth.

He was still talking. 'There's IVF, Faye. We could use my sperm and egg donation...find a surrogate.'

Without even thinking about it, Faye heard herself divulging, 'I harvested some of my eggs...'

'What?'

She nodded. It was as if that piece of information had always been there, but she'd pushed it down so deep because she'd never thought it would be of any use.

'After I had the operation, my ovaries were...*are* still intact. I was advised to freeze some eggs because I was so young. To be honest, I was so traumatised at the time that I hardly noticed the couple of months they spent stimulating and then collecting eggs. And I still have my ovaries, so even if those eggs aren't viable any more I could go through the process again.'

Primo looked shocked. 'But do you not see that this gives us a chance to have a child of our own, Faye? How could you not have realised that?'

'Maybe because when it was offered up to my husband as an option he dismissed it out of hand, saying, "I'm not having some stranger give birth to a child of mine." He had a similar opinion of adoption.'

She looked at Primo.

'After the divorce, I shut down. I buried any hope of having a child and kept my relationships strictly superficial, so it never came up. And then, when you and I married... I just assumed it wouldn't become an issue because we would be divorcing in six months.'

Without even realising it Faye had retreated back behind her desk, as if seeking protection.

Primo came closer...to the other side of the desk. 'First of all, your husband was a prize idiot. And I hope I never meet him because I'll be tempted to do him some damage. Secondly, I can understand why you behaved the way you did... But we have a chance, Faye, aren't you willing to explore that?'

Faye could see the satisfaction on Primo's face: problem sorted. And, yes, she could acknowledge that there might be a chance for them to have a family... But he hadn't lived with the demise of a dream for ten years. He had lost the possibility of having a family with her for only a week. And now he was learning that there was hope.

Part of Faye was angry with Primo—totally irrationally—because he wouldn't ever understand the pain of her grief. The devastation.

'Primo, it's not that simple. Just because the eggs exist, or can exist, it doesn't mean that we can create successful embryos or even find a surrogate.'

'There's adoption...'

Faye shook her head. 'Are you really willing to bring up someone else's child? And what if nothing worked and we were still alone? Without a family? Then what?'

He came around the desk, even closer. 'Then we'd have each other.'

Faye shook her head, terrified to let herself believe that for a second. 'It's not enough, Primo. We've been together a month. We still don't really know each other.'

'I know you better than I know anyone else in this world, and I know that you know me.'

'It was intense between us—'

'It's still intense, Faye. It's not going anywhere.'

She wanted to deny it, but she couldn't. She was aware of every minute movement he made. Every inflection of his voice. The humming electricity between them.

'Primo, I can't do this...'

He moved even closer, and now nothing separated them. If he touched her—

Faye sat down.

Primo went down on his haunches before her.

'Faye, what I'm trying and failing to say is that if we ended up alone then that would be okay. Because I don't want a family without you. It's you or no one. The dream only exists because of you, and that dream can be just the two of us, if that's what's meant to be.'

Faye's eyes prickled. 'You can't say that for sure, Primo, because we're not facing that wasteland. But I know. It wrecked my first marriage. And I've heard stories all my life about failed IVF, about adoptions that go wrong because people aren't honest about how much they want their own DNA in their children. It tears relationships far stronger than ours to shreds. You've only just decided that this is something you want...and you should have it. But not with me. There's not enough to sustain us if it doesn't work.'

He took her hands and looked at her. 'I love you, Faye.'

His words fell into a numb place inside Faye where she couldn't feel them. Or believe them. She was in self-protection mode.

'Why would you say that?'

'Because it's true. I fell in love with you and I didn't even know what it was. Because I don't think I've ever loved anyone before except for Quin.'

Faye stood up again, dislodging Primo's hands, moving behind her chair. He rose in a fluid movement. Watched her. She felt panicky because what if she believed him and he was just saying this to win her over...

'You don't love me, Primo, it was just amazing sex. And now you think we might be able to have a family. We're already married, and it'd be a hassle to divorce, and—'

'Stop.'

Faye clamped her mouth shut.

Primo said, 'I do love you. And, yes, I would like us to try and create a family. Because you're the one who has broken me apart and made me want things I never thought I wanted. A whole life, Faye. Not half a life.'

But the truth was that it might only ever be half a life. Faye could see into a future where in spite of everything she and Primo couldn't create that family. She saw how their desire would wane and how empty their lives would become. How he would realise that he didn't love her. And then he would blame her for being empty, useless, like her first husband had. And he would walk away and leave her like a piece of unwanted baggage. And even though she now knew she was enough, she knew she would not survive Primo's rejection.

She was barely surviving now, but in time she might just be able to claw back some sense of herself again.

And who's that? asked a small voice. *A woman skirting around the edges of life in case it hurts her?*

She shook her head, hands gripping the back of her chair like claws. 'I can't, Primo. I *won't.*'

'Do you love me, Faye?'

Her heart beat out the answer.

Of course. Yes. For ever.

But she couldn't speak. This was the last bastion of any kind of defence.

'Don't make me say it,' she pleaded.

Because he knew. Of course he did.

He backed away to the door.

He said, 'I won't. For now. But it's there, Faye, and you can try and hide from it, or deny it, but it's futile. There are no guarantees of anything in life and, yes, I think after realising that I want to try for a family, and the kind of life I never knew, it would be disappointing if it didn't work out. But all of that is secondary to the fact that without you none of it is even worth trying for. I'm not your first husband, Faye. I'm me, Primo, and I deserve the chance to show you how much I love you. For you, alone.'

When Primo was gone, Faye deflated like a balloon. She saw the packaged item he'd brought and went over and picked it up. She took off the paper. It was the Lara Lopez painting.

Faye put it up on a shelf and looked at it. It got her right in the gut. It was all there in its messiness. Life. All the pain and heartache and agony and tumult. But also the energy and the never-ending *hope* that made people get up every day and believe in something outside of themselves. And finally she saw it for the first time. *Love.* Big and terrifying and loud and potentially heartbreaking. But it was there. Like a beating heart. Never giving up. Hoping. Striving. Failing. Getting up and trying again. Doing better. *Trusting.*

She loved Primo. More than anything. More than her fear that he would walk away one day because she couldn't deliver him a child.

There was a knock on the door and she turned around, heart slamming against her ribcage. Just as she was thinking it couldn't be Primo, because he wouldn't knock, her assistant appeared and handed her a note.

'Primo wrote this just before he left and told me to give it to you.'

The paper was folded over and Faye opened it.
You're braver than this.
I love you.
P (Your husband)

That evening, Primo sat at a dining table with three other men in one of Manhattan's most exclusive restaurants. And he was bored silly. How had he put up with this for so long? He wanted to loosen his tie. Throw off his jacket. Upend the table. Smash plates and glasses. Demand that everyone see and acknowledge the pain he was in. The pain of loving a woman who had been so hurt by her past that—

His phone vibrated in his pocket and he took it out.

A text.

From Faye.

Primo felt like a teenager as excitement surged in his blood.

You're right. I am brave.

Primo tipped his head back and sent thanks to every god that existed. He texted:

You're braver than anyone I know.

I am pretty amazing.

You are.

Go ahead, take off your tie. I'm sure they won't mind.

Adrenalin filled Primo's body. She was here.
He looked to his left.

Cold.

He looked to his right.

Getting warmer.

He turned around and looked behind him and he saw her. She had her back to him, but there was a big mirror along the wall and she was watching him in the reflection.

Her hair was down. She was wearing that dress again. The one with the sequins. She was on her own, and he vowed in that moment that she would never, ever be on her own again.

He stood up from the table and said, 'Gentlemen, if you'll excuse me? There's someone infinitely more interesting and beautiful that I need to talk to.'

And he went and sat down with his wife.

Much later, in Primo's bed in his apartment, he and Faye were lying facing each other. They hadn't even managed to get from the restaurant to the car without making love.

Faye giggled a little at the memory. 'Do you think they have CCTV in that office?'

Primo grinned. 'I hope so. It'll be the scandal of the year. *Primo Holt and Faye MacKenzie Bring One of Manhattan's Most Respected Institutions into Disrepute.*'

'Faye MacKenzie Holt, you mean,' she corrected him.

They linked hands. Fingers entwined.

Primo said, 'Say it again, Faye. I need to hear it.'

Faye's heart squeezed. She hadn't fully acknowledged yet that, for Primo, handing himself over to someone after watching his own mother abandon him hadn't been easy.

'I love you, Primo Holt.' She pressed a kiss to his mouth.

'I love you.' She kissed his chin. 'I love you.' She kissed his forehead. 'I love you.'

'What made you realise you could do this?' he asked.

'The fact that my love for you is greater than my fear of you walking away. I'd always associated the grief I felt that I couldn't have children with my heartbreak over my husband's rejection, but I didn't love him at all. I just loved the idea of being married and having a successful life together...' She bit her lip, a faint lingering doubt niggling at her. 'What if it doesn't work and we can't have children? What happens to your legacy?'

Primo shrugged. 'Nowadays, I don't think succession matters like that. And we have a nephew and two nieces who, in case you hadn't noticed, are already running rings around their parents and who bear the Holt name.'

Faye felt relief flood her. She chuckled, thinking of Sol.

Primo became serious. 'I'm not going anywhere. Faye. Ever. No matter what happens. And I have a proposal.'

'We're already married.'

'Thank God for that.' Primo kissed her. And then he said, 'No, a slightly different proposal. I think we should give ourselves a year. A year of getting to know one another, living together, with no talk of children, or a family, and no trying anything. How does that sound?'

'Still trying to get me to move in with you?' Faye joked. But she felt emotional.

It was an amazing proposal. A chance to really get to know one another before they went near the subject of children or family. She hadn't even realised until that moment how much she needed some sort of show of trust from Primo like this.

'Oh, you're not going anywhere, Mrs MacKenzie Holt. Whether it's here, or your apartment, I don't care where we are—as long as we're together. And never apart for longer than about…an hour? Would that do?'

Faye buried her head in his shoulder, overwhelmed with love and emotion.

He tipped her chin up. 'So, what do you say?'

She smiled. 'I think that sounds just perfect… But let's add a little clause. If we want to talk about it in six months, let's talk about it then.'

Primo groaned and rolled onto his back, taking Faye with him so she lay over him. 'What is it with you and six months? Do I have to point out we only got as far as a month before the wheels came off and this marriage became a love-match?'

Faye grinned. 'Well, then, let's see where we are in a month. Because from where I'm currently lying, anything is possible.'

Primo rolled over again, and this time he was perfectly positioned between Faye's legs.

Just before he joined their bodies he kissed her and said, 'Bring it on. I can't wait.'

EPILOGUE

A YEAR TO the day since they'd had that first drink, Primo handed Faye a large and very old key. She looked at him as the fresh breeze came straight off the Atlantic made her hair fly into her face. And then she looked at the castle. The magical, fairytale Irish castle.

'What have you done, Primo?' she asked suspiciously.

'It's our first anniversary. This is my gift to you.'

Faye put a hand to her mouth and let out a helpless laugh of total shock and joy. 'You bought it?'

He nodded, delighted with himself.

She shook her head. 'This is the most outrageous, extravagant thing… How can I ever—?'

He stopped her words with his mouth—his favourite way to interrupt her. Faye melted into the kiss, wrapping her arms around his neck. For a man who had professed not to believe in romance or love, he'd become one of the most romantic men on the planet, and he told Faye on a daily basis how much he loved her. As she did him.

When they drew apart, she looked at him dreamily. 'You're a fool in love—you know that?'

He frowned. 'You say that like it's a bad thing.'

He picked her up then, and she clung on as he strode to the door and leant down to open it with the key. They went inside, where there was a fire blazing brightly in the reception hall, piles of turf beside it.

The housekeeper appeared and Primo put Faye down. 'Kathleen has agreed to stay on,' he said. 'As she and her husband live nearby and have looked after the castle for years.'

Faye shook her hand. 'Thank you, Kathleen.'

The woman smiled. 'It'll be good to have a family here again…it's been too long.'

Once, that innocuous statement would have caused Faye untold pain. But now she and Primo looked at each other and shared a secret smile. In the past six months they had managed to create five embryos with Faye's eggs and Primo's sperm. And they'd just received news of a suitable surrogate. The process of transferring the embryos—they were trying two to start with—would be happening soon.

There was every reason to hope that they would get their wish of a family, but even if it didn't happen Faye knew that they would be okay. Because their lives were richer and fuller than she could ever have dreamt. Their love was strong and deep and true, and it had the roots to sustain them.

This place would hold a family again even if it wasn't theirs. Because she could already see them welcoming Quin and Sadie, who had become their closest friends as well as family.

And in the end the fairytale castle did ring out with far more than just their nephews and nieces voices. Just over nine months after that anniversary visit to the castle their wonderful, amazing surrogate gave birth to twin boys: Callum and Max.

And then, two years later, she gave birth again, to a daughter: Hope.

Because Faye and Primo had never underestimated the power of hope, while also never losing sight of what they had. Which was enough. But now they had everything. And they didn't take it for granted for one second.

* * * * *

CARRYING A
SICILIAN SECRET

CAITLIN CREWS

MILLS & BOON

CHAPTER ONE

DIONI ADRIANAKIS DID not like a single thing about New York City, though she would die before she admitted such cultural heresy to anyone. It was crowded. It was almost entirely concrete. And astonishingly dirty and smelly, as was only to be expected, given the first two points.

Most especially, it was not a temperate and beautiful Greek island like the home of her childhood and her last few years. Nor was it the lovely finishing school she had gone to, high in the Alps, where serene views beckoned in all directions and one did not have to be debutante material to enjoy it.

But people were meant to love New York City. *Love* was one of the city's defining characteristics and Dioni had decided she would *adore it* based on its legend alone. Sight unseen, she had informed her brother that she wished to move here, he had consented, and off she'd gone.

Hoist with her own petard, really, she thought now as she rounded the corner onto her street in the West Village.

Or, more accurately, as she turned onto the street

where one of her older brother's properties waited. It was a lovely brownstone on a pretty street, as these things went. She had no complaints about it whatsoever. Everything in it was perfect and well-maintained. It even had its own garden, which she knew was a near unheard-of luxury here. Sometimes she would sit out in it and pretend she couldn't hear the city all around her. But when she opened her eyes, there were tall buildings in place of the sky, no stars in evidence, and she was still alone.

She started down the street, reminding herself that it was better not to worry too much over her laboring steps because she wouldn't be pregnant forever. A happy little thing she'd been telling herself that seemed less and less amusing the more pregnant she became. She had a good three months to go yet and she'd felt for a while as if she was trying to navigate the world, and this packed-tight city—in someone else's body.

What she did like about New York City was the ease with which she could indulge the mad cravings that had taken her over these past months. The trouble was that she had to go and fetch them herself, something she would have loved if she had her *old* body. But she didn't. And Dioni had told her older brother that she required fierce independence in this stage of her life, and therefore didn't want the staff he'd offered here, which she knew he would have been only too happy to provide.

The trouble was, any staff members here would be

loyal to her brother. Which meant they would report back to him.

She might not know what she planned to do, but she did know that there was no point bringing her brother in on the reality of her life until she had at least *some part* of it planned out. It wasn't Apostolis's fault that he was lovingly overbearing. It was simply who he was. Her hero, always, but he did have a tendency to take charge so there was nothing to do but trail along in his wake.

That had been fine when she was a girl. But Dioni was keenly aware that this situation was hers to solve. If there was any *solving* to be done.

And besides, how could she tell her beloved older brother exactly how and when and with whom she had gotten herself pregnant? She still couldn't figure that out.

Today she'd run out—well, she'd *waddled*—to get the particular cakes she fancied that were made at a bakery just around the corner. She could admit that it was that sort of thing that really did make New York special. Have a whim, cater to it within moments. She wasn't sure that made up for the total lack of natural beauty that she was used to, but it was something.

And there was something else, she thought as she walked on, her eyes on the figure who looked to be standing there at the foot of the stairs to her brownstone. There were so many people in New York City at any given time that it was impossible not to walk down the street without thinking she saw every single ghost of every single person she'd ever met.

Though the truth was, Dioni saw *this* ghost all the time, so she didn't have to wait for random strangers on a leafy street in the West Village to bring him to mind.

Her curse was that Alceu Vaccaro was the shadow cast over every breath she took.

No ghosts were necessary.

She took the opportunity to think of him objectively as she lumbered closer, and the figure that was almost certainly a figment of her imagination stayed where it was. She had known Alceu for what seemed like her whole life. Her brother, who had in many ways raised her while her father was off chasing the celebrities who were always present at the family hotel, was some ten years older than she was, and Alceu was his closest friend from his university days.

Alceu hailed from Sicily, an island of mystery and lore that he always spoke of in dark tones—though it was clear to her that a deep passion for his island lived in his gaze. She had always admired him, because who could not? He had grown up in what looked to her like a perfect fairy-tale castle set atop a hillside, surrounded by thick, reckless vegetation, and possessed of a commanding view of the rugged island and the sea beyond.

She'd seen all the pictures online, years ago. And more all the time in this age of drones that could fly where they would, privacy be damned.

What she had spent her months in New York asking herself was this: Had she always had a soft spot for him? A *crush,* if she was being honest?

The simple answer was yes.

But the real answer was harder to fathom, because it had never occurred to her that Alceu was aware that she existed. As a woman, that was.

Of course he knew that his best friend had a younger sister, but in the same way that he knew that the Adrianakis family were intimately intertwined with the Hotel Andromeda, that legendary former mansion that was considered by many to be its own character in a sweeping, iconic story of the Greek islands and the very, very famous people who came there.

And to be honest, the hotel was far more impressive.

Dioni was not down on herself when she thought such things. She knew precisely what place she held in her storied family. Her father was larger than life and had been known to call himself the embodiment of Greek hospitality, especially if the guests in question were rich, powerful, and famous. Her brother had their father's charm, but was also capable of thinking of others—like his lonely little sister. Her mother had been a woman of such grace and charm that even today, people felt the need to share with Dioni the many ways in which they had always felt touched by stardust in her mother's presence. Just as her father had when he was still alive.

Strangers never seemed to remember that Dioni had never met her mother, having been instead the reason her mother had died, in childbirth. She thought her father had wanted to make sure she never forgot.

Not that she allowed herself to think about deaths

in childbirth now that she was six months pregnant herself.

Which was to say, she thought about it all the time.

But Alceu was unlikely to have considered Dioni's inner life overmuch, assuming he thought about his friend's younger sister at all. What people normally thought about Dioni was that it was astonishing that she was related to her exquisite mother, her over-the-top, legendary father, and Apostolis himself, who had long been considered one of Europe's most eligible bachelors. So sophisticated. So charming. Never a hair out of place.

Dioni, by contrast, never had a hair *in* place. Her old headmistress had applied herself to the task, certain that she could tame Dioni's bedraggled hems, wild hair, and inability to even take a breath without looking like she'd rolled around in something distressingly humid.

I believe you're the only failure of my entire career, the poor woman had said at graduation, shaking her head. *I can't believe it myself.*

Then she'd tried to straighten the dress that Dioni was wearing, to no avail, as a kind of last attempt at making the proverbial purse out of a sow's ear.

There was no possibility that Alceu, who made Apostolis's perfection seem casual and faintly bedraggled by comparison, would ever notice a wild-haired little sow like Dioni. And even if by some chance he did, it would not be for *positive* reasons.

How could she have a crush on a man like that?

A man so remote he made the stars seem accessible and familiar?

And yet.

The thing about Alceu Vaccaro was that he made Dioni's heart hurt. And he always had.

She had always felt drawn to him, as if he was a source of light.

When nothing could be further from the truth.

Her brother had a way about him, and could certainly be charming when it suited him, but Dioni had never seen any evidence that Alceu could do the same. He was a grim, forbidding, deeply self-contained kind of man, and that should have been more than enough to have her running for safety. Instead, there was something about him that simply...sent her spinning.

Though inside her, when she was near him, there was a kind of glorious stillness.

And so she never would have called her reaction to him a *crush*.

Or any of the sophisticated words that she imagined her best friend Jolie would use to describe the situation. Jolie had always been the chic, knowing one between them. It was why Dioni's own father had married her, straight out of school. And no doubt why her brother had married her too, after their father had died, supposedly because it was in the will.

Though Dioni rather thought that had Apostolis wanted, he could have fought that.

She didn't like to think about Jolie too much these days, because she hadn't told her best friend about that unexpected connection with Alceu—however brief—or this pregnancy, either. How could she risk it? Jolie was now married to Apostolis and would certainly feel compelled to tell him that his only sister was pregnant. Thanks to his best friend.

That would lead to far too many questions Dioni didn't want to answer, and the kind of trouble she liked to avoid, after growing up with her father and his dramas.

And she was terribly afraid that Apostolis would think less of her once he knew.

She reminded herself that she had chosen all of this, and quite deliberately, as she made her way down the street. It was a quiet street, for New York City. It was usually empty, though she could still see that person standing there outside her building, making her whole body shiver. Almost as if she had somehow manifested Alceu into being, right here before her eyes.

When she knew better.

Alceu had made it very clear that what had happened between them represented a loss of control on his part, an unforgivable lapse of judgment to hear him tell it, and had left him with nothing but *pity*.

At first, that had been hard enough to live with.

It wasn't as if Dioni was bulletproof, after all. She did have feelings, it was only that she'd found a way to keep them to herself. Because in her family there were already far too many emotional outbursts. She had never fancied contributing to the show. It had always been easier to let the things her father said roll right off of her, leaving no marks. Her brother had always been there to assure her that she was better off ignoring the old man, so she'd tried.

But it was that word, *pity.*

It had stayed with her. It had sunk in, deep, and she'd discovered that when she was truly upset, garments simply stayed on her body the way they were supposed to. Her hair didn't bother to fall out of clips and bands to go follow its own bliss.

She had spent the first few months in New York City so sophisticated it hurt, yet with no one around to notice.

Dioni had taken it as a sign that she might actually survive this that she'd managed to clumsily drop her mug of tea all over herself last night—happily after it had gone cold. And today, she'd thought that she was looking smart until she'd seen herself in the bakery window. And the reality was all wild hair, her huge belly, and the hems of her jeans dragging on the ground—unevenly and clearly not *deliberately* frayed.

In other words, she looked her usual fright.

Evidently, that meant she was going to be okay.

Some people grow wan and pale when they've had an upset, Dioni had written in the letters she did not send to Jolie. *But I fear that I become dreadfully proper. I will know myself again only when I realize I've been walking around all day with my dress on inside out.*

She was laughing about that as she drew even closer to the brownstone and was struck even more by the still, watchful stranger's resemblance to her memory of the man she kept meaning to make herself forget.

But the thing was, there had been that storm.

It had been a tense and awkward day. It had been Apostolis and Jolie's wedding day and neither bride nor groom had even bothered to pretend that they were happy about the union. Dioni had therefore felt that it was her task to enjoy it for everyone. And as she and Alceu were the only guests and legal witnesses, she had dedicated herself to the cause.

She had planned an elaborate wedding breakfast, complete with cake and fizzy drinks, and despite Alceu's seeming lack of interest in the entire affair, she had enlisted his help, too.

In the sense that she had sat next to him and made it seem as if they were acting in concert. Instead of what had actually happened, which was that she kept trying to make it a happy occasion and everyone else had been in some or other state of horror.

And after her brother and Jolie took the opportunity of their wedding toasts to rip into each other, Dioni had intended to stay and sort it all out herself. Because she, after all, was the only person in the room who loved both of them.

But instead, while her brother and her best friend had been leaning in close, smiling with malice as they landed one verbal blow after the next, Alceu had escorted Dioni away from the danger zone.

Looking back, she still didn't know how he had managed that.

It had been so smooth. One moment she had been sitting there, literally gaping as Apostolis and then Jolie in turn made it sound as if their marriage should be a literal deathmatch. The next thing she knew she'd been led by the elbow out from the breakfast room.

Then she was in one of the sitting rooms, which had already been prepared for the hotel's guests, because there were always guests at the Hotel Andromeda. Though that day, said guests were off adventuring on a different island. That was how they'd snuck in a wedding.

And nature had done the rest, because it was vile weather that day. The storm had pounded down, the rain had seemed to dance sideways, and she could not remember a single other moment that she'd been *alone in a room* with Alceu Vaccaro.

Much less in a nearly empty hotel in the rain.

I wonder if they'll make it, she had found herself saying, moving over to the window.

They must, Alceu had replied curtly, and he was not staring out at the swath of cliffside and the stormy sea beyond. He had instead moved over to fix himself a drink. *There are legal considerations at play, which are always more likely to produce a strong union between two people than anything more fanciful could.*

I meant the night, Dioni had said. Then she'd turned from the window and frowned at him as he fixed himself a drink. *I think that's the most words you've ever said in my presence. Certainly the most you've ever said* to *me*.

She didn't think. She knew.

Alceu had taken his time looking at her again, but when he did, it had simply thrilled her. She had understood, then, that *thrilled* was the right word. He was so uncompromising. He was so quietly ferocious. Maybe it was no wonder she had never had any interest in the sorts of boys she'd encountered along the way, because always humming along in the back of her mind, there was this.

Him.

A man who seemed to her to be more like a mountain, impossible, unyielding, and wholly unimpressed with her presence.

That last part would likely sound bad, she knew, if she ever shared it with someone. But then again, she rarely met people who didn't know who she was, and they always acted much too interested. Only it always turned out that what they were really interested in was her father. Or the hotel. Or her brother. Or the legend of her late mother that they wanted to play out with her.

Alceu, by contrast, looked at her the way any high mountain gazed upon a person foolish enough to wish to climb it.

It stirred something deep inside of her. Because wasn't that why people climbed mountains in the first place? Because they were there?

There was all that storming tempest outside, right there at her back, and she understood with a deep kind of knowledge that seemed to come from the storm itself, or possibly from her own bones, that she was powerful or reckless, mad or daring in the same way.

That she was the kind of woman who stood in front of a man like him and thought *yes*.

It was the same impulse. One false move and she could tumble to her death.

But first, there in that sitting room, there had been the way that gaze of his moved over her.

Mountains and stars and the ache in her heart aside, Alceu was a remarkably attractive man.

So much so that there didn't seem to be any appropriate words to describe it. That dark hair that he kept cut short, as if he found the hint of any length a challenge to his authority. It only emphasized the harsh lines of his face, from his bold nose to his sensually stern lips that would not have looked out of place carved in marble. His eyes were dark and his brows almost too expressive, given how little he usually spoke.

She had thought, in that moment, that he'd felt like a lightning storm of his own in front of her. And that she would have given anything she had just to see him smile.

She hadn't dared imagine him laughing.

What words would you like me to speak to you, Dioni? he had said, and though the words had sounded as if they should have been a question, they had not been. They were a silken challenge, and there was a different sort of menace in his tone.

She had understood none of it.

What she had understood was that she could not have prevented herself from walking toward him then, or from stopping only when she'd gotten much too close. She had watched his eyes widen in a kind of arrogant astonishment, as those brows of his arched.

It wasn't that Dioni was bold, because she wasn't. Her father had often called her his jewel, but it was worth noting that jewel was meant to shine on others. It was not necessarily *in itself* anything more than a stone.

She had never had that sparkle. What she did have, however, was a lifetime spent walking around as her own mother's murderer. And yes, she knew that no one liked to use that word. It made people uncomfortable. But the fact of it remained.

If she hadn't been born, her mother would still be alive.

It had been clear to her early on that she could not cringe to and fro, apologizing for the very air she breathed. Dioni would forget to do it, for one thing. And for another, she was the only person who hadn't actually met her mother. So she could only piece together an idea of who her mother had been.

And in *her* head, all was always forgiven. Her mother was perfect and loved her deeply.

But as that was not necessarily true for anyone else who had known her, Dioni had chosen early on not to attempt to reach her mother's level of perfection. Possibly because she'd always known, even as a child, that it was unattainable.

It was also true that her father had found ways to remind her of that, too.

She'd had no other choice but to become good at living down to people's lowest expectations. Or as she liked to think of it, simply being who she was, regardless of the judgmental eyes upon her.

The result of that, all these years later, often looked like boldness. But what it really was, she thought now on a relatively quiet street in a very noisy city, was that she simply had nothing to lose.

So six months ago she had tipped her chin back and looked up at Alceu, that mountain filled with impassable ranges and desperately steep slopes, and she had smiled.

Do you know, she'd said, *I've never been kissed.*

I cannot imagine why you would consider that an appropriate topic for discussion, Alceu had replied in frigid tones. *With me, of all people.*

What if I am expected to get married one day, like my brother? How will I know?

Know what? Alceu had asked, the words bitten off in hard, grim pieces.

Anything, she'd replied blithely. *As I told you already, I've never been kissed.*

She had watched, fascinated beyond measure, as a light she'd never seen before gleamed hot in Alceu's stark gaze. He had not bent closer to her. He had not moved.

And yet she'd felt as if he'd expanded to fill the whole of her vision.

Let me make certain that you understand, he had said, very distinctly, *that I will not kiss you.*

But it had washed over her like heat.

And it had been true. He had not kissed her that night.

Sometimes she thought the lack of kissing was her biggest regret.

He had certainly showed her other things, far more catastrophically life-altering things.

But she woke up sometimes in her room here, sirens in the distance and no hint of the sea, and wondered what it would have been like to kiss Alceu the way she'd wanted to do.

Even now *kissing* seemed far preferable to what she was actually doing, which was still trundling along down the hard, faintly malodorous street, wishing that she hadn't told her brother she wanted to live in this great, hard place.

While drawing ever closer to that man at the foot of her steps who looked like Alceu, but couldn't be.

It just *couldn't* be.

And so she was only a few steps away when she was forced to admit the truth.

This man didn't simply *look like* Alceu. It *was* Alceu.

Dioni stopped dead, suddenly wishing that this was a far busier street. One where she could call out for help from passersby, or hail a cab.

But there were only the two of them.

Closer, he looked as perfect as always. As if he had been put upon this earth to wear clothing that exalted the sheer glory of his form in an exquisitely cut suit. Wide shoulders, narrow waist. He was a lean man who nonetheless had power pouring out of him from every pore.

As she had discovered, and vividly.

Though today there was something a whole lot like fury blazing from his dark eyes.

"Alceu," she said, and it wasn't until she said his name that she understood how nervous she was, how breathless she became in his presence. She had forgotten that, somehow. "I'm shocked that *pity* brought you all the way to New York. That seems like a long trip."

He lifted a hand and slashed it through the air in the universal signal to stop. Except in this case, it was also imbued with the kind of temper she would have sworn he could not possess. Not Alceu. Not this remote, inaccessible man.

"I think," he said, every word a frigid punch, "that you had better explain yourself, Dioni. And fast."

CHAPTER TWO

ALCEU VACCARO HAD not been so close to losing control of himself since—well.

Since the last time he had been in the presence of his best and only friend's younger sister, which made something inside him seem to roar.

But that was the trouble. There should be no roaring. There should be no reactions of any kind. That reminded him of his parents and their bitter theatrics and he had spent his entire life making certain that he was absolutely nothing like them or anyone else in his cursed family.

His late, venal, grasping father. His histrionic mother. His uncles, all of whom had met their bitter ends, and his grandparents, who were legends in Sicily for all the wrong reasons. In a place known for warring tribes and badly behaved people, his family had managed to distinguish themselves.

They had all been despicable. His mother still was. Alceu wanted nothing to do with them.

So he had decided, long ago, that it would all end with him.

He would not inflict himself on some poor woman

as a spouse. He would certainly not bring another member of his bloodline into being. He would repair what he could, make reparations for what he couldn't, and when he died, the diseased strain of Vaccaro genetics would pass forever into oblivion.

Because that is not at all depressing, Apostolis had often said.

Though Alceu had never thought so. *I consider it a liberation*, he had always replied. *For everyone else.*

He had been in Paris with his friend when Apostolis had let it drop that his sister had taken off for New York City, an urge she'd developed seemingly out of nowhere.

Alceu had not reacted well to that news.

Because much as he preferred to pretend that he could not remember any part of that wedding or its aftermath, the truth was that he remembered it entirely too well. He had learned a great many things about Dioni Adrianakis, and not all of it had to do with her responses to his touch.

For example, he had discovered that she alone managed to light a fire in him no one else ever had. When, in fact, every other woman he had ever gone near had seemed like nothing more to him than a little match, quickly extinguished. But that was his cross to bear.

The more germane thing he knew about Dioni was that she had no interest at all in ever leaving that island. She had waxed rhapsodic about how much she loved that she got to live there all throughout the painfully awkward run-up to Apostolis's forced wedding.

He knew her opinions of all the villages, each beach, and a great number of the local *tavernas*.

He could think of only one reason that she might leave.

It must have something to do with what had happened between them.

Or more likely, a hard voice inside had chimed in, *what happened after. When you dismissed her as if she was an embarrassment.*

He had done what was necessary, he assured himself now.

Again.

But because he had made certain that she would not pursue him in any way, he had decided that he could not go and see if she was all right himself. It would be unwelcome. It *should* be unwelcome. He was not even certain where the urge to check up on her had come from. Everything about Dioni was...disruptive. He could not make sense of it.

Alceu had therefore done what any man in his position would have done, and he'd had one of his men track her down and follow her to gather the necessary information. He had not told this man what he'd been looking for, because he hadn't known himself. He'd simply...wanted to see if she was all right.

An unaccountable urge by any reckoning.

He had been sitting there alone, in the folly of a castle that exemplified everything he detested about his family, when he'd seen the pictures of her.

Of Dioni—for it was clearly Dioni—

He had seen all the pictures, but he hadn't believed it until now.

Alceu *still* couldn't believe it.

He'd watched her walk all the way down the length of the street, and it had clearly been her from the moment she'd turned the corner. He'd tried to convince himself otherwise, but it hadn't stuck. It wasn't as if she was *unrecognizable*.

Not with that face that had haunted him for months now, a face that he imagined could have given Helen of Troy a run for her money.

But he could not accept that what he was seeing was true, not even with her standing right here in front of him.

Because Dioni Adrianakis was pregnant.

Six months pregnant, almost to the day, if he had to guess.

But he didn't have to guess. He knew.

She was studying him now as if she had tried not to recognize him, too, and everything about her… was infuriating.

She was dressed as if she was anyone. Anyone at all.

A pair of casual jeans. A T-shirt with a fox on it. Both stretched over her belly, so he had seen hints of a swath of her skin as she walked. It wasn't that he minded casual clothes, but this was Dioni Adrianakis and it should not have been possible to simply…come upon her like this. Where was her security? Where was her understanding that she was currently carrying the heir to two fortunes?

Then, of course, there was the *Dioni* of it all.

Her dark hair was clipped to the back of her head, but it never stayed there. Tendrils were falling as they would, and, as ever, she seemed wholly unaware of it. Her eyes were dark and fathomless, though even now they seemed to tip over into merriment a little too easily for his liking.

Pregnancy clearly agreed with her, and he hated that too.

She looked ripe. Sweet.

And the temptation of her mouth that he had managed to resist was right there. Much too close.

She was looking at him as if he'd said something outrageous.

"What is there to explain?" she asked.

There were many things Alceu wanted to say to that. He wanted her to explain what had happened that night, because he still could not account for it. He still could not understand how she had somehow managed to *become* that storm to him.

It had been bad enough in that sitting room, where she had been far more potent than the whiskey he'd pulled out in honor of his friend's lowest point yet. And instead had found himself discussing *kissing* with Dioni Adrianakis, of all people.

He would like her to explain how, when he'd left that room because he'd refused to be swept up in anything he couldn't control, no matter who it was or who was involved, he had somehow tossed open the wrong door and walked out onto a terrace drenched with rain.

And had been somehow unsurprised to find that she had followed him.

That, worse still, they had then locked themselves out.

The staff have all been sent on their way until later, she had told him, in that merry way of hers that he told himself made him livid, even in retrospect. *And I am not going to be the one to interrupt my brother at a time like this. Someone will come and open the door soon enough.*

He would like her to explain how sitting out a rainstorm had turned to sharing a bottle of the local handcrafted *raki*—far too potent—and ill-advised dancing.

He would like her to explain how any of this had happened.

"You are pregnant," he said, perhaps with the faintest hint of accusation.

She blinked at that, then looked down. Then she rubbed her free hand over the great swell of her belly. "You're very observant."

"By my calculations, we are talking about six months." He bit off those words, harshly. "When, pray, were you planning to tell me that you and I managed to conceive a child?"

She kept her eyes on her belly for a moment and when she lifted her gaze, he was surprised to see something like defiance there. "I wasn't."

"You planned to hide this?" Alceu could not take that on board. "Do you think this is some kind of prank, Dioni?"

"Why would I tell you?" She looked genuinely astonished, as if he was the one behaving outrageously. "You made it perfectly clear that you were appalled at what happened between us and wanted nothing more to do with me. I believe you said you *pity* me, and were ashamed of yourself for indulging—" She stopped, with a shake of her head. "There's no point talking about it. I heard what you said and acted accordingly."

Alceu had always prided himself on keeping his temper in check, but he thought he was as close to fury today as he had been since he was a university student. "You call this *acting accordingly*, do you? You picked up and moved across the planet, alone, to a city like this? Do you know the sorts of things that happen to foolish, sheltered women in places like New York? Every day?"

She regarded him for a long moment, and he disliked it. Intensely. The way she looked at him made his chest seem to contract.

"There are foolish and sheltered women everywhere," Dioni said, very quietly, which did not help the constriction in his chest at all. "Including, most notably, at my brother's wedding. But don't worry, Alceu. I'm significantly less foolish these days than I was."

"Where is your security detail? Who is watching out for you?"

And he only realized that he had moved closer to her when her chin tipped up, so she could keep meeting his eyes. "I told my brother to leave me alone. He has respected my wishes."

He reminded himself that standing this close to her led nowhere good. It led to streets in New York City and the reality of the baby she was carrying. Why compound the error?

But he didn't step back. "To what end, Dioni? Do you think you can keep this secret forever?"

"I was considering it," she shot back. "New York allows a person to be happily anonymous. My brother never comes here. It's entirely possible that I could just…"

"Raise the baby without him noticing?" he finished for her, incredulous.

And Alceu had to caution himself against reaching out and putting his hands on her body. It didn't matter that he wanted to, desperately. He knew better. Now he knew all too well where it would lead.

"The fact of the matter is that it's not Apostolis's business when or how or *if* I share this with him," Dioni said, with a certain calm that Alceu found far more offensive than the previous flare of defiance. "And it's not yours, either."

"I beg your pardon." He could hear the ice in his own voice. He saw it make her shiver. "Am I laboring under a misconception? Are you not carrying my child, Dioni? The girl who had never been kissed has had a host of lovers since that night, is that it?"

He was pleased—and ashamed that he was pleased—that he could see the color rising in her cheeks.

"You're the father," she said, as if she would love to deny it. She scowled at him. "But I'm perfectly capable of forgetting that when it comes time to sign a birth certificate. I don't need anything from you. I don't want anything from you." He stared at her, stonily, and her scowl deepened. And her voice took on a slightly belligerent tone. "I don't even want your *pity*, Alceu, so feel free to take that with you when you turn around and go back to wherever you came from today."

The fury in him was like a lightning bolt, and it struck him again and again.

"I do not believe that I will be doing that," he told her.

Then he took her arm, the way he had done once before, and led her up the stairs and into her own home.

When he had done the same thing after that interminable wedding breakfast, he had assumed that she was that easily cowed. He knew better now. There was a certain alchemy, a certain *chemical reaction* when his flesh touched hers. It was one more thing he could not account for. But he also could not deny it.

And he was not above using it.

This was how he found himself standing in the well-appointed foyer of a historic Lower Manhattan brownstone with the door shut tight between him and Dioni, and the world.

Which, if he'd thought about it at all, was really not the wisest course of action.

"I don't know how you do that," she was saying, forging ahead of him to move deeper into the house, tugging her arm free from his grasp. "It's impolite, at the very least, to be forever *propelled about* by the arm when you least expect it. And you do it too easily."

She walked differently now, and he found it mesmerizing. Her hips moved like a sinuous metronome, so different from the nervous way she'd darted about before. He followed her, not sure what that seething thing inside of him was, all of those lightning bolts— or how it might explode.

Though he had done enough exploding in her presence.

Clearly.

At the other end of a series of drawing rooms and studies, it was all light. She led him into a kitchen that stretched out into a glassed enclosure, bursting with plants. Beyond it was a lovely little garden, walled off from the rest of New York.

He might have liked the place, under different circumstances.

"There's no one else here," she told him without bothering to glance back at him. "So no one will ever know that you came today. You can turn around and go, Alceu, and that will be the end of it. No one will ever know who the father of my child is, my brother will get over it in time, and we can all carry on as we were."

"But I will know."

She turned to look at him, her hands braced on the counter before her, and a different sort of frown on her face.

"I will know," he said again. "And I don't know

what gave you the impression that I am the sort of man who shirks my responsibilities."

"All this out of *pity*?" Dioni shot back at him. "On behalf of both me and my unborn child, no thank you. We will be perfectly fine."

"It is not a matter of pity or any other emotion," he told her coolly, amazed that every time she threw that word at him—a word he knew full well he had used deliberately, to hurt her—it seemed to dig into him a little deeper. "You are an Adrianakis. Your child stands to inherit—"

"Nothing." She cut him off. "The hotel and everything in it goes to my brother and Jolie. And I am happy with that arrangement. You don't need to be involved."

"Your child is also a Vaccaro," Alceu continued, as if she hadn't spoken. "And I'm afraid that the child is the last heir to a vast estate. A curse *I* intended to take with me to my grave."

She digested that, and then her eyes narrowed. "I'm sorry, what are you suggesting? That *I* intended otherwise? Are you suggesting that the virgin in this scenario should have been in charge of the birth control? Really?"

He thought she was going to shout at him. Or light into him, whether raising her voice or not. And part of him welcomed that, because it would be a kind of proof, wouldn't it?

That she was overwrought. That she was out of control. That he had been perfectly right to draw a line under that episode on the terrace and more, had likely not been as much to blame as he'd thought he was, ever since.

But instead, Dioni laughed.

She laughed and she laughed.

He was offended. Then he was baffled. Then there was something else inside of him, some scratchy sort of clawing feeling that had him questioning whether he'd ever before been *laughed at*.

Alceu rather thought not.

Not by a woman. Not like *this*. His mother, Marcella, always used her pointed laughter as a weapon, but this was something else.

Dioni looked as if she actually thought that this was funny.

She laughed so hard that tears streamed down her face, and in her usual careless fashion, she pulled up the collar of the shirt she wore and scrubbed at her eyes. Then let it fall again, as if using her garment as a tissue was the most natural thing in the world.

He found himself staring at the splotches of liquid right there on the collar of her shirt. As if the secret to the universe waited for him, just there, if he could only decode it.

But then she reached over to that brown paper bag she'd been carrying and pulled it toward her across the gleaming countertop.

He watched, in what he could only term *bemusement*, as she lifted out a little box and set it on the counter. She unfolded the cardboard edges to open it up, then fished a plastic fork from the bag so she could dig in.

It was a hefty slice of cake, he realized in the next moment. Something green and pink, with icing and fondant and all manner of bells and whistles.

She put the first bite in her mouth, chewed with her eyes closed, and then let out a moan that he was quite certain he had heard before.

His body was positive that he had.

He felt himself shudder into a kind of high alert as she took another bite and moaned again, with the same delight, so that he could feel it deep in his sex.

But she was not looking at him. She scarcely seemed aware of him at all.

Her eyes were closed tight and she was feasting on takeaway cake with a plastic fork as if it was ambrosia from the gods.

Nothing about this made the faintest sense to Alceu.

He had been born perfectly aware of his place in the world. His family's wealth had allowed them to escape a great many consequences of their legendary and historic vile behavior, but it could not do much to alter public perception. No one would dare these days, but when he'd been a boy it had not been uncommon for strangers to grab his arm and let him know exactly what they thought of his father. His mother. His entire twisted family tree.

Alceu had quickly realized that the accusations were true. Each and every one of them.

And so he had made certain that his life was a monument to iron control.

By the time he'd met Apostolis, there were very few things that he could not arrange to his liking.

By the time they graduated from university, the idea that something could *not* be managed to suit him was laughable.

And from that moment until now, there was only Dioni to suggest that he was not, in fact, impermeable to the temptations that felled weaker men.

He had told himself, these last six months, that it was unforgivable. That she had done this to him with some witchery he would never understand, as he'd never expected to lay eyes on her again.

But now he realized that the real problem with Dioni was *this*.

The heedless joy she took in forking in bite after bite of her ridiculously over-the-top cake. The fact she didn't mind the plastic fork, when he was quite certain that there were ample utensils in this well-appointed kitchen.

She didn't care that her appearance was less than perfect. She was perfectly happy to wipe her face on her own shirt and carry on. She was not sophisticated in the least, and it wasn't that Alceu looked for a certain sophistication or elegance in anyone. It was that the presence of those things generally indicated a certain commitment to some or other notion of excellence.

If Dioni knew what the word *excellent* meant, Alceu would be surprised.

Shocked, in fact.

And yet he was transfixed.

With every bite she made another deep, sensual noise. And with another woman, he might have suspected that the point was to make him react in the way he did.

But he suspected that this was actually far more insulting.

It was entirely possible that she had forgotten he was here.

That lightning seemed to strike him harder. Deeper.

In his reaction to his family, and the family reputation, and the distinct understanding he'd had for the whole of his life that he could never make up for the sins encoded in his blood, Alceu had made himself as much an object of his own control as everything else.

He was fastidious. He always looked ruthlessly perfect. He prided himself on the perfection of his manners, his propriety, and his excruciatingly correct behavior under any and all circumstances.

She had already proved him wrong on that count once. He had polluted the one good relationship in his life—his friendship with Apostolis—by touching her. By proving himself the hypocrite he had always feared he was, because of *who* he was.

Now it was happening again. This time she did not even bother to look at him, such was her sorcery and worse, his reaction to it.

She made him feel something he hadn't felt since he was a very small child.

Helpless.

Except this time, that helplessness was also wrapped up in the wild pleasure he had taken in her body.

He could remember the rain. The wind. The crash of the sea in the distance. He could remember fighting himself out on that terrace, still not fully realizing what it was that was rising in him, one dangerous heartbeat at a time.

It's like music, Dioni had said, and it had meant something that she wasn't looking at him. That her eyes were out toward the sea, the storm.

Maybe he'd made a noise. Both of them were damp from the rain that the wind threw their way, even though they stood beneath the vines of the pergola.

She looked over at him, her dark eyes dancing. *Can't you hear it?*

And then she started moving, dancing to music only she could hear. And yet the longer she moved, the longer she danced, the more he could hear it, too.

When she spun around and around and around, and then tripped—because of course she tripped, this was *Dioni*—how could he do anything but catch her?

He could still remember it so clearly.

Her eyes, sparkling. Her skin, so hot despite the coolness of the rain and the wind, burning his palms.

The way she laughed as if there was nothing more delightful on earth than this foul weather to mark the most cynical wedding that he had ever attended.

The way she looked at him as if he was not a creature of iron and stone, atonement and sorrow.

She looked at him as if he was made of light and air, as if he, too, could dance with the rain, unfettered and free.

He had done none of those things.

What he had done was, in many ways, worse, because he could still feel every touch, every taste, as if they were tattooed into his flesh.

Now that same rush of helplessness was taking him over again, and he hated it.

Why should this woman be the only creature on earth who had power over him?

Why should this bedraggled, stained, *careless* woman be the only one alive who could get under his skin without even trying?

He liked women who exuded so much sophistication that they might well be mistaken for marble statues, not a woman so chaotic that even one of the finest finishing schools in the world had failed to smooth off her edges.

How could this be happening?

It was an outrage. He wanted, desperately, for this to be a mistake.

But the hardest part of him told him otherwise.

And in any case, there had only ever been one solution to the Dioni problem. He was only sorry he hadn't understood that from the start.

Therefore, when she took the very last bite of her cake and then stared at the empty box as if heartbroken that she'd demolished it so quickly, he did the only thing he could.

The only possible thing there was to do.

"Marry me," he gritted out.

CHAPTER THREE

DIONI HAD OBVIOUSLY fantasized about this moment upwards of a trillion times, give or take.

Even before she knew she was pregnant, she had done her best to salve her wounds—and her pride—by imagining Alceu groveling to her in a thousand different ways. Though she had not taken as much pleasure as she'd expected she would in her daydreams of him crawling about on the ground, or throwing himself prostrate before her, or falling to his knees theatrically to beg her forgiveness.

Because, she had long since concluded, the sad truth was that the Alceu she liked—the Alceu she had always liked, and far too much for her own good—was proud and coolly arrogant and wholly uncowed by anything or anyone.

It was a shame that she couldn't change him, even in her own head.

Nonetheless, she had let her fantasies run wild. And as time went on, and her situation became more unavoidably real, the daydreams had shifted. Maybe she ran into him by accident somewhere. Maybe she had a child who so resembled him that word got back to him, somehow—though not via her brother, because even in her dreams she hadn't worked out how she was going to tell Apostolis about any of this. There was an infinite variety of scenarios, but they always ended with him seeing her again and counting himself a terrible fool. *She* would pity *him*. He would come to her, awash in declarations, and he would beg her to marry him—

But not like this.

Because this was all wrong. She was enormous, which was fine because she was pregnant but was so *ungainly*. She was covered in princess cake crumbs. Instead of finding her in her depressed, effortlessly elegant mode, she was her clumsy, messy, tattered self.

This, naturally, was when he chose to ask her— well, *tell* her—to marry him.

And there had been no declarations. There had been thinly veiled accusations to suggest that she'd deliberately gone and gotten herself pregnant to spite him. There had been temper. And it had all led to an *order*, not a request.

"Are you *demanding* that I marry you, Alceu?" Dioni asked into the quiet of the brownstone all around them, as if she thought calling it what it was would shame him, somehow, into rethinking his approach.

Instead, he scowled. "You are carrying my child."

"You say that like that's a revelation. And I suppose it is, for you." She shrugged, and tried to brush some of the crumbs off the wide shelf of her belly, then gave up. "But I've had six months to resign myself to the paternity of my child, and at no point during those six months did I think that marrying you would be an option. Or a good idea."

Or on offer, though she did not say that.

He studied her for what seemed like a pitiless age or two.

"Nonetheless," he said.

She waited for him to expound on that, but he didn't. He just stood there, maddeningly fierce, those rich, dark eyes of his seeming something like ferocious as he gazed at her. Almost as if her failure to fling herself at his trouser cuff and weep with gratitude was a personal betrayal to him.

"*Nonetheless* is neither a complete sentence nor a reasonable answer," she pointed out.

"What do you imagine are your options here, *camurria*?" he asked quietly, though she did not pretend she couldn't hear the steel in his voice. It was stamped all over him. "I doubt very much that you would have gone to the trouble to run across the world and hide from reality if you did not know exactly where this was headed all along. Why bother to pretend otherwise?"

Her heart was beating too hard in her chest and it made her breath feel tight. And the last thing she needed was for more of her body to hurt in new and unexpected ways, but she couldn't let herself focus on the ramifications of what he was saying. So she parsed it instead.

"You called me that before. *Camurria*. I looked it up." She glared at him. He stared back, impassively enough, save for that dark fire in his gaze. "Apparently, it's Sicilian for *pain in the ass*. But I suspect you know that."

"If the shoe fits," he replied, silkily.

"I'm not a shoe," Dioni tossed back at him. "I'm not an object that you can claim, now, when you wanted nothing to do with me six months ago. Nothing's actually changed. The fact that I'm pregnant is because of you, but this baby has nothing to do with you. I will raise my own child, precisely the way I want, and I don't need any help or interference from anyone."

And she told herself that was what she wanted, more than anything. When the truth was more that it was what she'd come to accept that she was going to get—whether she really wanted it or not.

That was the reality she'd spent months coming to terms with here.

He was a wild card at best.

"But this is a fantasyland you are describing, and you know it." She could see that something had shifted in him. That whatever emotion had led him to propose—though she doubted he even admitted he had such things, or maybe he didn't know he was capable of emotion—in that particularly rough-sounding voice was gone.

Now he was the Alceu she had always known. Contained. Stern. *Absolutely certain* of himself.

What was wrong with her that he made her shiver, deep inside, in the parts of her body that only he had ever touched?

That she was still so wildly attracted to him, while

she was carrying his child inside of her body, made the heat between her legs seem to bloom. Soft, wet.

Extremely disappointing, she thought.

"I think that a proposal is supposed to involve a question of some kind," she told him, and she did not question why it was she was entertaining this. She should send him on his way. She should not have let him come inside in the first place. "Not an ill-tempered command tossed out over a kitchen counter."

"I would think that the punishment suits the crime, does it not?" he retorted in a tone that really, she thought, should have made her furious.

Instead it made that blooming inside of her deepen. Then expand.

And maybe the best way to describe Alceu's effect on her was like an illness. His wildfire power over her came upon her without warning, robbed her of little bits of herself, and left her shaking for days.

He was debilitating.

What she needed to do was make him leave and get back to her very important work of daydreaming about various ways he really *should* grovel before her. It turned out that she found that notion far more appealing, suddenly.

She tossed her takeaway cake box into the appropriate trash receptacle. She brushed another round of crumbs off of her shirt, into the sink, and made herself count to ten.

Twice.

Because surely she could do with a little calm.

When she turned to face him again, he still hadn't

moved an inch. But then, he didn't have to, did he? He filled the room all the same. As if the din of the city all around them, audible even through the walls and windows, was his name—pressing in upon them.

Branding her the way his touch had, months back.

"I am going to pretend none of this happened," she told him. "You're welcome to do whatever you like, but I certainly hope it includes taking yourself back home to Sicily, where you can sit in your castle and brood as much as you like. I hear you're very good at it."

She went to sweep dramatically from the room. But she miscalculated.

Maybe it was because sweeping hither and yon was best done in the appropriate sort of dress. Or in any kind of dress at all. Raggedy jeans that kept catching at her heels didn't quite give the same impression, and even if they did, Dioni was still and ever herself.

So really, it shouldn't have surprised her at all that she tripped.

And she would have gone flying and done a header into the floor had Alceu not reached out as if he'd anticipated her every move, and simply…caught her.

As if she weighed no more than a feather.

As if it had been a foregone conclusion that he would catch her like that, so easily.

As if it was *inevitable*.

Alceu gazed down at her. She could see every striation in his dark eyes. Every shade of brown in the world, each one of them magical. He held her in his arms as if they were in a gorgeous, achingly cinematic film, as if the music was swelling and the audience was gasping and everything had been leading to *this*.

His stern, uncompromising face seemed fiercer this close. She really ought to have been afraid, though she wasn't. Dioni could not seem to keep herself from lifting a hand—it was almost as if it moved of its own accord—and tracing the bold, ruthless features before her.

The face she knew better than her own, having dreamed of it so often.

And something about those sensual lips of his—so austere, so reserved—shifted.

They did not quite *soften*. There was nothing about Alceu that was *soft*.

He muttered that word again. *Camurria.*

"Careful," Dioni said, though her own voice had gone all husky. "Or I will start to imagine that is an endearment."

His dark eyes blazed and warmed her, everywhere.

Then, at last, he lowered his mouth to hers.

And he had been inside her body. He had knelt between her legs, out on that rain-swept terrace. Then he had licked his way between her thighs and taught her things about herself she had never dreamed could be possible. That she could writhe like that, heedless of anything but him. That she could lose herself entirely, the whole of her being focused on what he did with his mouth, his lips, even his teeth.

Alceu had held her over him on one of the chaises, tucked away from the worst of the weather. He had lifted her up as if she were insubstantial, settled her against the hard heat of him, and then slowly, painstakingly, he had lowered her down and surged into her.

One delirious centimeter at a time.

He had felt and seen the precise moment when she'd flinched, because the pain of entry was like a punch where a person least wanted to be punched. And Dioni had watched the way his gaze had gone something far darker than merely possessive. She had felt the way his hands wrapped around her hips and gripped her, so tight and sure that she could only move as he bade her.

Then, once she had seated herself astride him—and he was so deep within her that she had understood what *wholeness* meant and had never been quite the same since—he had taught her how to move.

Dioni had felt that too, every stroke, every thrust and reverse. She had felt the friction, the astonishing heat.

When she wasn't imagining him groveling, she was imagining that. The press, the pull. Her softness and his hardness.

The glory of it all, a spiral of jubilation and greed that had swept her away.

She had felt every part of him, and had marveled at the way he seemed to know exactly how to angle himself so that she could not help but fall apart.

Over and over again.

Dioni had felt more sensation than she'd ever believed possible out there in the rain. She'd imagined that she would never know anything better, or more disastrous—

But this kiss was better than all of it combined.

This kiss was a *revelation*, and she understood why.

It was his mouth descending upon hers. It was *him*. He was the one holding her in that low, romantic swoon of a position. He was the one who traced the seam of her lips with his tongue, made that low sound in his throat, and then deepened the kiss.

He was the one who shifted her so he could pull her up against his body and then tilt her head so that he could kiss her at a better angle.

And then it was all deeper, better, *wilder*.

Dioni could think of nothing she wanted more in all the world than to kiss him back.

Forever. Then again.

As if there were infinite variations and he intended to explore each and every one of them. She could feel her belly pressed to him, and something about that was shockingly erotic. That the baby they'd made was so obviously *there* between them and still he kissed her with a sensual, carnal intent that taught her entirely new ways to find him *thrilling*.

On and on it went, with new angles to try and different ways to use their mouths, until they were both panting. And her hands were fists against his chest, ruining the perfect lines of his suit. And her hair had fallen down all around her, but not of its own volition this time.

Because his hands were deep in the mess of it, gripping her skull and guiding her head where he wanted it to go.

She understood that when he finally pulled away it was because it was that—or possibly expire on the spot.

"Oxygen," she managed to pant out. "Oxygen is good."

And for a moment, Alceu simply rested his forehead against hers. And they breathed together.

A fantasy she had not thought to have, and that would now haunt her, she was sure.

But before she was ready, he stepped away.

He held her there at arm's length and gazed at her as if he was truly taking her in for the first time. Her mouth, wet from his. Her hair in a careless tangle that spilled over her shoulders. Her narrow shoulders and big, round belly.

Dioni could track the way his face changed as he looked.

How he grew more and more stern the longer he gazed down at her. Until he was frowning down at her—still holding her by the shoulders as if he thought that if he let go, even a little, she would run.

Or, maybe worse in his eyes, fling herself upon him.

And the more breaths she took, and the more she settled down, she had to acknowledge that his concern was not misplaced.

"You understand that marriage is the only option, do you not?" Alceu asked, and darkly, but he did not leave her any room to respond. Wise man. "It is not a matter of *pity*, but of propriety—and this is nothing to celebrate. You would do well to pity yourself."

He let go of her then and stepped back, and Dioni was not sure if she was bemused or insulted as he immediately began setting himself to rights. He smoothed down his shirt and his coat. He even ran a hand over his hair, as if anything could make it look out of place.

And he continued to frown at her as he crossed his arms, which on anyone else—meaning, on her—would wrinkle everything immediately.

But this, of course, was Alceu Vaccaro.

Sheer, ferocious male perfection.

So she licked the taste of him off her lips and endeavored not to smile when he scowled at her.

"The Vaccaros are well known in Sicily and for all the wrong reasons," he told her in that same dark tone. "There is not a single ancestor in my family tree that I do not view without abhorrence. I come from a long line of monsters, each one more dedicated to proving themselves the worst. Most preferred not to ruin their own lives, but made certain they ruined the lives of others, cutting a wide swath across the island and well into Europe." He looked something like *pained* for a moment. "Marrying you constitutes the breaking of a vow, and many will see this as yet one more example that despite everything, a Vaccaro always shows himself. A Vaccaro always proves that he cannot be trusted."

Dioni found herself drifting, focusing on his mouth as it moved instead of the words he was saying. And he seemed to realize that because he made a low, growling sort of sound that had her gaze snapping to his.

But if he expected contrition, he would have to contend with his disappointment, because all she did was smile.

His scowl deepened. "The house that I grew up in is a monument to narcissism and greed. It was built to stave off enemies, and these were not imagined enemies. I find it embarrassing, but I've made it my life's work to take that building and the property it sits on and make it over into something good. If you expect a life of ease, you will be greatly disappointed."

And then he raised his brows as if he expected a response. Immediately.

"I assure you, I understand the point of this lecture," Dioni said, mildly. "I, who have not yet accepted your proposal, would do so only because I am a gold digger of the highest order." She waved her hand, taking in the kitchen they stood in, gleaming and beautiful. The gardens beyond. The entire brownstone itself, which was an extraordinarily luxurious property. "As is self-evident, I should think. I would do anything to escape this cruel and terrible life."

"I understand that you are used to a pampered life," he growled at her. "Perhaps you forget that your brother is my closest friend."

Dioni never forgot that, little as she wished to think of Apostolis just now. Apostolis, who was always so kind to her. Apostolis, who had always made time for her. Apostolis, who had supported her when she'd wanted to go off to school, even when her father had initially balked.

She particularly did not want to think about his friendship with Alceu and how this situation must certainly test it, once her brother found out. Maybe she was deluding herself that she could keep it from him much longer, but the idea of telling him made her stomach hurt.

Especially if he was understanding. He forgave her everything and had supported her always and this was how she'd repaid him?

It did not bear thinking about.

"I did not exactly grow up in a workhouse, I grant you," she said instead, rolling her eyes as if she was far more at her ease than she was. "But you seem to forget that for all the legends that swirl around my family, we have always been in trade. I have been working at the Hotel Andromeda since I was a girl. I am not unaccustomed to work, Alceu, though again, I don't recall volunteering to help rehabilitate your image on an island I've never visited." She smiled then, and widely. The very picture of beneficence. "Though I will say that this is quite a novel approach. No actual proposal, all dire warnings. Truly, it's the stuff of which romantic poetry is made. I salute you."

"This is what I am trying to make clear to you," he all but threw at her, that same arrested fury in his gaze that she remembered from the storm they'd shared. "There will be no romance. You already carry my child. The Vaccaro line continues, I am no better than those who came before me, and unless I can raise our child to put an end to this once and for all, it will carry on as it always has. I have failed. This— you and me and what must happen now—is nothing but damage control."

He stood there, arms crossed, telling her all of these

dire things in what she could tell was perfect serious-
ness. He believed every word he was saying.

This time it was her heart that hurt, and more than
the way it usually did where he was concerned.

Because he was doing this while he was standing there ramrod straight, as if facing his own firing
squad. Only the gleam in his gaze told her that he was
not anywhere near as calm as he pretended.

Or perhaps he believed he was. She imagined he
always believed he was.

But then, none of it mattered anyway.

Because he had kissed her.

And so she knew, now.

Because her whole life she had been chaotic.
Clumsy. Usually stained. Always a bit raggedy.

But when he kissed her, deep inside, she went still.

Still and bright and beautiful.

It was as if all the pieces that made her Dioni were
little more than chunks of coal, but when his mouth
was on her, all of that fused and became the diamond
she'd been *meant* to be all along.

That was what it had felt like, that calm, endless
glow from within while his mouth teased her and
tamed her, taught her and remade her.

That was what *he* felt like, as if he was the glue that
could hold her together.

"Dioni," he said gruffly. "You must marry me."

And she agreed. Of course she must, though not for
any one of his dire and depressing reasons.

She did not have to know a single thing about him,
his family, or the Vaccaros' reputation in Sicily to

know that he was wrong. Whether he could ever accept it or not.

Because she was a motherless child who was the reason for her own lack, and she knew a thing or two about redemption and forgiveness.

She did not believe in *irreparable*.

"Thank you for asking so prettily," she said.

"Dioni." Her name was a stark growl and it shivered through her like another crushed bit of coal turned diamond gleam.

"Yes, Alceu," she said quietly. "I will marry you and live a life of despair in your villainous castle. Oh, happy day."

But inside, what she felt was nothing short of joy. She watched the way his expression changed again, something almost haunted moving over his stern face, stark and unmistakable. She watched the way he loosed his arms, and stood straight again.

She realized that for all his bluster, he hadn't known how she would respond.

And deep inside, that stillness glowed, and she knew.

You are going to fall in love with me, she thought.

And it was so impossible, so wildly unlikely, that it could only be true.

Dioni intended to see to it herself.

CHAPTER FOUR

SICILY WAS A wild tangle of mysteriously treacherous and beautiful mountains, gleaming seas in all directions, and old, half-ruined cities that whispered of ancient secrets yet to be uncovered.

And yet everyone Dioni encountered made it clear that she was going to be unhappy in such a magical place.

They'd flown directly from an airfield outside Manhattan and she'd pretended not to notice the way that Alceu had ushered her onto his waiting jet as if he'd imagined that, given the opportunity, she might abscond at the first opportunity and charge off into the greater New York area.

She had almost pointed out to him that she would be running nowhere, whether she wanted to or not, because she was *six months pregnant*.

But instead, she'd found it almost endearing that he'd imagined it was a possibility.

The whole flight over, he was brusque and broody, muttering about the work he had to do and pounding away at his laptop in what she felt was a largely performative manner. Because she knew his business partner—her brother—and was fully aware that the work they did to rehabilitate faltering companies involved other employees and therefore did not necessarily require his hand on the wheel at every moment.

If I had to guess, she had written in another letter on her mobile that she would not send, I would tell you that this is Alceu flustered. Maybe it's what men do when they are beset by feelings. Because anyone else would sit here and think that he was a wall of granite, but I know better. Because I know that whatever I felt inside, he felt it too. You might think that's nothing more than the rambling of a delusional virgin who went ahead and got herself pregnant straight out of the gate with the most inappropriate person possible.

She had considered that for a few moments, sitting there as the plane winged its way across the Atlantic. She had thought about Jolie and the miseries she'd suffered while married to Dioni's father. And how different it was, that thing that sparked between Jolie and Apostolis, no matter what the two of them had believed at first.

Then again, maybe you would understand all too well.

Once they made it to Sicily, they landed on an airstrip close to the sea. Dioni stood on the tarmac, breathing in the scented breeze that made her think of deep greenery and long swims into summer evenings. Then she was packed into an all-terrain vehicle that Alceu himself drove, navigating old, winding roads as if he'd carved them into the mountainside himself.

For a long while she could see the sea, the same sea,

more or less, that eventually found its way to the island where she'd grown up. Then, as the road wound around and around, it disappeared. There was only the thick vegetation on all sides while everything got steeper and more treacherous and beside her, Alceu seemed to turn to stone.

Until, at last, he drove them out of the woods and all the way up a rocky outcropping that was boldly thrusting itself off the side of the mountaintop, unencumbered by any sense of its own danger. There was only one road, with cottages and outbuildings scattered along the way in a copse of trees here and a field there, but all she could focus on was that grand castle—really more of a fortress—that stood tall and imposing right there on the furthest edge.

The pictures from the drones had not done the place justice.

It was perhaps the most dramatic building she'd ever seen, and that was saying something when she'd grown up in a very famous hotel, but she suspected Castello Vaccaro had been built for an actual, practical purpose. It looked impregnable and easily defended. The approach from the road left them out in the open as they approached the battlements. Inside the thick walls, she assumed there would be the sorts of amenities that one expected from an old hereditary estate like this.

But it was clear that *this* particular approach had been built to impress. Or perhaps *intimidate* was the right word.

Alceu, who had maintained a dark silence the whole

way, chose to carry on with it as he drove her up to the walls, then in through the gates that opened at his approach. Then closed—ominously—behind them. He parked in the forecourt, throwing himself out of the vehicle and stalking around the front to help her out, something she was forced to accept as she was too unwieldy on her own to get herself out her door before he could get there.

Once she was standing with her feet on the stones, he stared down at her. His eyes too dark, his mouth a hard line. And she could not begin to fathom the look on his face.

She thought he was about to say something, but instead he turned, then inclined his head abruptly. That was how she knew that someone else was approaching.

Because you are standing in a castle *and the only thing you see is still him*, she chided herself.

"Welcome home, *signore*," came a stiff voice.

Dioni turned to see a woman she assumed must be a housekeeper, given the uniform she wore, standing before them with a disapproving look on her face.

"Concetta, this is Dioni Adrianakis," Alceu told her. Dioni watched the woman's eyes fall immediately to her belly, then rise again, narrowed. "We will be married shortly."

The woman crossed herself and muttered something in Sicilian that Dioni did not have to know to understand meant that she thought terrible mistakes had been made. By Alceu himself, if her frown was any indication.

Oddly, she found that almost endearing.

Because, as she'd had ample time to think about on the plane ride, her expectation when she'd thought realistically about the dreams she'd had that involved marrying this man had returned to the same theme. That the disappointment and dismay at such a union would move in the opposite direction. She'd been certain that the general reaction would have been that she was not good enough for him. That she, in all her usual disarray, would in fact be a disheveled stain upon the Vaccaro name.

If she looked at it that way, this was all nothing short of delightful.

He was the mistake.

Clearly his housekeeper thought so. "I will show you to your rooms," Concetta said to Dioni, shooting that narrow gaze at Alceu. "I can only hope you know what you're doing."

"*I* certainly don't know what I'm doing," Dioni confided to the other woman, who looked shocked that she was speaking to her. "But I hope it involves food."

Other staff came out then to handle the luggage, all of them staring at Dioni and frowning at Alceu and muttering things beneath their breath that they clearly wanted Alceu to hear. Dioni, meanwhile, wondered why none of them seemed to notice that the sky was a marvelous blue above them. The sunlight danced down into the forecourt, making the stone of this fortress gleam. They were all acting like it was a dark and terrible place when, as far as she could see, it was beautiful.

Even more beautiful than it looked in pictures.

"I hope you're going to give me a room with a view," she said merrily as the staring continued and Concetta made no move to lead her off to any rooms. "Not something in the dungeon."

Nobody laughed at that, so she had to laugh herself.

"There are no dungeons," Alceu said in a repressive sort of way, though that only made her laugh more. "Most people are wise enough to realize that the whole of Mount Vaccaro is its own prison, long before they make it to the *castello*."

"Of course," Dioni murmured, though she still couldn't control the laughter bubbling inside of her. "My mistake."

What she really wanted was to ask him if she was going to get to spend time in his bedroom, but she didn't. Somehow she imagined that he would not be receptive to that line of conversation, especially not with an audience.

But she hardly saw the point of marrying the man who'd gotten her pregnant if she couldn't touch him.

She stopped worrying about that as Concetta, responding to a lifted brow from Alceu, finally led her inside. Because the castle was beautiful from the outside, but she knew full well that the interiors of such places could better resemble the Dark Ages.

But this place was even more gleaming and inviting within.

"Was the castle a hovel, or something?" she asked as they walked through an exquisitely rendered gallery into a hall that was filled with light, making it seem as if they were part of the endless sky.

Concetta frowned at her. "A hovel? Hardly. This has been the home of the Vaccaro family for centuries and they have always liked their comforts."

"It's just that if it's a prison, it's an awfully lovely one," Dioni pointed out. "I can't say that I'm an expert on incarceration, but I'm quite certain I have never seen so many Italian masters gracing the walls of any local jail."

The older woman glared at her. "Just because something is pretty does not mean that it does not have knives beneath," she said, in tones of the direst warning. "As you will find out soon enough, when you meet the *signore*'s mother."

"His mother?" Dioni was captivated. "I don't know why I imagined that Alceu was an orphan."

"He would be better off." Concetta sniffed.

And she set off on a twisting route through the castle, delivering Dioni at last to a set of rooms that no one on the whole of the planet would consider anything but gorgeous. Concetta left her there so she could look around—*and perhaps freshen up*, the other woman had suggested, which indicated that Dioni was as bedraggled as ever.

She didn't bother to confirm the inevitable in any of the dizzying mirrors.

Instead, she took in the high ceilings and the windows that were like doors, opening up onto the walkable, crenelated walls that functioned more like terraces with parapets set at each corner. She drifted out to stand outside, feeling the wind against her face. Her room was almost at the very edge of the cliff—

or more accurately, the place where the castle and the cliff were one. As she looked out, she could see the lush tangle of greenery they had driven through to get here, all the way up the side of the steep slope, so thick that there was no hint of any road. In the distance, the blue of the Mediterranean beckoned, as if to remind her that she was not so far from home, after all.

"We can do anything, you and I," she murmured to the baby she carried, rubbing her hand over a mighty little kick from within. "Just so long as we can see the water."

So she felt something like fortified when she turned around and saw what had to be the most beautiful woman she had ever beheld, lounging in the floor-to-ceiling window she'd used as her door to get outside.

She was strikingly voluptuous. And wanted everyone to know it, Dioni could see, based on the skin-tight gown she wore though it was barely midday. Her hair was jet-black with a dramatic wing of white that swooped low over one eye. Her eyes were a very familiar fathomless bit of darkness, and her lips—which might have seemed stern if unadorned—were painted a shocking red.

"You must be Alceu's mother," Dioni said.

Ruby-red lips pursed. "And you must be the sacrificial lamb, led bleating to the altar."

"Will there be bleating?" Dioni asked. "Things must be different in Sicily. I grant you, a proper Greek wedding certainly has its own interesting rituals. But no bleating, as far as I'm aware."

The woman moved with serpentine grace. She came

closer, flicking her dark gaze all over Dioni, until she felt as if she'd suffered some sort of clinical examination.

"It will all end in pain," the woman said. Darkly. "You will see soon enough."

"I'm Dioni," Dioni told her in as friendly a tone as possible. "And you are...?"

"I am Marcella Maria Vaccaro," the woman told her, with the sort of enunciation that suggested that trumpets should have sounded. "Alceu is my son, and so I know him as only a mother can. He is pretending he is something other than what he is, and he does so to his detriment. You will see. Like it or not, you will know the truth."

"The truth of what?" Dioni rubbed her hand over her belly at another insistent kick. "Your grandchild? We only have about three months to go, and then the baby will be here. Like a truth all on its own."

Marcella moved closer still, but did not regard Dioni's belly with any maternal warmth. On the contrary, she looked as if she thought the child might reach out and bite her.

"I always knew that he would fall, as they all fall." She shook her head so her dark hair slithered this way and that. "Fate comes for us all, in the end."

She looked expectantly at Dioni. Dioni smiled back.

Marcella let out a small huff, turned on her heel, and slunk off.

And Dioni did, then, indulge in the *faintest* bit of worry she'd made a terrible mistake.

But she dismissed it.

Because there was no changing course, and anyway, there was far too much to see, do, and absorb over the next few days.

Alceu made himself scarce—though in fairness, that was easy enough to do in such a large, rambling place. She would get the sense of him, like a disturbance in the air—a kind of rippling sensation, or possibly heat—lingering in otherwise empty parts of the castle. As if he had been there only moments before and the intensity of his presence remained.

She would find herself breathing a little faster, a little deeper. Her heart would set itself to hammering. And it would take her some while to get her breath back under control.

Dioni spent her first day or two simply exploring. She did her best to build a map for herself. Like how best to get from one side of the castle to the other when there was a courtyard in between. It was true that she had grown up in a kind of luxury, and that even her school had adhered to standards far beyond the reach of many. But this was certainly her first time in an *actual castle*.

It was difficult not to act like she was some sort of princess, though she was far rounder and less nimble than the singing, dancing princesses she'd loved to watch when she was young.

Then again, Concetta and the rest of the staff were universally dour and disapproving, which only made her more inclined to act as if she was a one-woman musical.

"The acoustics of this are marvelous," Dioni said on

one occasion, finding herself in what had once been a grand ballroom. She tried out a few bars of the first princess song that came to mind, about letting it go, and sighed happily. "I can only imagine what it must sound like with an orchestra here. Singer. Dancers going this way and that."

When she swirled back around to face the housekeeper and the two maids who were accompanying her today—with her arms out wide, like a proper princess would do mid-song—they were all staring at her with the same expression on their faces.

Discouraging expressions, it went without saying.

"People do not *sing* here," Concetta said oppressively.

One of the younger women bit back a laugh. "What would there be to sing about?"

The other one had a sort of musing look on her face. "It would be one thing if it was a dirge, don't you think? Or a proper elegy."

Dioni had laughed. At them. "I think this place could do with a whole lot more singing," she told them. "And I certainly like to sing. So I suppose we will all have to come to terms with that reality."

"It will change you," Concetta assured her, and the other women nodded. "The Vaccaros are creeping poison and none survive it intact."

The housekeeper appeared to be hale and hearty, and had been in the employ of the family for at least the last forty years. Suggesting that it was a slow-creeping poison, indeed. But after that interaction she took it upon herself to take her tours alone. She found the libraries—a whole set of them, one linking to the next. They were arranged around a kind of atrium that was filled with fruit trees, bright and bursting with blooms and fruit. She stood in the very center, her face tipped up to the soft morning light, and wondered how anyone could find this place anything but magical.

When she opened her eyes, she thought she saw movement high above, as if someone was up on those battlements. Or had been, only a moment ago, looking down.

Not someone, she corrected herself. *Him.*

Something inside her wound tight and hummed, and she found herself daydreaming—again—about that kiss in New York. His mouth on hers, so demanding. So marvelously incapacitating.

It was a wonder she could think about anything else.

And she couldn't see anyone up above her now, but she knew, all the same.

Alceu was not as immune to her as he pretended.

Or anyway, she amended, he came to look at her. Who could really say if that was an immune response or not?

She picked her way back through the series of libraries. One was stuffed with novels. Another was full of carefully arranged reference books and a wide, round table in the middle, sporting a map of the world with Sicily placed dead center. She took her time in the next, a bright, museum-like space featuring precious first volumes in seven languages, all set behind glass doors that indicated these books were to be admired, not loved.

It was then, suddenly, that she became aware of someone else in the room.

She could admit that when she looked up, her heart leaped, and she hoped—

But it was not Alceu.

It was, once again, his mother.

"It is a good thing you like a library, I suppose," Marcella said. She was dressed similarly to the first time Dioni had seen her. It was well before noon, yet she wore an evening gown that appeared to have been painted onto the generous curves of her body. Dioni did not have to be an expert on fashion to recognize that the bold jewelry she wore was not exactly appropriate for the morning.

To say nothing of her vampire lips, still in that shocking red.

"I love libraries," Dioni said brightly. "And this house has so many to choose from. It would take me a lifetime to read my way through."

"That is about what you can expect." Marcella drifted in, casting a derisive sort of look at one glass case, then another. "A Vaccaro wife is little more than a collector's item. Chosen to sit aside, off on a shelf, good for a bit of breeding, and then left to her own devices. And you have already accomplished the first part of the business."

Dioni had the urge to hold her belly, as if to protect the baby from Marcella, but that didn't make any sense. It was only words. "That sounds like a lovely life. Books, my baby, endless solitude. I have to say, since everyone has been at pains to tell me how terrible it is here since I arrived, I did expect something a bit more onerous."

Marcella sniffed. "You are so optimistic. But then, you are very young."

"I'm not that young," Dioni protested.

"It would not matter if you were eighteen or eighty," Marcella declared, though she, herself, appeared something like ageless. "These walls are a curse to all. You will find out, child. Like it or not."

And by the time she vamped back off to wherever she'd come from—like, perhaps, a crypt—Dioni could acknowledge that she was becoming ever so slightly tired of all these proclamations.

She was still thinking about that later that very same day as she enjoyed yet another meal all by herself. Today she was trying a selection of Sicilian delicacies like cheesy *arancini*, an aubergine *caponata*, and *pasta con le sarde* out on her formidable wall terrace with the steep mountainside and the sea in the distance as company. Every bite was a symphony, fresh and perfect, and then she glanced up to see Alceu there at last.

And every time she saw him it was like the first time.

Dioni told herself that she was getting used to those ripples he left behind him, like a wake, waves crashing into her and riptides carrying her away though he was nowhere in sight.

But she was not used to *him*. To the simple fact of his presence, and how it both enticed and overwhelmed her. At once.

He was dressed as formally here, in his own home,

as she had ever seen him anywhere else. She wanted to ask him about that. She wanted him to tell her if he even knew that he did these things, but other topics were a little too heavy on her mind.

"Is there a particular reason that every person I've encountered here over the last two days, and specifically your mother, has gone out of their way to tell me how terrible it is?" she asked.

Without much heat, because the *arancini* were little balls of ricotta and rice, fried to perfection, and it was impossible to work up a temper with such goodness on her tongue.

"I told you," Alceu replied in that dark, brooding way of his, as if they weren't standing here draped in golden sunshine with the hint of the sea in the air. "This is a place of darkness."

Dioni stared at him. She kept staring and then tilted her head, just slightly, and let her gaze go with it to take in the sky above. The view. The expansive brightness in every direction, cascading down the steep mountainside and stretching out across the Mediterranean.

Then she shifted her gaze back to him. "Yes," she agreed. "The darkest."

His brow creased at that, but he did not come any closer. He stayed where he was, standing in the doorway in a manner that she would describe as stiff if it was anyone else. But he was not *stiff*. He was Alceu and he might have been still, but he was also impossibly graceful, even wrapped in his usual forbidding cloud.

"My doctors will be arriving shortly," he told her after a moment. "They will perform the necessary examination and blood test so that we can determine both if the baby is healthy, and that it is mine."

She knew that she should have been offended at that. Maybe she was, a little bit. "Is there some doubt?"

But the truth was, a larger part of her was something like tickled that he imagined her life was exciting enough to allow for the possibility of two lovers. Or even more, for that matter. Not for the first time in her life, she wondered what sort of person she would have been if she'd been adventurous. If she'd set off when she was done with school and tossed herself headfirst into the kind of scrapes and mistakes and wild, impractical joys that so many of her classmates had.

Her trouble was, she had always thought that while those stories sounded so exciting when told to her later, the truth of them always seemed to involve sticky nightclubs, gritty, packed beaches in places like overrun Ibiza, and deeply regrettable nights that turned into long, nauseatingly hungover mornings.

It had always seemed a lot more fun to stay home.

But that didn't make it any less entertaining to imagine herself a different sort of woman. And better yet, to imagine that Alceu thought she was just such a woman. She decided to take the entire line of questioning as a compliment.

"It is a matter of legalities," he told her darkly.

"I fully understand," she assured him, with a wave of her hand. "After all, it makes absolutely perfect sense that after having waited all those years to lose my virginity, I would take the loss of it as a starting pistol and hare off into a sea of men, sampling every single one of them that I encountered."

"New York City is not exactly known as a place of quiet retreat and contemplation," he replied. Coolly.

"I'm touched that you think I'm so energetic." She rolled her eyes and decided she would, in fact, have another *arancini*. "But by all means, let's make sure that everything is nice and tidy and legal."

"I have already had all the documents drawn up." Alceu's gaze moved over her as she chewed, then swallowed. His frown deepened, but she thought she saw a flash of that heat she recognized. Her body reacted as if he'd touched her. "Once the doctors have presented me with the results, I expect that we will both sign, and we can then marry. I have the priest ready to go, tomorrow morning."

"I thought this would all be a process." Dioni ordered her own body to behave. It did not. "Don't banns have to be read, sacraments discussed, conversions suggested?"

"I think you know that the rules are not the same for those who can afford to change them," Alceu told her. "A sad but true fact of the world."

"So, if I'm following," she said, staring at the bright, fresh fruits that made her second plate so happy, "the intention was to end your bloodline with you so that you could make certain that no more abuses of power occurred. Unless and until you discovered that you could use that power for your own whims."

"Yes, Dioni," Alceu said, and this time, there was something in his voice that made her shiver into a kind of watchful stillness, different from that other kind that glittered her up and changed everything. "You've caught me. I am, like all of my ancestors I so despise, little more than a hypocrite. Nonetheless, we'll be married in the morning."

"This is all very romantic," she said after a moment, and it was more difficult than before to find that light-hearted tone. But she managed it. She popped a bit of the fruit into her mouth and told herself that the first hit of tart sweetness was just the serotonin booster she needed. "My heart is aflutter."

She thought he would turn and stalk off at that, but he didn't. Instead, he moved closer, coming out from the shadows of the castle into the bright, direct light on the terrace.

And he kept coming until he stopped at the edge of the table, so that she had to crane her neck back to look up at him.

Not that doing so was a hardship, but it didn't help her settle any.

She was sure that he could see the way her pulse beat hard in her neck. The way her eyes blazed a bit, because she couldn't seem to muster up any other kind of response when he was near. Or maybe it was simply that she had been building towards seeing him these past couple of days, ever since walking away from him in that forecourt. She'd been sensing him in empty rooms. Imagining him up above her in fragrant, peaceful courtyards.

Maybe part of her still believed this was all a dream.

He glared down at her as if he was a breath away from a full-on scowl, so dark and forbidding was his expression, as he reached into the pocket of his coat and pulled out a small box. Then he snapped it open, placing it on the table between them.

Dioni took her time looking away from the dark magic of his gaze, down to the mosaic top of the table. Where there was a ring nestled in the dark velvet box.

She stared at it.

Not because she didn't recognize the fact that it was a ring, or understand what it must represent. She hadn't thought there would be rings. In this strange little situation of theirs, she hadn't thought about *rings* at all.

But the presence of one, here before her so unexpectedly, made the enormity of what was happening hit home.

"Does it not suit you?" Alceu asked, and his voice sounded...frozen. "I'm certain I can find something more to your taste."

He reached out as if to snatch the ring back and she moved without thinking it through, slapping her hand down to cover the whole box. So that when he went to take it back, he grazed her hand instead.

And that was a whole different kind of fire, flaring to life inside of her. And jumping between them, she could tell. She could see it in the way his dark eyes gleamed.

"I didn't say I didn't like it." She lifted her palm and peered at the ring again. "I doubt there is anyone alive who wouldn't like so many diamonds in one place."

He let his extended arm drop to his side, though she was sure that he felt as caught in this bright little fire of theirs as she was. That he was just as unable to do anything at all but feel the same burn inside, and remember.

"It was my mother's," he told her.

And this time, she could call his voice—his whole demeanor—the very definition of *stiff.*

She smiled at him, then down at the ring. "Is it poisonous?"

And she watched as something perilously close to a smile moved over his stern mouth, then disappeared. Making her want nothing so much as to chase it, to bring it back, to bask in it some more.

"A reasonable question," he agreed, and it felt like warmth, this quiet little moment between them. "But I assure you, it is not. This is the first ring my father gave her and it was little worn. It has been passed down in my family for generations. Almost universally, its owners remove it, usually in fits of rage. It has been thrown from the battlements. It has gone down more than one drain. And yet it always finds its way back."

"So it is less a gesture toward a harmonious and fruitful marriage, and more an introduction to a family curse." Dioni reached in and picked it up before he could follow the family tradition with this ring, as she suspected he wanted to. That frown on his face seemed to suggest that a good toss from the walls was imminent.

"What it is, *camurria*, is tradition," he told her darkly. "For good or for ill."

She held the ring between her thumb and forefinger, looking between its shimmering intensity and his.

"No bended knee?" she asked softly, from a daring place she would have said did not exist inside of her.

If asked, she would have said there was no possibility she would ever be bold enough to tease anyone. Especially not this man. But she had already experienced his thunder. His wildfire. All those flashes of lightning, all that danger and rumbling.

She told herself she was prepared.

First, there was that stark astonishment all over his face. Then the arrogant rise of his brow.

And then, to her amazement, he held her gaze— stern and forbidding—and sank to one knee.

It should have looked silly on him. A man so powerful, so austere and contained, making such a universal gesture of obeisance.

But this was Alceu.

On him, kneeling down only made him look more powerful.

He reached over and took the ring from her. Then he took her hand, and she didn't know if she was frozen solid, or paralyzed, or simply in such disbelief that this was actually happening that every system in her body was trying to shut itself down.

All she could do was stare as he held her hand in his and smoothly slid the ring into place.

"You will be my wife," he said with great portent,

his voice seeming to echo deep in her bones. "May God have mercy on both our souls."

And that did it.

That broke the spell and Dioni laughed, tossing her head back while she did it, and when she looked at him again there was a different sort of arrested expression on his face.

A different gleam in his gaze altogether.

"Really, Alceu," she said. "You might want to consider opening a line of greeting cards. Surely the world is desperate for this level of sentimentality. I am swept away."

She thought he would rise quickly, but he stayed where he was. It was as if he spent half of his life on his knees and found it comfortable. And he stared at her in that same fulminating way, as if he could see straight through her, to the darkest recesses of her soul.

Her trouble was, she wouldn't mind if he could.

"You will be my wife," he told her, more intently this time. "And it is not the lark you seem to imagine it, Dioni. For one thing, you will be the object of pity the world over."

"If you say so." She shrugged when his brow creased. "I think you're drastically underestimating your appeal."

"I am not a cruel man," he told her, with that same intensity. "But cruelty is in my blood, my bones."

"So you have said," she murmured. "In a great many ways, though you have not specified what sort of cruelty you mean."

He seemed taken aback by that, as if it should have been obvious. As if the cruelty of his bones and blood should have been evident at a glance. "When I was a young boy I became enamored of the chickens in the yard. The cook kept them for eggs, but I liked them. I suppose you could say I considered them friends."

Dioni found that her throat was constricted as she tried to imagine Alceu as a small boy, playing with chickens, of all things—and as she tried to imagine that, she was also trying to ward off her sense of foreboding.

"My father threw one of his dinner parties," Alceu continued. "I was not usually permitted to take part in them, but that night he insisted that I get dressed and attend." His eyes seemed to sear straight through her. "Can you guess what he served?"

"Alceu…" she murmured.

"He told the whole party that it was important to teach children the circle of life," he told her in that same remote tone with his eyes blazing. "But even then, I knew the truth. I knew that he didn't care about *life lessons*. He found a way to hurt me, so he did. That was the lesson. That is who raised me, Dioni. There was only one way that I knew to make certain that no part of him would ever be passed on." That fire in him seemed to reach higher, though he did not move. "Alas."

And she wanted to say something comforting to him, but she was certain that he would not be receptive to it. She nodded sagely instead. "I will make a note. No chickens."

Alceu did not laugh, but then, she had not thought that he would. He scowled, and she fancied that it was a slightly less ferocious version than usual. "I can only try my best not to model the behavior I witnessed all of my life," he told her with all of that intense dignity of his. "It was never my intention to lay a finger on you, yet here we are. Neither did I ever wish to have a child to bear the burden of the bloodline. Still, I will do what I must to give you some semblance of the life you deserve, and to do all that is possible to make certain that our child is nothing like the rest of the Vaccaros. It is the least I can do after permitting things to get to this stage."

She realized her hand was still in his, and she no longer liked it as much as she had, so she it snatched back. "Yes, of course. You were simply the tide that rolled in and swept me out to sea. I had nothing to do with it. I was barely there."

He rose then, another quiet feat of grace and off-handed athleticism. No one should be able to move like that, she thought. It was simply unfair.

Particularly when she wasn't happy with him.

"I owe you an apology," he said with terrific formality that made her want nothing so much as to thump him one. "I should not have kissed you in New York. I take the blame entirely. It sets the wrong example."

"Once again, you seem to be under the impression that I was not involved," Dioni pointed out. Perhaps from between her teeth. "That is not how I remember it."

"The physical part of our relationship is over,"

Alceu told her then, looking down the length of his body to where she was sitting, as if he knew full well that he was delivering a blow. "I hope you like the rooms that have been made available to you. If you do not, you may choose from any other apartments in the castle. Any but mine."

She considered that for a moment, the breeze that teased at her face only reminding her that she was flushed. That his very presence did that to her, but he was acting like that didn't matter.

"I'm not sure what's made you imagine that I'm a good candidate for a nonsexual marriage," she said, as carefully as she could. When she could hardly hear herself over the frantic pounding of her heart. "But I am not."

"You are whatever I say you are," he replied, starkly enough that she sucked in a breath. "I am sorry if that offends you, but it is the truth. And I did warn you. This is a prison, and in a prison, not a single one of us gets to do as we choose. You'll see."

Then he stood there, as if waiting for her to have some kind of explosive reaction—and maybe that was the reason why she bit it back.

Instead she curled her fingers tight, feeling the ring on her finger. A hard, cold intrusion for all that it still glittered and caught the sun.

When she still said nothing, he nodded as if they had come to some agreement, and then turned and headed back inside.

And Dioni had no idea if he lurked in there to watch her reaction or not, but she had to assume that he did.

Because she thought that she would rather die than give him the satisfaction of watching her react to the bomb he'd just dropped on her.

She shifted her thumb in her fist so that she could wrap her fingers around it and play with her ring at the same time. She let her mind race around as it would. There was no point having fights with him when he so clearly wanted them, and certainly not now, right before their wedding.

Because Dioni knew that they would be signing those documents tonight. She had never been that woman he seemed to imagine she could have been. She had only and ever been his.

She also knew that she would marry him tomorrow, no matter what nonsense he came up with in the meantime.

Deep in that still place inside her, bright and warm, she knew.

So she sat there, slicked through with temper and longing and yet no second thoughts, and made herself smile out at the view as if none of this hurt at all.

Because he was going to fall in love with her any moment now.

He *was*.

CHAPTER FIVE

IT WAS A small affair, as he supposed shotgun weddings tended to be, even in these so-called enlightened times.

If, that was, anything involving the Vaccaros could be said to be *enlightened*.

Alceu stood in the tiny chapel halfway down the mountainside that had served as his family's church for centuries. It was in pristine condition—not a great shock, given that most of his ancestors might have reasonably assumed that they'd have been struck down upon entry. The priest stood at the altar, somehow managing to both look pointedly at Dioni's belly as punctuation to every sentence and yet seem deliberately unaware that the ceremony was anything but perfectly normal.

Maybe no weddings were "normal."

The last one Alceu had attended could certainly not claim that title. He was surprised the Hotel Andromeda yet stood.

His mother lounged in one of the few pews—having, he was certain, chosen the one that bathed her in the red light from the stained glass window above.

She was dressed in what could only be described as mourning attire, complete with a mantilla over her head that somehow failed to disguise the brightness of her lipstick. Across the aisle from her and keeping to the more decorous shadows, Concetta sat ramrod straight in her perfectly pressed uniform, looking distinctly dubious.

Oh, happy day, Dioni had said.

And yet his bride appeared in the chapel doorway like a ray of light.

She was holding a pretty bouquet of flowers that she must have picked on her way to the church, because he knew that there had been none ready for her. He had decided that speed trumped tradition. Just the same, he had done nothing in the way of a wedding gown, either, and yet she had managed that, too. Her dress was the color of champagne and flowed over her, accentuating the reason that they were here today.

Except he found himself looking less at the accoutrements and more at the sheer beauty of her. Alceu would have said that she was excited, but he did not see how that could be possible under these circumstances. Yet the evidence seemed plain enough. Because she was glowing. *Beaming.*

She nearly bounded down the aisle, that smile of hers taking up far too much room on her face and the chapel itself, carving its way deep beneath his ribs.

He could admit that there was a part of him that had expected her to fall at the rules laid down yesterday. That same part of him was something like irritated that she hadn't.

They recited their vows, one after the next, and when the priest indicated that Alceu could kiss his bride, his wife, it was his turn to face the things he'd told her. Head-on.

While Dioni only gazed up at him, her smile growing wider by the moment.

"So quickly do we find our vows are elastic," she murmured, for only him to hear, as he leaned in and pressed a furious kiss to her lips.

It was nothing like that kiss in New York and yet it still seemed to rampage through him, laying waste to all it touched.

Afterward, the deed accomplished and their doom complete, he walked with her back up to the house as his ancestors had done from time immemorial. Too many of his forebears to count had escorted their new wives up the side of the mountain, then led them behind the stone walls that never let Vaccaros go.

There was a huge part of him that wanted only to raze the whole of it to the ground.

Alceu walked silently, deeply aware of the solemnity of the occasion and the ghosts all around him, keeping step with him as he—the one who had been so certain he would put an end to these terrible traditions—turned out to be no better than the lot of them.

And yet beside him, Dioni kept marveling at the view. She stopped every time she could look back down the mountain, out toward the sea. She picked more flowers. She marveled at the light on the water far below. She listened to the birds singing and hummed along. There was a skip in her step, and it took very little time indeed for her hair to fall down from where it had been pinned up in the chapel. The hem of her champagne dress dragged in the rich brown earth. There was a smudge of something he assumed was pollen on her cheek.

Dioni didn't seem to notice or care.

Alceu noticed. And the fact that he could not pretend that he did not care infuriated him. He kept on walking, grimly determined to make it back to the castle before he forgot himself.

Before he indulged himself in her, all sunshine and light, that musical laugh and the way she seemed to throw her arms wide and take in all aspects of this cursed place until he was forced to see it through her eyes. Until he was forced to wonder why he, too, couldn't revel in the way the trees arched above them like a canopy. Or the way the sun filtered down through the branches, creating patterns on the earth. Or even the way the castle rose up above them, as beautiful as it was staunchly defensive, built to keep the family's well-deserved enemies at bay.

When they finally made it to the cool embrace of the stone walls, he was grateful.

But it was far harder to walk away from her than it should have been.

He noticed that too, and cared far more than was wise.

Later that night, while he was doing his best to work in his office, he found himself drawn to the faint sound of music winding its way in and around the stone walls.

Like memories of joyful times these stones had never known.

It was like his brand-new wife was haunting him.

And yet he couldn't seem to keep himself from following the ghost of her, walking down one long, empty hallway into the next, following the melody that grew louder as he moved.

Eventually, he found himself in the old ballroom that he had refurbished with the same level of attention to detail that he'd given the rest of the castle, though he had no intention of ever throwing something like a ball. As he approached, he found himself in the grip of a kind of apprehension, as if he wasn't at all sure what he would see when he looked inside.

Would it be Dioni after all? Or was he truly, fully engaging with the dark promise of this place at last? Could he expect to see actual ghosts inside?

He didn't know if he was pleased or disappointed or both when a glance within showed him only Dioni.

All alone, her hair all around her like a tangled cloud and her eyes closed.

And she was singing.

He knew he recognized the song, though he couldn't have said how. He was mesmerized by the way she moved, holding her belly as if she were dancing with their child. Her eyes stayed shut as she swayed and swirled, letting her voice and the song she sang move her around the floor.

Until suddenly she stopped, as if she sensed him the way he did her, though he did not wish to examine that possibility or admit that he did exactly that. Then she opened her eyes, and stared straight at him.

It was their wedding night.

Suddenly that was the only thing he could manage to think.

And it seemed that she could read his thoughts, or she shared the same bright images of what *normal* wedding nights looked like, because he stood there watching—in no little awe and too much desire—as her cheeks flushed red.

He was suddenly aware that he was not dressed as he normally was, in one of the suits he wore as his armor, to distinguish himself from his barbaric relatives. Instead, he was wearing little more than a pair of soft trousers suitable for late nights of privacy and a T-shirt to match. He could see that she noticed. But then, he could hardly pull his eyes away from the nightgown she wore, a slinky, silken affair that highlighted how much her breasts had ripened, how round she was, and how unearthly her beauty was.

How his friend had ever let her out from under lock and key was a mystery to him.

Not that he wished to think of Apostolis at a time like this.

"You should be in bed," he told her, and his voice sounded harsh as it echoed back at him.

"I couldn't sleep," she replied. "Perhaps the curse of our marriage has already set in. I will admit that I was not expecting it to take root in the form of insomnia." But she smiled as she said it, rubbing at her belly. "Or perhaps I'm extremely pregnant. One of the two."

She did not tell him to approach her, and he meant to leave—and yet somehow he found himself crossing the floor until he was there before her. *Right there*, looking down at her as if this was a different sort of marriage altogether.

When he could not allow it. When he knew better.

"You should not look at me like that," he scolded her, his voice too rough.

But her smile only widened. "Like what?"

"So wide-eyed and innocent, as if anything good can come of this."

He growled that out, but even that did nothing to shake her. If anything, her eyes softened more, and that led him to imagine what else might also have softened, and that was precisely why he needed to wheel himself around and quit her presence immediately.

But he did not move.

"Good has already come of it, Alceu," Dioni said quietly.

She reached out then, the ring he had given her yesterday catching the light of all the chandeliers above and sending it spinning, turning, *dancing* in all directions. And he felt that same whirling kaleidoscope inside of him when she took his hands, pulled him forward, and then settled his palms on her belly.

"Dioni—" he began.

But she didn't let go of his hands.

He was fairly certain she actually *shushed* him. And in the next moment he couldn't remember either way, because he felt her belly move beneath his hands.

Alceu had never felt a sensation like it before. But he knew what it was.

The doctors' report had been unequivocal about the thing he'd already known. This was his child. She was carrying *his* child.

His son.

And here, now, on this wedding night that should never have happened, his son was kicking at him. Saying his own kind of hello.

As if they were truly a family, after all.

Alceu felt an immense wave crash through him. Sensation. Emotion.

An ocean of longing, regrets, and something as acrid as grief.

He pulled his hands back, shattered.

As if he had never known himself until this moment.

And he would never be whole again.

"I wish that I thought this was a good thing," he said, and his voice came out little more than a rough whisper. "But I can only look back on my own childhood and wish that this had never come to pass. No child should have to go through the things I did."

Her gaze shifted to something almost solemn, and he thought she held herself a bit more stiffly, as if he had hurt her. But if he had, she didn't show it in any other manner. "What is so terrible about this place? What happened to you, Alceu? It can't all have been chickens, can it?"

It was so late. And it was only the two of them,

standing here surrounded by echoes in an abandoned ballroom polished to a shine by his own hands. He should know better than to allow the kind of intimacy that he could feel wrapping around them.

He *did* know better.

Because it was so late. Because outside the windows, there was nothing but darkness for kilometers in all directions. Because he knew that everyone else in the castle was fast asleep.

Alceu had never been *torn*. He did not *shatter*. He had known his mission in life since he was small.

This was an aberration and he could not make sense of it.

He could not understand why it was only Dioni who brought this out in him. Only Dioni who he could look at, think of the right thing to do, and then…not do it.

Tonight was only the latest example, and not nearly the worst. There had been ample opportunity for him to walk away from her on the terrace outside the Hotel Andromeda.

But he had moved closer instead. And tonight he stayed where he was, which was the same thing. "I have no memory of my parents ever getting along," he told her shortly. "They had despised each other, always, as far as I was aware. But I have heard many stories of their younger years, when they confused that dislike for passion and made all of Europe witness to their explosions. Their theatrics." He blew out a breath, yet couldn't manage to make himself stop. "As it soured, they took lovers and flaunted them at each other, trying to cause the most damage. And they did. Over and over again. Since all they cared about was hurting each other, they paid no attention to the destruction they left behind them as they went. My father bullied and raged his way through his life, leaving only the walking wounded behind him. My mother's many lovers fared little better when she was done with them."

He stepped back, looking for condemnation, but all Dioni did was gaze back at him.

"I hope," she said, quietly, "that no one judges me for my father's behavior. You already know that he married my best friend. And while she and I never talked about it too closely, he was not exactly kind to her. He was Spyros Adrianakis and his legend was the only thing that mattered to him. Are you expecting me to judge you for your parents' behavior?"

Maybe he was, because it threw him that she did not. Even as he understood that if she had, it would have helped. He would have been able to step back, to rethink.

Instead, he kept going. "I was only a boy when I realized that my parents did not contain their little games to the mainland," Alceu told her. "Eventually I would learn the truth. My father was obsessed with power, and exerted his over everyone who came into contact with him, little caring if that meant he ground them underfoot. My mother, to this day, enjoys nothing so much as worming her way into other people's marriages, for sport and entertainment. Then sitting back, laughing all the while, at the wreckage she leaves behind. But then, as a child, all I knew was that when I walked into a village I was greeted by people who spat on the ground, crossed themselves, and whispered that I was a devil."

"That doesn't make you one," Dioni said at once, frowning. "It makes you a pawn, perhaps."

Alceu couldn't say that he liked that description. But he couldn't argue with it, either.

These were not things he discussed. These were not stories he told.

But this was his wedding night.

This was Dioni, who could not seem to be dissuaded from looking at him as if she could, by the force of her gaze alone, make him *good*. When he knew better.

And so he had no choice but to tell her the rest.

"The summer before I left for university I met a girl from the village at the base of the mountain." His voice was hoarse. This wasn't a story he had ever told anyone before. Not even her brother. "Her name was Grazia. I believed that I could rehabilitate my family name by engaging with the villagers. I helped build houses, I volunteered, and I tried to show that I was not like my family. And I thought that I was making strides, especially when I met her. She was a sweet, kind, happy girl." He hated this story. There was a reason he never told it. "Grazia and I had an understanding when I left for university, and I counted the days to my return at Christmas so that I could see her again." He shook his head, the memories too vivid, even now. "I had it all planned. I would propose. We would marry and she would come abroad with me.

Then we would come back and, together, we would show the whole of Sicily that the Vaccaro family could be trusted again."

He didn't want to say these things. He didn't want to think about that time.

But there was nothing around him but ghosts, and Dioni, and the child she carried that meant that there would be a future despite everything.

And she said nothing, still watching him intently, so he could not seem to help but go on.

"When I came home that Christmas, everything was changed." His throat was dry. He made himself swallow, but it didn't help. "My father had taken her to his bed. Sweet, kind Grazia never stood a chance. Because he could not abide even the faintest hint of happiness. And because there was no greater way to exert his power over me."

"Alceu..." Dioni only whispered his name, her eyes wide. "I'm so sorry."

"She didn't matter to him," Alceu bit out. "He made certain I walked in on them. Then he laughed. And then, when she ran from here, overwhelmed with the shame of it, and *accidentally fell* from the cliff to her death, he only shrugged." Alceu stared at her, so she would understand that he was not exaggerating. He could still remember his father's laughter. The dismissive wave of his hand. The deep, disgusting understanding that it was more than likely that Grazia had jumped. "He told me that I should know better than to mess about with peasants."

He heard the shocked noise she made then and he

moved closer, wrapping his hands around her shoulders. "That is when I knew for certain, Dioni. This family is sick. We are a cancer upon the earth and always have been. There is nothing good here. No good can come from us. No good can remain."

"You are not your father," she said after a moment, as if it was an effort for her to remain calm. "And our son will not be like him either, Alceu. He will be like you."

"And you think that's better?" He let out a bitter laugh, dropping his hands and stepping back, aware that he was not entirely within his own control when he rubbed a palm over his face. "What is good about me, Dioni? I impregnated my best friend's beloved younger sister on his wedding day. I do not exactly qualify for sainthood."

She frowned. "That is not exactly what I—"

He shook his head and backed away. "The sooner you resign yourself to the fact that this is a cursed enterprise, the better. When the child is born, we will decide how best to protect him from the ravages of this bloodline. But I'm afraid it is too late for you or me."

"Alceu—"

"You must keep your distance from me, Dioni," he told her, and he could hear that his voice shook, gravelly and grave. "I beg of you."

He thought that settled it.

Because what else did she need to hear? How else could he illustrate the horrors that awaited her?

And so he was unprepared, a week later, to stagger from his office in the middle of the night into his bedroom only to find the wife who haunted him without even trying lying in his bed.

Completely naked.

"What the hell are you doing?" he managed to grit out, though all the blood in his body had surged to the hardest part of him.

She stirred, looking sleepy until she saw him, and then she smiled.

That burst of bright sunshine, even in the middle of the night, that made every last part of him ache.

"What does it look like I'm doing?" she asked, and then laughed, to really plunge the dagger in deep. "I'm seducing you. Obviously."

CHAPTER SIX

SEDUCTION WAS NOT exactly in Dioni's wheelhouse.

If anything, she found the fact she was even *trying* such a thing funny. She had grown up mostly unconcerned with her body, since no one paid much attention to the clumsy, scruffy, mostly overlooked daughter of legends, and so she could run and swim and wander about as she liked. At school she'd discovered that she was not only supposed to care deeply about her looks, but feel shame about it all, and she'd tried. But it was much nicer to curl up with biscuits and books.

She had never *tried* to employ feminine wiles in her life.

Dioni hadn't actually known she possessed any. Not until the night of her brother's wedding.

And yes, she supposed that her behavior could have been seen as *seductive* that night, but she hadn't thought about it that way at the time. She had wanted him, but that hadn't been anything new. It hadn't been *an action item*. And *wanting him* wasn't anything new, either. She had simply wanted to dance in the rain. The way she often did, on her own. There had been something about the rain and the storm that had called to her. It had felt to her the way that he did.

It had been unconscious, was the thing.

But the same could not be said about tonight.

Because Dioni had spent a long time thinking about the things he had told her on their wedding night. She had spent the week since then going over and over how he'd left her standing there, in the middle of an empty dance floor.

She hadn't felt much like singing, really. Not since that night.

But she had also completely disagreed with his conclusions. About everything.

Allowing the terrible things that had been done to him and those he cared for to wreck him was understandable. Yet if he never moved on from those things, he was allowing himself to remain wrecked forever.

Staying still was only an option if a person was in their grave.

Or maybe, she had thought earlier tonight, lying in bed and rubbing lotion into the parts of her body that were still expanding and growing, it was simply the space that she was in. Everything inside of her was shifting, changing, shaping itself into something else entirely.

That was what she wanted. The shift, the push. Creating room where there was none.

Her body knew how to do it. Why shouldn't she let it take her where she wanted to go?

And the more she thought about actually doing such a thing, actually getting up and going to him and *being seductive* because he wouldn't, the more she found herself something like incensed. What was the point of them being married at all if she was simply sent off to some far reach of his massive house? What was the point of any of it if she was simply expected to accept what everyone else said about him, this place, and her future here?

Not to mention the implications for their son.

Dioni had never thought that she would get a chance to touch Alceu, and yet she had. She had certainly never expected to fall pregnant, or to marry him. Those things had happened, and she wasn't precisely upset about either of them.

How could she be when even now—while his mother slunk about muttering her dark incantations all over the place and everyone here seemed entirely too preoccupied with their expectations of woe and lamentation—she still felt that same clear stillness inside.

Nothing had changed that.

If anything, it was stronger than it had been in New York.

And Dioni had grown up in the shadow of a man who thought entirely too much of himself and what he believed others thought about him. She had learned quickly that if she wished to claim any space for herself, she would have to go ahead and do it.

She was the one who had prevailed upon her father to send her away to school in the first place. If she hadn't, she was fairly sure that Spyros would have forgotten to bother, and who knows if she would have ended up with any kind of education at all? And she was the one to insist that she should stay at home after school. Partly because she loved the hotel and her family's legacy, but also because she wanted the opportunity to continue to live with Jolie. To maintain their friendship despite the unusual circumstances.

After all, she had told her friend on the night before her wedding, *not everyone gets to call their best friend* stepmother.

So tonight she'd gotten out of her bed and put on that nightgown she'd been wearing in the ballroom. And then, even though it was a long walk, she'd wound her way through the hallways, moving quietly so that she attracted no notice from anyone. Not even the staff.

It was like she was one of the ghosts of this place. And she liked the feeling of it, almost as if she was light on her feet, when she knew better.

She had passed his office, there at the start of the hallway that she'd been told led to *the* signore*'s private rooms*, and had seen him working there, though it was late. He'd been frowning down at his laptop while making notes on a pad in front of him and she could have stood there, looking at him, forever. But she'd moved on before he could look up and see her, slipping down the hall and beginning her search for the man's bed.

Because even the unknowable Alceu must be in possession of a bed.

Dioni had never been this deep into his private area of the house before, but she would have known these were his rooms even if she was blind. It all smelled faintly like him, that hint of citrus and spice. She'd felt her breath go shaky and her whole body shiver into awareness as she padded her way through the suite until she eventually found his bedroom, set there at the corner of the house.

Inside, she'd paused to look out the windows that, like hers, opened up onto the walls. She could see little but darkness, and the lights of the villages clustered down at the foot of the mountains.

By day, she was certain that he could see almost all the way to her island.

And somehow, thinking of home made her feel at home. She'd pulled the nightgown up and over her head and then she'd made her way to the bed, a large, imposing affair set against the far wall, while carefully aesthetic antiques stood about like sentries.

First she'd gotten under his sheets, but then she'd thought that she would make far more of an impact if they were tossed aside, so that the point of this gambit was immediately clear.

That being her nudity, which, now, she could see was doing exactly what she'd wanted it to do.

"Is it working?" she asked him.

But she could see that it was. That arrested look was all over him. He could not seem to keep his eyes on her face, too busy with drinking in her curves. And she was certain she saw his hands twitch as if they wished to reach out on their own.

"Is what working?" he managed to get out, though he hardly sounded like himself.

"My seduction." She moved to prop herself up on one elbow, a perilous affair given that her center of gravity had shifted. Then she lifted a hand to her hair, shaking out the knot she'd put in it, so that the black mass of it tumbled down all around her. She could smell the scent of her shampoo filling the room and she could see that he did, too, because she watched it work its way through him—from the flare of his nostrils to how he shifted the way he stood.

And that dark, furious, glorious look he aimed at her, as if he wasn't sure if he was dreaming, Dioni knew that she would remember forever.

It wouldn't be possible, no matter what he said, to feel more beautiful than she did now.

And that was a good thing, because he did not exactly start singing hosannas.

"I thought we agreed," he gritted out instead.

"We did not agree," she corrected him. Gently, she thought, for a naked woman who clearly deserved a different response. "You made a great many decisions and then left the room before I could respond."

"Surely you heard me, all the same."

She sighed a little and as she did could feel her body move. Just slightly, but it was enough. His eyes tracked the movement and if she wasn't mistaken, he swallowed. Hard.

"You made your case," she told him. "But I reject it."

"It was less an argument than a statement of intent, *camurria*."

"I know what it was." But she decided that she

would not categorize it. Because she doubted he would like the things she would call it. It would involve a discussion of ghosts. Of the sins of the father and her belief that anyone could change their life if they wanted to, no matter what lurked in the past. "But Alceu. It isn't practical."

"Because you believe anything about what happened between us is *practical*?" He sounded incredulous. "I think perhaps your current state is affecting your mind, Dioni."

"My current state?" She nodded, sagely. "You mean the fact that we are married. I agree. It is affecting my mind. Because, according to you, the worst has already happened. *God have mercy on both our souls*, and so on. So I don't see why we have to continue to punish ourselves. I'm already pregnant, Alceu. The damage has already been done, according to you. Why must I be banished off to a guest room?"

He was shaking his head, but she could see the way that pulse of his pounded in his throat. "What are you suggesting?"

She sat up, and it wasn't elegant, but he looked mesmerized all the same. "Well, for a start, I thought it might be fun to see what it was like to both kiss *and* have sex at the same time, instead of separating those events by six months and a baby."

This time there was no doubt that he had to swallow, more than once, as if to clear his throat. And that gaze of his was nothing but fire.

"That would be a mistake." His voice was low.

It wasn't easy for her to move her body so that

she could get to the edge of the bed, and then stand, but she did it. Then she walked toward him and she felt like a fertility goddess, because that was how he looked at her. As if he had never seen anything so beautiful approaching him before. As if he couldn't conceive of it.

That was what she held on to. Because she didn't know what she was supposed to do when he was saying one thing to her, but everything else about him was telling her the opposite.

"Surely the mistake has already been made." She watched him watch her, and it made that curious, wonderful heat inside her turn into something more like a naked flame. "What would happen if instead of damning ourselves forever, we danced in it, instead?"

Dioni drifted closer to him, though he looked something like tortured.

"Dancing is what got us in trouble in the first place," he said, in a voice that almost sounded bitter, but she could see the flash of fire and heat in his gaze.

"You can't get me pregnant," she pointed out. "We're already married. It's currently a secret, but it won't always be. Whether or not you take me to bed tonight will make no difference at all in the grand scheme of things."

"If it would make no difference—" he began.

"Except," she clarified, "to me. It would make a tremendous difference to *me*, Alceu."

She was far too close to him now. Dioni reached out and helped herself to one of the buttons on his shirt, loosening it and then letting her fingers trail across the swath of golden skin that she found there.

And he made a tortured sort of sound, but he didn't push her away. He reached out to brush his hand over her jaw, her cheek. Then he moved his thumb restlessly over the arch of her cheekbone and the seam of her lips.

It was like the fire between them went molten.

"What is it you want?" he demanded, his voice little more than a whisper.

She loosened another button, and this time, leaned forward to press her mouth there. She felt the heat of his skin blaze against her lips. She felt the small jerking motion he made, an electric shock to him the way that he had always been for her.

Only then did she ease back and look up at him, her hands braced on his chest, and her big belly a round weight between them.

"You," she told him, though she knew it was dangerous to declare such things. It strayed too close to the heart of her. "Alceu, you must know that I have always wanted you."

Dioni watched him as he fought himself. As he struggled.

And then as he fell.

As whatever resolve he had built up against her simply shattered.

Until there was nothing remaining but that fire.

It was what she'd wanted. But seeing it, she had the stray thought that she'd had no idea how potent it was, this thing she'd come looking for.

That it could burn her into ash if she wasn't careful.

"You are the undoing of man," he rasped out.

But before she could respond to that, or simply revel in it, his mouth crashed down upon hers.

And it was even better than before.

It was a wild, impossible glory and everything in her spun out, greedily.

He kissed her and he kissed her, his hands rising to frame her face. He detangled her hair as he raked his fingers through it, kissing her more. His hands moved down her back, finding the span of her bottom and then drifting to her hips, as if noting the way they'd widened.

He shifted her around so that her back was to him and took himself on a tour down her neck, holding the great, round weight of their baby with one big hand.

Over and over again, he kissed her.

Alceu set her away from him and she looked at him quickly, expecting that he would stop this—but he didn't. He shrugged out of his shirt. He kicked off his trousers. Then he came to her, the look on his face so intense that she backed up of her own accord, until she brushed up against the bed. He kept coming. She sat down.

And this time, he did not offer her a ring. This time, he urged her to lie back.

When she did he spread her legs apart, draped them over his shoulders, then bent to lick his way into her heat.

Dioni shattered immediately.

It was an immediate implosion that had her throwing out her arms, arching her back, and then—worse still, or *better*—she could feel the way he laughed against her flesh.

And he was still laughing as he shifted to grip her bottom as he held her before him like a feast.

Then he took his time, slow and deliberate, and tore her apart.

One extraordinary lick at a time.

And after she had shattered into so many pieces that she wasn't certain how she was meant to carry on, he began to move his way up the length of her body, lavishing attention on every centimeter he found.

Any stray thought she might have had about the comparisons he could make between her body six months ago and now were swept away in the obvious enjoyment he took in her as he went. She had no doubt at all that he found her enchanting. Engrossing.

And in case she thought to wonder, he kept murmuring it as he went.

"I have never seen a woman more beautiful," he muttered at one breast, tasting it and holding it. "*Chi si duci.* You are too sweet," he told her when he found his way to the other, and made her moan.

He shifted his weight to one side so he could hold her there, laid out on the bed with him. Then he kissed her, his naked skin against hers.

Dioni had never felt anything so divine.

She wanted to revel in every part of it. The hair on his chest that made his skin rougher than hers, so that all she wanted to do was bury her face in it. And maybe rub herself all over him, everywhere. The blazing heat of him. The way his skin looked next to hers, the muscles in his forearm next to the smoothness of hers.

But he was kissing her, turning her face to his and plunging his tongue deep enough that she could taste herself in his mouth.

It made her shiver all over again.

And then he rolled them over, pulling her on top of him so she could settle there astride him the way she had once before in the pouring rain.

But everything was different now.

She straddled his hips and for a moment, all thoughts of fertility goddesses fled. Because she felt so exposed, as he was staring up at all the parts of her that had gotten so rounded, so heavy—

But he sighed. *"Zuccareddu,"* he murmured. *"Bellissima."*

Then he reached between them and at last—*at last*—she felt the thick, wide head of the hardest part of him deep in her sensitive folds.

He rubbed himself there, laughing in that dark way that thrilled her, everywhere, and she began to shake. Then she shattered again as he pressed himself against the center of her need.

As if it was the first time, she flew apart—

And she was still shaking with the force of it as he shifted her, holding her as he slid his way deep inside of her.

Dioni didn't have time to come back down from the stars before he started to move.

She stayed there, bright like a comet.

And for a long while, possibly forever, there was only this.

The way he thrust, claiming every part of her. The way he gazed up at her, something fierce and possessive, greedy and dark all over his handsome face.

There was the way he gripped her like he would never let her go, so hard that she hoped he left fingerprints behind.

She rocked herself against him, moving with his grip, and meeting his thrusts so that both of them were moaning out their pleasure—

Because it went on and on.

And every time she shattered, it got better. Deeper. Wilder.

Until, at last, Alceu took her up to another peak, hurled her off of it, and followed, blazing like a comet all his own beside her.

And when they both found their way back to earth, back to flesh instead of fire, he rolled with her. He took her down to the bed beside him so he could kiss her forehead, her cheeks, her mouth.

She was still quivering, and making little noises in the back of her throat involuntarily. He lay there beside her, that huge, hard length of his body pressed to her side and one arm holding her pregnant belly.

Dioni could feel her breath match his. She could feel the heat of him, deep inside her body, all over her, and beside her. As if they really had become one.

She wanted to stay awake as long as possible, though her eyelids were heavy and her body wanted nothing more than to slip off into oblivion.

But she fought it, because she wanted to enjoy this. Before he said anything. Before he made more declarations.

Before he tried to take back what had happened, or minimize it.

Right here, right now, Dioni wanted to do nothing at all but bask in Alceu and the shockingly effective seduction she'd executed here.

And love him, whether he knew it or not, for as long as she was able.

Before he discovered her secret and made her stop.

CHAPTER SEVEN

ALCEU COULD FEEL too many dark thoughts pressing upon him, coming in fast, but he kept them at bay.

He could tell that Dioni was not sleeping, though she was lying there beside him, quietly enough. He found he couldn't drift off himself. Instead, they lay there together, in the embrace of darkness all around, and he knew that he should be awash in regret. Recrimination.

The usual self-flagellation that followed his loss of control—something that only happened with this woman.

But he couldn't quite get there. Not just yet.

He shifted beside her, stroking the heat of her belly with his palm. When she looked over at him, he traced the shape of her lips, something tugging at him inside when they curved. Then he moved, rolling her with him so that he could lift her up and carry her.

"I am far too heavy to be carted around like this," she said, but she looped an arm around his neck and held on while he proved her wrong.

"If I cannot carry my wife and child, what kind of husband am I?" He meant that lightly, or he thought he did. But his voice came out far darker than he intended, blending in with the insistent press of the night outside.

And he could feel all the things he didn't want to start thinking begin to turn into words, then bite at him, but he didn't want them. Not now.

Not yet.

He carried her through the dark bedroom and did not turn toward the bathroom suite. Instead, he carried her outside to the battlements. Out on a wide part of the wall, as part of his renovation of the castle, he had put in an expansive outdoor shower. It was more properly several showerheads, there where the dark seemed closer than it was and the stars far brighter. When the water poured out, soft and warm, it was something like erotic.

"Who would have thought that a man so stern and uncompromising was secretly sensualist," Dioni murmured as he worked up a thick, soapy lather on her skin. He used his own hands, smoothing his way over every part of her voluptuous form.

As if he was not so much washing her as committing her to memory.

And there was something about what she'd called him—stern, uncompromising—that sat on him wrong, though he knew that he went out of his way to appear to be both of those things. That was how he wanted the world to see him. An upright man of fierce morals, despite his name.

It was that *she* had called him that, he understood. That she saw him in that way, when for her, he had already bent far more than he had ever imagined he might.

But he did not allow himself to pursue that line of thought any further. He knew where it would go.

Instead, he lathered her in the thick, fragrant soap that he preferred, until every last part of her skin smelled like him. There was something in him that he did not wish to acknowledge directly that thrilled at that notion. That wanted nothing more than to mark her in every way he could. His ring on her finger. His son in her belly. His scent so deep in her skin that she could not breathe without thinking of him. Of the feel of him moving deep inside of her, haunting her as sure as the tight clench of her haunted him.

He said none of these things either.

Instead, there beneath the stars, he took her mouth beneath the shower spray. He slicked back her hair with his hands, finding his way to the glory of her mouth.

It was carnal, demanding.

And he could not stop himself. He didn't *want* to stop, and he knew that was the real trouble. He moved her toward the built-in bench so he could take her hips from behind, then thrust himself deep inside her slick heat once more.

It was a blistering shot straight out into the cosmos, and he wasn't certain how much of him remained when they were done.

He started the process of washing her all over again. Only this time, when he'd made certain that she was tended to and fully relaxed, he bundled her up the softest towel he could find, carried her back in, and laid her in his bed once more.

Dioni curled into him and was asleep almost immediately.

But Alceu found that he could not rest. Or perhaps he did not want to, because he knew what waited for him once he did. The darkness that knew his name was far too close, and too insistent.

Later he stood out on the battlements, watching dawn break far off in the distance, out where the ocean was nothing but a thick line against the sky.

He was not foolish enough to imagine that he could pretend this had not happened. Or that it had not fundamentally changed them, and more, made a mockery of all the rules he'd attempted to put into place.

There could be no going back, he understood that.

But that didn't mean he had any idea how to go forward.

He stood there for a long while. And when he finally went back inside the castle, the sun was only just beginning to peek over the horizon.

Dioni was beginning to stir, so Alceu called down to the kitchen, and had food brought up. Because he might have been keeping his distance from her since he'd brought her here, but that didn't mean he wasn't fully aware of everything Dioni was doing while under his care.

Alceu took his duties and responsibilities seriously.

One thing he knew was that she was ravenous, particularly when she woke up.

He suspected that she would be even more so this

morning. Sure enough, when Concetta wheeled in a cart stacked with plates of Sicilian pastries and pistachio granita, plus Greek yogurt, spanakopita, and other breakfast items, he saw Dioni smiling before she even opened her eyes.

After Concetta left, with only a single dark look his way to indicate that she had feelings about the fact he was not alone, Dioni wrapped herself in the top sheet. Then she pulled it with her from the bed like a makeshift gown as she came outside to join him on the wall, where the day was shaping into typical Sicilian perfection all around them.

She looked out at the landscape that was arrayed before them, treetops and the mountain's steep slope and the watching, waiting sea, and sighed happily.

And Alceu was tempted to see the world the way that she did, all blue sky and a pretty view. Or maybe it was that once she sat down at the table, looking as if the breakfast before her was the result of a magic spell and she was swept away with joy, he could not help but notice that the sky really was a glorious shade of blue. The great tangle of the trees was green and pretty. The birds were conducting a concerto in the branches, the sun was warm and the breeze was light, and the scent of the sea danced in and around everything, as if making tides from the mountain air.

He almost felt as if he was drunk again as she dug in, tasting everything as if she'd never seen food before, and moaning with that joy that he was always surprised did not occur only when he was inside her.

"I do not think that I am a sensualist," he found

himself saying when he had intended to sit there in a dignified, perhaps appropriately forbidding silence. "Or perhaps I am not the only one."

She smiled at him, looking dreamy-eyed and something he was deeply concerned was *happy*. "It's not an insult, Alceu. If you ask me, it is the only way to live. Because otherwise, what's the point of all these marvelous things we get to do and feel and experience?" When he only stared back at her, she sighed. "And when I was a girl, I learned that moments of marvel were fleeting and unlikely to be repeated, so if I wanted to enjoy them I needed to make sure I committed myself to them. Immediately and fully. The truth is, it's a practice like anything else."

He found that he could not stand the notion of the childhood she wasn't describing in full, but he could picture all too clearly, knowing far more than anyone should have to about the late Spyros Adrianakis. And how he had conducted himself in the little fiefdom that was the Hotel Andromeda.

"My father considered himself something of a sensualist, I suppose," he said, and he didn't even know where the words came from. It should have seemed like a violation to mention that man when he had dedicated himself to wiping his memory from the earth, and yet somehow, because it was Dioni, it was fine. Even necessary.

And she didn't react badly. She only nodded, and seemed to watch him more intently as she continued to feast on pastries.

Alceu picked up his espresso and leaned back in

his chair, looking out at the mountainside but seeing far into the past. "One time—I must have been a teenager—I caught him with one of his lovers. They were cavorting about on a boat that we were all staying on for a so-called *family holiday* off the coast of Sardinia." He made a low noise of remembered disgust, as much for those long-ago days when there was still the pretense of *family* anything as for what he'd seen that day. "His lover ran off into her stateroom, where she was staying as a guest of my mother, you understand. Because my father liked to steal his toys from others. I thought he would shout at me, or push me around as he liked to do. But he felt it was a teaching moment. He lounged about, naked, and forced me to stand there as he explained to me that great men have great appetites. That these were sensual delights gifted by the gods to those who deserved them. And only fools, the weak, and poor men who were not smart enough to improve themselves did without."

"That sounds like a narcissist, not a sensualist," Dioni said, and so matter-of-factly that it took Alceu back. Because it wasn't an insult. She wasn't screeching the way his mother liked to do. She was saying it as it if was obvious. And she kept going. "If I had to guess, I'd say that he could see the joy you took in life and wanted to make certain that it was twisted for you. Poisoned beyond recognition."

"It's as if you met him," Alceu said, and then frowned down at his own hand when he found that he was rubbing his chest.

"In a way, I suppose I have," Dioni said. She wrinkled her nose. "He sounds a great deal like my father, to be honest. Shockingly, surpassingly, almost operatically self-involved."

"And yet your brother often marveled that you stayed so long in his company."

He should not have mentioned Apostolis.

It was a dangerous road to start down, but Dioni only glanced at him. "I did not stay for my father. I stayed for Jolie. My poor friend who had no choice but to marry a man like him." She blew out a breath. "Or rather, she did have a choice because there are always choices, but it was a terrible one. I stayed in solidarity. And however little I might have enjoyed my father's last years, I will never regret spending that time with my friend."

"She must be a very good friend, then."

He watched her smile, though there was a sadness there. "She's the best of friends." Dioni looked down at her plate. "And I have been lying to her for six months. When she learns that, she will be hurt. But I could not see a way around it."

"Because you believed, on some level, that you could...what? Wish your pregnancy away?"

Dioni shook her head. "What I knew was that if I told her, she might feel duty-bound to tell my brother. And if she told my brother, he would sweep in and make decisions for me. And I didn't want him to do that. He's been doing that my whole life."

Alceu frowned at her. "Your brother wants nothing but the best for you."

"Don't you think I know that?" She laughed, but

there was something in her voice. It made him sit up a little straighter. "He has been so kind to me my whole life. Yet neither he nor I ever talk about the fact that he plays the role he does in my life because my birth robbed him of his mother." Alceu stared at her and she smiled again, though he had never seen such a bittersweet expression on her face before. It made something inside his chest...catch. "I killed her, Alceu."

If she had flipped the table and gone for his throat, he did not think he could have been more surprised.

"It is my understanding that your mother died in childbirth," he said, very carefully.

This was not news to him. He had heard this before, and had even discussed it with Apostolis from time to time. At university, certainly, and no doubt since. It had always seemed an academic discussion to him, though he had been sympathetic toward his friend.

But the prospect of a woman dying while giving birth seemed wildly different to him now. It was his child in her belly. It was *Dioni* he would lose.

It all seemed a far more perilous enterprise than he had previously considered it.

Because now it would be personal.

"I accept the truth of it," Dioni said and she sat back in her chair, too. She pressed her hands into the curve of her belly, as if assuring herself that it was real, that the baby within was still there. "I have always been very clear about what actually happened. It is everyone around me who wants to make it euphemistic. But you see, I've always believed that if my mother could, she would forgive me and tell me that it was all worth it. Because that's what mothers do, isn't it?"

Alceu thought that it was very unlikely his mother would do anything of the kind, but he did not say anything. He was not entirely sure that he could have if he'd wanted to.

"And now that I am close enough to being a mother myself, I know it's true," Dioni continued, with a certain soft urgency.

"You must be terrified," Alceu found himself saying.

Her dark eyes found his and held. "I am not." Though it was almost as if she was testing out the words as she spoke them aloud. "That might change the closer I get to it, I grant you. I suppose that if I allow myself to think about it, it would be overwhelming, so I choose to believe that particular history will not repeat itself. Maybe I believe that no history repeats itself unless we allow it. And if that's the case..."

She trailed off. And he let her, because he didn't want to follow that trail to its inevitable conclusion.

Because he wanted, much too badly, to take what she said to heart. To believe it. To change the history he had always worn like his very own hair shirt.

All those things he ought to have been considering pressed in upon him again, but he shoved them aside, more ruthlessly this time.

Because the child would be born soon enough, and the reality of how he would need to be raised—to avoid all the pitfalls of the family name—would take precedence. Having failed to prevent the bloodline from continuing, Alceu would have to do the next best thing and make certain it polluted as little as possible.

This was a moment, this thing between him and the wife he'd never wanted. This was a marvel, it would not last, and he decided in the brightness of that deep blue morning that he would let it play out as it would.

Because it couldn't last.

And so for the next few weeks, for the first time in his life, he simply…allowed his life to carry on at its face value.

The business was in one of its fact-finding phases, meaning that they were in between projects and looking for new opportunities to help struggling businesses get back on their feet. It was an enjoyable phase, allowing him to follow threads and fancies wherever they took him, looking at the kinds of projects that made him feel as if—despite the undeniable fact that he was a Vaccaro—he was putting good out into the world. He and Apostolis conferred when they found promising leads and sent ideas back and forth, and he allowed himself to enjoy that part of the process as much as he always did.

He also continued researching possible uses for the castle. The trouble was, Europe was littered with the ruins of grand legacies in the form of castles and keeps, and it took money and vision to transform them into something else. It wasn't that Alceu lacked those things, but he needed to be sure that if the castle was to remain standing, it stood for good.

And outside his office, he allowed the marvel of it all to continue, because he knew it was temporary.

He did not move Dioni into his side of the castle officially, but she never slept in the guest rooms. They woke up every morning wrapped around each other. He took great pleasure in feeding her and in making certain that each day started well. Blue and bright, for as long as possible.

When he found her again in the evenings, she was filled with stories about the adventures she'd had during the day. She had started venturing into the villages. To see them, she said. To wander about the markets, sit by the sea, and get a feel for the local culture.

Neither one of them mentioned the story he'd told her of the village girl who had lost everything because of her association with this family.

And besides, as he kept reminding himself, these days could not matter because they could not last.

"Every village is unique, and yet the same," Dioni was saying tonight, at one of the dinners his mother insisted upon, claiming she liked the opportunity to be civilized. Alceu thought it was more likely because she thought she could exert her influence on the newest member of the family. "It's always fascinating to explore them and get a sense of how they are different than the others, and what remains the same. This is true in Greece as well."

"It is not necessary for you to do that," Marcella said, frowning. "They are villages. They do not require *study*."

"It might not be necessary, but I enjoy it," Dioni replied cheerfully. "I was talking to a fisherman today, who told me—"

"A fisherman?" Marcella let out one of her slithery laughs. Alceu could feel it wind itself around and around until it felt like it was clamped to the base of his spine. "What on earth could *a Vaccaro* have to discuss with *a fisherman?*"

Alceu had learned by now that his wife was a master at not reacting to provocation. She didn't change her expression. She didn't get tense. She only smiled.

"I don't know anything about fishing for a living, Marcella," she said in that same merry way of hers. "And the man I met is something of an expert on the subject. So we had a great deal to talk about, it turns out."

Alceu saw his mother shift position in her seat, every part of her radiating disapproval, which he knew boded ill. So he adroitly changed the subject, talking about some or other world events, while promising himself for what had to be the hundredth time to stop allowing these dinners to take place.

He felt as if he was exposing Dioni, not to mention his unborn child, to a pit of snakes.

Moreover, there was no joy in these forced appearances. When they ate together, just themselves, it was as if the food itself became part of the symphony of their lovemaking. One feast leading into the next.

She was a banquet he would never tire of. He understood that too well.

He was so busy thinking about all the ways he'd had her the night before, and plotting how he planned to have her tonight, that he missed the start of whatever conversation his mother and Dioni had begun.

But he certainly heard the sharpness in Marcella's tone as she leaned forward, narrowing her eyes at Alceu's wife.

"You cannot possibly be so naive, child," she said in her purring, nasty way. "I assume it must be an act, or I can only fear for you." She waved a hand, her talons painted in a dark red that matched her lips. "Do you truly imagine that this honeymoon of yours is the marriage? You must know better. Do you think you signed all those papers for the fun of it? If you leave him—and you will long to—you take nothing. Not even the children you bear. That is how they keep you."

"Mother, please," Alceu began.

But Dioni was leaning forward too, her dark eyes intent on his mother. "That is very true, Marcella," she said in her quiet way. "A mother's love knows no bounds. She will put up with anything, won't she, for the love of her child—never thinking of herself at all."

"Do you think to shame me?" Marcella laughed. "You have no idea what I feel for my son. Or what I have suffered in this family. I could have chosen any man in Europe. Princes fought for my hand. I gave up a *throne* for this vicious little family, so don't you tell me about *a mother's love*."

"That is enough," Alceu ordered her.

Marcella turned to him then, her eyes narrowed, but he could see the hint of glee in them. Because though she enjoyed claiming herself the victim in all things, what she truly loved was this.

The opportunity to show she was as vicious as any other Vaccaro.

"You are a greater fool than your father ever was," she said now, making a meal of the words. "At least *he* did not pretend that he was led around by anything but the little head in his trousers. You're making moon eyes and wafting about like a lovesick calf. You know what happens to calves, my darling son?" She leaned in to enunciate. "They are slaughtered."

Alceu was readying himself to handle that in the way it deserved when he was stopped dead—

Because Dioni was laughing.

That boundless, blue-sky laughter that made everything in him dance. And made his mother sit back in her chair in shock.

And still Dioni laughed, the way she had in New York. It was as if she'd gone over to a window, thrown it open, and let all the light of the stars inside.

"I'm so sorry," she said as she wiped at her eyes, all that laughter in her voice. "This is all just so over-the-top, isn't it? What I love about you, Marcella, is that you're so *operatic*. It makes me wish that everything was so dire and laced with doom and portent. That we could sing arias into the night, die spectacularly, and rise again tomorrow to do it all over again."

She smothered another bout of laughter while across the table, Alceu watched as his mother's mouth dropped open.

"This is so much better than my family," Dioni continued, in a chatty sort of way as if there had been no hint of darkness here. She'd managed to spill something down her front, though she seemed unaware of it. And as ever, the simple twist she'd put her hair into, which should have looked elegant, was instead falling down on one side. There was no reason at all it should make him want to smile. "My father was very much in love with the sound of his own voice. He was never the least bit *fun*. All of his stories were about reflected glory, this movie star, that politician. It was never *calves to the slaughter* over the fish course." She laughed again. "Honestly, I feel deprived."

Marcella, Alceu noted, did not say a word for the remainder of the dinner.

And he found himself lingering at the table with Dioni long after his mother had pleaded a convenient headache and stalked away.

"You handle her masterfully," he said. Quietly, not certain where that dark and brooding urge to confide in her was coming from. "So masterfully that I can only wonder how it has never occurred to me to treat her in the same way."

"This castle is like the Dread Pirate Roberts," Dioni said softly. "Do you know that story?" Alceu shook his head. She smiled, resting her arm on the swell of her belly. "He was a great and terrible pirate who ravaged the seven seas, as you would expect. And when he took a captive, particularly one he took a shine to, he would order them about all day and then every night say something to the effect of, 'Well done, but I'll almost certainly kill you tomorrow.' And that could go on for ages. That's what it's like here. No matter what actually happens, everyone carries on as if at any moment the castle will be struck down from above. Or perhaps simply crumble off the side

of the mountain and fall into the sea. *At any moment.*"
She smiled at him, her eyes seeming more fathomless than usual in the candlelight. "And yet every day
here dawns the same. The most beautiful blue skies
over mountains and far-off beaches. It's peaceful up
here. Everything is lovely. No matter how much your
mother vamps about, that doesn't change. Maybe it's
time that the Vaccaro family accepts the fact that despite their very best efforts, they might just end well,
after all."

Alceu felt a great wash of sensation, deep inside. It seemed to flood him, taking him over, until
he hardly knew what he was about. He stood, then
walked around the table until he could stop by her
chair, lean down to brace himself on its arms, and
then set his mouth to hers.

It was a wildfire, and the flames danced higher
every time they touched.

One conflagration led to the next, until it was all
the same blaze.

He tugged down the rest of her hair. He liked it all
around her, flowing and unruly.

He kissed her and kissed her, as if that alone would
scour him clean of all the shadows, all these memories, all these burdens he'd agreed were his long ago,
when he'd had no idea what any of it might mean.

When he had been sickened and heartsick and had
wanted nothing more than to hurt his father in return
for what he'd done to Grazia.

He kissed her until the heat was too much and then

he bent down, lifted her up, and carried her through the castle to his bed.

Where it turned out he was as hungry for her as if he'd never touched her before. He spent all night learning new ways to adore her, and in the morning, watching her enjoy her breakfast so much made him take her to bed all over again.

Alceu could not concentrate on work that day. All he could seem to remember was the way she'd laughed and laughed, and how that laughter had done the impossible. How it had stopped Marcella in her tracks. How it had changed everything.

He was terribly afraid that it had changed him, too.

Or maybe that wasn't *fear*, that thing like dawn deep inside him, threatening him with light.

He went to find her when he knew she would be taking her lunch and found her in the library of novels, sitting on a sofa surrounded by stacks of books.

She looked up and smiled wide, as if immediately delighted to see him.

He still could not get used to that automatic response. It still made something in him seem to dance.

"I never see you at this time of day," Dioni said merrily, waving him to a spot beside her on the sofa, and he took it, because he could not refuse her anything. Another problem he knew he would have to deal with, and soon. "The baby and I were enjoying some of my favorite books from childhood."

And then she showed him each one, describing them all to him, sounding as passionate about the books she chose as she was about the things she ate. Or the things they did in bed.

Or the way she tipped her face into the sun whenever she was outside, and breathed deep.

Alceu felt as if the insides of him were clawed into pieces, flayed open in some catastrophic way that must surely lead to disaster—

But he didn't do a thing to stop it. He sat there, watching this calamity approach him as if he had no choice at all but to let her change him.

Change for *her*, something in him suggested. *Try that.*

He didn't want to try anything, but as he sat there he could feel the whole of his chest begin to ache. He opened his mouth to make all of this worse—

But at that moment, the door to the library swung open.

"If you'll excuse me," Concetta said in her very formal housekeeper's voice, which would have been surprising had he cared about anything but his wife. "You have some visitors."

Alceu glanced over, already disinterested. Beside him, one hand on her belly and the other brandishing one of her books, Dioni looked up—and then went still.

And for a moment, they both stared as the apparition of the doorway slowly resolved itself into two distinct people.

A man. A woman.

Both of whom stared back at them with similar looks on their faces. Shock, first and foremost.

A kind of dawning horror on one, a considering sort of recognition on the other.

Then it all seemed to flare into temper, like an electric charge that made the whole castle seem to flicker in its wake.

"What," bit out Apostolis in a clear fury, taking in his sister's rounded form and then turning his gaze toward his best friend, his gaze a mix of outrage and betrayal, "in the bloody hell is going on, Alceu?"

CHAPTER EIGHT

DIONI SHOT TO her feet, swiftly if not at all elegantly, because she had never seen that look on her brother's face before.

"What does it look like, Apostolis?" she demanded, something like a sob constricting her chest. Because she was terrified that he might rush Alceu at any moment, turning this into something violent. And then what would she do? The very idea of the two men she loved most in the world at each other's throats made her feel sick, and yet, hadn't she known all along that this moment would happen—sooner or later? Wasn't that why she'd run off to New York City in the first place? She tried to draw Apostolis's attention, scowling at him. "And why are you asking him? I am very clearly the one pregnant."

Her brother turned that arrogant, astonished, furious glare on her. "This is impossible. Tell me I am misunderstanding what I'm seeing, Dioni. Tell me this cannot be what it looks like."

Beside him, Jolie murmured something that Dioni couldn't hear. And she wanted nothing more than to look at her friend to make certain that they, at least, were all right, or *could be* all right—but she didn't dare look away from her brother.

Her heart sank as he continued to glare at her. That sob in her chest started to *hurt*. Because she had spent all of her life being protected by Apostolis. He had cared for her. Looked out for her. He had always treated her as if she was a kind of delight to him, a light in an otherwise dark family story. He had protected her all these years, and never once in all that time could she recall him being anything like *disappointed* in her.

She did not think she could bear it.

But she was not a little girl any longer. She would always be his little sister but she was fully grown, married, and soon to be a mother. Shortly she would be raising her own child and the truth was, though she loved her brother dearly, he had not been her parent. He had shouldered those responsibilities in many ways, yes, but he should not have had to take care of her like that.

That he'd had to do so anyway didn't change the facts of things.

Or how those facts had changed.

And Dioni was a woman, not a child, who had astonishingly vast love inside of her for her husband that she would not get over no matter how angry Apostolis was about it.

None of this was his business, though she wouldn't have minded his blessing.

And even as her heart sank, another part of her was glad, because now he knew. And now Jolie knew, too. Whether it was painful or not in this moment, it was a relief. Everything was out in the open and that meant there'd be no more hiding—the way she'd been doing since not long after the night of her brother's wedding. And had certainly been doing since she'd come to Sicily.

Almost, something in her whispered then, as if Alceu had intended to keep all of this a secret all this while. Because she didn't think he'd had any plan in place to introduce the fact of their marriage and impending parenthood to anyone, not even Apostolis, at any point. If he did, he'd never mentioned it to her.

Maybe they had both wanted to preserve Apostolis's good opinion of them as long as possible.

But she couldn't worry about that now. She kept her gaze on her brother and reminded herself that this needed to happen. She regretted that they had to go through this first, but it was the only way.

Alceu was Apostolis's best friend. She was the little sister she suspected he still saw as a girl. There had never been any version of this moment that wouldn't come with tension.

Dioni opened her mouth to lay it all out for her brother and her own best friend when, beside her, Alceu stood. To her surprise—and, she could admit, a rush of pleasure—he wrapped his hand around the nape of her neck.

A sign of possessiveness that made everything inside her...dance.

He might as well have set off a bomb. Apostolis's gaze went blank, then wide.

Then even darker.

Beside him, Jolie smiled.

"Dioni and I are married," Alceu announced in his forbidding way. "We are expecting our son in a couple of months and I know you will both join us in celebrating this great joy."

There was another deep, intense silence.

Dioni could hear her own heartbeat, like a drum. She could feel his hand on her neck and the way the heat of him coursed through her until she had to repress a shiver.

And for a moment, it was as if the four of them were frozen into place, as incapable of moving as if they were carved from ice. She might have thought she was if it weren't for Alceu's hand on her neck.

But then the ice shattered and everything got loud.

Her brother was shouting. Alceu was not shouting back, but he wasn't backing down, either.

"All this time you were nothing more than a snake in the grass," Apostolis threw at him, after a spate of furious and insulting Greek that Dioni hoped neither Alceu nor Jolie could follow. "I trusted you!"

"I have no excuse," Alceu replied after a moment, sounding…if not precisely *unbothered*, then certainly not bursting with the sort of *certainty* about the two of them she might have liked to hear in this moment. She tried to tell herself she was imagining it as he continued. "The fault is mine."

Clearly she was not imagining it. That fatalistic tone of his that made everything in her curl up in a tight bristle.

Dioni turned to stare at him. And she was aware as she did that she was more upset with that cool, emotionless statement than with the yelling, suggesting she wasn't quite right herself. She found she didn't care. "The fault is yours? As if you did this by yourself?"

Both her husband and her brother ignored her, making that bristling, thorny thing inside her seem to sink its claws in deeper.

"You defiled her," Apostolis went on, and that he was quieter did not make it any better to hear her brother say such a thing. As if she was unclean, which was a problem for him even though he wasn't looking at her, but at Alceu. "I've spent my life taking care of her, and I thought you understood that. What it meant. Why I did it. And yet all the while, you were just as bad as your own—"

"He did not seduce me or take advantage of me in any way," Dioni broke in, before he finished that sentence the way she feared he would. "Quite the opposite. If you cared that much about it, maybe you should have paid more attention to what was going on around you while you were pretending to hate Jolie at your wedding."

"At my wedding," her brother repeated, taking a step toward Alceu, looking even more murderous than before. "You stood up for me. You were my best man."

Tension emanated out from Apostolis and an eruption seemed inevitable—but Alceu, again, only inclined his head. "There's nothing I can say to explain away these facts, I am afraid."

Apostolis stepped closer and Dioni moved forward as if she thought she could personally intercept him with her body.

Well. What she thought was that she *would* intercept him and he would have to toss her to the ground to get past her. She did not think that even now, even in this state, he would do that.

"What is the matter with you?" she demanded, loudly, of her hero. The brother she had looked up to, always, and had never had so much as a single harsh word for in all her life. Maybe later, when this moment was solved and lived through, she would mourn the loss of that innocence along with all the rest. "Can you hear yourself, Apostolis? This is your best friend. Your business partner. He is, and has always been, a good and honorable man who you yourself have always said you would trust with your life. And have."

When Alceu made a noise beside her, she waved her hand at him, dismissively. "We are not entertaining your family's obsession with making themselves out to be the most evil people who have ever eviled. We're talking about reality."

She looked back at her brother and pointed her finger at him. "Did I scream at you when you decided to marry my best friend?"

Apostolis looked as if she'd plunged a knife straight into his heart. She felt as if she had, and couldn't say she enjoyed the sensation, but she didn't back down.

"That's completely different," her brother protested.

"Completely," came Jolie's arch voice, then. Her husband turned to look at her as if she was holding a second knife, yet all she did was lift a shoulder, the very picture of elegant nonchalance. "Perhaps you've forgotten that Dioni and I are the same age. You certainly do not treat *me* as if I'm an infant."

Jolie ignored Apostolis's glare and moved forward to take Dioni's hands in hers, gripping her tight. "Congratulations. I am delighted. So is he, or he will be, when he comes to terms with the idea that you have not been a seven-year-old girl in need of a hand to hold in quite some time."

And it wasn't until her friend hugged her, hard, that Dioni realized that she was long overdue for a big, long, messy sob. This, clearly, seemed like the very worst and very best moment to give in to that urge.

But she couldn't hold it in. So she…let it out, heedlessly.

She buried her face in her hands and let the tears fall as they would.

Dioni cried and cried. She cried for a good long while. Because her best friend was here and her brother knew and everything was tense and broken, but she had to believe that it was better.

Even if it didn't feel anything like *better*.

And she had been pregnant forever. She was huge and uncomfortable and unwieldy, but she had also never felt more beautiful in all her life. And she was having a son. She would be holding a chubby little fist in hers soon enough, and she adored him already though she hadn't even met him yet, and she wanted his life to be as beautiful as she could make it no matter if he hadn't been planned.

And she was so in love with her husband that she couldn't see straight. It got worse by the day. Every time he touched her. Every time he looked at her. Every time he said her name, it made her love him more and made that stillness, that certainty that she was in the right place with the right person, expand within her—but *he* wanted only to *take responsibility* for her.

For her and the child they'd made.

And that wasn't the same thing at all.

When she looked up again, Jolie had cleared the library of men. She had steered Dioni back down to the sofa. Now she sat beside Dioni and kept her arm tight around her friend's shoulders, the way she had always done. The way Dioni had done for her, too, on the few occasions either one of them gave in to emotion.

She didn't say anything. She didn't try to rush Dioni through the storm. Jolie sat with her and helped her weather it.

It hurt to think how long it had been since they'd seen each other. It *hurt*.

"Well," Dioni said ruefully as the last of the tears subsided, wiping at her face. "That went about as hideously as I expected it would."

"I think," Jolie said with great confidence and a squeeze, "that when the smoke clears, we'll all find this very funny. It's the surprise of it all that's overshadowing everything at the moment, but that won't last. You must know that the two of you are his favorite people. It will dawn on him that there could be no better man for his sister than Alceu." She smiled.

"And if it does not, I will be certain to hasten that dawn along."

A rush of something sharper than simple guilt washed over her then, and Dioni turned toward her friend so she could look at her full-on. "I wanted to tell you a thousand times. I wrote you letters, sometimes five times a day. I've saved them all on my mobile, but I never sent them."

"I wish you had," Jolie said simply.

There were no recriminations. No expressions of hurt feelings. That was all she said.

But it was enough.

That guilt didn't go away, but it was gentler, then.

Dioni let out a sigh. "I couldn't tell you, much as I wanted to. It was right after your wedding, and things were not... I wasn't sure how things were between you and Apostolis. I didn't want to tell him, so I couldn't bring you into this and worry that you'd feel you *had* to tell him."

"I wouldn't have told him," Jolie protested. But she considered that for a moment. "To be honest, I'm not sure what I would have done. I've kept secrets from him before. I don't know that I ever will again. But I suppose the real question is, why were you afraid to tell him?" She frowned. "Did you think that he would stop loving you, Dioni? He might rant and rage, but he would do anything for you. Surely you must know this."

And so Dioni poured it all out to the one person she thought would understand, as she had long wished she could. That she knew that he would try to fix it. That she needed to fix it herself, whatever that looked like. That her brother was wonderful, but if she was going to be the mother of a human being—and it appeared she was, and rather soon—she really, truly, needed to sort this all out for herself.

"I thought I would simply live off in America for as long as possible, then present a fully grown child to him when I came home and refuse to answer questions," she said. When Jolie laughed, she shrugged. "I planned to be mysterious for the rest of my life because I certainly had no intention of telling Alceu about any of this. And if I didn't tell him, why would I tell anyone?"

When her friend made a face at that, as if not wanting to tell Alceu was an unreasonable position, she explained. How that night—Jolie's wedding night—had gone. The things he said. The fact that he had used the word *pity.*

"I would not have told him either," Jolie said, rolling her eyes. She let out a laugh. *"Men."*

Dioni nodded, more relief washing through her then, because Jolie understood exactly how crushing it had been. To be *pitied* when she had been wildly and madly in love. "Imagine my surprise when he appeared in New York in all his state, as if I had gotten pregnant on purpose to spite him, and demanded that I marry him."

"I can imagine that." Jolie smiled, sitting back against the sofa. "Just as I can imagine that you somehow failed to mention to him that you've been in love with him for the whole of your life."

"Not *in love*," Dioni corrected her, flushing slightly. "Have I had a certain tenderness toward him? Yes. Have I been, at certain times, preoccupied with him? Also yes. But what do those things amount to, in the end?"

"Apparently, they amount to a wedding and baby boy, though not necessarily in that order."

They both laughed then, leaning into each other as they did, and it was suddenly as if there had been no separation between them. Dioni talked her friend through every detail of the last seven months. And in her turn, Jolie told her how things were going at the Hotel Andromeda, and in her marriage, and all the secrets that she was no longer keeping because she and Apostolis had truly found their way at last.

"You seem happy," Dioni said, when that had never been something Jolie had expected or even aspired to. "Are you truly happy?"

"I am finally living up to my name," Jolie said, and she looked it.

And it was a gift, Dioni thought, to lose herself in something other than her own worries and daydreams and fears, for a change.

"You have always been the most optimistic person," Jolie said much, much later. "It's inspiring. I have to imagine that this might all work out all right."

"For you, I'm sure it will." Dioni shook her head. "What I worry is that Alceu truly believes that he's a villain. No matter what he does, he is certain that his true nature will take hold."

Hadn't she seen it earlier? In that fatalistic manner

he'd adopted, as if he *wanted* Apostolis to take a swing at him? Or would not have been surprised if he had?

It had her skin feeling too tight, all over.

"I'm no expert on the subject," her friend said after a moment. "But what I can tell you about love—or what I know of it in the short time I've experienced it—is that it must be built on forgiveness or it is something else entirely. I don't mean that if he is hideous you should bear that. I mean that *he* must forgive himself. For whatever he imagines he has done or might do, just as you must do the same. Just as all of us must see ourselves in the mirror and understand the truth we're looking at. Because I think, in the end, that's what intimacy demands. We must see ourselves to truly see each other."

And Dioni told herself there was no reason for that notion to make her want to sob again, for hours.

There was no sign of Apostolis or Alceu, so as night fell, Dioni took Jolie out into the bright green courtyard that took on a deeper emerald in the last of the light. And they ate their dinner there, while the stars slowly came into view. They talked late into the night, the way they had in school and the way they had sometimes when they'd lived at the hotel together.

The way Dioni had believed, in New York, they never would again.

As if they could do as they pleased. As if there was nothing but time.

As if the only thing that mattered was the joy they took in each other's company, the stories they told, and the space they held for each other.

"Like sisters," she said, leaning back to look at the Milky Way sprawled out above them.

"Like sisters," Jolie agreed, pressing her shoulder to Dioni's.

And so, by the time she found her way to bed, Dioni felt brand-new.

Remade.

More than capable of finally telling her husband that she loved him, like it or not.

Assuming, of course, that Apostolis hadn't killed him before she could.

CHAPTER NINE

ALCEU LET APOSTOLIS rant at him for a long while.

There was something freeing about it. Liberating, even—because there was no one else who would dare. He couldn't think of the last time anyone had tried.

That kind of shouting had died with his father, long ago.

Alceu found himself bracing for impact. Would Apostolis take a swing at him? Would he throw something? He was pacing up and down the length of Alceu's office and he certainly had the opportunity.

Maybe there was a part of him—and not a small part—that wanted it. The bright burst of sensation, of pain. Blood and bone, adrenaline and temper.

Those were things he would not hate himself for feeling, he thought.

But Apostolis never lunged for him.

And when his friend finally wound down, Alceu simply poured him a whiskey, took a pull of his own, and said nothing.

"It this how it is to be?" Apostolis asked then. "You plan to simply stand there, offering no defense for your behavior?"

"And if I did offer some kind of defense, what would that look like?" Alceu studied his friend. "Do you wish for me to express regret that I married your sister? That would indicate that it was some kind of terrible mistake. When the woman we are discussing will shortly become the mother of my child and I do not think you would care for it if I had not made her my wife." When Apostolis glared at him, he sighed. "Do you really wish to discuss the details of what happened between your sister and me, Apostolis? Is that truly what you want?"

"It is not."

They sat in silence for some time after that.

Alceu stared out the window, and found himself thinking of that salon in the Hotel Andromeda where he and Dioni should never have been on their own. He thought about Dioni herself. Her dragging hems and hair that never stayed put. And about her tears, more specifically.

As if all that sunshine and happiness, all those smiles, had been nothing but a performance all along.

The very notion made his bones ache, as if he had gone brittle overnight and might shatter at the faintest touch.

Because he thought that he could bear anything. That he had. That he would continue to do so until the last of his cursed bloodline quit the earth for good.

But now there was Dioni. And their baby.

And it turned out that Dioni's unhappiness was the one thing he could not abide.

It made him want to tear down the castle all around

them with his hands—or, perhaps, he simply wanted an excuse to explode. To prove he was every bit as bad as his father had been, as Apostolis had *not quite* said several times already.

Alceu did not need it said.

He felt it keenly.

He might as well start laughing and telling Apostolis that this was what Vaccaros did. That girls were his for the taking. That the peasantry were otherwise pointless, and he would sample them as he chose, like so many amuse-bouches.

Alceu could feel his father all over him, then, like a second skin. He could remember how the old man had reacted when news of Grazia's death had reached the castle. A shrug, then a laugh, as if it was nothing to him what a young girl he'd ruined might do.

You are only angry because I got there first, Giuseppe Vaccaro had said slyly. *I am disappointed in you, Alceu. Did no one tell you that village girls are to play with, not place on pedestals?*

Somehow, he had not attempted to kill his father that day. And he had always thought it ironic that his heart had been what killed him, seeing how little Giuseppe had ever used that organ. Over time, Alceu had understood that he had likely been more in love with the idea of Grazia than the reality of her, but then, he had never had the opportunity to get to know her the way he'd wanted.

And yet here he was anyway. A despoiler of virgins, exactly like his father.

As if there had never been any point in trying to

make himself something different. As if he'd been cursed from the start.

He thought he would have preferred it if his friend really had taken a swing at him.

Apostolis drank another whiskey. And then he looked at his oldest friend and business partner, and smiled. Ruefully, but it was a smile all the same. "I suppose there could be worse brothers to have."

"A ringing endorsement."

Apostolis lifted his glass in Alceu's direction. "I might, at any point in time, punch you in the mouth. Just so we're clear."

"Understood." Alceu nodded, and it was harder than it usually was to remain calm. But then, he had only ever unleashed himself with Dioni and that was why they were in this mess. He could not risk doing it again. Not with her and certainly not in any other arena. He was already tainted with his father's mark. He did not know why he'd imagined he could ever be clean, no matter how bright Dioni shined. "It will be well-deserved, should it happen."

"More than well-deserved," Apostolis agreed. He swirled his whiskey around his tumbler. "You did not bother to ask for my blessing, but I will give it to you all the same. As the urge to murder you fades, I believe that I want nothing but the best for the both of you. I have only one concern."

"If you intend to question my ability to provide for your sister," Alceu said, sardonically, "I invite you to speak to my business partner. He will tell you that I am more than capable of taking care of her and the child."

"Very funny." But Apostolis was frowning at his drink. "In all the years I've known you, you have been adamant that you would never marry, never have a child, never even date a woman long enough for her to think about such things. And yet here you are."

Alceu wanted to drain the whiskey bottle, but he did not allow himself such indulgences. He could not trust himself. How many times did he need to prove that to himself?

"Here we are," he agreed.

"I would hate to see my sister hurt, Alceu," his friend said quietly. "I hope you know what you're doing."

"What I can tell you," Alceu said, though the words seemed to wrench open a place inside of him he had no desire to look at more closely, "is that it is never my intention to hurt Dioni. If there is a way for me to avoid it, I will."

His friend inclined his head. "Then I know it is as good as done." He set his drink down and then smiled when he looked up. "You told me years ago that I could drop by at any time. Aren't you glad that I decided now was that time?"

Alceu was shocked that he smiled at that, but he did. "As a matter of fact, I am. I did not like the idea that I was lying to you, if only by omission. But now it is done."

It was done and there was no undoing it. That sat in him like stone, but there was no changing it.

Some part of him had known that since he'd seen the surveillance photos of her.

What he could not understand was why, knowing that he had already made such a mess, he had only made it worse since she'd come here. He had prided himself on his militant moderation in all things since his university days. Grazia's death had taught him that emotions were foolish, dangerous, and could be used as weapons.

Worse, his intensity was as poisonous as his father's dark pleasures, and came to the same end.

He did not drink to excess. He did not carouse. He had kept all of these extreme behaviors locked down tight, until Dioni.

Even now, he could not account for his own behavior.

And much later, after he made certain that Apostolis and Jolie were settled for the night in one of the many guest suites, he found himself wandering the halls of the castle as had long been his habit.

He knew every brick. Every stone. He had taken every bit of it apart and put it back together as if performing an exorcism and yet he still couldn't seem to come to terms with what this place meant. What it was to him.

Who he would become if he stayed here. Who he had already become because he *had* stayed here.

And now, worse, he was already worried about what this place would do to his son.

Not to mention the woman who could not seem to understand her own danger.

He found himself down in the old ballroom again,

though it seemed much emptier than he recalled it. He could not remember it being used for years. Not since his father was still alive, and had bullied half of Sicily into appearing at the lavish parties he had used as traps for the unwary, all games of dominance and spite.

Now, all he could see was Dioni, dancing by herself and holding her hands on the baby belly before her, making up her own music as she went.

And all he could think about was his best friend in the entire world and the look on his face when he'd said that he knew Alceu would not hurt her.

Apostolis had truly believed that. The same way Dioni had seemed to mean it when she'd said he was a good and honorable man.

How could they not see the rot within? When so much of it had already gotten out?

Alceu let out a breath and when he turned to go, he was unsurprised to find his mother standing there, staring at him with her usual malevolence. Sometimes he thought she tracked him through the castle, looking for opportunities to offload her bile on him.

He wanted to laugh, to ward her off the way Dioni did. He wanted to make some joke about her creeping around at night, though the only thing that came to mind was the possibility he knew was already whispered about in the villages—that Marcella Vaccaro was some kind of vampire.

But somehow the hilarity wouldn't come tonight. No jokes. No laughter.

No attempt at a lighthearted smile.

Alceu was far too raw.

"I knew it would come to this," Marcella seethed at him, shaking her head so that her jet-black hair slithered about like a premonition. "You can't escape your blood, Alceu. It is *inside* of you. It makes you who you are—no better than your father. In some ways, I expect you are much worse. Giuseppe never pretended to be anything but rotted straight through." She smirked. "You think you're a good man, do you not? There is nothing more dangerous."

He looked away from her, toward the ghost of Dioni on the smooth, gleaming floor. To the gleam of the chandeliers above, picking up light where there was none, a lot like she always did.

Maybe he was rotted well enough, because everything in him *hurt*.

"Everyone thinks that I renovated this place out of some innate sense of love," he told his mother. "Or some regard for the family legacy, at the very least. They think that I consider this castle some kind of jewel, and set myself to polishing it." He laughed then, though it was a bitter sound. "But the truth is, I hated it. I still hate it. Yet I made certain that I put my fingerprints on every single stone, every single corner, every cornice and buttress. So that it was no longer a monument to our history. So that I could make it mine, and then get rid of it, one way or the other."

"Burn it to the ground," Marcella challenged him. "Go ahead. You will still be you, Alceu."

"Still the better bargain between the two of us, Mother."

She let out a laugh to rival his. "You think that I married your father like this? Like the harpy you see before you now?"

She came closer, and then she was too close. She reached out and put her hand on his arm, and he let her. Maybe he needed to look down and see her talons. Maybe he needed to recall exactly what had happened to him and how she had hastened it all along.

Maybe it was pretending he could control his memories that had led him here, because if he hadn't, would he have allowed all this to happen?

If he hadn't, would he have known enough to walk out of that wedding breakfast at the Hotel Andromeda? Alone?

"I am what the Vaccaros made me," Marcella told him, like a threat. "Think of that, while you listen to your happy little wife sing her songs and dance her way through this dark place. And think of this. One day, there will be no difference at all between her and me."

That was one of his darkest fears, but he refused to give her the satisfaction of reacting. Instead, he stared down at her impassively. He watched her dig her nails into his forearm, then release him with a snarl.

"You will see," she warned him darkly, and then she spun around and swept out of the room.

Leaving him with a dark ballroom and chandeliers that could only reflect back the shadows all around them.

And so Alceu knew, then, there was only one thing that he could do.

He felt like a condemned man as he made his way through the castle that too many of his ancestors had left their fingerprints on. He passed room after room filled with ghosts and scandals and long-dried tears. And he knew by now that Dioni did not see these things here. She could not feel the darkness in the walls and pressing in the windows no matter how many times he pointed it out to her.

Just as he knew that she would not bother to go to sleep in any bed but his.

That ache in his chest was becoming too familiar.

He made his way to his rooms and she was there, curled up in his bed the way she always was, now.

There was a large part of him that wanted to claim that she belonged there—but that was the trouble. That urge. That tide of something like desperation that wanted more than anything for him to be a different man.

The kind of man who could deserve a woman like her, sunlight and sweet songs, in his bed. In his arms. In his *life*.

The truly galling part of this was that Apostolis and Dioni, two of the best people he knew, were wrong about this. His mother was right. They had both lived this story. They knew how it ended.

Because it only ended one way.

Over and over again.

He had always been kidding himself that he could change that trajectory.

For some while, he stood in the moonlight at the foot of the bed and watched her sleep. And he even imagined that he could leave her there. That he could let her sleep and let her know from some distance what he had decided.

What he had been *forced* to decide, for all their sakes.

He let himself imagine that he could simply do what needed to be done, and remove himself with no further blurring of lines and intentions—but it seemed his mother had been right about him all along.

He was no better than his father.

He was weak, through and through.

He could not help but fail to meet his standards, no matter what he wanted to do.

Because Dioni lay naked in his bed, just as she had that first night. The sheet was crumpled at her feet as if she'd kicked it off, and so the moonlight caressed her curves like a lover.

And no power on earth could keep him from going to her.

From sliding into bed beside her and running his hands all over her satiny flesh and feeling her heat beneath him. Nothing could keep him from caressing her, everywhere, and waking her up to pleasure. From making her spin and sob and cry out his name.

Over and over again.

When he was deep inside of her, he understood that he would never feel whole again. That he never had before.

That he had been lost at sea seven months ago. That his surrender that night had been total—that he had drowned then and had spent all this time trying to pretend that he had been treading water instead.

It would have been kinder all around to simply slip beneath the water then.

But he hadn't.

He couldn't.

Somehow, deep down, he knew he never would. Not while she lived.

And when he finally tired even himself out, dawn was already breaking outside. And though she slept, it was a fitful thing.

He knew because he watched her.

Alceu did not bother to sleep himself. He wanted to soak in every last minute here. He knew he would treasure these moments, that he would take them out like a hoard of jewels across the years that yawned ahead, look at them in the light, and remember this goodbye.

When she woke up, he did not have food waiting for her. He stood there, fully dressed, keeping his expression grave. As if this wasn't killing him.

But the point was her, he reminded himself, not whatever he might feel.

Because he knew too well that his *feelings* were toxic.

"This looks ominous," she said.

She didn't smile. He thought nothing could have wounded him more.

Still, he pushed on. "I'm going on a trip," he told her, very matter-of-factly. "Your brother and I have some things to tend to in various corners of the globe, including a very boring charity ball that you will likely see in pictures. You will not be coming with us."

"Because I am pregnant?" she asked, though she looked…cautious.

"You are very pregnant."

"Yes," she said. "The *very* makes all the difference."

"While I am gone, I will have the staff move you into one of the cottages." And then, because she only blinked at him as if it didn't make sense, he said, more roughly, "I don't want you in the castle. I don't want you in my bed, Dioni. Must I be more direct?"

And he watched as he accomplished the very thing he had told her brother last night he would try not to do. He watched the effect those words had on her.

He watched himself hurt her and he didn't take it back.

And it was cold comfort indeed to know that hurting her now would save her far greater pain in the future. That it was a kindness to do this now, though he doubted very much she would agree.

"What are you talking about?" she asked, her voice barely above a whisper.

"Everything will be set up for you and the baby," he assured her, and if his voice was colder than usual, well. That too was a gift, little though she might realize it. "The doctors will be on hand. You will want for nothing."

"Except you," Dioni said quietly. "I will want you. My husband. The man I love."

He stared back at her, that tide in him too high, because he could not have heard her correctly.

She swallowed, naked and regal and his, and yet

out of his reach. "I love you, Alceu. You must know that I always have."

And Alceu felt as if he was cracked wide open. As if those words were an explosion, deep inside. He couldn't take them on board.

He couldn't allow them to take root.

"I have been pretending that this might be a manageable situation," he managed to grit out at her. "But nothing has changed. I married you for the protection of the baby I made with you. You are both under my protection now and always will be. But the rest of this?" He slashed his hand through the air, as if that could keep his body from its typical reaction to the ripeness of her body and those wide, dark eyes. "It is no good. All of it will end in pain."

"Being afraid is no good reason—" she began to argue.

"Not my pain, Dioni. Yours. Our son's."

His voice was harsh. He could hear it in the room. He could see it all over Dioni's face.

But that only made his resolve harden. "I'm not willing to risk that. I told you this from the start. And I take responsibility for what has happened between us. I knew better. I should have stopped it."

She rose from the bed then, uncurling herself to stand and then moving toward him, her hand outstretched.

"If you can't keep your hands to yourself, and I don't believe you can, I will remove the temptation," he said, like he was handing down a sentence from on high, and her hand dropped to her side. "When I'm here, you will not know it. You will lack for nothing, but you and I cannot continue like this."

"Alceu..." she whispered.

But he turned to go.

He made himself turn and then, harder still, he made himself walk away from her.

Because this way, she would be safe. The child would be safe.

He could not let anything else matter...especially not that shattered, jagged emptiness where his heart should have been.

CHAPTER TEN

"I wish you were coming with us," Jolie said, after a strange sort of breakfast together. Dioni felt...split in two. She wanted nothing more than to tell her friend everything that had happened. All the things that Alceu had said to her earlier—but she didn't.

Partly because she held on to a little bit of hope that Alceu had been...emotionally overwrought, perhaps. That he would think better of it all as the day wore on.

But even more than that, she felt strongly some things had to be only hers and Alceu's, even if it hurt. Not hiding from her friend, but keeping faith with her husband.

Even if he wasn't interested in the role.

"I wish I could too," she said instead, and rather than try to make up a reason why she couldn't—something she thought might make her burst into tears—she ran her hands over her belly. "I'm not sure I really fancy giving birth midflight, if I'm honest."

Not that she was *quite* there yet.

Jolie only smiled. And later, when she hugged Dioni goodbye, she bent down to kiss her belly. "I can't wait to meet him. He will be so loved."

"Every day of his life," Dioni agreed, feeling emotion flood her eyes.

Then she felt that very specific prickle all over her body, and looked up to see her husband standing there, waiting with Apostolis because of course they were all leaving together. Right now, whether she liked it or not.

She imagined Alceu thought that meant there would be fewer scenes.

Dioni was tempted to throw a fit just to prove him wrong.

But she didn't.

Because she had *dignity*, she told herself.

When really, she thought, it was because she had no strategy. Not yet. She had no idea what to *do* about the line he'd drawn in the sand.

After what had happened with Alceu at the Hotel Andromeda, she hadn't launched herself into action. Not immediately. First she'd taken to listening to some of the saddest brokenhearted songs she knew, to wallow and then heal. Then, when her period hadn't come, she'd been something like paralyzed for a week. Two.

Only when she'd started to worry about things like morning sickness and *showing* had she launched herself into action.

So here, now, she let her brother hug her and give her his usual bossy advice, which she knew full well was his love language. "Make sure you sleep," he told her, more than once. "And you must eat."

"Apostolis. It would be difficult for anyone alive to be better fed than I am."

He looked down at her with affection. "I understand

why you didn't tell me immediately," he said gruffly. And then he smiled. "See to it that you never do such a thing again."

"I wouldn't dare," she replied, smiling back, though she felt far too emotional.

Apostolis put his arm around Jolie and began walking toward the front door, and there was a part of her that wanted to watch them. To see the evidence of the happiness her friend had claimed they had in the way he bent to kiss her temple, and the way they leaned into each other as they moved.

But all she could really think about was that this was her last private moment with Alceu. Surely he would say something. Surely he would indicate that he'd heard what she'd said, that he knew that she loved him. That she was *in love* with him, and surely that must mean *something*—

"The staff has already begun carrying out my instructions," he told her coolly. "I have put you in the finest cottage, which, I trust, will suit you. It can accommodate the typically sprawling Sicilian family, so I think it will be more than adequate. And the doctors will keep me apprised of the child's progress."

Her heart was thumping at her, but what she really didn't want was that emotion she could feel pricking at the backs of her eyes to come flooding out. He would only take that as evidence to support his case, she knew.

"Are you forbidding me from contacting you?" she asked instead. "Is that why you're telling me with *such significance* that the doctors will talk to you?"

And if she stepped back from all this and observed

this moment like it was happening to someone else, she supposed it was fascinating, really, the way he could turn himself to stone as he stood there.

"There is no reason for you to contact me."

"I understand that you have a genetic predisposition to melodrama, Alceu, but this does seem to take it a bit too far, don't you think?"

And oh, she hoped he would never know how much it cost her to keep her voice calm and sweet.

"I meant what I said, Dioni." He didn't use that word, *camurria*. That insult that she had long since come to think of as the sweetest endearment imaginable. "There will be no more giving in to temptation."

And when he turned to go, she could have yelled. She could have screamed the castle down around them, maybe. She was sure she had those things inside of her, so she wasn't sure where the strength to stay quiet came from.

The strength to simply hold his gaze until *he* dropped it.

The courage to simply stand there, pitiless, and allow him to abandon her and their baby in real time, with no pretense that he wasn't doing precisely that.

But the trouble with that was that he did it anyway.

And then she was left there, standing in a doorway and clinging to the wall while it seemed the world spun around and around, heedless of how dizzy it made her.

She made herself move after what seemed like an ice age, wandering deeper into the castle, of half a mind to simply lose herself in the libraries again.

But she was intercepted by Concetta.

"If you will come with me," the housekeeper said, sounding almost apologetic, "I will get you settled into your cottage."

And once again, she could have fought. But what would it gain her?

So instead it was all a long, slow march out into the forecourt and then through the castle door. Then back along the rocky outcropping with only the music of what she was certain was her mother-in-law's spiteful laughter on the breeze.

Concetta led her to one of the cottages, though Dioni could see that Alceu had not lied about its size. It was set back from the others, with the more wooded side of the outcropping all to itself, and what looked like gardens left to their own devices. *Like me*, she thought.

Once she let them lead her inside, the staff bustled all around her, though she could not have said what they were doing. She still had that sense that everything was a blur.

Maybe it was only that she *wished* it was.

And when she finally jolted awake from whatever daydream had her in its grip, she was screamingly hungry again. She was also alone.

The cottage was bright and lovely and pretty, filled with books and art and perfectly cheerful in every way, which made Dioni want to practice that screaming again. So loud that she might knock that castle down into pebbles. So fierce that it might send this whole outcropping of dark Vaccaro history tumbling down the side of the mountain.

But she did no such thing.

She had spent her whole life being quiet and unassuming, because why attempt to have a bigger personality than the infamous Spyros Adrianakis? Why attempt to compete with a circus like that?

Dioni found herself standing in the living room, her hands folded before her and some sort of strange smile on her face. Some terrible parody of something *quiet and unassuming*, she supposed.

It reminded her of when she'd first made it to New York. When she'd dismissed all the staff, made grand proclamations about her independence, and finally found herself standing all by herself in the townhouse.

Alone at last.

But back then, she'd had the pregnancy to come to terms with. She'd had all those dreams and daydreams about Alceu. All the various fantasies she'd entertained of seeking revenge, or accepting him back if he apologized, or a thousand other twisted little scenarios that she'd known would never come to pass.

Now she still had her baby on the way, but there were no fantasies attached to it.

She thought of all the things he had said to her. All the words he'd used, and that look on his face, and how stony and distant he had been when he'd left. Dioni supposed she should take all that at face value.

But instead, all she could think was that he was *such* a liar, because she knew how it felt when they moved together in the dark.

She knew how he groaned out her name.

She knew what it felt like to dance through the heavens while holding on tight to him.

There was no question. He was lying, though she wasn't sure he was aware of it. Dioni believed that Alceu thought he was protecting her, but it was clear to her that the person he was really protecting was himself.

And Dioni was so sick and tired of being *protected* that she really did let out a sound that was as close to a scream as she'd ever come.

It didn't rattle the art on the walls, but it felt good, so she did it again.

And she thought of all the times in her life that she'd cheerfully acted impervious to insult, neglect, or indifference. She thought of her childhood years of staying out of her father's way on the one hand, and bearing the guests' intrusive commentary regarding her mother on the other. More, that she had been *expected* to do those things.

Because Apostolis might have protected her as best he could. But he hadn't been able to save her.

"He couldn't save himself," she muttered out loud.

It had taken Jolie to do that.

Dioni thought of the years, one after the other, on and on, that she had simply carried on and thought she was happy. Maybe she had been, because it hadn't been a bad life. She'd lived at the hotel. She'd helped with the admin and had occasionally lent a hand in a staff shortage. She'd volunteered in the villages and danced in *tavernas* in the summers, and she'd gone swimming in the sea whenever the fancy took her.

She had read books as she pleased, and she'd had her best friend *right there*, and her brother had always remembered to call her to see how she was. The hotel was always packed with guests, some of them wildly interesting, and so there had always been decent conversation, laughter, long walks to look at the stars, and all the rest of the sorts of things that could make any life spectacular.

But all of that paled next to these last weeks, here on this mountain with the man she loved.

Because it was one thing to be happy without knowing that there could be more. It was one thing to play at a life, even such a lovely one. It was another to truly feel *alive*.

And now she knew the difference.

She thought about her father as she rubbed her hands over the places where her son kicked at her, as hungry as she was. Already she knew that the love she felt for a baby she hadn't even met yet far exceeded anything her father had ever felt for her. He hadn't wanted children. He wanted an heir to pass the hotel along to, and so Dioni was nothing to him. A silly thing to flit about, a jewel in his crown, but not a crown he wore often. Or at all.

She thought about her brother, and how it had been so clear to her that Jolie was perfect for him, because she challenged Apostolis. She pushed him. She did not simply accept his magnificence like all of those women he had been linked to in the paper always did.

Or the way his younger sister always had.

And once again, setting a record for annual tears, Dioni cried.

Because she had always been alone, perhaps, but she had never felt that way.

Not until now.

She cried and she cried, until she exhausted herself. After an emergency raid of the kitchen to get some food in her, she sobbed some more. Then she slept on one of the sofas in her new living room and woke sometime in the middle of the night, the moon shining in to fill in all the corners of the room, and perhaps in her, too.

Because she lay there with her eyes swollen, feeling faintly ill and wrung dry, but something like *replete*.

Dioni took one breath. Another.

She let the moonlight dance all over her, silver and sweet.

Then she shuffled into her small kitchen, drank a lot of water and ate a little bit of food, because the baby needed it.

She went back out to the couch and slept till morning.

And when she woke up that time, she was furious.

Dioni felt nothing but a kind of towering rage, except instead of clouding her, it brought nothing but clarity.

The kind of clarity that felt a great deal like a knife edge.

She wandered around the cottage until she found a suite with her things in it. Then she took a long shower, and took even longer dressing herself. Only then did she begin making her arrangements.

It took a number of phone calls and a heart-to-heart with Concetta, but by the time afternoon rolled around, she was ready.

She walked back over to the castle, breathing in all

of these scents that had become so dear to her. The flowers, the trees. She took in the warm sun, the rich earth. The view down the mountain and across the sea. The birds that looped in lazy circles above her, some calling out, some singing.

She walked over to stand near the castle gate and waited for the car to be brought round, and she wasn't at all surprised when Marcella materialized beside her.

"Running off, are we?" purred the older woman. "I did try to warn you."

"Were those warnings, Marcella?" Dioni asked. "How funny. They sounded a whole lot more like feverish prophecies to me."

Her mother-in-law ignored that.

"This is how it begins," she told Dioni instead, sounding triumphant. "Maybe this time he will chase you, as men do. You will think it is because he cares what happens to you, but you cannot kid yourself in this way. It is the bloodline, always."

"He thinks his blood is a poison, Marcella," Dioni pointed out. "So I somehow doubt he'll be racing about after it."

Marcella smirked. "Once the child is born, the truth will come out. Perhaps at first you will weep over his temper, because that is all you will see. As time goes on, you will find that you dream about that temper. That you wish you could have it back. Because in its place there will be nothing but the deadening indifference." She drifted closer, so close that Dioni could smell the perfume she wore like a shield. And could see the faint bit of creping at her neck. "So you will do what you can to get his attention, however and wherever possible. Negative attention, positive attention, it won't matter. These Vaccaro men are narcotic. Even when you know that it will kill you, you cannot walk away. Even after he dies, you will find yourself engaged in a pitched battle with his name. Tarnishing it as best you can, as if that might haunt him from beyond the grave."

"Marcella…"

But the older woman laughed. "I tell you, foolish girl, this is how it begins. And I should know. I *was* you, once. The die is already cast."

Dioni looked at her mother-in-law. Really looked at her. She tried to see the girl that Marcella must once have been. Pretty, with prospects. A woman who even now, even riddled with bitterness, still dreamed of that prince who might have saved her if she'd chosen him instead of Giuseppe.

And she supposed that she could see exactly how she could become her mother-in-law's clone. How *easy* it would be. How comforting, even, to imagine herself forever lost in a battle with her husband. One he did not even have to be alive to play.

Because that felt better than the truth.

She did not laugh, not today. Instead, she moved closer and took her mother-in-law's hands in hers, ignoring Marcella's shocked expression and the way she tried to recoil.

"You're going to have a grandson soon," she told her, her voice serious and her gaze direct. "He will not care about your behavior from before he was born.

What he will want from you is a *grandmother*. He will not listen to the stories that are told about you. He will deny them if asked, because all he will see when he looks at you is love, Marcella." The other woman took a breath and held it, and that made Dioni believe that she was actually reaching her. She went with it, squeezing her hands. "That is, if you decide, right now, that you think that's what he deserves. And I hope you will, because deep down, that's what you deserve, too."

"H-how maudlin," the older woman stuttered, but she did not pull away.

"And I will need a mother," Dioni told her. She did not break her gaze. "Because I have never had one. I don't know anything about raising a child, but you do. And for all of this slinking around, muttering dire warnings over the dinner table, and evening gowns before breakfast, your son is a fine man. Whether that's because of you or in spite of you, it doesn't matter, does it? You are involved all the same. Imagine, if you will, what it might be like if you *helped* me."

And for a moment, then, Marcella looked stricken. She looked away quickly, composing her beautiful face into the mask she preferred. "I'm the least maternal woman alive," she said, though she sounded something like shaken. "Ask anyone."

"I don't care what anyone thinks," Dioni told her fiercely. "*I* will care about two things only. What *your* son thinks of you and what *my* son thinks of you. All the rest is up to you, Marcella."

Her mother-in-law stepped back, looking pale, and

her breath came too fast. "Fine words indeed when you are running away. You can talk all you like about breaking cycles, but what you're doing is perpetuating one."

"I'm not running anywhere," Dioni told her, quiet and fierce. "Quite the opposite."

When the car came, she nodded to the older woman, held her gaze a moment too long, and then climbed inside.

In the back seat, her doctor waited. Dioni smiled when she spotted him. "Flying is generally considered to be safe, but an abundance of caution never hurt anyone, I am sure," he said.

"Wonderful," she replied, and settled back against the seat, thinking through the next steps that needed to occur for her plan to work the way she wanted it to, proud that it hadn't taken her *weeks* this time.

When they landed in Vienna a couple of hours later, she was ready, having dressed herself on the plane.

She took a car to the grand old house that had been converted into some kind of museum in the heart of the Innere Stadt, the center of the old city, and did not allow herself to consider her feelings at all until she was climbing the stairs. Her determination was fueling her more surely than anything else ever could, and she decided that her feelings didn't matter.

Not until she could share them with the person who had caused them, thank you.

Inside, she offered a dazzling smile to the attendants who waited there in the lobby. She told them who she was and watched them step out of her way, eyes wide as they took in her giant belly.

Dioni walked further into the house, following the gleaming lights and the sound of a string quartet. She allowed herself to be swept up into the glittering, old-world charity ball, the sort that were put on all the time in graceful places like this, comprising a very particular social circle for a certain set of people.

She knew exactly which set, because she recognized some of the faces here. Old school friends. Socialites and celebrities. And, as always at these things, the sort of truly powerful people who did not operate in spheres that ended up in papers because they owned those papers. Lavishly appointed rooms like this were the places where they were instantly recognizable, but not outside in the streets.

But she didn't care about any of them. What she was looking for was a little knot of people she eventually found in a far corner, having what looked like the sort of friendly conversation that was actually business in a place like this, though it was important for all parties involved to act as if it wasn't. Genteel negotiating was the only sort allowed in these balls, because outright negotiation would be considered gauche.

Then again, all the same people considered her gauche, too.

It was the hair that she could feel was finding its way loose from the twist she'd put it up in. It was the hem of the dress that she was sure was unsewing itself as she moved, and she had to be careful not to go too fast or it was a certainty that she would do an inelegant header.

Not that anyone would be surprised.

Though she did take some comfort from her lack of elegance. At least she wasn't *that* filled with despair tonight.

If this was temper, Dioni decided she liked riding it.

Accordingly, she marched across the ballroom floor. She nodded at the raised eyebrows and the familiar faces. She made no accommodation for her enormous belly and found it gratifying, she could admit, to see the way that people leaped out of her way.

As she moved closer, it was Jolie who looked up and smiled. Because it was Jolie, of course, who had volunteered their whereabouts tonight and had directed Dioni straight to them.

Just as it was Jolie who now took her husband's arm and held on to it so that as Dioni bore down upon their group, he could not intercede.

They both knew Apostolis well.

"Good evening," Dioni said merrily as she joined the group, stepping close to her husband and sliding her arm through his. "I'm so sorry to be late." She could feel the way that Alceu stiffened beside her. She could feel his startled glare on the side of her face. She smiled at the people, who she vaguely recognized as some or other billionaire, his heiress wife, and a set of minor nobles. She smiled even more widely at them. "What a pleasure to meet you all. I am Dioni Vaccaro. Alceu's apparently secret wife."

CHAPTER ELEVEN

ALCEU WAS IN a state of shock.

And it did not help that he had been standing there, pretending to engage in the typical sort of boring cocktail conversation that Apostolis had always excelled at—and was even better at now, it had to be said—while thinking instead of Dioni.

Of the way she had looked at him the night before last, with such adoration, as she'd woken up to find him with her. He could taste her in his mouth. He had been certain a hundred times already that he had heard her laugh, or smelled her fragrance—a mixture of the soap he preferred and the lotions she used, always mingled with arousal.

Apostolis had already lifted a brow in his direction, more than once, as a sign to attempt to put a smile on his face. And he had tried.

He had *tried* to try, to be more accurate.

Now she was right there beside him. *Touching* him, when even looking at her was a weakness.

And yet for all that she was smiling, there was something like steel in her dark gaze.

He wanted to pick her up then and there, and carry

her out. He wanted to get his hands on her, his mouth on her. He wanted to lay her down on any flat surface and make them both sigh.

He wanted a great number of things that polite company—and her brother's presence—forbade him.

"What are you doing here?" Apostolis asked Dioni when all Alceu could seem to do was glare down at her. "Should you be flying anywhere in your state?"

"She should not be," Alceu said darkly.

"*She* flew with medical supervision, naturally," Dioni said lightly, smiling at the other guests.

"Because *she* is not a child," Jolie chimed in.

"Though," Dioni said with that laugh that drove him mad, "she *is* finding that she quite likes referring to herself in the third person."

And Alceu could not abide it. He could not make any sense of this dark wave inside of him, something tidal and primal, roaring up from the depths of him in a way that should have scared him. But it didn't.

He felt it was the only possible reaction to this moment. To standing here in this dry, tedious business event that Apostolis had insisted they attend because he liked to play the part of careless Greek tycoon only to go around saving people from the unsavory practices of those he met in such places. It was a *reasonable* response to find the woman who haunted him with every breath right here before him. In flesh and blood.

When he had made it clear that she was to stay back in Sicily, sequestered in the palace.

"Excuse us," he said, perhaps a bit gruffly, as he

took her arm the way he had before and tugged her off from the group. And even though that had a high likelihood of leading to that punch in the face Apostolis would still be only too happy to deliver to him, he didn't care.

"They're still newlyweds," Jolie said with the kind of laugh that made others laugh with her and lean in closer. "Isn't it romantic?"

That wasn't the word that Alceu would have used, if asked. It sat on him strangely. It made him feel things he wanted nothing to do with—so instead of engaging with it, he pulled her out into the center of the crowded dance floor.

There were strings playing haunting melodies. There were couples in formal attire. He thought he glimpsed a tiara here, a famous necklace there.

But none of that mattered.

Only Dioni interested him.

He held her in his arms and glared down at her, not certain if he wanted to kiss her...or kiss her and *then* demand to know what, precisely, she thought she was playing at.

"I'll ask you again," he said, though *not* kissing her felt like an attack all its own. "Perhaps you can offer me a better answer than the one you gave your brother. What are you doing here, *camurria*?"

Alceu had not meant to call her that name. He had decided that he never would again, in fact, and then there it was. Right on his tongue whether he liked it or not.

"Well, Alceu, I considered the things you said to

me," she replied with a smile. "And I decided, pretty quickly, that you're an idiot."

And she let her smile go sweet.

So sweet that it took him a moment to hear what she'd actually said. "I beg your pardon."

Dioni's smile changed, then, and he hated it. He knew it was his fault that it was anything less than sunshine.

But she kept that dark gaze on him, still shaded with steel beneath. "I am not going to play these little games with you, Alceu. As I told your mother today, more or less, it is time to decide who you want to be."

"You told my mother...*what*?"

There was a certain patience in the way she looked at him. A certain knowing kindness that made his ribs hurt. It didn't seem to matter that her hair was coming out of its fastening and her nail polish was chipped and clinging to uneven nails.

All that mattered was that she was looking up at him.

As if, despite everything, she believed in him.

"Do you want to be the kind of father yours was to you?" she asked him softly. "Or do you want to be a *real* father to your son? Do you want to be what he overcomes in life—or do you want to love him so wildly and so wholly that there is no possibility that he can become anything but the person he's meant to be?"

"I have no idea what you're talking about."

She leaned forward, fiercely, and pulled her hand from his. Then she thumped him in the center of his chest, seemingly unaware or uninterested in the stares she got from the people around them. She didn't even seem to recognize that she was suddenly standing still in the middle of the crowded dance floor, calling attention to them both.

It was something Alceu was certain he should care about—and would at any moment, given his lifelong dedication to seeming perfection at all costs—but he didn't.

Not then. Not yet.

Not when she was looking at him with so much passion flooding her face.

"Of course you don't know," she said, sounding something like ferocious. "Because everything you are doing is about fear." He must have made some sound because she angled herself closer, or would have, if her belly hadn't been there between them. "I don't want that, Alceu. I don't think you want it either."

"Dioni—"

"I'm in love with you." And she said it so matter-of-factly, then. As if it was a fact, not a feeling. "I've been in love with you for a long while. Do you really think it makes sense that I held on to my innocence as long as I did, then tossed it aside on a whim? Do I strike you as that kind of person?"

Everything hurt. He had to force words from his mouth and was half-afraid they would come out as something else. "I haven't given the matter much thought."

She poked her finger into his chest again. "That is such a lie. Every time you do this, every time you say something so harsh, I assume that it's that father of yours coming out of your mouth." He felt as if he had turned to stone, but she was still going. "You think that you're making it better, somehow, by telling me these things. But you might as well be slinking around in inappropriate clothing with your mother. That's what it sounds like."

He blinked at that, thrown off-balance, and he hated that feeling the way he always did.

But it was as if she knew it, because she moved closer, or as close as she could. She pressed into him, gripping his arms.

Alceu expected that she knew that she was the only thing anchoring him to this moment. To this planet.

"I can't understand why this is so hard for you to comprehend," he gritted out in a low voice. "I'm trying to *save* you, Dioni. You keep bringing up my mother—but she is the object lesson here. Do you want to end up like her?"

"What on earth makes you think that I would?" Dioni shook her head as she looked up at him. "How dare you think you could be the ruin of me. Or that you could *save* me. I am perfectly capable of saving myself, and have done so when necessary."

"You are misunderstanding—"

"I do not need you to be noble on my account," she told him, and that passion was still all over her face, but she was no longer speaking in such a fiery manner. And there was that steel again, right there in her gaze. "That is not what I need from you, Alceu. What I want from you, what I *need* from you, is simple."

"Dioni. *Camurria.*" He felt more than off-balance now. He felt as if the marble floor was melting away beneath his feet. As if there was no solid ground. As if there was nothing but this woman who had come out of nowhere and wrecked his whole world. "Nothing about you is simple."

"Because you're in love with me," she told him, her gaze intent on his. She did not smile, though there was the hint of that sunshine he craved in her gaze. "Madly, wildly, impossibly in love with me. What do you think would happen if you let go of that control you hold on to so tightly? I'll tell you that *I* think it would be the worst of all things for a Vaccaro." Her mouth cured then, only slightly. "You might actually be happy."

Once again, Alceu felt that wild sea tug at him. It was sensation, emotion—too many things he did not wish to name, tumbling him over and over again. Like some kind of terrible riptide, snatching him away from what he'd always thought was the safety of shore, and hurling him out into open water.

Pitiless. Merciless.

Except Dioni lifted her hand and pressed her palm to his cheek. "A fate worse than death, I know."

"And what if I am in love with you?" he managed to get out, his voice so hoarse it felt like he was lighting himself on fire. "Don't you realize that I can think of no greater curse for you to bear?"

And Dioni laughed.

Sunshine and blue skies. Birdsong and deep green forests. That was what she sounded like.

That was how it *felt*, that laugh of hers.

Like running down the mountain as a boy, *alive* with a wild joy simply because he moved so fast. Simply because he *could*.

And because he had been too small, once, to know anything about his family but that. The mountain. The castle. The long, jolting drive to the sea.

That and running until his lungs nearly burst, laughing that off, then running again.

Dioni's laugh raised the sort of dead who should never have gone to their graves. It made him want to run again, to dance. To render himself breathless and then breathe only her.

Only her. Only this.

She sobered, wiping at her eyes and smearing her makeup, not that she seemed to notice.

"Then we will have to be cursed together," she said, catching her breath when he ran his thumb beneath one eye, then the other. "Let's take all of your mother's dark prophecies and all of your family's poison, then mix them up all together and make a life out of them. You don't have to know how to do anything, Alceu. I don't know myself. All we have to do is *try*."

"Relationships require good models, and I have none," he told her sternly. "I'm not sure you do, either. How can we be anything but a disaster?"

"We will decide," she said, very surely and solemnly, her gaze on his. "You and I will decide right now. We will decide that no matter what, we will work it out. There will be no more running away. There will be no more ranting on about *resisting tempta-*

tion. There will be no more misplaced nobility, or tedious lectures, or pity. We will be done with that, you and me."

He sighed, only dimly aware that there were still people all around them. That they were still in a ballroom. That her brother and best friend were not far. But how could he care when she was still speaking to him like this? Like she *knew* how it would go.

"I think you are optimistic," he said, still much too gruffly, and perhaps he was afraid of the things he wanted. What if that had been the trouble all along? "But what if you're wrong?"

"Then we get to be human," Dioni said, her voice rougher than before. "We will try, we will do our best, and if we get it wrong we will start over again." She blew out a breath. "Do you know what I've been doing on my visits down to the villages?"

"Taking up fishing, I presume."

She smiled, but her eyes told a different tale, and one that made everything in him tighten.

"I found her family," Dioni said quietly. "Grazia's mother and father are still there. And a great many brothers and sisters and cousins. But it was her parents I spoke to most."

And if she had detonated a bomb, or slapped him across the face, Alceu did not think he could have been more shocked.

He was reeling again, and he was no fonder of the sensation. "You should not go sticking your fingers in wounds like that," he managed to say.

"There is no ill will, Alceu," she told him softly.

"Not toward you. They knew exactly who your father was. Just as I knew who *you* were. And they knew their daughter too."

"You should not…" he started again.

"They know who to blame," Dioni told him, urgently. "And everything else is the sadness, the grief, for what was lost. *What a waste.* That's what her mother said. Grazia was a happy girl with a future ahead of her, by all accounts, when your father got his hooks in her. Why should there be no futures at all, all these years later? Why should you suffer for your father's sins? Surely the best revenge of all is to live well, Alceu. Even in Sicily."

He could feel the dance moving around them. It was as if they were one more pillar in the middle of this ballroom.

It was as if he was still out to sea, bobbing up and down in that open water with no sense of where the shore was or how to swim there.

But Dioni had just shown him that if he looked up, he could see the stars.

And when he looked at her, he saw galaxies.

So he took her hands in his. Then he leaned down and set his mouth to hers.

And then kissed her, with all of the longing and need, the wonder and hope, the terror and the desire inside of him.

"I will disappoint you," he told her. There against her mouth.

But this was Dioni, so she smiled. "I will disappoint you right back. And then we will laugh. Perhaps we will fight first, then find our way to each other again. You will make me cry. I will hurt your feelings. And over time, we will do less of that, I hope. And more listening. Learning. *Loving*, Alceu."

"How can you be so certain?"

"I read a lot of books," she said, her eyes sparkling.

"You forget that I knew your father. *How* are you sure?"

"Because," she said, her voice low and only for him. Just as she had been. "My mother gave her life for me. It was a gift, and I believe it was meant to be shared. We will not squander it, Alceu. We will savor it. No matter what it takes."

"No matter what it takes," he heard himself agree.

Then he kissed her again, and again.

And only stopped when the music did, and only long enough to lean down, and lift her in his arms the way he liked. Then, without a single thought for anyone who might be watching them—or considering a punch in the mouth—carried her off.

Straight into that happy ending she was so sure they had coming.

CHAPTER TWELVE

LIKE HIS FATHER, Tolis Vaccaro was born in his own sweet time, and was unyielding and uncompromising from the start.

Dioni loved him to distraction, immediately and completely, and not only because she lived through the birth and *got* to meet him. But it was Alceu who was besotted.

And it was as if that was all he needed. As if it took Tolis to make his heart open wide like that.

"I love him," he said as they all lay together in the bed, the baby between them and all of that awe on Alceu's face. But he was looking at her. "And oh, Dioni, *camurria mia*, I love you too."

She laughed, and then she kissed him. "I know you do, you impossible man. I have always known."

And after that, after the stone statue that was Alceu crumbled and became a man, all things that seemed impossible before became doable.

Marcella did not exactly turn into the gray-haired stereotype of a grandmother overnight—all baking and cooking and the like—but she, too, fell in love with the baby.

"It is as if," Alceu said when Tolis was an intense eighteen months old and they were taking the family walk that had become their nightly habit, "she is trying to redeem herself."

"I hope she does," Dioni replied happily, watching his mother—still dressed inappropriately, but less so—walk with the determined little boy who insisted he needed to walk himself everywhere.

"Of course you do," Marcella purred. She looked back over her shoulder and lifted a shaped brow. "Vaccaros must always have an exit strategy."

"I will confess that I have none," Alceu told her, his mouth at her ear. "That is how much I love you."

"I am happy to hear that," she said, tilting her head back to look at him. "Because I love you too."

Especially because, by then, they had another baby on the way.

She and Alceu spent more time in the village at the base of the mountain, so that he, too, could spend time with Grazia's parents. Because time had not stopped as their daughter's life had. And they bore him no ill will, though they also liked that he had no intention of acting the way his father had. Ever.

"We have always known that if it was up to you, the ending would have been different," Grazia's father told him on one of those occasions. "And this is a good thing. I have told everyone I know that if a Vaccaro can be different, it is you."

"I promised her first," Alceu told the old man, his voice rough. "That was the only reason she agreed to talk to me."

"She was her mother's daughter," Grazia's father said, his eyes damp. "Hardheaded."

Dioni would always think that was what finally got Alceu to make a decision about what he would do with the castle. He did not tear it down. He did not burn it.

Instead, he kept his promise and made it over into a kind of retreat center for those seeking solitude. Peace. A reset.

It was *not* a hotel, though Apostolis laughed uproariously every time he came to visit his namesake, because he couldn't believe that there were now *two* famous hotels in the family.

And he never did get around to punching his best friend—long his brother in name, and now in fact—in the mouth.

Possibly because even an Adrianakis could see that the castle had become a place of serenity. A place to lose oneself in the silence, the sea and the sky, and to come out whole.

Dioni and Alceu moved their growing family to the cottage she'd stayed in only that one night, bringing the surly staff with them, and slowly, they all learned how to smile more. How to dance. How to laugh uproariously and chase the little ones around and around in the garden.

"My darling *camurria*," Alceu murmured to her in the bedroom where they hid away from their brood and reminded themselves of all the reasons why they could never manage to keep much more than a year between them, "you are appallingly fertile."

"Don't pretend you don't like me pregnant," she

whispered as he rolled her beneath him and let his hands move where they would.

"There is nothing I don't like about you," he replied, letting his teeth graze down the side of her neck. "But I will always love you ripe."

Dioni found that, unlike many women, she loved being pregnant. She thought it might be because they had left the castle and its curses and its legacies behind. They lived in the cottage now. Marcella lived in another cottage, and dressed in fewer and fewer evening gowns as the years went by. Their children were funny and adorable and frustrating and *theirs*, and there was no history bearing down upon them.

They spent as much time as possible with Apostolis and Jolie, and the cousins that they soon provided. On pretty Mediterranean evenings, the four of them would sit together in Greece or in Sicily, laughing as the sun sank gracefully into the sea and their children argued over which was better, a whole castle or the Hotel Andromeda —that the whole world could agree was *legendary*.

But it was not old buildings made of stone and dead men's dreams that Dioni and Alceu talked about when they crawled into bed together and tangled themselves up in each other the way they always did.

It was the dark eyes of their children. Their shouts of laughter and howls of injustice. Their unique and fascinating little personalities and the young men and women they became as they grew.

Funny. Interesting. Beautiful in ways that Dioni found healing, and frustrating, and endlessly entertaining.

The family neither she nor Alceu had ever had, so they doted on the one they'd made.

Sometimes he disappointed her, but she disappointed him too, but they didn't dwell on these moments. Sometimes they fought. He could be stone and darkness and she was never afraid to poke, and that was not always the right mix. Feelings were hurt. Tears were shed.

But they laughed much more than they cried.

They listened far more than they got loud.

They ruined each other nightly and saved each other repeatedly.

And always—always—they loved each other.

Heart and body and soul.

A great many years later, Dioni and her husband walked with their fingers interlaced through the grounds of the castle, the gardens long since planted, and these days, bright and vibrant with flowers.

They walked down the hill together, though their knees ached and they laughed about how much more slowly they moved these days. Just as they laughed about Alceu's habit of issuing proclamations that made the children clasp at their chests and claim they'd *been cursed at last*. Just as they laughed at the fact that Dioni was as clumsy and bedraggled now, with her hair white, as ever.

Nothing changed and everything changed. There was a party up at the castle that night that their children, their children's spouses, and their own grandchildren were throwing for them.

But together, alone, they walked down and stood

in the tiny chapel where they had said those vows so long ago.

Because fifty years was a happy ending no matter how they looked at it.

"What can possibly be left?" Dioni asked her love, gazing up at him as they held each other on that old altar.

"The only thing that matters," Alceu replied. He kissed her, with all the love and passion, hope and wonder, desire and longing they had always had between them and always would. Because happiness really was the best curse of all time. "Forever, my dear *camurria*. Together, just like this."

* * * * *

If Carrying a Sicilian Secret
left you wanting more,
then be sure to check out the first installment in
the Notorious Mediterranean Marriages duet,
Greek's Enemy Bride*!*

And why not explore these other stories
from Caitlin Crews?

A Tycoon Too Wild to Wed
Her Venetian Secret
Pregnant Princess Bride
Forbidden Royal Vows
Greek's Christmas Heir

Available now!

MILLS & BOON®

Coming next month

BILLION-DOLLAR RING RUSE
Jadesola James

'Am I that obvious?'

'Weren't you trying to be?'

'Don't be so eager to rush a beautiful thing, Miss Montgomery.'

'Val,' she corrected, her heart thumping like a rabbit's. If this was happening, she couldn't let it happen with him calling her *Miss Montgomery* or, worse yet, Valentina. Not with his liquid, rich voice simply dripping with all the dirty things she presumed he could do to her—it was bringing to the surface something she wasn't ready to explore. Not with him.

And yet, her thoughts were going in directions she couldn't control, while she sat in the booth, heart thudding, mentally grasping at them as they floated beyond her fingertips into places that sent back heated, urgent images that took her breath away with their sensuality. His mouth on her neck, his lips on hers, the softness of his breath on her ear. His hands on her breasts, hips, bottom, thighs. Stroking. Exploring.

Gripping.

Her face bloomed with heat, and it left her body in the softest of exhales before he *finally* kissed her.

Continue reading

BILLION-DOLLAR RING RUSE
Jadesola James

Available next month
millsandboon.co.uk

COMING SOON!

We really hope you enjoyed reading this book.
If you're looking for more romance
be sure to head to the shops when
new books are available on

Thursday 27th
March

To see which titles are coming soon, please visit
millsandboon.co.uk/nextmonth

LET'S TALK
Romance

For exclusive extracts, competitions
and special offers, find us online:

f MillsandBoon

X @MillsandBoon

⊚ @MillsandBoonUK

♪ @MillsandBoonUK

Get in touch on 01413 063 232

For all the latest titles coming soon, visit
millsandboon.co.uk/nextmonth

Afterglow Books is a trend-led, trope-filled list of books with diverse, authentic and relatable characters, a wide array of voices and representations, plus real world trials and tribulations. Featuring all the tropes you could possibly want (think small-town settings, fake relationships, grumpy vs sunshine, enemies to lovers) and all with a generous dose of spice in every story.

♪ @millsandboonuk
📷 @millsandboonuk
afterglowbooks.co.uk

#AfterglowBooks

For all the latest book news, exclusive content and giveaways scan the QR code below to sign up to the Afterglow newsletter:

SCAN ME

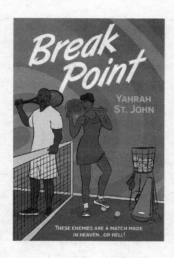
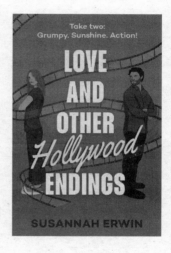
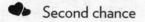
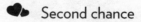

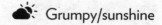

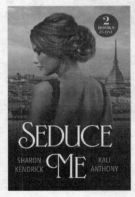

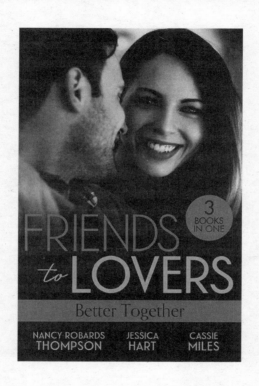